# Content Warnings

Narcissistic/Manipulative Ex

Attempted Murder

Drug Abuse (Off Page)

Surprise Child

Military PTSD

Claustrophobia

Sexual Asphyxiation

Explicit Language

# Dedication

To the woman who won't let a man define her. The woman who chases her success and doesn't let fear of failure hold her back. To those who want to get trapped in a tiny cabin during a snowstorm with a hot and mysterious cowboy and give the town something new to talk about.

# *Chapter One*

THEY SAY EVERYBODY DIES famous in a small town. Dahlia is the woman whose boyfriend cheated on her and got the other woman pregnant. No matter how hard she works and how successful Dreaming of Dahlias is, that's what people think of when they look at her.

She's moved on so why can't the rest of this town?

"Dahlia!" Carly, Dahlia's employee and best friend, shouts from outside her office. "Your one o'clock is here!"

"I'll be right there!" She flips her wrist to look at her watch, and sighs. Dahlia places a napkin in the current wedding binder, marking where she left off. It's the busy season at Dreaming of Dahlias and she feels like she's been ordering flowers like clockwork.

Seeing Peter with his hands in his pockets leaning against the checkout counter brings back the memory from earlier this week when she took his order for a special anniversary arrangement for his *wife*.

Carly wears her fake customer service smile and swaps places with Dahlia behind the counter. "He insisted to speak with you," her best friend hisses into Dahlia's ear. "I can totally handle it."

Dahlia takes a deep breath and smiles at her best friend. "Do you care to unload the boxes we just got in? They're in the back."

Carly cuts Peter with a side-eye glare, before disappearing into the back room.

"Dahlia," he says, placing a hand on the counter.

"Peter. Here is the arrangement you ordered. Complete with a happy anniversary tag." She sets the enormous vase between them on the counter, conveniently blocking him from her view.

"Beautiful as always," he says, sliding it to the side. "Thank you." His gaze lingers on her longer than it should and she hates that even after all these years, it still stirs something in her. Probably disgust, that can get confused with desire all the time.

"Thanks. Is that all?" Dahlia clicks away on her computer, trying to make him take the hint that there isn't anything else to be said. The bell to her shop rings and Dahlia looks past the flowers and her stomach twists.

*This day couldn't get any worse.*

"Dahlia, Mom and Dad were wondering—" The man lifts his gaze and his cowboy hat reveals the same brown eyes as Dahlia's. He levels Peter with a glare that has her wanting to duck behind the counter and disappear, but she can't let him wreck her shop.

"What the hell are you doing here?" He jerks his gaze to Dahlia and points at the man. "What is *he* doing in *your* shop?"

"Tripp," Dahlia says calmly and steps out from behind the counter to stand between her younger brother and ex. "He ordered some flowers and he was leaving." She glances over her shoulder and Peter smirks.

*Why me?* Dahlia doesn't have time to respond before Tripp stomps to the counter, grabs the vase of flowers and shoves them into Peter's chest.

"Get out," Tripp growls, his free hand clenches.

"What's going on?" Carly steps out from the back room, her long, blonde hair wrapped in a messy bun on top of her head. "Oh shit," she says with a gleeful smile and leans against the counter.

"Tripp. Peter," Dahlia says, trying to get their attention. The door rings, but she doesn't take her eyes off the standoff.

"Peter? Are you ready to go?"

"No fucking way," Carly whispers and Dahlia wants to crawl into a hole right there.

*And somehow it got worse.*

No. She won't succumb to this.

This is her shop. *Hers.* And she has the power here. Not Peter and certainly not his wife, Katherine, that he cheated on her with.

Peter's gaze flicks to Dahlia and Tripp sidesteps to keep himself between the asshole and his sister.

There are so many things Dahlia wants to say. Things she never got to scream and let loose because she picked the high road. But right now, with *him and his wife* in Dreaming of Dahlias, her skin heats and her mouth opens to tell him exactly what she thinks about him having the audacity to come into her shop and order flowers for his wife that he got pregnant while they were still dating.

"Daddy!" a child screams in delight, and Dahlia clamps her mouth closed. Peter's daughter bounds past Tripp and Dahlia, clueless of the tension in the room and wraps her arms around Peter's leg.

"Are those for me?" she asks with eyes full of adoration.

"No, sweetie," Dahlia says, moving to stand beside her brother. She looks from the child to Katherine still poised at the doorway; her smile sweet enough to draw in honeybees. "They're for your mommy. Why don't you take them to her and then go get something sweet at Malt and Toffee?"

Katherine's eyes narrow, but Dahlia keeps her smile plastered on.

*High road. I'm taking the high road.*

This has been her mantra since her life went sideways six years ago. She had her whole life planned out, down to when they would start a family and what the names of their children would be. Then rumors spread that someone saw Peter with a woman from out of town, and as small as her town is, it wasn't long before she knew the woman's name, birthday, and where she lived. By the time she confronted Peter she knew the truth in case he tried to lie his way out. The only information she didn't have was Katherine's social security number.

Dahlia refuses to let Katherine or Peter see her wounded. Her mask is a perfect illusion of happiness and full of content. There are even days she nearly convinces herself that she's absolutely fine. Drowning herself in work to the point she doesn't have time to analyze her inner emotions and turmoil.

"That sounds like a great idea," Peter says to his daughter. Dahlia turns as he leaves, going back to her computer and checking the inventory for the week. It isn't until the bell rings and only her, Carly, and Tripp remain that her brother's hands relax and he turns from the door.

"What the fuck?" he nearly shouts.

"Tripp, don't," Dahlia says on a sigh.

"Don't what? Why? Why in the world would you take an order for that asshole?"

Carly hops up on the counter and pulls a sucker from the candy jar Dahlia keeps for the kids. "That's what I said," she says around the hard candy in her mouth.

"Dreaming of Dahlias doesn't discriminate against its customers and we're the only flower shop in town."

"So let him drive *out of town*. Maybe he'll get lost and never come back. Maybe his breaks will miraculously stop working...or his engine will die and he'll get eaten by a bear trying to walk back home. I can make sure he never makes it back." Tripp's eyes widen with excitement and Dahlia can't stop the smile that lifts the corners of her lips.

"Stop. It's all in the past. What's done is done and I'm better for it. I've moved on and it's time the rest of this town does too." She tries to sound convincing, but Tripp and Carly don't believe her.

"And why was he looking at you like that?" Carly asks.

"Like what?" Tripp immediately goes rigid.

"Nothing," Dahlia huffs. "He wasn't looking at me in any kind of way. We don't turn away paying customers and we do it with a smile on our face. Okay?" She shoves past her brother. "Do you need something?"

"Aside from a good fight?"

Dahlia arches a brow and waits.

"Mom and Dad were wondering if you were coming for dinner tonight?"

"Why didn't they just call?" Dahlia asks, looking for her phone.

"They did. You didn't answer," her brother responds and Carly pulls Dahlia's very-dead phone from under some papers on the counter.

Dahlia takes it and places it in her back pocket. "Well, they could have called the shop. But, no. I have two weddings tomorrow that I have to prep for. Tell them I'm sorry," she says and walks to her office to nurse the migraine coming on. One of the weddings is Carly's first solo trip. Granted, her only task is escorting the order to the venue...Dahlia still doesn't like not seeing the flowers get to the wedding party herself.

"This makes the fifth one in a row you've missed!" Tripp shouts. Since her older brothers Sterling and Graves aren't around anymore, family dinners feel like there are ghosts lingering around the table and nothing is the same.

"I'll call them later this evening." Dahlia waves bye and heads to her office when the door chimes and two familiar faces waltz in. She immediately throws on her customer service smile and pretends the last fifteen minutes of torture never happened.

"Tonya? Marni? What are you guys doing here?" she asks the two women.

"We find ourselves in need of a wedding florist," Tonya says with a bright smile on her face.

Tripp tips his hat and looks at his sister. "Don't forget to call Mom and Dad. I'm not your messenger."

Dahlia raises her brows and glances at the door. Tripp grumbles under his breath as he walks away. She shakes it off and looks back to her customers. "Oh, a wedding! How exciting. So, which one is getting hitched first? I heard Curston Ranch has had an eventful year."

Marni moved back earlier this summer from the city and opened her own accounting firm. Most recently cattle rustlers came through and rumor has it there was a shootout at their ranch where they caught the men responsible. The Curstons were lucky, whereas Dahlia's parents lost everything.

"Both of us," Marni says confidently. "We're going to have a double wedding. We would invite the same people anyway so why make them come out twice when we could do it all at once?"

"So, you two are getting married together—like at the same time?"

"Yup," Tonya says, looping elbows with Marni. "And we would like to plan it as soon as possible. Like before spring."

"Spring is only six months away," Dahlia states, checking her mental calendar for openings.

"We know it's a big ask," Marni says. "But...well," her voice trails off and she looks at Tonya.

"What my future sister is trying to say is, she doesn't want to wait and neither do I."

"Why don't you come into my office?" Dahlia smiles and pulls out her planner and takes a seat behind her desk. Her pen slides down each page all the way to January. "I could squeeze you in on the 22nd. Do you have a venue or are you getting married on the ranch or—?" She lets the question hang in the air as she opens her binder and fills out their information.

"We're planning to have it on the ranch. It means so much to both of us," Marni supplies.

"The address?" Dahlia asks. She knows where the Curston Ranch is, but she likes to keep things as professional as possible with her paperwork.

Tonya gives her the information along with their phone numbers and then they talk about flowers and what arrangements they have in mind.

Their details are simple aside from two wedding bouquets, two grooms-men boutonnieres, and two mother corsages. Tonya made a face and snide remark about how they probably only needed one, but Marni insisted for two.

"If she shows, she'll have one. If not, it was what...twenty-five dollars?" she asks.

"More like thirty-five to forty-five dollars," Dahlia adds without looking up.

Marni blows out a breath, then shakes her head. "It's fine," she assures her friend.

"Okay. Two corsages," Dahlia says, adding it to her list. "And is the wedding inside or outside?"

Marni and Tonya look at each other, smiles spreading across their faces. "Outside," they say in unison.

Dahlia's pen stills. "Outside...in January...in Wyoming?" she asks, to make sure everyone is on the same page.

"We can't exactly ride our horses inside," Tonya jokes.

"I suppose not." Dahlia writes *outside* on the top of the form and circles it. "Do you know what flowers or decorations you'll be wanting?"

"Not sure. We love the rustic, western look, of course, but neither of us have really been into flowers."

"How about I'll email you with some options and you can look at these." She hands them her business card and some magazines with inspiration for arches, aisle decor, and bouquets. "Let me know what theme you're leaning toward and we'll pick out flowers and such. Okay?"

Marni smiles and takes the magazines. "Thank you so much for doing this. We really appreciate it."

"Of course. It's what I'm here for," Dahlia shrugs and follows them out of her office. Their wedding will be her first one of the new year, and it's outside. Her body shivers at the mere thought of setting up an arch outside in the snow.

Slumping in her chair, she pulls the drawer out where she keeps her headache medicine and takes three just to be safe.

She opens the Browns and Conleys folders. Carly will cover the Browns wedding and Dahlia will set up for the Conleys at Haynes Ranch up the mountain.

The ceremony will be inside the barn while the reception is inside the cabin. The Conleys requested an outdoorsy vibe inside for the reception. She'll add as much greenery as she can to enhance the outdoor textures to give them exactly what they asked for.

Haynes Ranch is a new venue. She searched their business website, and it looks beautiful, however nobody knows of the owner. When she went to scope out the location a month ago, the mysterious owner left the cabin unlocked for her to get a sense of the venue and an idea of where things were going to go.

Hunter Haynes.

He's not even from around here. And like everyone else in town, Dahlia is curious about who he is and what made him choose to buy a ranch that was falling apart, fix it up, and turn it into a venue of all things.

Maybe this weekend, she'll get some answers.

# Chapter Two

DAHLIA CLOSES THE HATCH to Carly's SUV. "Don't forget to get eyes on the wedding coordinator when you get there. And here's the binder for the Browns and check everything off as it is unloaded from the car."

Carly holds two large coffees and offers one to Dahlia. Malt and Toffee's logo adorns the cardboard sleeve and Dahlia inhales the familiar scent of her regular order. A hot Caramel Cinnamon Latte with whipped cream.

"I've got this," her best friend assures her. "But," She glances at her watch. "We should really get going if you want to set up before two-thirty for the Conleys."

Dahlia flips her wrist over. "Shit! Okay." She walks to her vehicle, patting herself down to make sure she has her phone. "If *anything* comes up, call me!"

"You just worry about telling me everything you find out about mister hot and mysterious!" Carly shouts across the parking lot and Dahlia's cheeks heat with the comment.

"Carly," she scolds, but her best friend laughs as she gets into her SUV and waves.

Dahlia starts her SUV and follows Carly until the road splits where Carly heads towards the Browns venue, and Dahlia goes left up into the mountains.

Her phone rings thirty minutes into her drive and she grabs it, worried something has already happened with the delivery. She answers the call without seeing who it's from.

"What's wrong?" Dahlia immediately asks, not giving the person on the other end a chance to say hello.

"Nothing, dear. Does something have to be wrong for a mother to call her daughter? Or for that daughter to even visit once in a while?" Bonnie, Dahlia's mother's voice, is sweet, but there is hurt in it too.

Dahlia bites her bottom lip. This is not a conversation she wanted to have today. "I planned to call last night. I'm sorry. Things got busy and—"

Bonnie cuts her off. "Tripp told me. Why didn't you call me? It's good to talk and get things off your chest. You can't keep bottling everything up, Dahlia. You're going to explode."

The GPS talks over her mother through the phone and she turns right as instructed. "There's nothing to talk about. I don't know what Tripp told you, but I'm sure he blew it out of proportion."

"He's your brother, and he's worried about you. It's just the two of you now, since—"

"Mom," Dahlia stops her before this conversation goes down a road that will lead to her mother crying and wondering what she did wrong to cause her two eldest children to not come around anymore.

"I haven't seen you in months. It's like you live at that shop of yours and I know you're proud of it, honey. But there is more to life than working all the time."

Dahlia's eyes close, and her head falls back into the seat. "I *do* live there, Mom. I'm trying to build something, and make a name for myself. I don't need a man to do that."

"You're a Brooks. That's your name. I know you have an apartment above your shop—I just meant—" Her mother's tone grows frustrated and Dahlia sighs, feeling guilty for being the reason.

"I know, Mom. I'm sorry I didn't call last night. We could get lunch tomorrow? The shop's closed and I don't have any weddings for next weekend. Does that sound good?"

Dahlia pulls into the driveway for the Haynes Ranch. It is a steady incline until she breaks through the top of a mountain and trees.

"It feels like a pity date, but I'll take it if it means I get to see my daughter."

Dahlia blows a stray curl from her face and puts her SUV in park in front of the cabin. "Great. I'll call you later to finalize the details. I have to set up this wedding."

She glances down at her black V-neck shirt and squawks at the white stain going down the front. She scrubs the dried whipped cream, but it doesn't give.

"*Finalize the details*," her mother mocks. "I'm not one of your clients. I birthed you for crying out loud."

"It's just a habit. I really have to go," Dahlia says, dragging the phone away from her ear as her mother goes on about how long she spent in labor and how painful it was. "I love you! I'll call you later!" she shouts before hitting the disconnect button.

Frantically, she searches her car for any kind of water or liquid to scrub it out, but there's none. Glancing around quickly for any prying eyes, she pulls her shirt off and flips it inside out. Checking herself in the mirror, she tells herself there are shirts made to look like they're inside out and this is totally fine.

She rests her forehead on the steering wheel and groans at the way this morning is starting. Reaching for her coffee, someone taps on the window and she jumps, nearly spilling the hot liquid all over herself.

She looks up to spot a man in a low-sitting cowboy hat and a green flannel standing beside her car.

*Is this him? The elusive stranger that folks in town say is on the run or a murderer?*

Dahlia hesitates as she reaches for her door handle. What if he really is a murderer?

She scolds her overactive imagination and pops the door open, and steps out.

Hunter can't help but look at her curves as she reaches across her seat for her phone. He's lived here for a little over a year and he's done a good job of keeping to himself. Being here, secluded in the mountains, has helped him more than what he thought was possible. And now it's time for this place to bring him in some money. That's where the wedding venue idea came from. Back home he was suffocating. Out here he can breathe and he's found peace.

Dahlia clears her throat, and he realizes he's still staring at her curves in her leggings. He quickly lifts his gaze to her beautiful brown eyes.

"You must be the florist?" he asks.

She studies his features. Could his blue eyes be those of a killer? They seem sweet enough. His hair is cut short around his ears, but his facial hair reveals that it's blond under the cowboy hat.

"Dahlia Brooks," she says and extends her hand to shake.

"Hunter Haynes," he responds and takes her hand.

His voice is deep, and she gets lost in the way his lips form the words. A white blur comes up behind Hunter and Dahlia jumps back at the sheer size of the dog that sits obediently at Hunter's feet.

"And this is Zip," Hunter introduces his dog, and it tilts its head to the side.

"Hello, Zip," Dahlia says and crouches. The dog sniffs her hand, then lowers his head for her to pet him.

"He likes you," Hunter states, and Dahlia smiles up at him, then stands.

"Are you nervous about your first clients?" she asks him, moving to the back of her car and opening the trunk. The back seats are folded down, and every inch of space is filled with flowers.

"Should I be?" he asks, glancing between her and the full car.

"In my experience, brides can be terrifying. This one venue I set up, the owner had to scrub bird poop off the dance floor. It was a concrete pad...outside." Dahlia slips her binder under her arm and grabs the first bucket with greenery in it.

"Well, there isn't any bird poop inside the cabin or in the barn," he chuckles and clears his throat. How is this stranger so easy for him to talk to? He hasn't felt this at ease around another person in...well, since he came back.

Hunter quickly steps forward, his fingers brushing hers where he grabs the bucket. "Let me," he insists and takes it from her.

"You don't have to help. I'm used to it," Dahlia hesitates, but Hunter doesn't back down.

They're filled halfway with water and he balks in surprise under the weight. To his dismay, she grabs the next one and leads the way into the cabin.

The front porch has large windows that let you see inside the cozy cabin, but the glass windows on the back of the cabin reach from the ceiling to the floor and are one-way glass. From the outside, you'd see yourself standing in the forest. The moment you step inside, it's like you're nestled in the woods. There's even a waterfall that is so peaceful and Dahlia imagines you'd see tons of wildlife while cozy in front of the fire.

It would be a beautiful place to experience the first snow of the year. The kind that comes down in large fluffy flakes and leaves a blanket of fresh white covering everything.

She places her binder on the table and flips open to a page, then plucks a pen from behind her ear and bends over the book and scribbles those details for future clients when they need a wedding venue. She likes to make everything a personable experience between herself and her clients.

"Is everything coming inside?" Hunter asks.

"Hmm?" Dahlia says, lost in her own thoughts. She tucks the pen back in its place and turns to Hunter, standing with his hands in his pockets. His jeans fit him perfectly and have just the perfect amount of excess material gathering around the top of his boots. She's willing to bet there is an athletic build under those clothes.

Her cheeks turn pink and she drops her chin, letting her curls hide her features when she realizes he's waiting for her to answer his question.

"Oh," she says and stands, her wild curls falling around her features. "Yes, but you don't have to help. Most places just pretend I'm not here."

*How could anyone pretend she wasn't around?* He wonders and drops his chin. He wasn't raised to just let a woman unload her car alone while he stood by and twiddled his thumbs. "You do whatever it is you do; I'll unload and bring everything inside."

Before she can protest, he's back out the door with Zip on his heels. She notices he has a limp when he walks and chases after him. "You really don't have to—" she shouts, but the door closes.

He's already pulling another bucket out of the back before she reaches her SUV. "Thank you, really. But I don't need your help," Dahlia argues and reaches for the container in Hunter's hands.

"Are you always this stubborn and headstrong?" he smirks.

Dahlia scoffs. "I'm not stubborn. I'm capable." She points her finger at his leg and his smirk falls. "Clearly you're hurting and I can handle it on my own."

Hunter's smirk falls, and he jerks the bucket away from her. "I'm fine," he says in a deep voice and brushes past her as he carries the flowers inside.

"Now who's being stubborn and headstrong," she grumbles and grabs another bucket.

When Hunter sets the last container of flowers inside, he retreats out into the crisp fall air.

Dahlia huffs and glances around the space. What is it about a man thinking a woman needs his input or help to achieve *anything* in life?

She must keep a professional manner. This is her brand—her business—she just has to play nice and finish her job. She pulls her phone out of her pocket and hooks it up to her portable speaker she always brings with her.

The moment the music fills the open room, her nerves settle and her creativity takes hold. This is where her passion lies, bringing an empty space like this to life with stunning arrangements and making it something magical.

The rest of the world fades away and time doesn't exist, which is why she sets alarms to remind her that there is a schedule to keep, otherwise she'd get lost in her work for hours.

# Chapter Three

HUNTER GRUNTS AT THE pain as he climbs down the stairs toward the barn. The colder weather always makes it worse, and his ears burn at Dahlia's comment about his limp. Zip licks the tip of Hunter's fingers to draw his attention back from his wandering mind.

"I'm okay, boy." Hunter scratches behind the dog's ears.

Music blasts from the house. Through the front windows, Dahlia spins as she grabs various pieces of greenery, swaying her hips to the music. Hunter hadn't planned to be here when she arrived. It's part of his contract for the venue. If anyone has any complaints, they can call him and he'll handle it from there. But he won't be one of the venue owners that is around for renters to complain to. He hates large crowds and chattering people.

That's another reason he moved way out here to the middle of nowhere and bought this ranch that was falling down.

He should leave right now. Dahlia has expressed she doesn't need his help, but something about her has him lingering longer than he planned. Maybe it's his years of being raised to be a gentleman and he's struggling with the thought of leaving her out here alone.

He didn't notice a ring on her finger or a tan line where one should be. Does she live alone? Is she single?

*For fuck's sake*. He groans and stalks off toward the barn to make sure everything is as it should be.

These are not thoughts he should have right now. She's here in professional business and he's here as a business owner. Nothing more.

He checks the lock to his personal shed out back. The last thing he needs is for a guest to get in there and cut off a limb with a table saw or a kid poking his eye out with a screwdriver.

Grabbing the broom from the closet, he sweeps the concrete floor once more to pass the time. It took him a year to get this place presentable and gave it its full potential. Inside, the barn doesn't even look like it used to house cattle and horses. It's sealed and insulated with its own heating and air system.

A glass chandelier hangs in the middle of a big open room. It's set up to either be the dance floor or reception area if the client prefers the barn over the cabin.

Personally, Hunter thinks it's too much, but brides want the beauty of a western wedding without the scent of a real working ranch.

Now it's time to see if it was all worth it.

***

"ARE YOU SURE EVERYTHING was perfect?" Dahlia asks as she places the finishing touches for the arch in the barn—if you can call it that. This place is nicer than her apartment above Dreaming of Dahlias. She places her phone on speaker and sets it down as she climbs the stepladder to get to the top of the arch.

"Yes, D. The bride loved her bouquet and there wasn't a flower out of place. Now tell me, did you meet him? What's he like?"

Dahlia sighs. How does she put into words her first experience with Hunter Haynes? He insisted on helping her unload her car, then just disappeared. She hasn't seen him or his dog since.

"Carly," Dahlia says in an exasperated tone.

"Oh, so he's cute? Green eyes that are full of mystery? What about his hands? You can always tell a lot about a man based on his hands."

Dahlia steps back down to the ground, and gathers the clippings and scraps of ribbon she left lying on the ground.

"His eyes are blue," she responds without thinking, and Carly squeals.

"So, you noticed! Oh, this is huge. What else?"

Someone clears their throat behind her and Dahlia's heart pounds in her chest. The tips of her ears burn and she hastily grabs the phone, hanging up on Carly and turns around.

"Blue eyes, you say?" the woman asks, her blonde hair pulled back in a high ponytail.

"Lauren!" Dahlia hisses and exhales in relief. "I thought you were—"

"The mysterious owner of this breathtaking venue?"

Dahlia straightens and tosses all her belongings into one of the empty buckets.

"Not you too," Dahlia groans. "What are you doing here this early?"

Lauren places a hand on her hip and arches a brow. "Honey, what are you doing here this late?"

*Late?* Dahlia checks her phone and curses.

"My bride and the bridal party will be here any minute," Lauren adds. She's a wedding coordinator and always makes sure not a single detail is missed.

"Shit! I lost track of time."

Lauren chuckles and grabs a pair of scissors Dahlia left on the floor, and drops them in her bucket.

"It's always good to see you, Dahlia. As always, you have this place looking fantastic."

Hunter has put so much work into this place, it's unbelievable. What kind of man has an eye for these details but doesn't come into town or talk to anyone? Is there a Mrs. Haynes behind the scenes that makes these decisions? But Dahlia didn't notice a wedding ring.

She pauses to look at her work from the back of the room. The chandelier is breathtaking. The exposed wooden beams and large windows on the walls still give you the feel of a rustic barn.

At the end of each chair down the aisle sits three glass vases with floating candles inside surrounded by greenery. A large wooden arch sits at the front of the aisle. On the top, left side, a large arrangement of soft pinks and natural colors adorn the wooden feature.

"It really does, doesn't it?" Dahlia says to herself. "Well, I'll get out of your way and I'll be back to get the vases tomorrow."

Lauren waves her off. "Don't be ridiculous. I'll drop them by the shop on Monday. You deserve at least one day to relax and not think about work."

"You're one to talk," Dahlia teases and Lauren rolls her eyes, but nods.

"Noted. We should both add vacation to our itineraries."

Dahlia carries the last remaining bucket with Lauren to her SUV and closes the door.

"I'll make you a deal. The day you take a vacation, I will."

Lauren laughs, and Dahlia looks around for any sign of Hunter.

"He won't be here," Lauren supplies.

"Who?" Dahlia asks.

"The mysterious cowboy you're looking for. He made it very clear that if we need anything to call and that he's left everything unlocked, so we shouldn't have any trouble."

Dahlia chews on the inside of her cheek. "That's...odd."

Lauren shrugs.

"Guess I'll head out then. Good luck today!"

Dahlia stops at the end of the driveway and glances behind her up the tall mountain. She thought her curiosity would be put to rest after meeting Hunter today. Turns out she's left with even more questions.

***

At Turnpike, the local fine dining restaurant, Dahlia sits across from her mother. Not as much fine dining as it's the only place in town that serves food aside from pastries and sweets. Once the sun goes down, it's the hottest place in town for live music and drinking.

Lunch, however, is a different crowd made up of farmers, ranch hands, and the occasional man in a suit looking for a greasy burger.

"You look tired, dear," Bonnie says.

"Gee thanks, Mom. That's what every thirty-year-old wants to hear." Dahlia picks at her fries.

"I didn't mean it like that and you know it. I'm just worried you're going to burn yourself out. You work seven days a week and sometimes right through the night to open the shop without ever sleeping. If Carly isn't enough, maybe you need to hire more help."

Dahlia wipes her mouth and sits back in her chair. "It's not that simple. I can't trust just anyone to do the work and do it right. I've trained Carly and still she can't do the wedding arrangements. If just one wedding goes wrong, that's my job—my reputation could take a huge hit."

Bonnie sighs and drops her chin. "That's really heavy to carry on your own, Dahlia. I know you love it. It's the way your eyes light up when you're creating all the beautiful arrangements you make. I'm worried one day you'll wake up and realize you're forty and still are married to your work and feel like you've missed out on so much."

Dahlia fights the urge to stand and leave the conversation all together. She knows her mom means well, but it's an exhausting hamster wheel she seems to be stuck on. Everything she says or does loops right back to the fact she's single.

"Mom. I love you. I really do. But please, can we not talk about my dating life for once? Can't we just enjoy a nice lunch and catch up about what's going on at the ranch and how *you* are doing?"

Bonnie concedes and takes a drink of her sweet tea. "Fine. Your dad misses you too and since we sold most of the land...he doesn't know what to do with himself. Working cattle was all he knew, but when Sterling left...and then Graves—" Bonnie clears her throat, but Dahlia doesn't miss the sheen in her gaze. "Walt couldn't have kept up with it all, especially after we lost all the cattle to those thieves. We couldn't just replace them. We didn't have the money. I think he knows that, but getting old is something nobody ever wants to admit. I swear if that man picks at one more thing in our house that needs '*fixed*', I'm going to go crazy." She laughs, but it's not the joyous type of laughter Dahlia remembers from her younger years.

Graves joined the army and, before that, Sterling decided this town didn't have enough to offer him. It's only Dahlia and Tripp now, and as much as Dahlia loved the ranch life, she couldn't make Dreaming of Dahlias a reality and run the family ranch. That wasn't what she wanted for her future. Granted back then, she also saw Peter in her future, so what does she know?

Bonnie stares out the windows toward the busy street. Dahlia's heart breaks not only because she misses her older brothers, but the amount of pain etched in her mom's features since they left. It's like she hasn't smiled since.

"How are Ma and Pa?" Dahlia asks, referencing Bonnie's parents.

"Tripp has been working the ranch with Pa. He refuses to sell. You know how upset he was when your dad and I sold. He tried every way to convince us, even offered to give us cattle for us to start over. We're too old for that." Bonnie chuckles. "Ma says they'll die on that ranch and your pa will most likely be out in the field with the cattle and horses when it happens. And yet," she adds, her tone shifting from saddened to pointed at Dahlia. "They still make time to come to Friday night dinner."

Dahlia sighs. "I'm trying, Mom. I'm really trying. Please understand that I'm not missing because I don't love you. I'm not leaving like Graves and Sterling. I'm right here."

She places a hand on her mother's arm and Bonnie looks up at her with tear-filled eyes.

"I know, sweetie. You kids are growing up and as much as I wish I could keep you tied to me and at home, this is how life works. It's just hard to adjust some days. Your father and I are both so proud of you, Dahlia. Never think we're not. All I could ever hope for my kids is their happiness."

"I am happy, Mom. With my life. With my work. I'm happy exactly where I am—with who I am."

Bonnie places her hand over Dahlias and smiles. "Then I did something right, didn't I?"

Dahlia's throat tightens, and she pulls her hand back to take a drink of her coke.

"You and Dad did so much right."

# Chapter Four

"MAYBE I SHOULD GO this time. Then we'll get some answers and actually learn something about this man," Carly says as she helps load up the box with the bridal and maid of honor bouquets.

"Maybe he just wants to be left alone? Ever think about that?"

Dahlia checks the boxes on her sheet and closes the hatch. "I just find it super weird that he moved all the way out here and hasn't even introduced himself to the town—or like the businesses he'll be working with. A.K.A. you. Let me come. Maybe we'll find the skeletons in his closet and put an end to the mystery of Hunter Haynes."

Dahlia shakes her head. "First off, he introduced himself the last time I was there and I need you here. Tomorrow is the Christmas Parade and there's still a long list of things to get done. I'll be back this evening for any last touches after I finish setting up for—" She flips through her book for the name of her clients.

"Wades," Carly supplies.

"Yes—them. The Wades wedding."

Carly places a hand on Dahlia's shoulder. "Are you okay, D? You seem...tired."

Dahlia chokes out a laugh. "Why does everyone keep asking me that? What makes this year any different from the other six years I've been running this shop? It's Christmas and I'm a florist. It's in our job description to look tired at every major holiday."

Carly drops her hand and gives Dahlia a solemn look. "Someone has to look out for you. You're like a plant that you forget to water or set in the sun. Speaking of, have you eaten today?"

*No*, Dahlia sighs. "I'll grab something on my way. Seriously, I'm good. I'll be back by five!"

Her best friend sighs and Dahlia waves as she leaves the shop.

***

A WHITE WEDDING OVERLOOKING a ranch covered in fresh snow sounds like the most beautiful scene she could ever imagine. Until she's trudging through snow taller than her boots, carrying the floral centerpieces, garland, candelabras, candles, and everything else she needs for this wedding, into the cabin at Haynes Ranch.

She drops the last box a little harder than intended, and cringes. The last thing she needs is for something to break. Then she'd really be in trouble.

"Rough morning?" Hunter asks from the door, and Dahlia jumps at the sound of his voice. Zip sits at his side, his tongue hanging out and paws covered in snow.

*Is he talking to me?*

Dahlia blows her wild curls out of her face and looks up from where she stands with her hands braced on her knees. Her cheeks are flush and sweat trickles down her spine from the strain of getting everything inside from her SUV.

"Nope. Not at all. I live for this," she says while trying to control her breathing. After shedding out of her puffy jacket, she aggressively pulls her hair tie out of her messy bun, to grab the escaped pieces and put it up again.

"It's snowing," Hunter says casually as a smirk tilts the left side of his lip. His blue eyes sparkle with amusement, which only fuels the fire in her veins. He's disappeared without so much as a *nice to meet you*, and today he's showing up—to what—make jokes?

"Really? I hadn't noticed." Dahlia waves her hands at her soaked pants and boots. "You might want to shovel a path for your guests. I'm just saying."

Hunter chuckles and she notices the snow shovel in his hand as he walks out the door. She arches a brow at the peculiar cowboy. Is he trying to become acquaintances now? After showing no sign of even being friendly before?

She stretches her neck and pulls out the bride's file, placing it on the table to make sure not a single detail gets missed. When her music comes through her speaker, she's transported to a different head space and gets to work.

Outside, Hunter scoops a shovel of snow from the driveway and tosses it to the side. If he got the tractor, this would go faster, but the work keeps his mind and hands busy while Dahlia is inside. He pauses when he spots her twirling around the floor with the handful of white *roses*? He isn't sure. He wasn't raised by a man who brought his wife flowers and never had a reason to step foot into a florist shop. But watching her work mesmerizes him, just like it did the first day.

She's so aggressive and he finds that intriguing. Every girl he's been with has been meek or pouted when things didn't go her way. He has a feeling Dahlia would put up a delicious fight.

Zip barks and Hunter realizes he's standing there with the shovel in his hand, staring at the house.

He internally scolds himself.

What does he have to offer someone like her? A woman with her life figured out and not afraid to go after her dreams?

His chances of a happily ever after died when he came home. He didn't move here chasing fairy tales, either. There's a reason he doesn't mingle in town or make friendships. He's meant to be alone—minus Zip. And that's the way he wants it.

He finishes shoveling the walkways from the parking area to the cabin. Given the weather, it's probably best this client reserved the cabin. Hunter fixed several venue locations on the property. There's one with the lake as a backdrop, an arch nestled in the woods with wooden benches. On the far side of his property is an arbor overlooking the valley and mountains with a stone paved floor. The various options are one reason he bought this ranch. The place that took the most work was the barn; everything else was just a matter of getting seating and coverage.

Hunter carries the shovel back to the shed between the barn and the cabin. His heart stops when he passes the window and spots Dahlia standing on top of a ladder, stretching as high as she can, reaching for the exposed wooden beam above her. She's looped greenery around the beams, and this seems to be her last piece.

*How reckless can one person be*? A fall from that height and she'll surely break something...and he would've let it happen.

Hunter races up the steps and opens the door. Dahlia startles. Her balance falters, and Hunter's eyes go wide.

She drops the greenery and crouches, her hands clutching the top of the ladder as it wobbles. Hunter rushes across the cabin just as the ladder tilts sideways and Dahlia free falls. She screams and Zip barks a high-pitched yelp. Hunter wraps his arms around her before she hits the floor. She lands on top of him and the air is knocked from his lungs.

He keeps his arms wrapped tightly around her shaking body and catches his breath. Zip whines and presses his cold nose to Hunter's cheek and Dahlia props up and gets lost in his blue eyes. Her skin heats not just from embarrassment, but from being pressed against him. She's acutely aware of every part of his body that is touching hers.

Hunter lifts his hand to tuck her escaped curls behind her ear, and Dahlia's gaze flicks to his lips. He drops his hand to the floor and lets his head fall back, staring at the ceiling.

"You're incredibly reckless, and stupid," he states.

Dahlia blinks and shoves back to stand and glares at him as he gets to his feet. "Where the hell did that come from? You barely know me aside from saying random shit that makes zero sense." She grabs the ladder and puts it back in place.

"Oh, no you don't," Hunter orders and grabs her arm, jerking her back away from the ladder.

"Seriously? What has gotten into you? Go back to hiding or whatever it is you do anytime someone shows up. I have this under control."

She yanks her arm free and reaches for the ladder again, but Hunter grabs the metal frame and moves it away from the exposed beam behind him.

"Do you call nearly falling to your death, under control? Ladders literally have warnings that say, '*do not stand*', at the top. It's there for a reason, to keep you—" Hunter shakes his head and shifts his train of thought to one not driven by his emotions. "Do you realize how expensive it would've been to clean your blood up off this floor if I hadn't caught you? Not to mention, the wedding wouldn't have happened, and that's money out of both our pockets." Hunter folds the ladder and Dahlia grabs his shoulder, spinning him to face her.

"Well, you were here, so I guess I should thank you. But I will be putting that ladder back up and fixing that dangling monstrosity." She points at the exposed beam with a garland of greenery swaying above them.

Hunter's hand tightens around the ladder frame and Dahlia squares her shoulders, ready for a fight.

"This is my job and I'll be damned if I let a man tell me how to do it. The ladder...please," she adds.

"No," Hunter nearly growls.

Dahlia huffs and stomps her foot like that is going to deter him.

She rubs a hand across her forehead and counts backward to calm herself before she says something she'll regret. A ladder locks into place and she spins. Hunter is adjusting it under the hanging greenery and puts one foot on the rung.

"Uh, what are you doing?"

He climbs up three more steps. "I'm taller than you. I don't have to stand on the top, so tell me what it is you need done and I'll do it."

Dahlia scoffs. "You can't—but I—" Hunter reaches the greenery and glances down at Dahlia, whose hair is falling around her pink cheeks.

"Use your words," he encourages in a tantalizing tone.

*Holy fucking shit. Why is that so hot?* Dahlia clears her throat and tries to regain her composure. One minute he's complaining about her ruining his payday, the next he's saying stuff like that?

"Dahlia?"

He has his elbow propped on his knee and he gazes down at her like he has all the time in the world.

*Professional. I must remain professional. There is absolutely no way he has my stomach flipping just from looking at me.*

"Just make it look like the rest. Loop it around until you reach the end so it covers the entire beam, then drape the cord down the backside so it'll be out of view for the camera."

After he's done, Dahlia runs an extension cord from behind the altar and conceals it with tape on the floor that nearly matches the color of the wood. She plugs it in and the wood beams light up with a soft glow along with the garland draped across the stone mantle over the fireplace that will be their backdrop.

"Wait for it," she whispers as Hunter climbs down and folds the ladder. She strides to the light switch on the opposite side of the room and dims the lights low, but not completely off. The room warms with the yellow lights, and Dahlia gasps at the scene. "Imagine the candles lit in the aisle and on the tables."

She gestures to the standing candelabras at the end of every two rows and the tables in the other room set for the reception. The soft twinkling lights reflect in her brown eyes as she looks around the room in wonder.

"This is my favorite part," she whispers.

"It's beautiful," Hunter says, not taking his eyes off Dahlia. A soft, slow song comes through her speaker and her breath catches at the way he's staring at her. How is this the same man who just yelled at her for being reckless and stupid?

He looks like he's about to say something, but a blaring alarm cuts the song off. Dahlia jumps out of the trance she fell into.

Hunter grabs the ladder and whistles for Zip, who made himself comfortable and was nearly asleep on the floor. He reaches for the doorknob and pauses.

"I should've asked before, but...are you okay?" he asks.

She tosses her tools in her bag. "Thanks to you," she admits, and he nods. "Are you okay?"

His lips curve into a tight smile. "Yeah. I'm fine."

Dahlia watches until he's out of view down the steps and takes a deep breath. She's heard of men giving you whiplash, but Hunter Haynes is something else. And worst of all, she can't shake the way he looked at her with soft lights. His gaze held something, and she wanted more than anything in that moment to explore what exactly it was.

# Chapter Five

DAHLIA LEANS AGAINST THE back porch beam of her childhood home. Her parents used to own as far as she could see. Now beyond the fence that lines the property belongs to someone else. She brings her hot chocolate to her lips and takes a sip.

Graves hasn't called. Sterling did long enough to say Merry Christmas. Bonnie's face lit up from hearing his voice, but it broke Dahlia's heart when he hung up and her mother excused herself. She came back later with red-rimmed eyes.

Dahlia scrolls through her contacts until she gets to G.

Her thumb hovers over the name and she takes a deep breath, then touches the screen.

"Hey," she says after the voicemail beeps. "I don't know if you ever listen to these, but it's Christmas, and I thought..." her voice cracks and she leans her head on the wooden beam. "I miss you, Graves. We all miss you. I just wish you'd call to let us know you're okay...I love you."

It's been two years since Graves disappeared. Two years of Dahlia leaving voicemails and wondering if he's found whatever he was looking for. When he came back, like most veterans, he wasn't the same. He didn't fit in the way he used to and, versus letting his family help, he left a note that he needed to do this and left.

"I don't know why you do that," Tripp states as he steps around the corner of the house.

"What are you doing?" she snaps, wiping a stray tear.

"He left us, D. Sterling isn't any better. They abandoned their family, and all everyone does is cry about it." He sips his whiskey and Dahlia inhales and forces herself to not get baited into another argument with her younger brother. Especially not on Christmas.

"Just leave it alone, Tripp. Don't you have a girlfriend somewhere that needs her diaper changed?"

"At least I can get a date," he snaps, and Dahlia rubs her temples. He always gets mouthy with whiskey.

"I'm not doing this today."

"Whatever. We're leaving anyway," Tripp shouts his goodbyes through the house and his truck doors slam close. Plastering on her fake smile of everything is fine, she goes back inside.

Ma and Pa sit in the pair of rocking chairs closest to the fireplace, with Bonnie and Walt across from them on the couch. They're lost in conversation as Dahlia observes her shrinking family. She was always closer to Graves. He understood her ambitions and dreams for the shop. Sterling was a womanizer and only cared about how many dates he could get with his charm.

Looks like Tripp is following in his footsteps.

"Mom," Dahlia says softly, interrupting the conversation. "It was a delicious meal, as always. I think I'm going to head out."

Bonnie pushes to her feet. "Are you sure, honey? Is everything okay?"

Dahlia nods. "I'm just tired."

"Probably from all the work you've been doing," Ma interjects. "You need to slow down. You're going to run yourself into the ground."

"I love you too, Ma."

Bonnie cups Dahlia's cheek. "I'm fine, promise."

\*\*\*

CHRISTMAS LIGHTS DECORATE EVERY shop downtown. Even Turnpike has a Santa hat on its flashing open sign. It's like walking into a commercial with the blanket of fresh snow. Light flurries fall when Dahlia steps out of her parked car and she sighs at the sight of what she's accomplished.

She's just gotten out of a hot shower when her phone rings.

*Beau*. That can only mean one thing.

"He's drunk, isn't he?"

"Hey, kid," Beau answers. "He won't be driving home, if that's what you're asking. Tried to sneak the Wilkes girl in here, too. I called her daddy and I bet you can imagine how that went over."

Dahlia sighs and leans her head into her door. "I'll be right there."

By the time she gets back in her car and drives to the other end of town, it takes less than five minutes. Turnpike is relatively empty compared to normal. Given the holiday, most people are with their families. The ones who come here, don't have families—or, well, are like her brother—who think he has some major shit to work through.

She spots Tripp in the back, stumbling around a pool table with some other guys. Making her way over to the bar, she sits and Beau brings her a beer.

"How are you holding up?" he asks, leaning over the counter.

Dahlia takes a swig and turns her back to Tripp. There is no sense in trying to get him to leave before he's ready. He'll just make a scene and that's not something she wants to add to her family's plate right now.

"As good as I can be," she responds, letting the weight of everything drag her down.

"Still no word?"

She shakes her head. Most people in this town have stopped asking about her brother, but Beau asks every time. It's hard to not feel like family in a town as small as hers. Beau watched her and her siblings grow up, graduate, then move out. It's a rite of passage when he lets you come through those bar doors for the first time.

Someone shouts from the pool table and through the mirror behind the bar, Tripp raises a fist in the air. Dahlia sighs.

Hunter sits alone in a shadowy corner, nobody paying him any attention. From the moment Dahlia walked in, he's kept his eyes on her. He's thought about going to say hello, Merry Christmas, something. He's shocked to find her here of all places on a holiday. A woman like her struck him as someone who would be with her family or curled up under a blanket with a bottle of wine. Definitely not in a bar.

A man moves to sit beside her, and Hunter drops his gaze. Guess that's why she is here. Makes sense that someone like her would have a boyfriend. He takes another drink of his beer and Zip sighs at his feet.

At the bar, Beau plants his hands on the bar top and glares. "What do you want?" His tone is harsher than when he talks to Dahlia. She glances beside her and wants to face-plant into the bar top.

*Could this town get any smaller?*

"If that's how you talk to all your paying customers, you're lucky to still be in business," Peter remarks and leans closer to Dahlia. "What's a girl like you doing in a place like this?".

"Seriously?" Dahlia snaps. "Shouldn't you be home with *your family*? It's Christmas." She doesn't look at him as she speaks, keeping her eyes on Tripp through the mirror.

"Katherine's parents don't like me all that much. It is either stay home and fight, or hide out here until they go back to South Dakota. Seems like I'm not welcome here either," he says with a sigh, tossing his glass back. "Another." He gestures his empty glass at Beau.

The bar owner glares at him before walking away from Dahlia.

"And what could they possibly not like about you? The fact that you got Katherine pregnant while you were dating another woman or that you're a coward that runs away to the bar instead of facing his problems?" Dahlia's eyes go wide. She did not mean to say it. She was thinking it, sure, but it just...slipped out before she could stop herself. Chugging the rest of her beer, her skin heats from his gaze.

To her surprise, Peter laughs and slaps his hand on the counter. "Baby isn't holding punches tonight. Look out, world!" he shouts and leans in, his chest nearly brushing her shoulder. "Maybe if you had this fiery attitude when we were dating, I wouldn't have cheated on you. It's sexy as hell."

She spins and shoves him back with both hands to his chest. "What the fuck?!"

He crashes to the floor and takes a couple of bar stools with him. All eyes in the bar are on her, and her ears burn.

"Dahlia?" Tripp slurs and stumbles his way through chairs to get to her side. When he reaches her, he spots the man trying to untangle himself from the barstools. "Oh, it's on."

Dahlia grabs her brother's arm. "No, Tripp. You're both drunk. Let's just go."

"I've been waiting for years for this. I'm not leaving until this sack of shit learns a lesson," Tripp says. He's way past listening.

"Tripp," Beau bellows. "I think it's time for you to leave, son."

Peter gets to his feet, his red, glassy eyes glaring at Dahlia.

"What are you looking at, fucker?" Tripp takes a step forward and shoves Dahlia to the side. She lands against the bar and loses her balance. Strong arms grip her around the waist and help get her feet back under her. Hunter looks between her and the two getting ready to brawl.

"Are you okay?" he asks and all she can do is nod, his blue eyes shadowed by the brim of his cowboy hat.

*Has he been here the whole time?*

"Wait here," he instructs, and Dahlia blinks at his back as she tries to make sense of what she is seeing.

"And who the hell are you?" Peter slurs. He and Hunter stand at the same height, but Hunter keeps his hands in his pockets.

"Hunter, a friend of Dahlia's. Seems to me you've overstayed your welcome."

Zip growls at his side. Peter glances at the canine and fear flashes in his eyes.

Tripp turns to face Hunter. "I got this under control. Why don't you go back to wherever it is you came from? You don't belong here. This is our town and we're going to settle this like men."

Dahlia shoves her way past Hunter and stands between her brother and Peter. "Don't be stupid. We're going home before you get yourself thrown in jail. Now."

Tripp scoffs and reaches to push Dahlia to the side again, but Hunter grabs his arm. Tripp clenches his fist and swings at Hunter.

He blocks the blow and Dahlia screams to get her brother to stop. His punches are sloppy and Hunter has no problem dodging them and staying on his feet. "I don't think he's listening," he jokes as Dahlia's cheeks redden.

"Hunter," she groans and grabs her brother's drawn back fist. In a drunken haze, he spins and swings for Dahlia. Hunter grabs his shirt, hauls him back, and lands a solid punch to his temple, knocking him out cold. He fights through the rage and refrains from hitting the bastard again for going after Dahlia.

"Oh, my God! What the hell was that?" Dahlia shoves past Hunter and kneels by her brother. Peter glances from Hunter to Tripp and lifts his hands.

"Beau, my tab?" Peter asks, still eying the white German Shepherd.

Beau sighs.

"What did you do that for?" Dahlia asks Hunter.

"He was going to hit you," Hunter states, his fists still clenched at his side. Is she dating this abusive asshole? And what else has he put her through behind closed doors? Will he retaliate for what Hunter did tonight? Uneasiness rolls in his stomach, and he places a gentle hand on Dahlia's shoulder.

"If you're in danger, if he...hits you..."

She brushes his hand off and stands, huffing. "He's my younger brother who doesn't know how to control his liquor and has a short fuse. That—"

She points at Peter who walks out of the bar. For once, someone in this town doesn't know everything about her life. He doesn't know the embarrassing tale of Dahlia Brooks and she doesn't want him to. "He's nobody. What am I supposed to do with him?" she asks, pointing at Tripp.

*Her brother*, Hunter realizes. Knocking him out probably wasn't the best impression. He hauls the unconscious man to his feet. Tripp mumbles something, but his head falls to the side. "I can help you get him where he needs to go."

She places her hands on her hips and stares up at him. The fire in her brown eyes heats his blood. "It's the least you could do since you made the problem worse."

Hunter's lips part and shock resonates through him. "Made it worse? He was going to punch you."

She scoffs. "Tripp is just hot headed and with Peter—let's just say a fuse doesn't exist at all. I guess we'll take him back to my place. Let him sober up." She pulls her phone from her pocket and slips her card out of the back of the case. "What do we owe you, Beau?" she asks.

The bar owner shakes his head. "After the night you've had, it's on the house."

Hunter gets the feeling that Peter isn't just *nothing* like Dahlia hinted at.

"I owe you," she says and pulls her keys from her pocket. "I'll take him from here." She reaches for her brother, but Hunter doesn't let go.

"I'm not letting you climb a ladder alone, and I'm certainly not letting you carry the weight of some man. I don't care if he is your brother. You lead, I'll follow." He whistles and Zip sticks to his side as they walk out of the bar.

# Chapter Six

"I'm curious how you planned to get him up the stairs and into your room by yourself," Hunter teases as Dahlia walks him back out through her shop.

She smiles. "Honestly, I would've left him in the car and let him figure it out. I didn't want you to think I was a horrible sister."

They stand on the sidewalk; the snow has stopped falling and everything looks untouched minus her tire tracks from Turnpike.

"I think he would've deserved it," Hunter says with a smirk. Dahlia shivers under the cold, but she doesn't show any sign of wanting to go back inside. He sheds out of his topcoat and drapes it over her shoulders.

It smells like a wood burning fire and a hint of spice. Dahlia pulls it tighter around her body, thankful for the shield from the cold night air.

"You really don't know who that was at the bar?" she asks, genuinely curious.

"Should I?"

She shakes her head. "Since you're not from around here, I guess not." Her voice is thick with the emotions of the day and she angles her head to hide her features from Hunter.

"Are you okay, Dahlia?" Hunter asks, his tone soft, and he places a hand on her arm.

She nods. "It's Christmas. Everyone should be happy on Christmas." Her voice is hollow, and it tugs at his chest. The urge to wrap her in a hug is nearly overwhelming, but he's worried he'll only make it worse.

She steels her features and rolls her shoulders back. "Thank you for helping me get my brother inside and for preventing a bar fight I suppose. I could take you to your truck?"

"I don't mind the walk. It's a gorgeous night." Wonder fills his blue eyes, but Dahlia doesn't have the energy after today to do anything other than fall asleep.

She shrugs out of his jacket and hands it back to him. "Merry Christmas, Hunter."

"Merry Christmas, Dahlia."

He waits until he hears the click of the lock to her shop before shrugging on his jacket and walking to his truck. The snow crunches under his boots down the sidewalk. By the time he makes it to Turnpike, the open sign flickers out and he lets Zip jump across into the passenger seat.

Dahlia watches as he drives down the street, the soft glow of his taillights flash as he passes her shop. He knocked her brother out with one punch. And the way he moved to dodge every one of Tripp's punches, it's like he was trained in hand-to-hand combat. And why was he alone in the bar at Christmas? Does he not have a family to go home to or to come visit? Surely he didn't spend the holiday by himself.

*Who is he and where did he come from?* Dahlia stands in the window with a blanket wrapped around her shoulders long after Hunter is out of view.

"Dahlia!" Tripp shouts, then retches. She sighs and her shoulders fall forward.

"I'm coming," she says, grabbing water, aspirin, and disinfectant on her way.

This is going to be a long night.

*** 

Dahlia makes room for the Valentine's Day decorations. Even though it's only the beginning of January. As soon as the Christmas trees come down, the hearts, roses, and all things red go up.

"Nobody warned me that working at a flower shop would make you dread the holidays so much," Carly complains as she decorates the front of the shop with the new red, pink, and cream planters filled with house-plants, coffee cups with nauseating sayings on them like *you're the sugar to my coffee*, and red hearts that go everywhere.

Dahlia works on the display window, one of the vital parts of having a shop on Main Street.

"Right?" she agrees. "If a man ever gets me flowers, I think I'd actually laugh. This is probably why I'm doomed to be single. If a guy thinks flowers are a grand gesture, his bar is too low."

They both laugh.

"So, what is this I hear about a tall mysterious man dragging Tripp out of the bar?" Carly inquires.

Dahlia sighs and drops her hands to her side.

"That was fast," she mumbles.

"Small town," Carly shrugs although Dahlia expected nothing less.

"Tripp and I got into it at Mom and Dad's. He went to the bar. Beau called me. Peter was there. He called me sexy. I pushed him. Tripp tried to fight him. Hunter knocked him out, and that was it."

Carly stands with her jaw hanging open and her hands suspended mid-air where she was putting a door swag on the wall. "Say what, now? I need all that repeated, slower and with more details. Hunter Haynes was there?"

Dahlia huffs and jams a dahlia into the foam of her free-standing design. "Yes, he was there. He moved with practiced precision. Tripp never got a hit in and then with one punch, my poor brother was unconscious on the floor. Peter didn't even try anything after that. It was actually funny—later, when I thought back on it."

Carly squeals. "Hunter Haynes swooped in and was your knight in shining armor! How freaking sweet."

Of course, her hopeless romantic of an employee and best friend would see that side of the story. "It wasn't like that."

"Uh yeah, it is *like that*! He knocked a guy out for you and came to your rescue. Have you called him? Reached out? Anything?"

Dahlia wrinkles her nose. "Of course not! We have a professional working relationship. He was just being nice."

Carly places her hands on her hips and gives Dahlia a look of you've-got-to-be-kidding. Dahlia rolls her eyes and continues working.

"What did Peter say that made you shove him? It had to be bad..." Carly presses.

"I think he was coming on to me? It was weird. Then he said if I had this much fire when we dated, then he wouldn't have cheated on me. Like it was my fault, and I drove him to Katherine."

"That asshole!" Carly shouts.

"Then Tripp was drunk off his ass trying to fight him, and it was a whole mess. Seems this town has nothing else to talk about other than my love life."

She puts the finishing touches on the giant heart made of red, pink, and white dahlias. Stepping back, she admires the work and checks her watch. It's after ten and they still have loads of work to get done.

"Let's call it a night. We'll start on this early in the morning. I'm starving and exhausted."

Carly concedes and Dahlia locks the door behind her.

Alone in her apartment, she scrolls through social media. Haynes Wedding Venues pops up and Dahlia clicks the ad, scrolling through the different locations on his ranch. She opens up the '*About Us*' portion and her brows furrow at the lack of details. There is literally nothing about Hunter or who he is.

Her thumb hovers over the contact us tab. How pathetic are you to reach out to someone via their business page? Most of the time she doesn't think Hunter can stand her, but then the other night...when he gave her his coat...is she reading more into it than she should?

It could mean nothing.

It could mean something.

And she's reminded why she hates dating and men in general. All the not knowing, the over analyzing every move or thing said. And she isn't even dating Hunter.

Fine. She'll take life into her own hands and settle this once and for all.

She clicks contact us and it pulls up a form with an email inquiry.

No phone number.

Nope. She will not do that. She won't stoop to sending an email like it's 2008. Instead, she sends a text to one person she knows will have Hunter's number. She'll claim she left some vases at his place and needs to pick them up.

Within minutes she has a reply from Lauren with a winky face and the mysterious cowboy's number.

There's still time before she reaches the point of no return.

Before she can talk herself out of it, she hits call and stares at the phone still in her hand as the first ring comes through.

Then the second...the third...and—

"Hello, this is Haynes." His sultry voice comes through the phone.

Dahlia's mouth opens, but nothing comes out.

"Hello?" he asks again, and she clamps her mouth closed and throws her phone onto the couch then strides across the house and closes her bedroom door.

Hunter stares at his phone and then checks the time. It's after eleven at night. Zip stretches out beside him on the bed and he rubs a hand down his neck and the dog sighs in contentment.

He stares at the contact saved in his phone.

Dreaming of Dahlias.

He saved it when it was sent over with the first wedding contract under emergencies, in case he needed to contact her, of course.

But now she's calling him...

Perhaps it could've been a mistake? Pocket dial or what not? It's not like she said hello or answered him. Could she need something?

Should he call back? It could be an emergency...

He smirks and props his arm behind his head and lays back on his pillow.

A flower emergency? It was an accident. Had to be. There is no other explanation as to why she'd call him. She doesn't even like him, barely thanked him for helping with her brother. Not that he needed a thank you, but he hoped the situation would have softened her hardened exterior she seems to wear around him all the time.

Who is the real Dahlia Brooks? The only version he's seen is the one who hides in her work. He catches glimpses of who he imagines she might be while she works. Those moments when she gets lost in the details of designing. The way her gaze softens when she stands back and admires how all her hard work came together.

Hunter stares at his phone until the screen goes black.

If she really needed him, she would've left a message.

Friends. That's all he has to offer someone like Dahlia. There isn't any point in reading into this because he won't let it go anywhere.

He can't.

He couldn't make it work before and nothing has changed that he could make something like an actual relationship work now.

Sighing, Hunter places his phone back on the table and stares at the wood ceiling, accepting that he'll never be anything more to Dahlia Brooks than friends—if he can even achieve that.

# Chapter Seven

THE BLISTERING ICY WIND bites at Dahlia's cheeks. She grips the reins tighter and holds her hat down to keep it from blowing away. A calf sits in her lap, offering little heat from its tiny body.

"Is that all of them?" Pa shouts, his lips blue, and Dahlia worries if this is the storm that takes him out of this world. He has a calf of his own that was born maybe hours ago.

Tripp carries a third one in his arms over to his horse Dahlia is holding and drapes it across the saddle.

"I think so! I didn't see any others!" Tripp responds over the howling wind.

"We need to head back! It's getting worse!" Dahlia says, handing her brother his reins. He swings up in the saddle and maneuvers the calf over his lap.

This is the worst winter storm they've seen in years. It came so quick and so fast; ranchers didn't have time to prepare. When Tripp called saying he needed another set of hands at Pa's ranch, Dahlia closed up shop with the impending storm and came as quickly as she could.

She may not be a rancher now, but it's in her blood, and she knows the value lost from just a few calves if they don't make it.

The black calf across her legs barely has the energy to fight. It's so cold. The accumulating white blanket of snow across the ground is up to the horses' knees in some places and it's a slow process to get back to the ranch.

Inside the barn, Dahlia's parents have heaters, fresh hay, and towels to get the babies warm and dry. When Dahlia climbs out of the saddle and pulls her calf down with her—they are too late.

Tears burn in her eyes and she hands it off to her dad. There isn't any time for grief or sadness. The other two calves are relying on them to survive. When the heater and towels aren't enough, Pa grabs one and Tripp takes the other. They go inside and place the calves in the bathtub, using the warm water to get their temperature up.

Dahlia sags against the door frame, exhaustion, unlike anything she feels from her shop, drags her down. The cold has seeped into her bones and no matter what she tries, she can't get warm. The storm rages outside and she finds the tea kettle and fills it with water before placing it on the stove.

"Mother nature is a fickle bitch," Ma grumbles, startling Dahlia from her spaced out trance.

"She can be ruthless," Dahlia mutters.

"Poor babies don't stand a chance in this. I'd imagine your pa will want to go back out there in a few hours to see if the storm has any other cows in labor."

*Going back out again?*

Dahlia rolls her muscles and rubs her hands together.

"I'll go out and check the horses to prep for the next ride out." She gives her ma a soft smile and kisses her cheek.

"Ranching can be as rewarding as it can be a slap to the face."

Dahlia nods in agreement. For her the good days didn't outweigh the heavy feeling of losses like this one. The calves that don't make it cling to her and always have. She always thought she was too soft for this life.

This winter proves she was right.

They carried a total of ten calves to the barn before the snow stopped falling. Only one died, but the others were close. As long as the weather holds, Pa said they can go back out in a couple of days. They'll hope their mommas accept them back or they'll have bottle calves to raise.

There was a rotating shift of who sat out with the calves overnight. The whole family stayed at Ma and Pa's ranch, alternating with who slept. After three nights of sleeping on the floor, Dahlia is too tired to fix dinner for herself, and slides onto a stool at Beau's. Turnpike is having one of its livelier nights, but she doesn't look around for familiar faces. She wants whiskey and a hot burger to warm her up and then drag herself home for a hot bath and her bed.

"Rough day?" a deep voice asks. She rolls her chin across her hand to glance to her right. Hunter sits on the barstool beside her.

"It seems that's how our conversations start, doesn't it? I'm having a rough day, morning, something and you just pop up out of nowhere."

Hunter smirks and takes a sip of his whiskey.

"Take that as a yes. Your brother giving you more trouble? I don't see him here tonight."

Dahlia fails to suppress a yawn and waves for Beau. "No, he's at the ranch. The storm got worse than we expected and we nearly lost ten calves to the cold." She bites her bottom lip and drops her hand to her lap. "We lost one," she whispers and sighs.

"I didn't picture you as the ranch hand type," he states.

"What? Did you think I was a delicate flower?"

His smirk turns into a chuckle. "I don't know what I think yet." Taking another sip of his whiskey, he asks, "So, your family has a ranch?"

He wishes he could take the question back as soon as it slips out. When he watched her walk in, her lips turned down, etched with sadness, his chest ached at the weight on her shoulders. He should've left it alone. It's not his place to fix whatever is broken with Dahlia Brooks. He doesn't need to get to know her. But the longer he watched her sit alone at the bar, it hurt to see her so—lost looking. He just wanted to lighten the mood if he could.

Beau sets her whiskey down and Hunter's eyebrows raise in surprise at the drink stronger than beer.

Dahlia sighs and swirls the amber liquid around her glass. "My grandparents own a ranch. Pa refuses to sell even though he can't do it all himself. If they call and need me, I go." She shrugs and tosses back her whiskey, hissing as the burn goes down.

"But you don't like it?" he asks, careful to keep his gaze on his own glass.

"I never saw that future for myself. That's why I chose the flower shop. Ranching is too—" she struggles to find the word and finishes her glass of whiskey. She turns her head to look over at him, and her brown eyes draw him in. They're full of so much pain. He's never seen Dahlia like this. Not even when he had to knock her brother out and take him home.

"It fucking sucks," she says, her eyes welling with tears and her throat tightening. "It's too hard, and it hurts too much."

Her heart feels like it's breaking. It's like everything is piling up and she is on the verge of falling apart. The calf today in the snow was the final blow to the dam she's built around her heart.

Graves.

Sterling.

Peter.

Tripp.

She's exhausted. When is it her time for someone to take care of her? A tear slides down her cheek and she hastily wipes it away, straightening her spine and planting her hands on the bar top.

"Whew. Sorry about that," she says, her hardened exterior snapping back into place like an elastic-band.

Before Hunter can stop himself, he places a hand on her knee and Dahlia jolts from the contact. Her eyes widen and she shies away from his touch.

"Dahlia," he says, his voice thick with concern.

She shoves off the stool and digs for her card in her pocket. "I'm tired. Beau, can you make that burger to go?"

The bar owner nods and looks to Hunter like he's to blame for the change of heart. "Sure thing."

"You don't have to do that. I need to be heading home, anyway." Hunter stands and Zip gets up from his laid-out position and sits at his side.

"I'm not doing anything. Like I said, I'm tired." Dahlia gives Christy, the bartender, her card and pays for her meal and drink. "I'll see you around," she tells Hunter.

"I'll walk you out," Hunter says, standing and leaving cash on the bar top.

He moves too quickly for Dahlia to argue and holds the door open and she steps out into the freezing night. The shock of the cold air seizes in her lungs and she wraps her arm across her front tightly while the other clings to her food container. Hunter beats her to her driver's door and pulls it open for her.

"Are you sure you're okay? If you need anything, I could—"

Dahlia cuts him off. "No. I'm fine. Absolutely fine. Just need some sleep. Have a good night, Hunter." She pulls her door closed before he can respond, worried that if she lingers in his presence her facade will fall away, revealing the broken person she works so hard to hide. Hunter shoves his hands in his pockets and watches as she drives away.

He climbs into his truck and starts the engine, waiting for it to warm up. He palms his phone and stares out his windshield at the blinking open sign of Turnpike. Friends text friends all the time, right? He is nothing more than a friend checking on her. He unlocks his phone screen and pulls up Dahlia's number, and opens a blank text message.

She sits in her SUV, resting her head on the steering wheel as heat blasts against her skin. Her shoulders shake as uncontrolled tears roll down her cheeks. Dahlia lifts her head and stares at herself through the rear-view mirror.

"You get five minutes, Dahlia Brooks. Then you're going to get your shit together and stuff it all down."

Her phone dings in her pocket and she pulls it out, hoping it's not Tripp saying they need more help. The message is from an unknown number and she opens it.

**It's okay to ask for help.**

Dahlia looks behind her down Main Street, but it's empty. Another message comes through.

**If you want to talk, you can call me.**

She quickly backs out of the message and compares the phone number to the one she called the other night.

It's him.

He texted her and said she can call him? She won't, of course. Because what would she say? Spill her guts as to why she's a snotty mess right now?

She types out, *thank you*, then deletes it. What does she say to that?

"I can't deal with this," she mutters and locks her phone, slipping it back in her pocket. After locking herself in her apartment, she runs a hot bath and takes her food with her to the bathroom. A small table sits beside her garden bathtub and she eats her burger while feeling warm for the first time in days.

The unanswered texts from Hunter sit between them like a line drawn in the sand. If she responds she's opening up a new level of friendship, she doesn't know if she can risk her business—or even wants to, for that matter.

After several minutes of no response, Hunter sighs and puts his truck in reverse, backing out of Turnpike and heading home. He tells himself the want he feels to be there for Dahlia is because she was hurting and she's a friend. But as the sinking feeling of disappointment settles deep in his gut, the longer his message goes without a response, he knows there is something more and he needs to be careful.

There is a fine line between friendly conversation and actions. Tonight he was so close to crossing it when that first tear ran down her cheek.

# Chapter Eight

"DREAMING OF DAHLIAS. How can we help you?" Carly answers the cordless shop phone at the counter.

Dahlia is putting the final touches on Marni Foster's wedding bouquet in the back room when her best friend peeks her head around the corner with a very concerned look on her face.

"It's for you," she says, and Dahlia looks up from the bouquet in her hand. She takes the phone from Carly and pinches it between her shoulder and ear.

"This is Dahlia."

"Hello, this is Marni Foster," Marni responds. Her tone has Dahlia dropping the bouquet to her side and grabbing the phone with her free hand.

"Hey, is everything okay? I was finishing up your bouquet, actually."

There's silence for several heartbeats, and Dahlia wonders if the line disconnected.

"Hello?" she asks.

"Sorry, I'm here. We hit a snag this morning on the ranch. The farmhouse had a waterline freeze and bust... We are going to have to postpone the wedding."

Dahlia glances at the bouquet hanging in her hand. Her heart plummets at the thought of Marni asking for a refund. This wedding was huge, mainly because there were two of all the vital pieces. She's spent countless nights making sure every detail is perfect and now she won't be able to see it all come together.

"...there's no way we could find another venue this short of notice and I understand if you can't refund it. It is what it is."

"Wait," Dahlia says, an idea forming in her mind. "If we found another venue that wasn't the ranch, would you still want to go through with it?"

She walks into the front and hands Carly the wedding bouquet before shuffling through papers on the counter, looking for her phone.

"I'd have to talk to Tonya, Connor, and Hocks, but what can you find two days before?"

Dahlia pulls up the unanswered messages Hunter sent her the night after she broke down at the bar.

"You find out if they'd be on board and I'll make some calls," Dahlia tells her and hangs up the phone.

Carly rolls a sucker around her mouth and arches a brow. "That's not a good news face," she tells her best friend.

Dahlia huffs and shakes her head, her finger hovering over the call button.

"The wedding is off, unless—" Dahlia's voice cuts off.

Carly pulls the sucker from her lips and stands straighter. "Oh no..."

Dahlia nods. "Unless I can call in a favor, and the two brides and two groomsmen agree."

Carly perks up and a slow smile creeps across her lips. "It's about time you give that man a call."

"Shut up," Dahlia grumbles and takes a fortifying breath before pushing the call button.

It rings twice before Hunter answers.

"Haynes," he answers, his voice colder than it was when he talked to her at the bar.

"It's me," Dahlia says. Her nerves rattle in her voice.

*Get it together. This is a business call. Nothing more. Act like it.*

"Miss Brooks. How can I help you?"

*Miss Brooks? Okay, this is getting weird.*

"Um, well—" She swipes her hand on her leggings and glances at Carly before walking to her office and shutting the door. She stands in the middle of her cluttered bliss and sighs. "I should've responded to your text. I'm sorry."

"Is this a business call? I have work that needs to be done."

Her cheeks redden.

*Fine. If that's how he wants to play this. Perfect.*

"It is actually. I have a client whose venue fell through because of a busted waterline. I was calling to see if you had any openings on Saturday."

There's a pause.

"As in two days?" Hunter questions.

"Yes."

There's a shuffle from the other end. "I have nothing booked this weekend. They'd have access to the barn and the cabin."

"That's great. I'll let her know and call you back to confirm."

Before he says bye, she disconnects the call and strides back out of her office as soon as the shop phone rings again.

"Dreaming of Dahlias," she answers.

"It's Marni Foster calling you back. If you can find us another venue, we'll take it."

Dahlia smiles in triumph, her eyes lighting up with the news. "Actually, I found one. Haynes Venues has a barn and a cabin both open this weekend."

\*\*\*

WHEN SHE GETS TO Hunter's with her car loaded down for all the things she needs to save this wedding and make it a masterpiece, Hunter is on the tractor in front of the cabin shoveling snow from the driveway and parking lot. Her stomach flips at seeing him after how he acted over the phone.

Business. Strictly business.

She grabs the Foster and Curston binder from her passenger seat and tugs her jacket tighter around her before stepping out. Zip sits on the cabin steps, watching his owner then looking at Dahlia, but doesn't make a move to come over to her. The snow stopped falling days ago, but it looks like Hunter hadn't touched it until now. He catches her gaze and tips his hat before returning to the task and shoveling snow off to the side.

Dahlia drops her chin and walks to the back of her SUV and pops open the back. Marni and Tonya unanimously chose the barn as their wedding venue and reception area. Dahlia carries everything inside and turns on her music, tuning out the rest of the world and her uncertainties and does what she does best.

When Hunter finishes moving all the snow, he takes the tractor back to the working barn out of sight of the wedding venue. He doesn't need anyone complaining about a green eyesore during their photographs. Zip runs alongside him until he parks the tractor and gets in his truck. His hand tightens on the steering wheel and he debates going to see if Dahlia needs help or to just stay out of sight like he planned. If she wants to keep things strictly business, he can do that.

So, he'll stay away.

Dark gray clouds set in the distance over the mountains and by the ache in Hunter's leg, he's willing to bet there's more snow coming in tonight. He checks the weather and sure enough, snow is due to move in around five in the afternoon. Zip whines when Hunter doesn't move the truck.

Hunter smirks and fires up the engine, and drives across his ranch to his home. If Dahlia needs anything she has his number. She'll just have to call.

***

DAHLIA STARES UP AT the ladder at the bare top left corner of the arch. It takes both hands to hold the spray of flowers and she can't climb without being able to hang on.

She stomps her foot and wants to strangle something at what she is about to do.

"Dreaming of Dahlias," Carly answers the phone with the perfect customer service voice.

"Are you busy?" Dahlia asks.

"We're selling hearts like crazy!" she says with enthusiasm.

Dahlia drops her head. "That's great!" she responds, knowing Carly said exactly what she thinks Dahlia wants to hear, but that means there is only one other person she can call.

"Did you need something?" her best friend asks.

"Oh no! I was almost finished here and wanted to check on you."

Carly talks to a customer away from the phone.

"I'll see you later." Dahlia hangs up and bites her lip and throws an air punch.

She glares at the betraying floral piece and groans as she walks the length of the barn back outside. All signs of the tractor, Hunter, and his truck are gone.

*Freaking fantastic.*

Dahlia pulls up Hayne's Venue's contact on her phone. The name is a small screw you for the way he referred to her as Miss Brooks. Defeated, she hits the green call button. With the phone on speaker, she paces outside the barn and grows anxious with each passing ring. If he doesn't answer, she's left to figure this out herself and she has no idea how she can do it alone.

"Haynes," he finally answers, and Dahlia is fuming with annoyance.

"Where the hell are you?" she snaps, spinning around with her free hand stretched out wide.

"Enjoying a hot coffee?" His voice is smug across the phone and Dahlia wants to scream.

"You're in town?!" How is she possibly going to get this arch done before the Curstons and Fosters show up?

"No," he says flatly. "I'm at home."

She jerks her attention to the cabin across the driveway, preparing herself to say the words she hates above all else. Her tongue sticks to the roof of her mouth as she swallows. "I need your help," she whispers.

"You cut out. I didn't hear you. What did you say?"

With an exasperated sigh, she brings the phone closer to her mouth. "Would you...*please*...come to the barn and help me with this last piece?"

"I'll be right there." He doesn't wait for her response before he hangs up. Dahlia watches the cabin for movement or any sign of Hunter making his way to the barn, but she doesn't see any at all. Does he think it's funny to mess with her about something so important?

# Chapter Nine

DAHLIA SHIVERS IN THE cold and goes back inside, wondering if Hunter really is coming. What feels like an eternity later, the roar of an engine approaches and she rushes to the door, her hair a frizzy mess.

Hunter steps out of his truck, a wince crinkling around his eyes as his boots hit the snow. Zip launches out of the seat behind him and freezes at the sight of Dahlia.

"Where have you been? I called you forever ago!" She grows more anxious with each passing minute. This arch has to be complete by the time the Wedding party arrives.

Hunter arches a brow and sucks on his teeth. "You called me fifteen minutes ago. Where's the fire?"

She huffs and spins on her heel, stalking back down the aisle to the ladder. Hunter follows behind her, ordering Zip to stay just inside the entrance, not wanting him to mess something up.

Her work never ceases to amaze him. When his eyes land on the arch, the fiery woman, who he can't get out of his head, stands with her hands on her hips.

"What are you doing? I need you over here."

Hunter smirks. "You need me? Never thought I'd hear those words coming for you."

Rolling her eyes, she climbs up the ladder. Once she reaches the top of the arch, she looks down and points to a large spray of flowers and some brown fluffy stuff that sticks out in all directions.

"Hand me that," she orders.

Hunter doesn't budge.

"Please…" she relents.

He sheds out of his winter coat and carefully lifts the arrangement. "What the hell is this stuff?" he asks as the fluffy part sheds on his shirt.

"Pampas grass. It's like the craft glitter of the florist world. It sheds, sticks to everything, but is so dang pretty." She grunts under the weight and lifts the arrangement above her head to the top of the arch.

Hunter brushes the remnants off his shirt and glances up when Dahlia mutters a string of curses.

"This isn't working!" she shouts, and Hunter rolls his lips to keep from smiling at her frustration. "You're going to have to come up here."

She straddles the top of the ladder, hooking her feet on the step and brace to keep her balance.

Hunter grabs the ladder and climbs. His body brushes along Dahlia's shoulder, and he places one hand on the arch to keep his balance. Her forehead comes to his chin, and he gazes down at her, quickly looking away when he notices how low her shirt sits along her breasts.

"What do you need me to do?" he asks.

She passes the arrangement to him and he's forced to use both hands to balance it.

"Hold this where I had it and I'm going to strap it in place."

His body shakes slightly as he tries to find his center of gravity. She made it look so easy up here reaching above her shorter frame like a ballerina standing on her toes.

Hunter stretches his arms tall, his frame towering over Dahlia slightly.

"Yes," she mutters, already concentrating on the ties around the floral foam. One of the pieces of pampas grass brushes across Hunter's mouth and he spits at the texture clinging to his lips.

"Almost done," Dahlia says as his muscle's tighten at the suspended angle.

"Any day now," he remarks.

With one final tug, Dahlia drops her hands. "Okay. Moment of truth. Let go."

Hesitantly, Hunter drops his hands from the arrangement, placing one back on the arch and Dahlia sighs in relief. She turns, momentarily forgetting how close Hunter is and her breath catches when she stares up into his beautiful blue eyes.

His grip tightens on the arch, keeping him in place and from reaching for her. Pampas grass clings to her curls and shirt, but she doesn't seem to notice. She shifts under the intensity of his studying stare and clears her throat.

She's a strong, independent woman and she *will not* melt for some man in a cowboy hat.

"You're in my way," she remarks dryly, and Hunter pushes off the arch and climbs off the ladder. Zip sits from his lying position when Hunter's boots hit the floor, but his owner gives him a signal to stay put.

When Dahlia is off the ladder, he shoves his hands back in his pockets.

"Perfect!" she squeals, and Hunter hates how her excitement makes him feel. When she grabs the ladder to pack it up, Hunter steps forward, taking it from her hands and effortlessly snaps it closed. She stares at him warily before grabbing the rest of the tools she borrowed from his shed.

"Careful with this door," he says as he swings the shed door open. "The latch is loose and if you bump it just right, it locks on its own," Hunter warns. Dahlia looks at the piece of metal standing straight up that is used to latch across the door to keep it from falling open.

"Good to know," she says, stepping inside the small room. It's barely big enough for both Dahlia and Hunter to stand without brushing shoulders every time they move.

She drops an armload of things on the workbench along the side of the room and the door closes behind them. Hunter sits the ladder down to lean against the wall. He cringes as Dahlia haphazardly puts things back where they go.

"Here, I'll do it," he says, trying to interject when she puts the pliers where the hammer is supposed to go.

"No, no. I got it." She reaches across his outstretched arm and puts his cable ties back in the wrong drawer.

"You certainly helped yourself, didn't you?" he asks. It's meant to be a joke, but his body is tense.

"I'll replace the ties I used, but isn't that what these are here for? To be used by the venue clients?" Her curls fall like a curtain around her face, hiding her tinged cheeks.

"Well, yes—I didn't mean—just let me get it." Hunter reaches for the wire cutters she's about to place in the wrong drawer and Dahlia steps back.

She's too quick. It throws her off balance, and she trips over her feet. Hunter tries to grab her, but her failed attempts at regaining her balance make it impossible. Her shoulder slams into the opposite wall, shaking the small room Hunter built onto the barn for the shed. He's there to catch her as she bounces off the unforgiving wall, her face a mask of embarrassment and anger.

"I'm fine," she says through gritted teeth and shrugs out of his embrace. "Here." She hands him the wire cutters, intent on leaving this small space and Haynes Ranch. She doesn't know if she'll ever come back. Perhaps it is time to let Carly take the lead on some weddings. She can do them all right here, so Dahlia doesn't have to deal with this insufferable man anymore.

"Dahlia," Hunter says, his voice tender and she wants to slap him for feeling sorry for her. Her shoulder hurts like a bitch, but really it's her pride that's hurt more than anything. What is it about him that makes her so...unsteady? It's like when she's around him, he pulls all her self-doubts and brings them to the surface.

She doesn't answer him or stop. She pushes the wooden door—but it doesn't budge. With more force, she shoves her body weight into it. Still nothing.

"No, no, no! This cannot be happening!" At the sound of her raised voice, Hunter quickly closes the distance between the workbench and the door. Dahlia moves to the side as he takes her place and grunts as he pushes on the door. The metal latch clanks from the outside and refuses to budge.

Hunter sighs and drops his shoulders. "It's locked."

"No, it can't be!" Dahlia pushes him back aside and tries again with no luck. Hunter leans on the workbench and crosses his arms, watching her act like a mouse caught in a trap. Her voice continues to rise in pitch as she repeats the word no and beats on the door like that will magically get it to open.

Hunter's humor fades when her demeanor changes from desperate to panicked. Her pleas sound broken through trembling lips.

"Dahlia," he says, trying to draw her attention, but she doesn't hear him. She can't over the roaring in her ears. Hunter grabs her shoulders and spins her to face him. Her brown eyes are large and tears stain her cheeks. Her body trembles under his hands and he recognizes what is happening.

"I need you to breathe for me." He emphasizes by taking a deep breath and letting it out slowly. Her eyes dart around, not focusing on any certain point.

"Come on, Little Flower. Look at me, focus on my hands on her arms, the slight pressure through your soft sweater. Listen to the sound of my voice. You can do it."

Finally, her brown eyes land on him, but she still seems so far away, lost in the recesses of her mind.

"In and out," Hunter repeats and her breath stutters as she tries to inhale. "Again," he encourages.

Her chest rises, and it nearly brushes against his body. "Thank you," she whispers, her voice so quiet he barely hears it.

Hunter's brows furrow with a list of unasked questions. The dim light of the shed shines on pieces of pampas grass in her hair. Slowly, he lifts his hand and pulls the pieces free from her luscious curls and lets them fall to the floor.

"It really gets on everything, doesn't it?" he teases. Dahlia glances out of the corner of her eye as he plucks another piece free.

A small smile tugs at the corner of her mouth. He carefully brushes the back of his hand across each cheek to wipe away her tears.

"Are you okay?" Hunter asks, his voice low and husky. "Do you want to talk about it?"

"I don't like feeling trapped—it's—"

Zip barks outside, cutting her off. The metal latch scrapes and the door swings open, flooding the small shed with more light.

Lauren's brows raise at the sight of Hunter and Dahlia pressed close to each other in the small room. Dahlia's eyes are red and she quickly steps back, wiping at her face.

"What happened here?" Lauren asks.

Dahlia doesn't respond. She rushes past the wedding planner, grabbing her jacket and phone, and is out of the barn before Hunter steps out of the shed.

"Dahlia," he calls after her, worried if she is okay to drive. By the time he gets outside, her SUV is halfway down his driveway.

# Chapter Ten

"I'M SURE IT'S NOT that bad," Carly assures Dahlia as she lies on her couch with a glass of wine.

"Oh, it was *that bad*." She recalled the events that happened with Hunter. "Which is why you're doing the weddings there from here on out."

Carly lets out a nervous chuckle. "Yeah, please don't do that to me. Have you met these brides? They're terrifying."

Dahlia groans and lays upside down on the couch, her hair dragging along the floor.

"There's more," she states, barely above a whisper. "Remember when we were kids...in the cave?"

Carly's expression goes grim, and she downs the contents of her glass. "Yes, of course. Why?"

"I was back there today." Dahlia's thoughts go back to when she was younger. Carly and she rode horses up in the mountains for a trail ride and curiosity got the best of them when they stumbled upon a cave entrance.

Dahlia traveled the deepest when some rocks gave way separating her from Carly. She was stuck in utter darkness for hours while Carly rode back to get her parents and brothers to help move the rock and get her out.

"D." Carly's tone is full of everything she isn't saying.

The silence in Dahlia's apartment is heavy as they both get sucked into one of the most terrifying memories of their life.

Carly jumps up to her feet and slaps Dahlia on the side of her ass.

"Get up. We're going out."

"What? No, Carly. I just want to lie here."

Not taking no for an answer, Carly flips on the bright light in the living space and claps her hands together. "Which is exactly why I'm not letting you. You have nothing in here to eat and if I know you, which I do," she says proudly. "You haven't eaten since the breakfast I brought in this morning."

Dahlia glances at her friend, guilt written all over her expression.

"Exactly. So. Get. Up."

"Where are we going?"

Carly grabs a clean blouse and jeans from Dahlia's closet and throws them at her. "To get food and do some dancing."

Dahlia groans and knows when her best friend sets her mind to something, there is no changing it. "Fine. But I'm not going to have fun."

"We'll see about that."

\*\*\*

DAHLIA TOSSES BACK THE shot and Carly cheers as she orders two more.

"Shouldn't we pace ourselves?" Dahlia asks as a fresh shot glass is set in front of her before the burn of the first one hits her stomach.

"We're going to hit our peak first." Carly lifts the small glass and hands it to Dahlia.

Her nose wrinkles and she tosses it back, coughing as this one hits her throat. "Are we peaked?" she asks, hoping that is the last one for a while.

"Nearly," Carly says with a smile, and Christy, the bartender for the busy Saturday night, sets two beers down for the women to nurse.

Carly pulls Dahlia's phone from her pocket while she isn't paying attention and types in her lock code to send a message before she notices.

While Dahlia loosens up, Hunter sits in front of his fireplace, the wood burning low as he stares into the knots of the wood grain along the walls.

Zip huffs as he lays at his feet, his body long past exhausted from the day's events. Hunter keeps replaying the vision of sheer horror that filled Dahlia's features when the door locked. He knows the look well.

More than anything, he wanted to get her to open up to him. To at least give him a chance to show her he understands and maybe it would do her some good to talk to him about what was bothering her. First the bar with her brother, then the night of Christmas, and now today.

There is more to Dahlia than the strong woman she puts on, and he wonders if she ever lets anyone in.

His phone chimes by his bed, and he winces as he gets up, striding across the small space. It's probably another venue interest form coming through his email.

To his shock, it's a text from Dreaming of Dahlias. Did she forget something at the barn? Did her clients complain and now she's messaging him to give him a piece of her mind? He expects nothing less.

Sitting on the edge of his bed, he prepares himself for the worst and opens the message.

**Turnpike.**

He waits, wondering if another message will come through, but that's it.

One word.

He could call her. It could've been a mistake. An accidental text.

He walks to the door, debating with each step he takes.

He's too damaged. He won't be enough for her. She deserves more than what his life offers.

Stay. Go. Stay. Go.

By the time he reaches for his hat and coat hanging on the rack on the wall, he's decided.

"Let's go, Zip."

The gravel crunches under his tires as he pulls into Turnpike. The lot is full of cars and the music thumps from inside. He usually avoids this place Thursday through Saturday for this exact reason.

His skin itches with anticipation, but he turns off the ignition and steps out of his truck. Zip jumps down and sticks to his side. The frigid air burns his eyes, and he pops the collar of his coat to block the breeze.

He tips his cowboy hat as he steps past people on the porch. Once inside, he shifts uneasily at the number of people dancing and milling around the bar. As he searches for Dahlia, he sticks to the wall, keeping the crowd from being at his back.

He makes it to the far side of the bar and flags down the girl working for a beer.

Laughter overpowers the music playing and Hunter jerks his attention to the source.

There she is.

Dahlia's curls hang loose around her face as she sways and fumbles through the steps with a blonde woman. She's smiling so hard; her eyes are narrow slits and the sound of her laugh is the best thing Hunter's heard in a long time.

The blonde catches him staring and nudges Dahlia before pointing in his direction. Dahlia's eyes widen and she falters, tripping over her feet, nearly falling forward.

Hunter smirks and grasps the beer left for him at the bar and takes a long drink, then salutes the bottle in her direction. She weaves a crooked line as she walks to him, giggling like someone without a care in the world.

"Is that *the* Hunter Haynes? I thought you didn't come off your big mysterious mountain?" Several customers turn their heads to look at Hunter at Dahlia's loud words.

The back of his neck burns from the lingering gazes and he drops his chin. "You seem...drunk."

"I'm peaked!" she shouts and leans against the bar, bumping into Hunter's body as she does. Zip lays at the other side of his feet, and he lifts his head at the movement.

"Am I supposed to know what that means?" he asks, cautious of the sideways glances in Dahlia's direction.

"Why are you so grumpy all the time? You should let loose! Get on *this* level." She drags her hand down her front, accentuating her body.

Hunter raises his brows, and he takes another drink, trying to solve the puzzle that is Dahlia Brooks. "Is that why you texted me? To *get on your level*?"

Her brows pinch and she blinks when he's entirely too close to bring into focus. "I didn't text you," she slurs.

Hunter clears his throat and straightens on the bar stool. "Yes, you did."

Dahlia flips her hair and her blouse falls askew off her shoulder, exposing the soft skin at the juncture of her neck.

She leans forward, looking up at him through her eyelashes and he has a clear view of her breast pushed up by her bra. "And why would I text you?"

Hunter shrugs. "I was wondering the same thing."

She waves a hand at Christy for another beer. She fumbles with the bar stool as she tries to climb up and Hunter reaches a hand out, prepared to catch her if he needs to.

"Are you sure that's a good idea?" he questions when the glass bottle taps onto the wooden bar top.

She waves his arm away and drinks half the bottle before coming up for air. "I'm fine," she hiccups.

Hunter's curiosity of what made Dahlia text him dies with the sight of her drunken state. She isn't thinking clearly and probably won't remember any of this tomorrow. It's not like her message had any meaning. It was one word and he drove like she's already got him hook, line, and sinker.

Annoyed with his own wishful thinking that she might actually want his company and not whatever *this* is, he gets up from his bar stool and puts some cash on the bar to cover his tab.

"Where are you going?" she asks, spinning around and tilting too far to the side. Hunter grabs her hand, and she falls into his chest. Her breasts rise and fall, pushing against his jacket as she slowly angles her head back and looks up at him.

She twists her hand to hold his and leans into his muscular frame.

"Why did you text me?" he asks again, needing to know what impelled her to finally reach out to him.

"I didn't," she says again, her lips parted as her rich brown eyes bounce between his features, like she can't focus on just one spot.

Hunter sighs and goes to drop his hand, but she squeezes it so slightly, he thinks he imagined it.

"You could stay?" she offers. "I mean, you don't have to leave. Unless there's someone you need to get back to, or something you need to do. Never mind, you're right. You should—"

He cups her cheek and places a thumb on her plump lips cutting off her rambling. "Do you want me to stay?"

"I shouldn't." She swallows and offers a small smile. "We're professionals and all that. We have business relationships to maintain."

Hunter nods and goes to drop his hand again, but she clutches it to her chest, her eyes pleading from the words she isn't saying.

He tucks her curls behind her ear, his hand lingering as his fingers tangle in her hair. "Okay, Little Flower."

Her heart skips at the sound of those simple words coming off his lips. Even in her hazy state, she recalls him saying it earlier, but she was too panicked to grasp onto it.

"Do you dance?" she asks.

Hunter chuckles and glances down at his boots. "Not even a little."

Dahlia looks past him at the dance floor where her friend is going strong with a group of women as they slide their boots across the floor.

"Do you want to step outside? It's kind of hot in here."

He nods. "Sure." Whistling for Zip he follows her.

She takes two steps and has a Jack Sparrow sway to her walk. Hunter wraps a steady arm around her waist and keeps her snug against him as they make their way to the back door.

# *Chapter Eleven*

HUNTER HASN'T HAD NEARLY enough to drink for the cold air to feel anything but cold. While Dahlia spreads her arms and inhales the night air like it's her first breath of oxygen since she arrived at Turnpike.

"I hate the snow," she mumbles. "Did you know that?"

Hunter shakes his head. "What do you hate about it?"

Dropping her hands, she grabs the railing and leans forward, gazing out at the vast white fields and hills.

"Everything is dead, suffocated and frozen out. There aren't any flowers and nothing can thrive in it."

Hunter stares out at the back parking lot. He's never liked the snow particularly. He knew what he was signing up for when he moved to Wyoming, but that first long winter had him ready to bail on more than one occasion.

"Why are you here?" she asks, and he peels his eyes away from the landscape and over to her. "Why did you come here? I can't figure it out."

He sucks on his teeth and scratches the scruff on his cheek. "Why a florist?" he deflects.

"What do you mean?" she asks, her brows pinched and gaze accusatory.

"Why did you open a flower shop and want to become a florist?" Is it wrong of him to take advantage and use alcohol to get to know her better?

She texted him and asked him to come here. Surely she can't fault him for genuinely wanting to get to know her.

"Have you ever seen a seed?" she asks, and Hunter gives her an incredulous look. "Well yeah, okay, but like if you hold a seed in the palm of your hand...it's so tiny, so fragile, but that tiny piece holds so much life. It has the potential to grow and bloom into something greater than anyone would ever think could come from such a tiny speck."

The depth of her words draws him in and he turns to fully face her while her eyes light up as she continues.

"I wanted to be a part of something that incredible and beautiful. I wanted to take a living thing and make it better than it ever thought possible. I feel the most like my true self when I get lost in an arrangement, trusting my instincts to see the entire picture while working on one tiny element. Isn't that what we all want? To be a part of something greater?"

Her eyes shine as she gazes up at him. Passion pours from every part of her features, like she's just cut out her heart and showed him the innermost parts of what makes her tick. To anyone else, it just looks like randomly placed flowers and decorations, but to Dahlia it's clear her work is what fills her cup and she loves it without a doubt.

"And here I thought you just liked pretty flowers," Hunter says with a smirk and Dahlia's lips crack into a wide smile.

"They are pretty, aren't they?" she sighs and leans her butt into the railing. Her eyes get heavy and Hunter takes a step closer.

"Let me take you home," he offers. "Does your friend need a ride, too?"

"Carly? I forgot all about her!" Dahlia exclaims and lunges for the door. When she reaches for the knob, she misses. And again. And again.

"Why is it moving?" she whines.

"I don't think it's the door knob that's moving," Hunter remarks and opens the door, keeping her within grabbing range in case she falters. Zip keeps his place next to Hunter, even with the crowded room.

Dahlia giggles as they step back into the busy bar. She rushes to the dance floor and links arms with Carly. Her curvy hips rock and sway, captivating Hunter with how free she looks. He stiffens when someone walks up beside him. Without turning his body, he angles his head to see who is intruding his space.

He recognizes the man from the night he knocked out Tripp.

"I see what you're doing," the man states, and Hunter fixes his attention back on Dahlia.

"And what is that?" Hunter asks.

"She's drunk. This isn't her. She's not this carefree woman who does casual sex. I'm not letting you leave this bar with her so she can hate herself tomorrow."

"I don't think I caught your name," Hunter says politely, despite the way the stranger is talking to him. As if he'd take advantage of a drunk woman like that.

"Doesn't matter." The man steps closer and leans in. "Stay the fuck away from Dahlia."

Zip lets out a low growl at the tension and Hunter sucks in a breath, tilting his head to the side. He turns and faces the obnoxious asshole that acts like he has some claim on Dahlia. Hunter notices the glint of a wedding band on his finger. Could this be another one of her brothers?

Before he can ask, someone knocks into his side, wrapping their arms around him and he looks down to Dahlia, smiling and laughing. Her expression falls and morphs into white fiery anger when her gaze lands on the man.

"Peter. What the fuck do you want?" Her tone has Hunter tightening his grip and angling her slightly away from Peter.

"Dahlia, I'm going to take you home. We don't want you *doing* anything you'll regret." He uses a placating tone and emphasizes the word '*doing*' while turning his attention to Hunter.

"I can *do* whoever and whatever I want," Dahlia snaps. Her cheek brushes against Hunter's chest as she gazes up at him. "Take me home? Carly said she'll find a ride."

Hunter brushes her wild curls behind her ear. "Are you sure?"

Dahlia nods, not an ounce of doubt in her brown eyes.

"You can't be serious, D. Throwing yourself at some stranger. I've known you my whole life. This isn't you. When did you become a slut?" Peter's voice becomes a shout, and Dahlia's cheeks redden.

"That's rich coming from you," she hisses. "Tell Katherine she was the best thing to ever happen to me. Saved me from...this." She points her finger at the man and Hunter slowly puts the pieces together that he isn't her brother. He's her ex on a power trip of seeing the woman he let go be with another man.

Peter's brows furrow and his fists clench at his side. His gaze is solely locked on Dahlia and he steps forward as if to grab her.

In a swift movement, Hunter pivots her behind his back and faces Peter head on. Zip stands ready to defend his owner at his side.

"You saw what I did to her brother," he threatens.

Peter freezes, but keeps his fists ready. His jaw ticks, and Dahlia peers around Hunter's demanding frame.

"Honestly, I wouldn't mind a repeat show," Dahlia states, and Peter's glare shifts to her.

Hunter watches the debate flicker across Peter's gaze. At this point half the bar is waiting to see what will happen, the other half is too drunk to notice.

"No, man," Peter mutters. "She isn't worth it. Enjoy my seconds."

Dahlia makes a noise that chinks away at the armor Hunter wears when he's around her. He wishes the asshole would throw a punch just so he could finish it.

Peter walks away, giving Hunter his back like he doesn't take his threat seriously. Rage boils in his blood, but there are more important things right now than starting a bar fight. When he turns, Dahlia's eyes glisten and his muscles relax.

"Little Flower," he whispers, and Dahlia shakes her head.

"Take me home," she begs. She's barely holding it together and doesn't want to break here. Peter won't have the satisfaction of seeing he got to her.

Hunter takes her hand and leads her to his truck outside. Zip jumps in the back and once she's in the passenger seat, Hunter stretches the seat belt across her body and clicks it into place. She places a hand on his arm laying across her stomach and he pauses.

His hat shadows his features from the cab lights, but her warm brown gaze is full of something Hunter has never seen Dahlia show.

Desire.

He clears his throat and closes her door. His body shudders at the image of Dahlia underneath him with that same expression.

He can't tonight. He isn't that man Peter claimed him to be. But it'll take every ounce of his willpower to prove it, because he wants her.

He climbs into the driver's seat and starts the engine. Dahlia presses her forehead to the cold window for the short drive downtown.

"Park around back," she instructs when he pulls into the front. She doesn't need the town whispering about Hunter Haynes' truck being parked outside her shop all night.

Hunter drives past Dreaming of Dahlias and parks in one of the vacant shop spots. Before he can reach her door, she tumbles out, gripping the handle to keep from falling.

"Easy," he tells her, and she moves her hands to his arm, clinging to him for balance. He lets Zip out of the backseat and helps Dahlia to her door. She pats herself down and hisses.

"I left my keys with Carly." Letting go of Hunter's arm, she uses the wall as she leans down to a planter and tries to tilt it up.

Seeing her struggle, Hunter walks over and lifts the planter, and plucks the key from under the pot.

"Now you know my secret hiding place," Dahlia states. "You can come in whenever you want."

Hunter unlocks the door. "Only when you ask me to."

Dahlia giggles and practically falls into her shop. A hallway light flicks on, showing the stairs that Hunter carried Tripp up.

Gripping the railing with both hands, she counts each step as she takes it. Zip rushes ahead, annoyed with the slow pace, and sits on the top of the stairs.

"Oh, look at the puppy," Dahlia coos, crawling up the last couple of steps and sits next to Zip.

Hunter chuckles and Zip licks her nose as she pets down his neck and back. Her elated gaze falls to Hunter, and she cocks her head to the side.

"I can't figure you out, Hunter Haynes."

He shrugs. "I can't figure you out either, Dahlia Brooks."

She reaches for him with a wavering hand and he pulls her to her feet and helps her into her apartment.

He sits her on the couch and pulls her boots off one at a time. "You're going to feel rough tomorrow."

She smacks her tongue to the roof of her mouth. "I'm so thirsty. Oh! I have wine," she says in triumph, and Hunter places a hand on her shoulder, coaxing her back down.

"How about water for now?"

Her features twist in disgust, but she doesn't get up again.

Hunter hands her a bottle of water he found in the fridge and stands awkwardly in the middle of the living space.

Dahlia looks up at him over the brim of her glass. "You could sit with me?" It's more of a question than an offer.

"Do you want me to sit with you?"

She nods. Hunter slips out of his coat and sets it on the chair. He leaves ample space between them on the couch, and Dahlia slides closer, until he lifts his arm and she snuggles into his side.

She holds the bottle of water like it's a cup of coffee and Hunter traces lazy lines on her shoulder with his thumb and finger. The TV screen is black and there isn't any sound in the apartment minus the running heater.

Dahlia breaks the silence. "You could've punched him, you know. I wouldn't have minded."

Hunter sighs. "You might tomorrow, and I didn't want to do anything to make your situation worse."

"Hmm. I don't think it can get much worse than the whole town knowing a man cheated on you with another woman and got her pregnant."

Hunter runs his free hand along his thigh. "Yeah, I should've punched him," he says with a light tone and Dahlia laughs, but it's missing the carefree melody she had earlier.

"I'm not a slut," she murmurs. "In case you were worried about...you know."

"I wasn't," Hunter responds, the heat between them building until he's nearly sweating from it. If she makes a move, he'll turn her down. Only because she isn't thinking clearly and he's not that kind of man. But will she hate him for the rejection? Will whatever could happen between them be over before it began?

Dahlia thrusts her bottle of water into Hunter's free hand and pushes up from the couch. "It's so hot," she whines, tugging at her top.

When she lifts the hem to take it off, Hunter grabs her hands.

"I should go," he whispers. It's one of the hardest things he's ever had to do.

"What? Why? Is it because of Peter? I'm sorry if—"

He leans in and presses his lips to her forehead, cutting off her words.

"No, Little Flower. I should go before something happens tonight and you're not ready."

Her eyes shine and no matter what she says, he knows he made the right choice.

"I am ready...I—"

"If you still feel that way in the morning, let me know. We can go get breakfast, talk, spend some real time together. Okay?"

Her brown eyes flick to his lips and Hunter steps back before he meets her lust filled gaze once more. A man only has so much restraint. "Good night and for what it's worth, I hope you call."

# Chapter Twelve

DAHLIA ROLLS OVER IN her bed, then she's free falling and lands with a thud.

Jumping up to her hands and knees, she whips her gaze around her apartment. She's on the couch, not her bed, and she's in nothing but her bra and panties.

Her head rattles with each swift movement and she groans as she lays back on the floor, willing everything to stop spinning.

"You're being so loud," Carly groans from the recliner, and Dahlia crawls her way back onto the couch.

"What happened last night?" Slowly the memories flash and come into focus in broken fragments. Hunter was there...then he was here, in her apartment. Peter was an asshole, but Dahlia can't focus on that because Hunter was here and she's nearly naked.

Did something happen between them? It all fades to a hazy blur and she can't remember anything after getting here.

"You left with Hunter Haynes, that's what," Carly supplies what Dahlia has already figured out.

"I know that part. What happened...after," she whispers, as if someone in the small-town grapevine will catch wind of the story and spread the rumors before she even knows the truth.

"How would I know? I just got here a couple of hours ago."

Dahlia jerks her head up. "Where were you?"

Carly pushes her blanket off and stretches. "Getting some great sex," she says nonchalantly. "Did you and Hunter?"

Dahlia immediately shakes her head. But did they? She doesn't know. She can't remember.

Grabbing her shirt off the floor, she shrugs it on. "I don't know." Heat rushes to her cheeks and her face is caked with the makeup she didn't wash off.

"There's only one way to find out," Carly states. "Call him."

Dahlia scoffs. "I'm not calling him and being like, *hey so I was too drunk to remember last night. Did we do anything?*"

Her best friend shrugs. "Easiest way to get the answer. Or you can lay here all day in a self-pity party of doubts and wondering."

"Shit," Dahlia groans, placing her arm over her eyes.

"Exactly."

"No. I'm supposed to go to his ranch today to get the leftover vases and candelabras." Lifting her arm, she peeks at her best friend. "Unless you want to go?"

Carly shakes her head, a devilish grin spreading on her lips. "Oh no. Nope. You're going and figuring out what this is you have going on with tall, blond, and mysterious."

"I really don't like you sometimes."

Carly rolls her eyes. "You're the only person the mysterious man has talked to since he showed up. He barely comes into town and when he does, it's quick in and out without so much as a coffee. Who doesn't drink coffee while running errands? *Mysterious*," Carly says while wiggling her fingers. "Like, where did he come from? Why did he move out here alone? Who did he kill that he's on the run from?"

Dahlia stops and shakes her head. "Carly, I swear, your imagination is one scary place. Maybe he enjoys being left *alone* and working in peace. Not everyone needs relationships."

"Yup, he's perfect for you. Two people who hate people and try to socialize as little as possible. You could have your own bedrooms and only have sex when it's penciled into your schedule." She raises her voice to a nasal tone. "*Nine o'clock? Can't. Booked. How about lunch and a quickie?*"

"Carly!" Dahlia exclaims, her eyes wide and mouth open. Although the separate bedrooms don't sound like that bad of an arrangement. "Go home," she drags out as she points at the door.

"I'm only saying these things out of love. Your vagina needs me. It's screaming for help."

*Apparently, I got some last night and I can't remember if it was good or bad.*

Her best friend flashes her a smile and pushes to her feet. "You love me and it's Sunday, so I'm going to rot on my couch all day and process how much I drank last night."

"I hate you," Dahlia says into the couch cushion. She lays there until she can't handle how gross she feels any longer. A long hot shower and a steaming cup of hot coffee has her feeling somewhat human, and she still can't remember any more details of her night with Hunter.

During her shower, she checked to see if she was sore at all, but she wasn't. There isn't any proof or signs that say she got laid last night.

Her phone chimes and she checks the notification.

A text from Hunter pops up and her heart races as she opens the message.

**Snow's coming. You should wait till tomorrow to come back. Wouldn't want you getting stuck.**

His message squashes her excitement about what could have been happening between them. He doesn't ask how she's feeling, say he had a good time last night, or mention anything about what happened.

Fine, if he wants to act like last night never happened, so can she.

Dahlia scoffs and thinks of her four-wheel-drive SUV. She'll be just fine and it's cute that he thinks she needs him looking after her.

Her low battery alert sounds and she locks her phone and tosses it onto the bed. She'll just charge it on her way to the Haynes Ranch.

Her stomach gurgles as she climbs into her car. "Seriously, we just ate—" She glances at the clock on her dash and groans. "No, we didn't because I was drunk."

Food first. Then pack up from the wedding.

The loneliness of realizing Carly is right creeps up her spine as she drives. Her dating life is pathetic—nonexistent, actually. Why is it so hard to find someone who brings substance to her already happy life? She doesn't want to change anything about herself and loves her life just the way it is. There's comfort in the chaos, which means she probably needs therapy. But where's the man who can handle her crazy schedule and smile inside the vortex of her life beside her? Does that man even exist?

Could it be Hunter? She shakes her head and pushes that thought away. Nothing happened.

Nothing. Happened.

If she says it enough, she'll convince herself that whatever transpired last night was nothing more than a fever dream.

Dahlia is so far stuck in her head; she hasn't turned the radio on. Mindlessly, she uses her turn signals, stops at red lights—hopefully—and before she realizes it, she's turning into Hunter's driveway.

"Damn it," she whines and throws her head back into the seat. "I forgot food!"

The snow is already falling in heavy sheets of huge flurries. Any tracks left by the wedding party the night before are long gone. Dahlia pushes the button for four-wheel drive and sighs. "I'll just grab something at home tonight. I've waited this long."

She accelerates up the snowy driveway, her tires spinning sporadically, but she grew up here and knows how to handle a vehicle in the snow and ice.

Her stomach growls and her head pounds as the hangover sets in. A wave of nausea rolls through her and she squeezes her eyes closed. Her tires catch on the mounded snow, and she fights with her steering wheel.

She turns it sharp, trying to free her tires from the snow. It gives and propels her across the driveway into the ditch.

\*\*\*

"HE FUCKING JINXED ME!" Dahlia trudges up the steps to the cabin. Her toes froze halfway up the hill after her tires spun endlessly and she couldn't get out of the ditch. After slamming on the steering wheel, cursing the universe and digging around her catch-all of a purse, she found a smashed granola bar she licked from the wrapper. Hanging her head in shame, she got out to ask one person in this forsaken blizzard for help.

The hill is much shorter and no where near this steep in a vehicle. Her thighs burn and she pants with each step. This is why it would be a good idea to use that gym membership she pays for monthly.

"Hunter!" she shouts through chattering teeth and a shaking body at the cabin door. There aren't any lights on. Peering through the tall windows, her decorations are piled neatly on the floor, already taken down. "Asshole, why do you have to be so nice and right about everything?"

Dahlia pounds on the door again, but no answer. The snow is up to her ankles as she walks around to the back door and she jiggles the handle.

Locked.

Wrapping her jacket tighter around her, she whines in defeat, "I am really starting to dislike this man." Pulling her phone from her pocket, she prepares to do the one thing she had no intention of doing.

She taps her phone screen to unlock it, but it doesn't respond. She taps it harder and shakes it violently. "No! Damn it."

She forgot to plug it in when she got in the car because she thought of food. Which she also forgot because her raging hormones had her in la-la land, daydreaming about Hunter and how he could be the end to her drought.

A dog barks behind her and she jumps around, barely able to make out the white furry animal through the snow.

"Zip? What are you doing out here?" She crouches and holds her hand out, hoping to coax the canine closer. "Where's Hunter? You shouldn't be out in this."

He cocks his head to the side as if to say, *no shit. Why are you out here?*

Suddenly, he turns his head and barks into the woods. Dahlia reaches out to grab his collar, but she comes up short and the dog runs away.

"Wait! Come here! I'm trying to help you!"

Dahlia trudges through the snow after Zip. He stops just inside the tree line and barks at her again.

"Where are you going?" Dahlia pants, the cold air hurting as she inhales.

A blood-curling woman's scream breaks through the snowstorm and the hair stands on her arms. Dahlia freezes and spins, trying to find where she heard the person in trouble.

Zip growls and walks up beside her.

"It's okay," she whispers. "Let's just go back."

She steps away from the tree and the dog brushes against her leg, pushing her further from the cabin. Dahlia shivers and blows her breath on her hands.

The scream comes closer, and it sounds right in front of her. She loses all sense of logical thinking and turns to run in the direction Zip was going. He yips and barks, as if encouraging her to go faster. Every cell in Dahlia's body pushes her harder and to run with everything she has. Like death is right on her heels and if she falters, if she slows, then she's a goner.

Somewhere in these woods a woman is running from something and she's screaming like her life depends on it. A gunshot rings out. Dahlia falls to the snow covered ground and scrambles behind a tree.

*What the fuck?* The woman's screams go silent and Dahlia presses her back into the tree, darting her head side to side, waiting to see a gun aimed at her. *Did someone just get shot?*

She has to get out of here.

The dog barks incessantly, prancing on its feet.

"Shhh," Dahlia scolds, but it doesn't deter Zip. She pushes to her feet and glances around the side of the tree, careful to stay hidden. Holding her breath, she peers through the snow and gathers herself. She has to get back to her car. Then she can charge her phone, call Hunter, and get out of this freaking snow blizzard. After several minutes, she doesn't see anything. The dog whines and Dahlia decides it can take care of itself.

She presses her back into the tree and takes several deep breaths, counting to three. She spins away from the tree and runs as hard as her legs can go.

Raising her eyes from the ground, she screams, but can't stop her momentum before she's barreling into a dark figure obscured by the flurries.

Their hands clamp around her biceps and hold her upright.

"Let go of me!" She tries to break free, but the hands hold firm. The dog barks and whines from behind her. She squeezes her eyes closed. At least this way she won't see the killing blow. Maybe she could play opossum? Pass out and fake a heart attack? If her heart doesn't slow down, she won't have to fake it. She holds her breath and waits.

This is it. She's going to die in this snow because she chased after a dog who clearly didn't need her help. This man might as well have been in a white van with free puppies spray painted on the side. Hunter will come home and see her car in the ditch and that will be all that's left of her.

"What the hell are you doing out here?" the man's voice cuts through her spiral. "Zip!" he shouts, and the barking stops. "Dahlia?"

Her eyes spring open at the sound of her name. Familiar blue eyes stare down at her framed by black edges in her vision. Before she can respond, she blinks and everything is black. Then...she's weightless.

# Chapter Thirteen

DAHLIA LIES ON THE bed on the far side of the room. Hunter's cabin is small with an open floor concept. The only place you'd get any privacy is the bathroom. He sits in his chair beside his wood-burning stove and runs a tired hand over his face. Zip lays at his feet and raises his head every time Dahlia makes a sound in her sleep.

He can't believe she actually passed out on him. He barely acted quick enough to catch her and carry her inside. His leg aches and he massages his thigh, feeling the rough scars through his jeans.

Why didn't she listen when he said to wait until tomorrow? Or at least text him back she was coming regardless, and he'd been at the main house. At least that explains where Zip went and why he couldn't find him earlier.

And she never called.

After everything she told him last night and the need that burned in her eyes, she never called him.

Dahlia hums and rolls to her stomach, inhaling deeply. He stills, waiting for her to pop up and freak out. Zip jumps to his feet and trots across the room to the edge of the bed.

"Zip," Hunter whisper-shouts, but the dog ignores him and leaps onto the bed. Dahlia squeals and jumps, her eyes wide and cheeks flush as she frantically looks around. Sensing her anxiety, Zip pushes against her chest and whines, licking at her hands to calm her. Her curly hair stands in all directions and her brown doll-sized eyes lock onto Hunter, who hasn't moved.

"Are you going to kill me?" she asks with a steady calm, like she's already assessed every way this could go and it's not good.

"Am I going to kill—why on earth would you think that?"

"I heard the screams. There was a woman. A gunshot. Someone died out there." She points at the door. "Which means someone killed her." Carefully, she slips out of the bed on her sock covered feet and spots her boots by the door. "I won't say anything, just let me go. Please. You know me. We're friends." Her voice is low and quiet as she walks on her toes. Like she's worried she'll scare him—or more likely scared he'll grab the rifle by his chair and use it.

"Dahlia," he says, with his palms up. "How long have you lived in Wyoming?"

She's almost to the door. She'll grab her boots and then take her chances running for it. "All my life," she admits.

"And you've never heard a mountain lion scream before?"

Dahlia doesn't know what that has to do with committing murder. Hunter still hasn't moved from his seat and she grabs her boots and retches the door open—or tries. The knob doesn't turn and she yanks on the wooden barrier, but it's no use.

"Please...please," she sputters and backs into the kitchen table big enough for two people. Hunter pushes to his feet and winces as he steps toward her. "Just let me leave. Nobody has to know."

"I'm not going to hurt you, Little Flower. And I'm not a killer. What you heard was a mountain lion scream. I didn't even know you were out there. I was looking for Zip, who probably saved your life as a matter of fact. The only woman in those woods in danger was you." He internally scolds himself for using his secret nickname for her in this situation of all times. He's only let it slip three times and none of them he thinks she remembers.

She sides steps until the table is positioned between them and reaches for the butcher knife laying on the counter.

*Did he just call me Little Flower? He called me that last night...didn't he?* Dahlia's stomach somersaults and she bites on her bottom lip. Why does it sound so intimate and why is it doing so many different things to her body? He could be a killer, unless he's telling the truth. Picturing him feeling her up is the last thing she should be doing, but *Little Flower* has her mind racing.

Hunter's eyes remain locked on her as his hands tighten on the chair. "If you come at me with that, I'll have you disarmed in three seconds and pinned to the ground."

He drops his chin and the brim of his cowboy hat hides his darkening eyes.

"Put it down, Dahlia," he demands. "Unless you want to be underneath me."

Her breath catches and her fingertips graze over the sharpened metal. That threat shouldn't heat her skin and cause her to squeeze her thighs together, but it does.

This is Hunter she's having a stand-off with. She knows him, and has worked with him for a year. But what does she really know about him?

Her eyes wander to the dog with its ears perked from the bed. It whines softly and tilts its head to the side, the large white ears and snout trained on her.

"A mountain lion?" she asks.

"Yes."

"You're not a murderer or a killer?"

Hunter can't meet her gaze and he sighs. He stalks around the table and she's not sure what her next move is. He bypasses the knife and lays his hand atop of hers instead. One deep breath and her breasts would graze his chest. "You're safe."

Her lips part as she searches his blue eyes for any sign of deception. She pulls her hand from under his, and prays he can't see the reaction she is having to his touch, his closeness, and this entire situation. She leans against the counter and pushes her hair behind her ears. "What happened? Where are we?"

Hunter mimics her stance and Zip hops down from the bed and licks at Hunter's hands.

"I found you in the woods and then you passed out. This is my cabin...where I live."

She takes a moment to study the small space. A wood stove sits in the far corner with one recliner. There's the bed she woke up in across from the stove with the wall as a headboard. A closed door, she assumes, leads to the bathroom and then the kitchen they're in. This is more like a hunting shack than a permanent living space. "What about the cabin? The one I decorated?"

"It's too big. To many—" he pauses, searching for the right words. "It's too exposed. I prefer this."

She arches a brow and angles her body to face him, waiting to see if he'll elaborate what that means.

"Why didn't you call me? Or at least text me back and I would have made sure I was there. Saved you from," he waves his hand around. "This."

She shrugs and her stomach rumbles loudly. Hunter chuckles and her cheeks flush.

"Take a seat, Dahlia. I'll fix us something to eat."

*He's going to feed me? In this shack he apparently lives in?*

"Wait," Dahlia says, stopping him as he pulls a cast-iron skillet from the wall. "Last night..." Her ears burn and she drops her gaze to force the words out. "Did we...you know, do anything?"

Hunter keeps his back to her as he answers. "No. I took you back to your apartment."

"Then you...left?"

He nods, and Dahlia steps out of his way as he reaches into a cabinet. She sits at the table and watches as he moves through the kitchen.

When Hunter said he'd fix *something* to eat, she thought he'd meant something quick and simple. Not a full meal of steak, fried potatoes, corn on the cob, yeast rolls, and green beans—the homegrown canned kind.

The meat is juicy and tender and she pokes her tongue out to lick up some escaped deliciousness on her lips. She's always respected his privacy, but here, in these close quarters and nothing else to do to distract her thoughts, she can't help but wonder and want to know everything.

"You like it?" he asks around a bite.

Dahlia nods and smiles sheepishly at the man-sized bite she just shoved in her mouth. "I forgot to eat. Well, I remembered, then forgot to stop and get anything before coming here. That's probably why I passed out."

*Because that sounds better than saying it was from being terrified.*

"You haven't eaten after everything you drank last night?"

She shakes her head.

"Why does that not surprise me?" He leans back in his seat and she notices his hand sliding over his left leg. Dahlia takes a drink of the water he set in front of her.

"So, Mr. Lives-Out-In-The-Middle-Of-Nowhere, I think this warrants you telling me a little about yourself." Her palms sweat at the idea of seeing into his life, his past, and figuring out who exactly Hunter Haynes is.

"What does...exactly? You trespassing? Sending a vague text to meet you and then pretending you didn't?" He stands, grabbing her plate and takes it to the sink.

"Last night, I didn't—actually, blame your dog. I was trying to save it from freezing to death." She grabs her phone to check it and it's still a useless paperweight.

Zip barks as if he knows they're talking about him.

"Well, someone did and from your phone."

"Carly," Dahlia hisses, and Hunter turns his back to face the sink. So she wasn't the one who wanted to see him. Her best friend orchestrated the whole thing. He washes the dishes and his shoulders tense with Dahlia at his back. He knows she isn't a threat, but his subconscious is on edge either way. Gripping the cloth, he braces on the porcelain sink bowl.

"I'll dry," she states, brushing up from behind him.

He pulls himself together enough to clear his throat and nod. There's something about her. Maybe it's the fact she doesn't shy away from him and is the only person he has any sort of friendship with since he's been home. He studies her out of his periphery. He'd have to be blind to deny she's beautiful. Even then, he'd feel the passion as she spoke. He'd feel her beauty just from being around her. It goes so much deeper than the surface. Maybe that's why he wants to share parts of himself with her.

# Chapter Fourteen

"I SERVED TWO TOURS before I was medically discharged," Hunter whispers, so low she almost missed it. Instead of jumping to say '*I'm sorry*' or something of the sort, she takes the wet plate from his hand and continues drying.

Hunter looks at her out of the corner of his eye, but there's nothing on her features. If she's uncomfortable, she doesn't show it. "My team and I drove over a land mine during patrol. My leg got crushed...they couldn't save it."

Her hands flinch slightly before she regains her composure. She fights the urge to look him up and down. How had she missed that? Those times she caught him limping—she thought he was hurt.

"So, when you came back...you didn't have anyone to come back to?" she asks, careful to not press too far, but enough that she can make sense of why he willingly isolated himself.

"Not exactly." He places the rag over the sink divider and grabs a chair, sitting it beside the wood stove. Dahlia follows him and he sits in the chair, offering her the recliner.

How does he tell her he left his family a note explaining that he would call when he got settled, and he's yet to talk to them?

She draws her legs up in the seat and stares into the fire. The heaviness in the air settles around them. When she asked if he'd ever killed someone...the haunted look in his eyes tells her as much.

"You don't owe me any explanation," she says, breaking up the silence.

He tilts his head and squeezes his eyes closed, petting Zip's head. "I-I haven't talked to my family. When I got back, I couldn't sleep without hearing gunfire in the distance. When Mom tried to wake me up and I nearly attacked her... I decided leaving was in everyone's best interest. I keep telling myself I'll go back, or at least call to let them know where I am, but I haven't."

Dahlia doesn't know if she should reach out to comfort him or give him his space. Out of all the rumors, the town cooked up about the mysterious bachelor who moved to town, a military veteran who couldn't adjust to life after he came home, wasn't one of them.

He's just like Graves. The pain of her missing brother has her wrapping her arms around her body to keep herself together.

"And this place helps?" she asks. Maybe if she can understand Hunter, she can understand Graves too, and he'll come home.

He smirks and leans back from Zip. "Surprisingly. I think it's knowing that there isn't anyone around for miles. He helps too." He points at his dog laying at his feet. "The wedding venue was something to keep me busy and give me something to strive toward."

He drops his chin, heat rushing across the back of his neck. He hasn't told anyone the truth about how much he's suffered since coming back and trying to adapt to a *normal* life.

"The Sergeant I served with told me about this wonderful place he lived. Where the mountains seemed to sing in the morning and the peaks touched heaven. It was cheesy stuff we talked about around a small fire in the desert. Something to keep us sane until we got home. I knew I had to see this place when I came back. I never expected it would be where I found my peace."

Dahlia's blood turns to ice and her eyes open wide as she gazes at Hunter Haynes. Pa used to describe the ranch as heaven on earth and would tell stories about how he loved to ride in the early morning while the dew was still on the plants to hear the mountains whisper their songs.

It's not possible...

"Who was he?" she asks.

Hunter cocks his head to the side. "He? The Sergeant?"

Dahlia nods, an icy chill running down her spine like she's seen a ghost.

"We called him Grizz—"

"Graves? Graves Brooks?"

Hunter's brows furrow, and he places his elbows on his knees and leans forward. "Yeah...Brooks..." His jaw falls open, and he takes off his hat, rubbing a hand across his face. "Holy shit. You're the sister he talked about all the time."

Dahlia's thoughts bounce in a hundred different directions. This man across from her is here because of what her brother said. He served with her brother...they could've been friends. He talked about her all the time and now can't do her the common courtesy of answering her phone call.

"Do you know where he is? I've been trying to track him down. To check in. He disappeared one day and hasn't called since." Her voice is hollow and Hunter's excited expression falls. A single tear escapes down Dahlia's cheek and he wrings his hands together to keep from going over to her.

"Dahlia—I'm sorry. I—adapting back to normal life can be...difficult. He—"

"You should call your family." She cuts him off. "At least your parents. I know how much it sucks being on the other side." Dahlia keeps her voice soft as she speaks. She knows the pain her parents have gone through and if she can convince this man to do what Graves won't, maybe that's why fate has brought them together.

Hunter nods, and the atmosphere of the cabin grows tense. Graves did the same thing that Hunter did. And now Hunter is seeing it from a different lens. "You're right. I've debated inviting them this spring." He grunts as he moves his leg. "But I don't want them to see me as a coward or if they don't come at all..." Hunter's voice trails off and she hurts for him. Something about seeing a strong bodied man be vulnerable pulls on her heartstrings.

"You should invite them, Hunter."

His eyes lock with hers. "You know you're the only person I've told this to. Even my parents don't know what I went through. What if they don't understand? They look at me and they see the same kid they raised. I don't know if I can handle that."

The cabin grows silent aside from Zip snoring at Hunter's feet and the crackling from the wood in the fire. Hunter stares into the flames, lost in his own thoughts.

"Thank you," Dahlia says, her eyes getting heavy with the events of the last twenty-four hours, and she settles into the recliner. "For getting me home last night, for not letting me get eaten earlier, and giving me a new piece of my brother."

Hunter smiles softly and pushes to his feet. "Come on, Little Flower. You're taking the bed. I'll sleep in the chair."

*There's that name again.* She has to shove down the reaction it causes and snuggles deeper into the recliner.

"Nonsense. I'm not letting you sleep in the chair. It's your cabin." She pulls the quilt from behind her head and drapes it across her body.

Hunter arches a brow and strides over. He scoops her up in his arms and carries her to the bed.

"What the hell? You can't pick me up! I'm—"

"I know you aren't about to say what I think you are," Hunter purrs as he lays her gently on the bed.

*Too big?* She stares at him, stunned. Never in a million years did she think a man would literally whisk her off her feet.

Zip jumps excitedly and settles in next to her. "Sleep, Dahlia. That's an order."

How can he expect her to sleep after the double whammy he just served? Between calling her something as beautiful as a Little Flower and putting on his show of strength? Sleep is the *last* thing on her mind.

Something flashes in her eyes and she pulls the blankets back on the empty side of the bed. "Then you're sleeping with me, Soldier."

There's humor in her tone to mask the uncertainty of what she just suggested. She could be reading this entire situation all wrong. It's been so long since she's been *taken care of*. She could be blowing this all out of proportion.

"Little Flower." Hunter's voice drops to a husky whisper. "If I get in that bed, we won't be sleeping."

*Or not.* Dahlia's stomach flips and she squeezes her thighs at his promise. Her lips part and she has half a mind to beg him to prove his point. She fights the urge to crawl to him across the mattress. "Good." It comes out breathy and full of need. There's no hiding just how much she wants this...how much she *needs* this.

Hunter drops his chin and hides the tightness in his jaw. "I'm not..." he starts and has to take a deep breath. "I'm not the same—as I was before."

"Hunter," Dahlia says his name like it's the most important thing in the world. It's a melody coming off her lips and he glances at her, sitting in the middle of his bed. "Tell me what to do."

His cock hardens at her request, and he clenches his hands to hide the tremor. He's dreamed of touching her, of having her. But he never felt worthy enough to have someone as competent as Dahlia. Not when he is missing a limb and has to live secluded for his own peace of mind.

"I lost it below the knee," he admits through gritted teeth. His throat nearly closes at saying it out loud. The words come out strained, and he wants to turn away from her to avoid the pity look he expects in her eyes.

"That's not an order," she states evenly. Not acknowledging his comment in the slightest.

Hunter blows out a breath and rolls the tension from his shoulders. His blue eyes settle on Dahlia's deep, burning gaze.

God, he wants her too. "You like being told what to do, Little Flower?"

*Holy shit!* Dahlia's heart pounds in her chest. Wait, does she? She's never let someone else take control before. Honestly, no guy ever knew what they were doing enough *to* take control. But Hunter... She stares as he reaches for the buttons on his shirt. He is the kind of man that will know exactly how to *take care* of her needs.

"Never met a man up to the task," she says honestly.

His lips form a circle as he lets out a low whistle to the blow she just made on all men. "You want to know what I want you to do, Little Flower?" He has the first four buttons of his shirt undone, revealing a scarred muscular chest. Dahlia's fingers itch to touch his skin and explore the rest of this cowboy.

"You want to play by my rules?" he asks and his shirt falls to the floor.

She forgets how to speak, how to move. Fuck, she nearly forgets to breathe. He's perfection. He's toned, obviously, since he carried her inside from the snow. But it's not in an overly bulky way. It's working muscle, not *working-out* muscle. The kind you get from chopping your own firewood and living the ranch life.

He tsks and places a finger under her chin, bringing her lust filled brown eyes up from his bare torso. "You want to be fully satisfied? Fucked out of your mind until you feel like you're floating on a high so delicious you'll never come down?"

Her lips part, and she blinks, trying her best to reign in her screaming vagina.

"I want you to undress, slowly. Then you'll crawl over to me and lay flat on your back."

Her blood feels hot enough to burn her skin. *Holy shit*, plays in her mind on repeat.

"Now," he says, his voice deeper and pulls his hand back to place it on the bulge in his pants.

Dahlia blushes, but not from the way Hunter is making her feel. She reaches for her shirt and remembers the embarrassing excuse of a bra she put on this morning and when was the last time she shaved...well anything? It's not exactly high on her priority list this time of year.

"Come here," Hunter whispers and holds his hand out for her. She takes it and steps off the bed to stand in front of him. He lifts her hand and places it over scars on his bare chest. The erratic beat of his heart pumps under her palm. "This is what you do to me, Dahlia. When I see you, think of you, hear your voice—I'm a fucking mess most of the time. Trust me when I say there has never been a woman that compares to you."

His vibrant blue gaze flicks to her lips and he dips his head, lightly brushing his mouth to hers. "Put me out of my misery and take your fucking clothes off. I think we both have suffered long enough."

"Okay," she says, finally finding her ability to speak. She throws her self-conscious thoughts out the door. Could he be saying those things just for a quick fuck? Possibly. But she doesn't think he is. There's something in his tone that tells her this is as hard for him as it is for her. They're both laying themselves vulnerable and at the mercy of one another.

His eyes track her every movement until she's standing in nothing, but her underwear.

"Fuck," he groans and squeezes his cock. "You're stunning. Do you want me?"

"Yes," she whispers. She's already soaked between her thighs, just from looking at him.

"Good, because I want you so bad I can't stand it. Take those off, get on the bed and spread your legs for me."

# Chapter Fifteen

HUNTER PULLS DAHLIA TO the edge of the bed and runs his fingers across her soaked center. "Already so wet for me?" He slides his jeans and boxers down his thighs and his cock rubs against her entrance.

"Are you going to keep talking all night?" she groans and presses herself further into the mattress.

A throaty chuckle escapes him and he leans down, bracing his hands on either side of her head to hover over her body. "I love it when you get impatient," he growls and brushes his lips quickly across hers. Dahlia huffs and reaches down to grab his cock, just to prove how impatient she is.

Hunter takes her wrist before she achieves her goal and raises it over her head, pinning both her hands.

"I told you I'd have you pinned underneath me."

"Hunter," she mewls. No man has ever worked her up this long. Normally, they treat her like her clit is a push-to-start and barely get her turned on before shoving their cock inside.

"Yes, Little Flower?" he whispers, sliding the tip of his cock from her ass to clit.

"Fuck me, please," she begs.

He slides his hand between them and lines up with her drenched center. "Anything for you, Dahlia."

He keeps her hands secure above her head and he slowly stretches her wide as he thrusts himself deeply inside of her. She spreads her legs wider, taking every inch of him, reveling as he fills her.

Hunter picks up a steady rhythm and her hands fist and his grip tightens around her wrist. "Fuck," he rasps, and Dahlia bites down on her bottom lip as she arches her back.

"I know, I feel so fucking good," she repeats the line all men use in a teasing tone and he stills. Her eyes fly open and she looks up at the man staring down at her with furrowed brows. "I was kidding. Well, not really—I hope I feel really good. It's just—"

Hunter stands, keeping himself deep in her pink pussy. He grips her thighs and pulls her into him on the edge of the bed. "Is that what you want to hear?" He slams into her, his fingers digging into the soft skin of her inner thighs so she can't move across the bed.

"What?" she cries out, her words cutting off when he does it again.

"You want me to treat this like any other fuck?" his voice raises and Zip whines where he lays at the door.

"Hunter—I was kidd—" He presses his thumb down on her clit and her body fights the overwhelming sensation he's causing.

"You do feel fucking fantastic, but it's because you take me so fucking good. Like you were made just for me. This won't be like the boys who have tried to take care of you before. Because when I'm finished and you're too exhausted to stand, I'll be carrying you to the shower then bring you back, naked to this bed, and wrap my arms around you until we both fall asleep."

How he's able to form a coherent thought let alone speak while her mind is buzzing with an orgasm begging to be released, is beyond her.

Hunter slams into her again and she screams in frustration at being on the cusp of the edge, but him not letting her go. He moves gentle circles around her clit. Leaning down, he presses his lips to her collarbone.

"Do you hear me, Little Flower? What we have going on here is nothing compared to who you've been with in the past. And come tomorrow morning, you won't even remember any of their names."

She smirks. "Soldier, I forgot their names the moment you carried me to this bed."

His cock jumps inside of her and her pussy tightens in response.

"Good."

Hunter sucks on her nipple then stands, readjusting his stance. He lifts her legs to place her feet on his shoulders and pushes his thumb back down on her clit.

Okay, maybe she is a push-to-start because her body turns molten and her toes curl from the pressure.

He thrusts deep inside of her and grinds his hips at the perfect angle. Everything within her shatters and a sound she's never made escapes her tense body as ecstasy overcomes her.

"Holy shit!" she exclaims and Hunter leans forward, keeping her feet on his shoulders, and bringing her knees closer to her body. His pelvis slap against her as he chases his own release.

He forgets about the raging snow blizzard outside. The fact that he lives away from civilization because the memories are too much for him to stand. Having Dahlia here, it somehow feels right. For the first time since he's been back he feels...at peace.

His balls tightens when that thought crosses his mind and he buries his face in the crook of her neck as he comes.

Peace. He feels...grounded.

His body tenses when her arms wrap around him and she runs her fingertips up and down his back. Shuddering, his breath comes out shaky against her skin.

Zip barks then jumps on the bed, wedging his wet tongue and nose between their chests. Dahlia giggles as the dog's head successfully wedges between them and licks her chin.

"Down, boy," Hunter says between chuckles and pushes him back to the floor. He traces a finger down the side of Dahlia's cheek and tucks a curl behind her ear. To think all the hell he's endured has led him to this tiny town in Wyoming, to a woman who may have just stolen his heart in a snowstorm.

"Is this the part where you carry me to the shower? I don't think I'm a noodle yet," she says with a smirk.

He drops his head and nips on her bottom lip.

"I ain't done with you yet."

\*\*\*

DAHLIA NEVER KNEW SHE could come so many times and still be in one piece. Between her thighs aches and the bedding is messed with cum and sweat. Her curls tighten around the base of her neck and she breathes heavily alongside Hunter who collapses by her side.

"Okay... I'm a noodle," she moans in bliss and brushes her fingers across Hunter's cheek.

He chuckles and pushes himself up to sit, glancing over his shoulder at this incredible woman.

"Then I promised to carry you to the shower and take care of you all over again." He brushes his lips across her forehead and stands, sliding one arm under her shoulders and the other under her knees.

"No, I'll walk. I'll hurt you—"

"Little Flower, if you say one negative thing about your beautiful body, we're going back to that bed, so I can show you just how wrong you are."

Her cheeks heat and she stares up at him as he carries her with ease to the bathroom and sits her on the counter.

As he turns on the water, Dahlia gets her first look at Hunter's left leg. From the knee down are titanium bars that lead to an ankle joint and carbon fiber and foam foot. When he turns back around, he catches her staring.

"Does it hurt?"

Hunter shrugs as he moves to stand between her legs and tucks her curls behind her ear. His hand gently grasps the juncture of her neck and his thumb brushes along her jaw. "The scar tissue aches when the weather turns. On really rough nights, the whole thing hurts as if I still have my leg." His voice is low and husky. Exhaustion is clear in his tone.

Dahlia skims her fingers along his muscled chest and down his ribcage. Hunter leans into her gentle caressing touch while steam from the hot water fills the shower.

"Does it hurt now?" she asks.

Hunter shifts his weight. "I'm fine. But we both need to get cleaned up."

He helps her off the counter and leads her through the glass doors into the shower. "You go first. I'll change the sheets and fix the bed for you."

Before she can argue, the bathroom door closes, and she's alone. She sighs when she picks up his three in one body wash and shampoo. Her curls are going to be out for vengeance tomorrow, but she's pretty sure she has cum in her hair so sacrifices will be made.

When she's done washing her body and has all the remnants of their time together scrubbed off her skin, she turns off the water. Grabbing the towel off the rack, she wraps it around her body, although it does little to hide her curves. She grabs another one off the shelf over the toilet and wraps her hair up. Peeking out of the bathroom and the bed is freshly made and Hunter is nowhere to be seen. The fire in the wood stove is burning low, leaving a chill throughout the room.

"Hunter?"

No response and it's not like he has anywhere to hide here. She hangs her body towel on the rack on the bathroom door and slips under the clean, fresh silk sheets. They glide across her body and she pulls the blankets up around her chin.

Dahlia dances between the realms of sleep and barely conscious. She thinks she hears the door open, but can't be sure.

Hunter stands from the filling the stove and watches the steady rise and fall of the comforter on his bed.

*His.*

This was the last thing he expected after not hearing from her all day. He assumed she woke up, filled with regret—or embarrassment—and what *almost* happened last night never would again.

Like clockwork, Zip jumps up onto the bed and settles in at the end. Dahlia doesn't budge. He feels—lighter—than he has in a long time. The pressing weight on his chest is gone for the time being and he wonders if he has the wild and independent woman in his bed to thank for that.

Hanging his hat on the rack, he checks his rifle leaning by the door frame and clicks the safety on. He sheds out of his coat and sighs as his muscles barely want to function.

Sitting in his recliner, he unlaces his boots, sliding them off one at a time and makes his way to the bathroom.

Dahlia whimpers in her sleep as he walks by, and his lips curl up into a smile. He can't wait to crawl under those covers and mold his body around hers. This will be the best damn sleep he's ever had.

After tossing his clothes in the hamper, he leans against the sink. His leg aches from the incredible sex and he sighs in relief as he slides the sleeve down over his thigh and onto the socket of his prosthetic. Lifting his knee from his socket, he slides off his socks and liner.

Hunter stares down at the missing limb and thinks back to Dahlia.

*What do you need me to do*, she had asked and never once shied away from him? It was as if she craved the direction, like it made the sex even better. Hunter places a hand on the sink then to the wall until he reaches the shower and uses his arms to brace on the handles he had installed and half jumps, half lifts himself into the shower.

His eyes grow heavy as the hot water warms him up from going outside to get enough firewood to get him through the night.

By the time he slips under the sheet and blankets, he's already on the cusp of sleep.

Dahlia stirs, rolling over to face him. She brushes her fingers across his lips and he exhales a deep satisfied sigh.

Her fingers run down his torso, across the band of his briefs. Hunter shudders and his breaths become shallow. Dahlia slows her movements, working the muscles of Hunter's upper thigh in a massaging fashion.

Somehow, what she is doing feels more intimate than when he had his cock buried deep inside of her.

She massages over the kneecap, and Hunter's brows furrow. Tenderly, she presses her lips to his sternum and her fingers brush over the scar tissue below his knee. Hunter remains perfectly still as her fingers roll around the muscles and scars.

"How does that feel?" she asks, worried that he's suffering in silence and this isn't as relaxing as she hoped it would be.

"Fine," he says with a breathy voice. Dahlia slides her fingers back up his leg.

He places his hand over hers to stop her and pushes it back down. "Don't stop. It feels...really good," he admits. Opening his eyes, he looks down to get lost in the rich dark depths of her heavy gaze.

He moves his hand to trace circles around her nipple and palm her breast. Dahlia sucks in a harsh breath and bites her lip. Hunter takes her wrist and rolls her to her back as he hovers above her, pinning her hands above her head. He frees her hair from the towel and tosses it to the bathroom floor.

"You drive me mad, woman," he rasps, kissing her forehead, cheeks, and last, her lips. His hardening cock presses into abdomen and she spreads her knees, eager to take him. Hunter's lips curve into a salacious smile and he lets himself get lost in her again.

# Chapter Sixteen

Dahlia shimmies from under Hunter's arm. He lets out a snore as she picks up a blanket from the floor and wraps it around her shoulders. Zip hops off the bed and makes a beeline to the door, whining and scratching when she doesn't open it immediately.

"And he calls me impatient," she says with a smirk. She opens the door to a foot of snow blocking her path. Zip leaps, landing with nothing but his head sticking out.

He barks at the white stuff like it's just offended him, and Dahlia pulls the quilt tighter and tries to muffle her laugh.

"I love your laugh," Hunter mumbles, his voice thick with sleep. He pushes up out of the bed and swings his leg over the side. Her eyes linger a fraction of a second on his scarred thigh and missing limb. Something about him not hiding it today tells her last night was more than a *fuck* for him. He's letting her see the most vulnerable part of himself. If she doesn't have to hide her curves, he shouldn't feel the need to hide this part of him, either.

"Love?" She bites her bottom lip, and he stands, bracing himself against the wall. "Little soon for that kind of talk, don't you think?" She means it as a joke, but she can't stop the flutter in her stomach and the way her palms sweat. His morning wood is perfectly outlined in his tight boxers and even though she's sore from all the sex last night, she can't wait until more.

He smiles at her and runs his hands through his cropped hair. "Come on, Little Flower. I'll fix us breakfast. From the looks of outside, we aren't leaving anytime, soon."

Zip bolts back in, snow sticking to his fur, and he shakes at the doormat. Dahlia squeals at the snow, landing at her feet and freezing her toes.

"I'll check the fire first, *then* fix breakfast." He reaches for his liner, sock, and prosthetic.

"How about you stop trying to do everything for me and I'll tend to the stove? You know where everything is in the kitchen." Dahlia doesn't give him time to argue before she's grabbing the handle to open the door and add wood. She scrapes the ashes to the bottom first and opens the air vent for air to stoke the embers.

"You know how to do all that?" Over her shoulder, Hunter leans against the doorway, still not dressed, wearing an impressed expression.

"Shocked that a woman can take care of herself?"

He shakes his head. "No. I'm shocked that you have never heard a mountain lion scream and have lived here your entire life."

Her mouth falls open, and she pushes to her feet. "I was running for my life! Besides, camping never was something my parents did. When would I be around a mountain lion?"

His shoulders shake with laughter and he sighs, a genuine smile spreading his lips. "You lived on a ranch," he teases. "You going to come over here, Little Flower? Put me out of my misery of imagining what's under that blanket?"

Dahlia stands and drops the blanket to the floor. Something about the way Hunter looks at her makes her feel radiant and confident. His piercing blue eyes burn away any embarrassment she might have felt with any other man. He sucks in a breath, his biceps flex as he grips the door frame.

"Like what you see?" she teases. His gaze burns all the way to her soul, stoking a flame and heating her skin.

"Come here. Now," he orders and she nearly becomes a puddle on the floor.

His hands travel across her shoulders and down her arms. "Breakfast first. I can't have you passing out on me again." He smirks and Dahlia's jaw falls open.

"I did not—"

He arches a brow and she sighs. "Fine. Food."

Bacon sizzles in the skillet and Dahlia sits in one of his T-shirts at the kitchen table. Hunter wants to know everything about Dahlia. "Can I ask you something?" he asks.

"Sure."

Hunter glances at her over his shoulder, studying her reaction. "That day when we got locked in the shed. What happened?"

Dahlia fidgets with her fingers and wishes Hunter had asked anything else. Like the number of guys she's been with. But she's learned about his most painful memories, so she can give him hers. "When Carly and I were younger. I got stuck inside a cave and rocks fell and blocked the entrance. It was hours of me, stuck and alone in a pitch-black space, waiting for my parents to come save me. Graves was the first one to get to me."

Dahlia's eyes take a distant look and Hunter walks to her side. "I'm so sorry. I wouldn't have let you in there if I knew it was like that."

She shakes her head and takes his hand. "I can't hide from it. The panic attacks are so rare, I didn't even think about it until I was in the middle of one. Thank you, by the way. You knew just what to say."

"Plenty of experience," he says with a wince.

She doesn't know where they'll end up after their time in his cabin. But for the first time in her life, she wants to explore her feelings and this man further.

***

"WELL, THAT'S IT," DAHLIA announces as she closes the hatch to her SUV. She spent three days in Hunter's cabin. After the first day she opted for walking around in one of his T-shirts. That might have been the sexiest thing he's ever seen.

Now, she stands awkwardly in the snow wearing what he found her in. Do they act like the last few days never happened? Go back to be acquaintance's even now that she knows his secrets? Was everything that bloomed between a delusion of the blizzard and being forced to stay in that small cabin?

She worries her bottom lip and reaches for her door handle. She's never been in an awkward in-between of *'was this a one-night thing'* or *'does he feel like she does and wants more'*? All those things he said to her, the way he made her feel—how does she go back from that?

Hunter stands off to the side, staring down the long driveway. For the first time since he's moved here, the idea of being so far from civilization—from her—is painful. When he doesn't respond, she steps toward the driver door, but Hunter grabs her arm and pulls her back into him, pinning her to the side of her vehicle.

"What are you doing?" she asks, looking down at where his hips grind into hers.

He stares into her wide eyes. How does he form the words he wants to say? Would she call him crazy? Or run screaming? There is a knife in his gut and it's twisting at the thought of watching her drive away. But he can't keep her here. Not unless she wants to stay. And if she says no, then he doesn't think he'll be able to handle it. He's been pushing people away for so long. This feeling of wanting to keep someone close is foreign, and it scares the hell out of him.

"Hunter?" she says his name, and he blinks her back into focus. Dahlia cups his cheek and brushes her thumb across his stubble.

"I—" he clears his throat and steps back, dropping his gaze. "Be careful."

Her hand falls to her side and she swallows the sadness trying to claw up her throat as she opens her door.

She has never been the type afraid to say what is on her mind.

She's Dahlia Brooks. She owns Dreaming of Dahlias and has built a business from the ground up. To hell with the man who thinks she is just going to leave after having the best sex and act like nothing has changed.

Nope. Not happening. Not to her. She whirls and faces the cowboy with his dog sitting at his side.

"Hunter Haynes, I know you aren't about to send me on my way with what? A *be careful*? After everything we've talked about the last two days and what we've been doing in that shack in the woods? I have half a mind—"

129

He gently grips her face and presses his lips to hers, cutting her off. Her tense body relaxes, and she leans back into her SUV. His body is flush against hers, and she clings to his coat, debating taking this back inside and try leaving again later.

"You wouldn't have made it to the end of the driveway before I caught you," he says against her lips. He pulls back and Dahlia's scowl softens.

"Well, start with that next time," she huffs in annoyance.

Hunter places a knuckle under her chin and tilts her head up. "I don't think I'll ever get enough of you, Little Flower. This is just the start."

And now he knows what he has to do. Because he knows without a doubt, this *thing* with Dahlia is serious and he wants everything in his past put behind him to move forward.

He's ready to move forward.

***

A PERMANENT SMILE SPREADS on Dahlia's face as she drives back to her shop. Three days, three whole days of bliss with Hunter that feels like an alternate reality. Is it supposed to be this easy? Just to fall into a routine with someone and enjoy their company?

Granted, the routine was eating, sleeping, and fucking—but it was a routine, nonetheless.

When she pulls onto main street her smile falters at the cop car parked outside her shop along with several other cars.

Her heart sinks. *Did someone break in?*

Images of her shop in total disarray has her jumping from her car and racing for the door.

"And where did you last see her?" the cop asks Carly. Bonnie's arm is around her shoulder and Walter keeps his gaze fixed on a spot at the wall.

"Sunday morning. We went to Turnpike the night before and were both—well," Carly's words fade and Sheriff Jones nods.

"Did she say what she might be doing? What were her plans for the day?"

"Uh—"

The bell to Dreaming of Dahlia's chimes as a distraught-looking Dahlia stumbles into the shop. "What happened? How bad is it?" she blurts, and four pairs of stunned eyes blink at her. Tripp rounds the corner from the back stairs.

"Her purse and phone are gone. She probably tried to drive out in the snowstorm like an idiot." When he looks up, he spots Dahlia in the doorway. "Jesus Christ, D! You had Mom and Dad here worried sick. Nearly put Ma and Pa in their graves. Where the hell have you been? Did you have a nice vacation?!"

Dahlia glances around her shop. Nothing is amiss. Nothing is broken or destroyed.

"What is going on?" she asks apprehensively.

"I told you she was fine," Carly grumbles, and Bonnie drops her arm and shoots her a glare. The sheriff sighs and closes his notes on his phone.

"I'll let you guys sort this one out."

"Thank you, Sheriff," Walt says as he shakes his hand.

Dahlia shrugs out of her coat and sets in on her counter. "What's going on?" she asks, noting the heaviness in the air.

Tripp's features are red and veins protrude from his neck. He scoffs and waves his hand in her direction. "You're unbelievable." Stepping in front of his mom, he pulls her into a hug. "I've got work to do."

Bonnie nods and the bell chimes as Tripp leaves.

"Well, I think I'll just—" Carly points at the door and gives Dahlia a sympathetic look.

Once it's just Dahlia and her parents, Walt's glare turns on his daughter. "What were you thinking just up and disappearing? Not letting anyone know where you were?! Do you know how sick your mother has been? It was like..." His words cut off and Dahlia drops her head.

*It was just like when Graves left...and Sterling.*

"I'd never do that!" Dahlia defends, trying to catch her mom's attention, but she is looking everywhere but at Dahlia. "My phone died. I got stuck in a ditch. Then the storm got worse, and I got snowed in."

"Where?" her mom snaps. "Where were you holed up the past three days that you couldn't charge your phone or call someone?"

Guilt washes over Dahlia like she's been buried under five feet of snow. Not once did she think about anyone outside of that cabin? For three days her shop has been closed and her friends and family worried and not once did she think about any of it.

"I'm sorry," she says, dropping her chin. "I should have called. But I'm fine. I'm here. And I'd never just leave."

"Where were you?" Walt demands.

Dahlia wrings her fingers. She knows what will happen if she says it out loud. Somehow the whole town will know by noon, even if her parents aren't the ones to say it. It's like the town itself has ears.

"Dahlia Brooks, answer your father," Bonnie presses. Suddenly Dahlia feels like she's in high school again and is being forced to tell her parents which of her brothers broke the antique oil lamp in the living room.

"I'm an adult now, Mom. If I want to keep my private life private, I can. Demanding me to tell you—either of you—anything isn't going to work. Not that it's any of your business, but because I love you enough to trust that you will respect me as a person and your daughter..." She lets her words settle in before continuing. "I was at Hunter Haynes place."

# Chapter Seventeen

DAHLIA CHECKS THE CLOCK hanging above the entrance of her shop.

"Where are you?" she whispers, her toe tapping nervously on the tile floor. It took a whole two days before the town buzz was filled with rumors about Dahlia's three-day excursion, hiding out at Hunter's place.

Carly sighs and leans her elbow on the counter, popping a sucker from her mouth. "I'm so proud of you," she coos. Dahlia rolls her eyes and pushes off the counter to straighten the shop...again.

"So, you keep saying," Dahlia huffs. "I just don't get why everyone had to make it such a big deal. And why did he agree to meet my parents? He could've said no and saved us both the embarrassment. Tripp still won't talk to me, not that it's a big loss or anything."

"His story is so sad, you know. What if Graves is out there somewhere just like him? Finding a woman who makes him happy, meeting her family..."

Dahlia's hands tremble and she swallows the sadness building in her throat. She knows Carly is right, but it hurts to know that Graves could be trusting someone else over her—his sister who has always been there. Why wasn't she enough to make him stay?

The door chimes, saving Dahlia from having to answer and Zip bounds over to her, eagerly waiting for pets. She crouches and runs her hands over his white soft fur, then lifts her gaze to find his owner hasn't come any closer than the door.

He looks shy.

Carly clears her throat and jerks her eyes toward Hunter.

Dahlia smiles and stands. "Hunter, this is Carly, my best friend and employee here at the shop. Carly, this is Hunter Haynes, owner of Haynes Venues."

Hunter tips his hat in Carly's direction. "Nice to meet you," he says.

"So, you're the one who nearly had the entire town on a manhunt for my best friend?" Carly teases and Hunter's gaze shoots to Dahlia.

"Manhunt?"

Dahlia winces. She hadn't gone into detail about what happened when she got back.

"Oh yeah. Her family was ready to call the F.B.I., C.I.A., National Guard, whoever they had to, to find their precious little girl."

Dahlia laughs nervously. "Okay, Carly. That's enough. Are you sure you're okay with running the shop for a few hours?"

Carly rolls her eyes. "You aren't getting out of this Dahlia Brooks." Her smile turns to Hunter. "Good luck," she says with a singing voice.

***

DAHLIA SITS IN THE passenger seat of Hunter's truck as she gives directions to her parents' house. He's been oddly quiet since they left her shop. It's like they're reverted to the standoffish people they were before the snowstorm.

"What is it?" she asks, not able to take another second of the awkward silence pressing in around her.

The truck rolls to a stop as Hunter pulls off on the side of the road. He puts the truck in park and drops his hands to his lap.

Dahlia prepares for the worst. He's having second thoughts. He's regretting everything that happened and never meant to let it get this far. He was only meeting her parents to be nice.

"Just say it," she demands. "This was all a mistake. You know what—" she scoffs and grabs the door handle, wrenching the door open before Hunter can stop her.

"Dahlia!" Hunter shouts as she walks down the road. He jumps out of the truck and races after her. "Wait a damn minute. I never said *any* of this was a mistake. You're putting words in my mouth."

She whirls, her hands flying out in both directions. "Then what? What is it you've not been able to look at me—or touch me—since you showed up this evening? I thought we were past this hot and cold thing we had going."

Hunter grabs her hands and pulls them to his chest. Dahlia's big brown eyes gaze up at him, full of fear. And he's the reason it's there.

He holds her stare, demanding to get through to her. "I don't regret one thing that we did. I meant *everything* I said about this being so much more than a quick fuck. You mean more to me than that, Little Flower. But..."

"But?" she presses, needing to know what is holding him back.

"You told me how much your brother hurt your parents...what makes me any different from him? When they learn my story, they'll hate me. It didn't help that I held you captive *in my bed* for three days and they thought you were never coming back."

"Wait, is all of this because you're scared they won't like you?" Dahlia flattens her palms on his chest. That thought never crossed her mind. How could her parents not like him? They tolerate every girl Tripp brings in so why would her bringing a man home be any different?

"I don't have the best first impression," Hunter says with a chuckle. "I haven't done the whole meet the parents' thing—well, ever." He takes a deep breath and lifts his chin to look at Dahlia. "I guess now is as good a time as any to talk about past relationships. I had one girlfriend before I left for the army. So, this—meeting the parents, trying to impress people, I've never had to do it before."

Dahlia's nerves settle, and she leans into Hunter. He lifts his hand up to her shoulders and pulls her into a hug. "If it makes you feel better, the last guy I brought home cheated on me and got his girlfriend pregnant. Oh, and he still lives here with his little family."

"Peter," Hunter grunts, putting the pieces together.

"And Katherine," Dahlia supplies with a sigh.

"I should've punched him."

She laughs and the tension that was brewing in the cab of the truck dissolves with the melodious sound. Hunter takes her chin between his thumb and forefinger and her heart jumps at the way he looks at her.

"So, this is as weird for you as it is for me?" he teases.

"Absolutely."

He presses his lips to hers in a quick kiss and leads her back to the truck.

"Then we better get it over with," he says.

***

Dahlia squeezes Hunter's hand as they stand outside her childhood home. He admires the wrap-around porch of the ranch style farmhouse. She explained to him they sold the ranch and kept the home after their cattle were stolen last year.

"Ready?" she asks.

He forces a smile and straightens his shoulders and knocks on the door. Zip sits patiently at his side.

"Doors open!" Tripp shouts from inside. Dahlia turns the knob, and they shed out of their coats before walking down the hallway.

Walt sits in his recliner in the living space. Dahlia comes into view first and he gives her an apprehensive look when she doesn't stride in and make herself at home like usual.

Ma and Pa sit on the couch, Ma working on some needle point and Tripp watches T.V. on the love seat with a different girl than the last time Dahlia attended family dinner.

"Dad. Ma. Pa. I want to introduce you to Hunter Haynes." All eyes turn on Hunter as he steps into view from the hallway. Walt stands and strides across the room with an outstretched hand.

"I'm Walt. I guess I owe you a thank you for looking after my little girl here when she got caught in that nasty storm."

Hunter takes his hand and gives it a firm shake. "Of course, sir. It was my pleasure."

*If only he knew how he looked after me,* Dahlia thinks to herself and her cheeks heat.

Pa stands next. "This is Marvin Shayne, my pa," Dahlia says, and Hunter shakes his hand.

"You a rancher?" Pa asks.

"Not yet, sir. The ranch was pretty run down when I bought it, but I almost have it back to working order, then I plan to buy a small herd of cattle."

Pa nods his approval and Tripp pushes to his feet. His flavor-of-the-week offers Dahlia a soft smile, but Dahlia's focused on her brother's scrutinizing gaze.

"You're the man from the bar," he accuses. "The one who—" His features morph to anger and Dahlia quickly interjects.

"The man who made sure I got home safe after getting drinks with Carly." She eyes her brother, silently pleading that he keep his mouth shut for now.

"So, he's the reason you disappeared?" Tripp snaps, and Walt places a hand on his shoulder.

"Dinner's almost ready—" Bonnie steps into the living space, her hands wrapped in her apron when she spots Hunter with a dog at his side.

"Mom, this is Hunter. Hunter, this is Bonnie Brooks."

Dahlia clings to the hope that her mom will forgive her for not calling and actually give Hunter a chance. She brought him home to formally meet them and that has to count for something.

"Pleasure to meet you," Hunter says and all eyes turn to the woman of the household.

"Dahlia, would you mind helping me set the table?" she asks without responding before she disappears back into the kitchen.

Hunter shifts his weight and Dahlia gives him a reassuring smile as she follows after her mother.

Bonnie stands at the stove, pulling a casserole from the oven and sets it on the top. Dahlia stands beside her and reaches for the plates in the upper cabinet.

"Just say it, Mom. Whatever it is."

Bonnie snaps her rag and tosses it over her shoulder. "Why didn't you tell me you were bringing a guest? I would've—spruced up the house. Brought out the special dishes. Fixed myself up a bit."

Dahlia can't hold back the giggle that escapes her lips.

"Don't you laugh at me, Dahlia Cheyenne."

"I'm sorry," she sputters. "I thought you were mad at me or already decided you didn't like him."

"Don't like him? Honey, you haven't taken a chance since that nasty Peter hurt you. I was worried you would never open yourself up again. Unlike your brother, who seems to have a revolving door of women."

"Thanks, Mom. And Tripp will grow up...one day," Dahlia says with little confidence. "I should probably tell you...remember how Tripp got knocked out at the bar back at Christmas?"

Bonnie arches a brow.

"That might've been Hunter to stop Tripp and Peter from getting into a fist fight." Dahlia bites her lips and squints her eyes.

"I'm sure this will make for an interesting dinner then won't it?"

*That's one way to look at it.*

After the table is set, the family takes their normal seats. Hunter sits in the empty chair beside Dahlia. Walt was impressed with Hunter's business mind and how well he's doing with the wedding venues.

"Who knew a ranch could make money off something other than beef?" he jokes, and Pa scoffs.

"And it helps Dahlia's business, too. Your venues are drawing in a lot more weddings. She's been so busy we've hardly seen her," Bonnie adds.

"Mom," Dahlia says, her tone telling her mother that now isn't the time.

"I'm just teasing, dear. You know your father and I are very proud of what you've accomplished."

Dahlia fidgets with her hands in her lap and Hunter places a hand on her thigh.

"I do very well for myself," Hunter adds. "And I'm more than happy to work alongside Dahlia." He takes another bite of the delicious apple pie.

"So," Tripp starts and Dahlia tenses. "What brings you to our town? I mean why did you decide to start a business here? Where are you from?"

"Tripp," Dahlia hisses and he only shrugs.

Hunter looks to Dahlia for guidance and she lifts her wine, subtly nodding her head.

# Chapter Eighteen

SILENCE FALLS OVER THE dining room until Tripp stands and his chair clatters to the floor.

"Tripp," Walt bellows, but his son doesn't stop, his date following him in confusion.

Bonnie's eyes glisten and she clears her throat. "I'm sorry. Excuse me."

"Mom," Dahlia says, hoping to ease her pain, but she shakes her head. Walt goes after her, and all that's left is Hunter, Dahlia, and her grandparents. She places a hand on Hunter's leg. She didn't know how her family would react to hearing his story about coming to Wyoming, but it wasn't like this.

"So, you really knew our Graves?" Ma asks, her voice filled with awe.

"Yes, ma'am," Hunter responds. "He talked about this place all the time. I knew I had to see it for myself. I was sorry to hear about him leaving. I didn't know until I connected with Dahlia."

Dahlia stares after her family.

"I couldn't imagine trying to come back from something like that. We only hope that Graves is doing well and comes back when he's ready," Ma adds, reaching across the table to take Dahlia's hand.

"I should probably go check on Tripp."

Zip lifts his head as Dahlia walks away. She feels bad leaving Hunter with her grandparents, but she worries more about what Tripp will do or how he'll react. She finds his date standing by the back door.

"Where is he?" Dahlia asks.

The woman points out the door where Tripp leans against the fence in the backyard. Dahlia takes a deep breath and pulls a coat off the winter rack before heading out.

The snow crunches under her feet as she approaches, but Tripp doesn't acknowledge her until she's standing beside him.

"Cut the crap, Tripp. What really has you so bothered?"

He snorts. "You always had a way with words, sis."

"You never were one to sugarcoat things, so why bother?"

She nudges his shoulder with hers, and he smirks. "I thought you'd left, too," he says, barely above a whisper. "When nobody knew where you were, I thought you'd found Graves and went after him."

Dahlia's annoyance toward her younger brother softens with his admission. "I'd never just leave, Tripp. But no, I still haven't heard from Graves and Hunter hasn't either."

Tripp nods. "If he loved this place so much—to the point a friend of his moves out here—then why did he just leave us?"

Dahlia thinks back to Hunter and how he left his family. "He did the only thing he could to find a way to fit into life again. I guess talking with Hunter has shown me how to see it from Graves' point of view. Hunter said when he came back he wasn't the same and he needed a fresh start."

Her brother turns to face her, leaning one arm on the fence. "So, you forgive him then? Graves, I mean."

Tears burn Dahlia's eyes and she gazes out across the beautiful Wyoming land. "I'm trying. I really am."

Movement on the porch catches Tripp's attention and he jerks his head for Dahlia to look. "So, you like this one, huh?"

Hunter leans on the porch column with his hands shoved in his pockets. Zip stands halfway between him and Dahlia, turning his head back and forth.

Bonnie steps out on the porch, a shawl pulled tightly around her shoulders. Hunter stands straight at her appearance, readying himself for a harsh reality of how she doesn't want her daughter with a man like him.

"I need to ask you something," she says, her voice wavering like she's barely holding it together.

"Yes ma'am."

"Was it anything your family—is there anything your family could have done to make you stay? To make you feel more—at ease?"

Hunter drops his chin. The heaviness of her loaded question pulls down on his shoulders. "No," he answers honestly. "I mean maybe for a short while, but I think I would've always left, in the end."

"Do you plan to ever see them again? Do you miss them?"

Hunter sees so much of Dahlia in her mother at this moment. The vulnerable gaze she holds is the same one Dahlia had when she talked about her older brother.

"I miss them very much, and I think I'm getting closer each day to being ready to see them again."

Hope sparks in Bonnie's brown eyes, the same eyes her daughter has.

"What's going on?" Dahlia asks as she and Tripp reach the porch.

"I was just inviting Hunter to dinner next Friday night," Bonnie says with an elated smile. It's like her demeanor has completely changed since she exploded at the table.

"Mom, it's Valentine's Day. I'll be a zombie. What if I promise to make the next one?"

"Sure, sweetie. Just don't—"

"Work too hard. I know, Mom." Dahlia embraces Bonnie and meets Walt in the house.

"I want to thank you all for a lovely family meal. It's been a long time since I've had one and I didn't realize how much I missed it."

Walt places a hand on his shoulder. "I wish I could say it wasn't always this crazy...but it is."

Bonnie lightly slaps her husband on the chest.

Hunter takes Dahlia's hand and her cheeks heat at the small act of intimacy in front of her family.

"Are you ready to go?" he asks.

Dahlia squeezes his hand and says goodbye to her family.

Zip beats them to the truck and Hunter smiles over at her once he's behind the steering wheel.

"What?" Dahlia asks. "Why are you looking at me like that?"

"Just admiring the view of you in my truck," he states, reaching across the center console to hold her hand. His gaze is full of things he wants to say, but can't. He doesn't want to rush this with Dahlia and what happens when she sees the real him? The version of him he keeps locked down and only emerges when the memories are too much.

He needs to tell her. Especially with her staying at his place.

What if she isn't safe? Isn't that why he left home? Too keep the ones he cares about safe?

Dahlia places a hand on his arm, flashing him her bright smile and sparkling brown eyes.

And he knows without a doubt, he's falling for this woman—and it scares the hell out of him.

***

SWEAT BEADS ACROSS HUNTER'S brow and his heart races. He rolls and fights with the sheet until his legs spring free and he swings them off the bed. His foot presses into the cold floor and he braces his elbows on his knees, holding his head in his hands.

Dahlia sleeps peacefully at his back and he moves slowly so he won't disturb her. There's still several hours before morning, but after vividly reliving the loss of his leg and what all happened that day, he won't be able to fall asleep.

Zip hops off the bed as Hunter rolls the sock up his thigh for his prosthetic. The scar tissue where his leg was removed aches more than normal this morning and he winces as he steps forward. After getting dressed, the door quietly clicks closed behind him and he slings his rifle over his shoulder. Zip races around the ground, sniffing and following a trail Hunter can't see.

The woods are quiet this time of night. An occasional owl hoots somewhere high in the pines and Hunter breathes in the fresh air, desperate to flush out the lingering smell of burning flesh. The nightmares feel too real sometimes and it'll take him hours to get his body to stop shaking.

His subconscious is stuck back in that hell and he's on high alert, as if he's actively being hunted.

He used to come out here to flirt with the mountain lion. A game of cat and mouse. Something about hunting and knowing he's being hunted calms his buzzing nerves.

The night terrors haven't happened as often with Dahlia sleeping in his bed and getting thoroughly fucked at night, but when he's restless, they're worse. And the more he gets to know Dahlia—the more he falls for her—the more restless he's becoming. There's something he has to do, and it scares the hell out of him.

Being around the entire town, their shocked expressions at seeing him with Dahlia, meeting her parents, the way Peter seems to think he has this claim on her—his nerves are fried.

He walks and waits, listening for the lion's scream. But he's met with silence.

That's one thing he loves about this place is the silence. Back home, there was too much noise. Too many people. Too many expectations. Everyone acted as if his time away never happened and they could all just pick up where they left off with friendships—*relationships*. But he wasn't the same and he didn't fit into the hole he left in his family and friend's lives.

Graves must have felt the same way. Hunter gets it, he does...but seeing the other side of the coin today with Dahlia and her family and how hurt and worried they are, it made him realize he did the same thing.

If he's able to have a stable relationship with a woman he cares deeply about, shouldn't he call his parents just to let them know he is okay? Will it be too hard to hear his mother's voice when she inevitably cries?

By the time the sun rises and the sky changes from indigo to purple and pinks, he knows he needs to get back before Dahlia wakes up. He thought he knew what he wanted out of his future before he left for the army.

His whole life was planned out, even what to expect when he got back. Nearly dying was not part of the plan, and that changed everything for him. Now this curly haired, brown-eyed beauty in his bed is something he *never* saw coming.

# *Chapter Nineteen*

VALENTINE'S DAY COMES AND goes in a blur. Before Dahlia knows it, every heart and red or pink decoration is swapped out for the Spring Open House that the entire town takes part in. Bonnie sweeps the floor while Tripp helps Walt lift a heavy concrete planter to the sidewalk.

Dahlia clicks open her phone screen and stares at the picture of her and Hunter that was taken on Valentine's Day. The two of them locked themselves in his cabin for the weekend. When Dahlia posed for the picture, Hunter came up behind her and tickled her right when she clicked the button. Her smile is infectious and Hunter's looking at her with complete adoration.

"He has a pretty face to stand and stare at," Carly whispers into her ears. Dahlia shrugs her off and stifles her laughter.

"Don't you have wreaths to put outside?"

Carly winks and disappears to the back of the shop. The town is slowly coming alive with the rising sun, and Dahlia steps out to the sidewalk.

"This is where you want them, sweetheart?" her dad asks as Tripp scoffs.

"If she wants it moved, she can do it."

Dahlia waves her dad off. "It's perfect, Dad. Thank you."

Tripp clears his throat and gives her an expectant look.

"And you too, Tripp."

Her brother checks the time and taps Walt on the shoulder. "Susan's is open. I'm going to grab the apple-cinnamon donuts before they sell out!"

"Now wait a minute," Bonnie chastises. "Walt, go with him and get the girls something. Oh!" She stops him before he can walk away. "And get me one of those caramel, white chocolate coffees!"

Dahlia laughs at her parents and takes a satisfied breath. Spring is her favorite time of year. The snow, and the heartache that usually comes with it, melts away bringing new life, blooming wildflowers, and everything turns green.

The sun heats her cheeks as she stands on the sidewalk and she closes her eyes, soaking in the start of the warmer months. Carly and her take turns helping the first customers of the day as they shop and everyone wears smiles. The energy is contagious, and it fuels Dahlia's excitement for this time of year.

"Dahlia," a man says and dread washes over her. She plasters on her best smile and turns to face Peter.

Only he isn't alone.

"Peter. Katherine. I hope you enjoy the open house today."

Katherine doesn't smile, and she tugs on Peter's arm. "Sweetie, Lily is making a beeline for cotton candy and it's barely after ten in the morning. We should really—"

"You go. I have some shopping to do...for you," he adds, like it's an afterthought.

Katherine's eyes dart between Dahlia and Peter before she rolls her shoulders back and strides after her daughter.

"What do you want?" Dahlia snaps, growing exhausted from this game he's playing.

"I haven't seen you since Christmas—at Turnpike—with Hunter Haynes." His eyes rake over her body like he's seeing her in a new light.

"And it's been so nice," she remarks.

Peter chuckles and walks past her to look at a wreath hanging on her stand. "So what? Are you two a thing now?"

"You have some nerve even thinking that is any of your goddamn business," Dahlia whisper-shouts, careful to keep any prying ears from hearing.

Peter doesn't turn to face her, and that only adds to her irritation.

"Where is your boyfriend? I figured he'd be here...at your side...making your debut in the town."

Dahlia smiles and greets a couple who walk by. She invited Hunter, but with the crowded streets she knows the real reason he was hesitant to come. He promised he'd try if he got his work done in time, but Dahlia took that as code for he didn't want to hurt her feelings by saying no.

"He has work to do on the ranch for an upcoming wedding."

"Hmm." He flips the price tags on each wreath and Dahlia's eyes widen.

"You're jealous," she states in a surprised tone. "The fact I found someone and I'm happy has turned you into this weird jealous creep who keeps putting his nose where it doesn't belong."

Peter slowly turns, his hands shoved in the pockets of his jacket.

"Careful, Dahlia. Those are big accusations."

"Then explain it to me. Why the sudden interest of who I'm with and what I'm doing in life? You left me—which I'm super thankful for. You cheated. You're the villain in this story, or did you forget?"

He sucks on his teeth and his gaze jerks from Dahlia to slightly above her shoulder. Hunter stands a few feet away with Zip at his side in his army-green service dog vest. Hunter loosely holds his leash in one hand and Dahlia spins on her heel to see what stole Peter's attention.

"You came," she says, her eyes lighting up just at the sight of her cowboy. Hunter tears his gaze from Peter's seething stare to Dahlia. She looks radiant with her natural looking makeup and painted on blue jeans. They hug her every curve perfectly and her brown curls gently sway in the breeze, framing her beautiful face.

"You asked," he responds, because that's all it would take for him to do anything for this woman. "What did I miss?" He steps up to Dahlia's side. His blood warms as she slings her arm through his elbow and leans in closer before addressing Peter.

"Nothing at all. He was just looking at a wreath for his front door."

Hunter knows she's lying. He heard it all before Peter realized he was standing there. Dahlia didn't deny Hunter being her boyfriend, although they hadn't labeled it yet. And little Peter is jealous. It's cute really, because Hunter knows without a doubt he has nothing to worry about from his little flower. Maybe he needs to prove this to the asshole from Dahlia's past.

"Why don't we let him look in peace while we go inside for a few minutes?" Hunter asks, his expression giving nothing away.

Dahlia nods and leads Hunter by the hand into the shop. "Carly! We have a customer out front. Can you help him?"

Carly lifts her head from the register computer and spots Peter through the window. "Can I shove my boot up his ass?"

Dahlia rolls her eyes, but her smile is lighter than the forced one from outside. "We don't turn away paying customers and—"

"We always do it with a smile on our face," Carly mutters. "I'm certain I'd smile while my boot was up his ass."

Dahlia laughs and shoos her friend toward the front of the shop.

Once they're alone, Hunter steps in Dahlia's line of sight and places his hands on the counter, caging her in place.

"I don't like the way he looks at you," Hunter nearly growls, and Dahlia is shocked at his tone.

"Who? Peter? He's harmless. All bark and no bite."

Hunter shakes his head and keeps his hat low, hiding his haunted eyes. "People will surprise you when they feel threatened or get a hit to their ego."

"Why would Peter feel threatened? And trust me, that man's ego is so big nothing could hurt it."

Hunter looks up at her statement, his blue eyes flicking between her rich brown ones. "You don't see the effect you have on him—the kind you have on me. You were right, he is jealous. But there is something darker in his eyes. Something I've seen my fair share of. I need you to be careful around him, Little Flower."

Her smile falls, and she takes in the weight of his words. He's genuinely worried, and it puts her on edge. "I will, but I really don't think he'd do anything to physically hurt me. He's—Peter. I've known him since I was five."

Hunter cups a hand to her cheek and brushes his thumb across her bottom lip. "Maybe not physically, but if he hurts you, or even tries—" Hunter's jaw clenches and he doesn't have to say the words for Dahlia to get his meaning. She places her hand over his and leans into his palm.

"Thank you for coming," she says, trying to distract him from his line of thoughts. "It means so much that you're here."

Hunter's lips curve up into a smirk. "Well, I'm your boyfriend so—"

Dahlia's cheeks flush and Hunter's smirk widens into a toothy smile. "You heard all of it?"

He nods. "From the moment those beautiful lips formed around a very naughty word."

Her features couldn't get any redder and Hunter kisses the tip of her tinged nose, then her cheeks.

"So, does this make me your girlfriend?" she asks. Her voice comes out in a breathy whisper.

"I sure hope so, because I don't plan on letting you go—ever." Hunter hovers his lips over hers, waiting for her response. She threads her fingers through his blond hair at the base of his skull and pulls him into her, closing the distance between their lips and kindling the slow burning flame that seems to always be burning for him in her soul.

His hands slide down her back and cups her ass, squeezing and pulling her closer against him. "These jeans are begging me to peel them down your legs and set you on this counter," he says against her lips.

Dahlia gasps and her blood heats at the vivid image he just painted in her mind.

A throat clears and Hunter drops his hands while Dahlia struggles to get her feet under her.

Bonnie stands with a mischievous smirk and her arms crossed at the back room of the shop. "Advice from an old lady," she starts, and Dahlia's lips part and her eyes widen. "Don't get frisky where just anybody can walk in and certainly not where you're supposed to be checking out customers."

"Mom—I—we weren't,"

Bonnie raises her hand. "You most certainly were, dear. It's nothing to be ashamed of, but we don't need to give the town more to gossip about. And you have wreaths to sell."

Dahlia jerks her attention to the front window where Peter is talking to Carly about a wreath she's holding. He's staring at Dahlia and based on the red creeping up his neck, he saw more than he wanted, possibly more than her mom.

Hunter moves to stand at her back and Peter glances at Carly and nods, handing her cash, then taking the wreath.

Dahlia's brother and dad walk past him with their haul from Malt and Toffee. Tripp glares and his jaw clenches, but he doesn't stop. The sweet aroma of cinnamon, chocolate, apple, and coffee fills the shop in seconds.

"He just doesn't know when to quit, does he?" Tripp asks Hunter like they're old friends. When Hunter doesn't respond, he looks from his sister to his mom, then back at Carly who comes into the shop. "What did I miss?"

Carly starts to speak, but Dahlia strides forward, lifting a drink carrier from her brother's hands. "They smell delicious!" She hands the drinks out and takes the bags from her dad to disperse the sugary goodness. Once everyone has their drinks and customers fill the shop, Hunter takes her hand and pulls her to a secluded corner.

"Dahlia," he says, knowing that she is feeling more than she is letting on.

"I'm fine, Hunter. I just—" She won't admit that she saw the dark look in his eyes. It was just a flicker, barely there, but she knows what she saw. But she doesn't want to worry Hunter more than he already seems to be and besides, this is *Peter* she's talking about. If anyone knows him, it's her.

Maybe he's getting tired of his wife and in a couple of months he'll find someone else to fixate over.

"What?" Hunter asks, reeling her back from her thoughts.

"I didn't want to stop," she admits and desire flashes in his eyes.

He leans in closer, his lips brushing the shell of her ear. "Tonight, we won't have to."

# Chapter Twenty

DAHLIA'S LOOSE-FITTING SWEATER FALLS off her shoulder as she leans against her apartment window overlooking her small town with a glass of wine. All the shops are closed for the night. The hustle and bustle of Spring Open House still hums under her skin, but she smiles, knowing her shop had a wonderful day and how her town showed up and gave their support to shopping small this spring season.

She can't stop her business mind as it already jumps to prepping for Easter next, then fades into Memorial Day with arrangements for loved ones who have passed. Calloused hands slide over her exposed shoulder and pull her curls to the side.

Hunter kisses the crook of her neck and wraps his arms around her waist. "Did you have a good day?"

She hums in contentment and leans into Hunter.

"It went really good, and we sold out of so much stuff. I know I have no reason to worry, but I'm constantly waiting for the rug to get ripped out from underneath me with Dahlias. Like it's too good to be true and one day the money isn't going to be there anymore. After days like today, I feel like I can breathe and take a second to just bask in what I've accomplished."

She spins in his arms and Hunter tucks her hair behind her ear, trailing his thumb along her jaw and across her lips. "You're amazing at everything you do, Little Flower."

"Everything?" She tantalizingly lifts her wine to her lips and takes a drink.

He chuckles and plucks the glass from her hand, setting it on the living room table. "Do you have plans tomorrow?"

Dahlia tilts her head, confused by his change of conversation. "The shop needs to be put back together after today, but what did you have in mind?"

"I thought maybe since we don't have any weddings tomorrow, I could take you away for a bit. Show you a part of who I was before I lost my leg. But you'll have to trust me. Like really, trust me."

Dahlia's smile falters, and she tilts her head. "That's not ominous at all... What are you—"

Hunter quickly presses his lips to hers. "You'll just have to *trust* me."

She wants to press further, but his hands skim down her body and lift the hem of her sweater. His touch is hot against her stomach and her plump lips part and Hunter is desperate to taste her, to have her, to remind himself that he's whole. But he hesitates.

"What's wrong?" she asks, noticing the way his hands stop exploring her body, and he doesn't meet her gaze.

"I need to talk to you about something...about why I was late today." Hunter doesn't step back. He keeps his hands on her, afraid to let go.

"Weren't you working at the ranch?" she says with a teasing tone.

Hunter smirks, but it's void of humor. "Yeah, that was a horrible cover, wasn't it?"

"Hey," she cups his chin and guides his blue eyes up to meet her gaze. "I get it. You don't have to explain any of it to me. It's fine."

Hunter turns his face and kisses her palm, taking a deep breath, then looks at her again. "I called my parents."

Out of everything he could have said, she did not expect that. All thoughts of sex and wanting to rip Hunter's pants off slips away. "Hunter, that's great, but how did it go? Did they answer? Are you okay? What did they say?"

He chuckles at her enthusiasm and kisses her forehead. "Maybe we should sit down." Taking her hand, he leads her to the couch and sits, pulling her onto his lap.

Her sweater rides up her bare thigh and Hunter slides a hand under it to run his finger across the lace of her panties. She waits patiently while he gathers his thoughts and emotions.

"After having dinner with your family, I knew I had to call them. I tried several times, but I couldn't bring myself to dial their number. I see what losing Sergeant Brooks has done to everyone he loves and I don't want to be the cause of that same kind of pain."

"Hunter—" Dahlia starts, but she doesn't know what else to say. The agony he's been going through comes to the surface and her heart breaks when his blue eyes shine.

"Mom sobbed. I couldn't understand anything she was saying. Dad ended up taking the phone from her and—I've never heard my old man cry before." He sucks in a deep breath and clears his throat. "After the shock wore off, we talked for nearly an hour. They asked where I was, how I've been, and then if I was coming home.

"I couldn't lie. So, I invited them to come here for a visit in a couple of weeks. Mom protested at having to wait, but I want to talk to them more before they get here. And I'm...nervous. What kind of man is nervous about seeing his parents?"

His head falls back onto the couch and he stares at the ceiling.

"That's a huge step, Hunter. You haven't seen them in over two years. Of course you'd be nervous."

Dahlia's stomach twists as something she hadn't thought before pops into her mind. A tiny seed of doubt about what she is doing exactly with Hunter Haynes.

What happens if he goes home? Isn't that what she wants her brother to do? Come home? So why would Hunter's situation be any different?

If he goes home...where does that leave them? Perhaps this was always supposed to be temporary. She is a way to pass the time until he's ready to leave.

"Dahlia," Hunter says, his voice loud in her tiny apartment. His hand slightly tightens on her hip bone, worry churning in his gut at the faraway look in her gaze. Why is her brow furrowing? What is she worried about?

"Hmm?"

"What are you thinking?"

Her features relax and she smiles at Hunter, shaking her head. "I'm really happy for you. Maybe you'll even want to go back to Tennessee..." She bites her lip, hating that her insecurity slipped out before she could stop it. Embarrassed, she tries to push off Hunter's lap, only he wraps his arms around her, keeping her in place.

"Little Flower." His voice is soft and tender. "*If* I ever decide to go to Tennessee, it'll only be to visit. This is my home now. A fact that I'm sure my mother will have a hard time understanding."

Dahlia drops her head and the muscles in Hunter's arms flex. Pinching her chin between his finger and thumb, he lifts her brown eyes up to him, making sure she believes him when he says, "You're my home."

Her chest tightens and she tries to blink the welling tears back before they escape. The three words fill her heart until it aches, and it terrifies her. She's never felt this way for anyone, not even Peter, who she dated for years. There is something different between Hunter and her.

Something more.

Something foreign.

"Stay tonight," she whispers. What is brewing between them feels like it could slip through her fingers like sand, and that's what makes it so terrifying and exhilarating. "Please."

She looks past Hunter at Zip, who is snoring on the recliner like that's been his place to sleep all along.

"You'll never have to beg me to stay, Little Flower. Begging me to let you come...that's a different story." He grins, skimming his fingers over the top of her panties, then down between her legs. Teasing her seam through the lace, he softly kisses her neck, her jaw, up to her cheek and the corner of her lips. Dahlia whimpers and tries to move her hips to spread her legs and give him better access.

Hunter brushes his lips across the shell of her ear. "You have to say it, Little Flower. Tell me what you want me to do, *exactly*."

Her eyes flutter closed when he teases her clit, but he retreats and her eyes spring open. Her bottom lip pops out and her brows furrow. "Hunter," she whines, and he flicks her pouted lip.

"What. Do. You. Want?"

She opens her mouth then clamps it closed only to open it again, but no words come out. Heat rushes up her neck and cheeks at the intensity of his gaze. "Fuck me," she states.

Hunter chuckles. "I think you can do better than that. Beg remember?"

She pushes herself up from Hunter's lap and stands before him. "You want me to tell you what I want?" she asks, swaying slightly as if dancing to music.

"That's right."

Dahlia tells her smart device to play her playlist, and the music fills her apartment. Her hips swing to the slow, emotional melody, and Hunter's gaze doesn't leave her. He drinks her in and realizes she has turned the game on him and he might be the one begging.

Her lace panties play peek-a-boo from under her sweater as she lifts it and twirls, but it doesn't go above her stomach.

"I want you..." she pauses, as if lost in thought. "I want you to kiss me here." Her finger runs up the lace of her panties and taps over her where her clit is. "Then I want you to bite...lick...and suck until my legs are shaking and I'm a wet mess all over your face."

Hunter's breath quickens and his cock pushes against his zipper. She's torturing him. "Little Flower," he groans, his voice pained and he pulls at the crotch of his pants, desperate for relief.

"Then, once I'm a trembling mess..." She pulls her sweater over her head and tosses it to the floor.

Hunter bites his bottom lip and groans at the tease. She's bra-less and her breasts look delicious as she raises her arms and swishes her ass in a slow circle.

"I want you to put your hard, huge cock inside of my pussy and fuck me like you mean it."

Hunter can't take it. He pushes off the couch and walks Dahlia back until she is pressed firmly against the wall.

His mouth is hot on her lips, her cheek, her neck. He bites until he's worried she'll be bruised. Hunter bends, moving down her collarbone, sternum, each nipple, then he drops to his knees and kisses her stomach, below her navel to the lace panties.

"I want you," Hunter growls. "And I'll do whatever you want and more." Lifting one of her legs, he braces her body as he tosses it over his shoulder, exposing her pussy to him. He takes the lace fabric between his teeth and pulls it quickly, ripping her panties free. He slides them down her leg and out of his way. He'll do just as Dahlia asked, but just when she's about to come, he's going to make her prove how badly she wants it.

Her fingers thread through his short blond hair, and pull his face closer to her center. That's all the encouragement Hunter needs. He hungrily grips her ass, his fingertips digging into her flesh.

He licks up her center and Dahlia presses her back into the wall. The raging storm inside of her builds with each graze of his teeth and flick on his tongue. Hunter is relentless as he pulls whimpers and mewling sounds from Dahlia's soul.

He'll never tire of hearing her as she unravels underneath him. While sucking on her clit, he gazes up at her through his lashes and locks onto her burning brown gaze. His cocks aches to be inside of her—his home.

Dahlia's leg tenses over his shoulder and a smile lifts the corner of her lips. She's close—so fucking close.

Hunter pulls up, licking his lips and Dahlia's eyes go wide, her curls wild and untamed around her face.

"What are you doing?" she says with a need coiled so tightly inside her it hurts.

"Beg," Hunter states, his own restraint waning.

She scoffs and tries to move her leg in retaliation, but he refuses to let her go.

"You want to come, Little Flower? Want me to lick your orgasm as your body trembles pinned to the wall? If you want me too—" He kisses the inside of her thigh. "Give you the orgasm you're fighting for right now? Then beg."

Dahlia squeezes her eyes closed at Hunter's words. "Yes," she says. "Yes. Hunter, please—I need you. Please." Her words sound more like a mewl and Hunter nips at her leg in anticipation.

"I'll take good care of you, Little Flower." He flicks his tongue across her clit.

"Yes," she cries. "More, please. Don't stop."

He groans against her center and bites her clit, the vibration and pain sending her over the edge with a cry of ecstasy and Hunter swears there isn't a better sound in the world.

# Chapter Twenty-One

DAHLIA RARELY WONDERED ABOUT who Hunter Haynes was before she met him. For her, it didn't matter because she's fallen for the man he is now. Was he an athlete in high school? Was he a total nerd and on the mock trial team? Maybe he was a loner or perhaps he skipped school and barely graduated.

If she had met him back then, would she have thought he was a total tool and blow him off?

Granted, her history with Peter's screams that she didn't have the best taste in guys.

But standing beside the new *toy* while he pays the previous owner, she questions his sanity—and hers when he asks if she'd ever ride it with him.

She sighs, scared to step toward the piece of metal as if it'll jump out and bite her. She tries to picture a younger, carefree Hunter. He told her he had one before he joined the army, but when he got back—he couldn't bring himself to ride it or look at it. But he found one for sale that had a modified shifter he could work with his prosthetic leg.

A motorcycle.

He bought a motorcycle. It's shiny in a beautiful burned orange color with black pinstripe accents.

"So, what do you think?" Hunter asks as he walks up behind her, total excitement filling his voice.

"I think it's—nice?"

He chuckles, at her hesitancy. "Don't worry about me, Little Flower. I used to ride all the time and once I get comfortable with the new shifter I'll take you out for a ride—if you want. I won't force you."

"Super," she responds with a fake smile. The only experience Dahlia has with motorcycles is the few locals who ride around town. She's never been up close to one, let alone *on* one.

Hunter kisses her cheek. She hasn't seen this side of him. He's almost child-like. "You are kind of adorable."

He scoffs. "I am a man. The last thing we want to be called is adorable. That's saved for kittens and puppies." He wraps his arms around her waist and kisses her neck.

"I've never seen you this—happy." She spins in his embrace and wraps her arms around his neck. "So, Mr. Haynes, are you ready to take it home?"

His eyes sparkle and he kisses her deeply once more before sucking in a deep breath. Dahlia follows him to his truck, and he tells Zip to get in the passenger seat. Hunter plucks his cowboy hat off his head and places it on Dahlia's, and he laughs.

"What are you—"

Her words get cut off when he pulls out a baseball cap and slides it on backwards. She licks her bottom lip at how sexy he looks. Maybe she had it wrong about the motorcycle because as he swings his leg over, revs the engine and winks at her, she's never been more fucking turned on.

Dahlia follows Hunter back to town. After an hour she was able to relax with each turn Hunter made on the bike. He's like a different person than last year. He seems free. She still catches glimpses of the haunted, far-off look he gets, but it happens less. She wonders when his parents come to visit if it'll set him back, or keep him moving forward.

If Graves came home, would it help or cause him to lose the progress he's made? Is he thriving wherever he is like Hunter is? Or is he still lost and alone?

"Call Graves," Dahlia tells her phone that sits in the holder on the dash. She clings to the hope that this is the time he answers, just like always...but he doesn't. The generic voice mail comes through and her heart drops.

"Hey big brother," she starts, determined to sound positive and happy. "It's been a while since I've called. Sorry about that. The shop has been busy and well...I met someone. You'll never believe who it is, though. I guess I have you to thank for him actually, since you're the reason he moved out here. Yeah..." she chuckles. "He's not from around here, which I think is just what I needed. Tripp likes him, but Tripp likes everyone—well except the person we don't mention."

She sighs and adjusts her grip on the steering wheel. "I really hope you're doing okay and you're finding what you need. I understand why you left, or at least I'm starting too. You have to do what is best for you. Just know that I love you. If you decide to come home," Her throat tightens as she struggles to get out the words. "Or if you decide not to, just find your happiness, Graves. You deserve it."

After she hangs up, the tears fall. The harsh reality hits her that Graves may never come home. She may never see him again, and she has to accept that.

***

HUNTER STANDS AT THE base of a ladder as Dahlia secures greenery up the support beams of his barn to the rafters. It's slow going as they move from one to the next, but it'll be finished in time.

Greenery weaves around floating candles in glass containers on the reception tables. And the floral backdrop behind the wedding party's table turned out beautiful, with big white roses, pale pink dahlias, and an assortment of smaller pastel-colored flowers.

"How does it look?" she asks with her hands stretched high to secure the last piece in.

Hunter smirks as he stares up. All he's been able to focus on is her ass and if she moves just right, he gets a peek of her lace bra under her crop top.

"I love everything about this view." He grins and Dahlia looks down at him from under her stretched arm.

"I meant the decorations," she deadpans.

"Little Flower, I've been staring at your ass in those painted on pants for nearly four hours and I'm pretty sure I have the design on your bra memorized."

She scoffs, but can't hide the smile as she climbs down the ladder.

"Come on, Soldier. I still have to do the arch before this wedding starts."

She rolls her shoulders and twists her neck. Hunter knows this day is getting the best of her. She won't take a second to eat and he's barely got her to drink water. For someone who sells flowers for a living, you'd think she'd take better care of herself...at least hydrate properly.

"You'll get it done and it'll be spectacular. You always do."

She ignores him and keeps working. She'll be stuck in her head until the job is done, then desperately need a massage and a hot bath. He follows her with the ladder and sets it at the base of the arch.

The music from her speaker she always plays fills the barn with '*Spin You Around*' by Morgan Wallen and he can't wait to get her off that ladder and to his cabin, so he can do just that.

"Shit!" Dahlia squawks and Hunter pivots around the ladder to see flowers fall off the arch...again. She glances at her watch and knows that she is getting close to her cut off time. She just has to get these flowers to stay put.

"What do you need?" Hunter asks at the foot of the ladder.

"I don't know!" Her voice rises in pitch and she forces a deep breath. "I need something to keep this secure, but also something I can hide. The floral wire isn't holding."

"Okay, what about a different wire?" He glances around the barn, desperate to find a solution for her.

"I can't exactly use *barbed wire* up here, Hunter." Her tone comes out harsher than she intended and she drops her chin. "I'm sorry. You didn't deserve that. I'm just—" She climbs down with the flowers with the foam base in her hands.

*Think, Dahlia. This is why you're the best. You think outside the box.*

"What kind of wire do you have?" she asks.

Hunter rubs a hand across the back of his neck. "We have some old fence, *barbed-wire*, um...I think there was some chicken wire left from the last owner."

"Can I see it?" she asks excitedly.

"The chicken wire?"

She nods, and Hunter leads her to the storage room. He pulls out the unused roll and the gears turn in her head.

"This could work. Do you have wire cutters?"

Hunter shifts through a toolbox and hands a pair of cutters to her. "How will this work, exactly?"

"I'll show you, but can you bring the buckets of greenery to the arch? We'll need to make sure you can't see the wire from the front."

Hunter has learned to never question her masterful ways and does as she asks.

Without a minute to spare, Dahlia puts the finishing touches on the arch and stands back to admire her handy work. She securely placed the foam block and flowers in position, ensuring that not a single sliver of the chicken wire was visible.

"Perfect. Now we have to hurry to get this all back to my car before the guests arrive." She grabs the wire and cutters, while Hunter grabs two buckets of leftover flowers and greenery.

Chattering guests get closer from outside the barn and Dahlia's eyes widen. "Shit!" she whisper-shouts.

"Just put them in here until afterward. It's faster." Hunter holds the door open to the shed and they sling their stuff inside. The barn door rolls open and Hunter grabs Dahlia, pulling her inside the room and closes the door behind them. Zip stares at them with his head to the side.

Hunter crouches and whispers to his dog. Zip lays down and watches the door, but doesn't make a sound.

"What are you doing?" she squeaks, and Hunter places a hand over her mouth. He angles his head as if he's listening outside and places a finger to his lips. The voices are muffled as people walk by the door, completely oblivious of them hiding in the shed. Hunter leans in closer, brushing his lips against Dahlia's ear.

"Do we walk out and give the town something to talk about, or—" He moves his hand from her mouth and slides it down her throat and settles softly on her exposed collarbone. "Do we hide out here and be extra quiet until it's over?"

She's pinned against the wooden table. The air between them is charged and her lips part. She doesn't like the idea of giving this town anything else to talk about, but if she stays shut up in this tight space with him, things *will* get heated.

Hunter watches her expectantly, waiting for her decision. Dahlia's parted lips curve into a smile and she leans into him, forcing him to step back.

"What are you doing, Little Flower?" The heat in her gaze makes him squirm and his cock presses against his zipper.

"We're being extra quiet," she states, moving her hand down his torso to his crotch.

Hunter sucks in a breath and eyes her warily. "Oh, are we?"

She nods, unbuckling his belt and then popping his button and unzipping his pants.

"There are over a hundred guests out there. What if we get caught?" he asks, not really wanting her to stop.

"Then there won't be rumors about what we were doing locked in a shed." She slides his pants and boxers down, his hard cock springing free.

Hunter's blue eyes blaze and he grips the counter as Dahlia's tongue darts out and licks from the base of his dick to the tip. He groans and Dahlia pulls back, glancing at the door.

"Shhh," she hisses and Hunter smirks, mouthing 'sorry'.

Dahlia shakes her head and grips his cock, working her hand up and down. When the music starts, she takes him in her mouth.

Hunter bites his bottom lip until he's afraid it'll bleed, trying to keep quiet while Dahlia sucks like her life depends on it. She's trying to make him lose the fight. At some point she made this a contest. She's challenging him to keep quiet and making it nearly impossible.

His balls tighten as everyone cheers for the new couple. Hunter moans as he comes, the roar of the guests overpowering him.

Dahlia stands, a victorious grin spread on her perfect, swollen lips. "You lost," she teases, and Hunter pulls her flush against him.

"With you? I win every day."

# Chapter Twenty-Two

THE DOOR TO DREAMING of Dahlias chimes as it opens, letting the fresh breeze blow in. Dahlia is bent over a potted peace lily as she shoves a card pick into the soil for the funeral it's being delivered to today. A hand snakes around her ass and squeezes. She jumps and whirls with the plastic pick aimed at the person responsible, her eyes full of fury.

"Good morning to you, too," Hunter jokes, and Dahlia drops her hand to her chest.

"Christ! You can't do that to me. I nearly gouged your eyes out!"

He looks at the *weapon* skeptically. "Remember what I said last time you threatened me?" He steps in closer to her, forcing her calves to hit the pot. "I'll have you pinned right here before you can even blink, Little Flower."

Her cheeks flush and a stray curl drops to the front of her face.

"Holy shit. That was so hot," Carly sighs and leans against the checkout counter. "Are you sure you don't have a brother? Distant cousin maybe?"

Hunter tips his hat in Carly's direction and lets Dahlia shove him back a couple of steps. "I'm almost done here. Then I need to go home and shower," she tells him.

"Hot date?" Carly asks.

It's been months since Dahlia spent those nights in his cabin. Nights full of heat and passion. She certainly wasn't looking for a relationship in Hunter Haynes, or any man. But something happened between them she'll never be able to explain and she's not sure she'd ever want to. Like two lost souls finally beating as one and everything just made sense after that.

They make sense.

"I'm meeting his parents," Dahlia blurts and drops her chin to tug on her shirt, suddenly feeling self-conscious of every part of herself. What if they don't like her? What if they don't approve or, worse…demand Hunter leave and she was wrong to encourage him to reach out to them to begin with?

"Holy shit," Carly whispers in disbelief. "You—you're meeting *his* parents? This is serious then? No more bullshit?"

Hunter can't help but chuckle at her friend with her mouth gaping open. "I'll pick you up at five," he states, tucking his finger under her chin to get her attention. "They'll love you. Honestly, at this rate, possibly more than the son who abandoned them."

Her brows furrow and lips part to defend his statement, but he gives her a quick peck and smiles before rushing out the door with Zip at his heels.

"You're meeting his parents," Carly mutters, her eyes not fixed on any specific space, like she's still trying to piece together when this all happened.

Dahlia stares out the door after Hunter.

Yes, she is. And today.

"Dahlia?" Carly places a hand on her best friend's shoulder, who is still staring out the door Hunter left through.

When she looks at Carly, her gaze is full of uncertainty and the panic that grows with each second that gets closer to meeting Hunter's parents.

"Whiskey or wine?" her best friend asks, measuring how big of a panic she's actually in.

"Tequila," Dahlia whispers, and Carly's eyes widen.

"Okay—okay, we're okay. This is a normal thing you do in relationships. Right?" She rubs her hands up and down Dahlia's arms. "You're going to show up and treat the mother like a problem bride. Nobody messes with Dahlia Brooks and she lets nothing get to her. Got it? You're okay, Dahlia. You've got this."

Dahlia offers a crazed smile and doesn't feel like a confident florist at this moment.

***

HUNTER'S TRUCK ROARS UP the driveway to the main cabin used for weddings and receptions. He figured it would be best to let his parents assume this is where he lives versus his little *hunting shack*, as Dahlia calls it.

"You're shaking the whole truck." He squeezes Dahlia's leg, and she takes a deep breath, running her hand over her half-up-do, trying to smooth the frizz. "You look gorgeous, Little Flower. Way too pretty for someone like me," he scoffs. "I don't even have all my body parts. You're way out of my league."

"You know that doesn't matter to me," she states. It's been a thing he's had to work through at his own pace. That first night, he was terrified to touch her, or her touch him. Like he thought she'd be repulsed and leave. But time and time again, she's proved that she's exactly the woman he always knew she was. There isn't a more kind-hearted person in this world that compares to *his* Dahlia.

"Look at me." He cups her cheek and guides her brown eyes to meet his.

"What if this is a mistake? This is a big deal and they haven't seen you in years. I don't want to impose," she insists.

His thumb brushes across the blush accented her cheek bones. "You didn't have to wear make-up. You're stunning without it. But yes, this is a big deal. Dahlia." He clears his throat and places his cowboy hat on the dashboard. "I lost six years of my life in hell on earth. I didn't think I was capable of feeling anything except hate and fear. You keep me here, grounded, and I'm happy. You're my gravity. I want you by my side and to introduce you to my parents. For me, time doesn't factor into emotions. I spent long enough staring at clocks and counting down days. I'm throwing all reservations out the window. I'm done living scared. But I'd really love to have you holding my hand and reminding me of everything I just said when Mom and Dad show up."

She nods and places her hand over his. "Wouldn't you know it's my stubbornness you have to thank for us being together?"

He flashes her a smile and walks around to open her door. "Does that mean you'll be stubborn enough to stay?"

"What if I decide to never leave?"

She raises her eyebrows and his lips part, but no sound comes out. Dahlia quickly kisses him and opens the cabin door with her key. "Come on, Soldier."

He blinks after the curly-haired force. He's envisioned it enough. Waking up to her every morning, more than just the weekends or after a long night. Had she been thinking about the same thing? Was that her way of saying she'd say yes if he asked? His mind spins with the numerous possibilities.

Zip licks his cheek when he doesn't make a move to get out of the truck and he pushes down his rambling thoughts for later as a vehicle approaches.

\*\*\*

DAHLIA SIPS ON HER wine as she sits beside Hunter across from his parents. Lydia keeps a skeptical expression; her scrutinizing eyes judge every attribute of the cabin and Dahlia. Her graying, blonde hair is styled with so much hair spray, Dahlia bets it would crunch under her touch. When Hunter introduced her to his parents, his dad, Jared, pulled her in for a hug immediately.

His mom, Lydia, kept her distance and has ever since.

"You should have seen him!" Jared slaps his knee. His cheeks are as red as the T-shirt he's wearing as he tells the story about little Hunter trying to catch a greased pig at the county fair. "He dove—head first! When the pig dodged, the poor kid landed full-face in shit!"

Zip lifts his head at the raised tone before huffing and laying back down at Hunter's feet.

"Language," Lydia scolds and everyone's laughter dies. Dahlia sips from her wineglass. "So, Dahlia. Hunter hasn't said much about you, well I guess he couldn't have given he only called a month ago." She gives her son a sorrowful look and Hunter dips his chin, playing with the whiskey glass in his hands. "What is it you do?"

"Well," Dahlia says, setting her glass down. "I own Dreaming of Dahlias, the florist shop in town. I graduated from college with an art degree and became a master florist after that."

Lydia wears a modest high-necked dress and purses her lips at Dahlia's words.

"Mom," Hunter says, pulling the skepticism from Dahlia and toward himself. "I'm glad you're here."

That admission cracks his mother's hard exterior, and she reaches across the table, gripping her son's hands. "Of course I'd come, sweetie. We've missed you so much and Melanie—well, she—"

Hunter's gaze cuts to Dahlia and he shakes his head.

"Lydia," Jared says with a warning in his tone.

Dahlia glances between the tick in Hunter's jaw and his exasperated mother. Her heart sinks and her palms sweat. She only has herself to blame. She never thought to ask if there was anyone else he left when he moved away. But you know what they say about making assumptions.

"It wasn't just us you left, you know. Doesn't she deserve some kind of explanation? A phone call? Something?" Lydia asks. Jared places his hand on his wife's leg and Dahlia goes rigid. Hunter rips away from his mother and sits back in his seat, running an exhausted hand over his face.

Dahlia takes in the change in the room. Jared's smile drops and Lydia stares with hardened eyes and a furrowed brow at her son. Dahlia can't fight the urge to reach out and take Hunter's hand, to show she's there and he's okay.

He glances at her touch and intertwines his fingers with hers.

"Who's Melanie?" Dahlia asks, taking control of the conversation. If it is an ex-girlfriend or fiancé, she reassures herself, it's all in the past. His *past*. And none of it matters.

Lydia purses her lips and takes a steadying breath. "She's the woman Hunter promised he would come home to. Then he left the moment he got back."

Dahlia's chest tightens along with her fingers, and it doesn't go unnoticed. Hunter leans on his knees, refusing to loosen his hold on his little flower's hand.

"I told her I was leaving. I told her she deserved to find someone who cared about her, because I didn't. How much clearer did you want me to be? Did you really travel all the way here to bring this up?" Hunter's voice turns cold.

"Son, of course not. We're just happy you called." Jared offers a soft smile and drapes an arm around his wife's shoulders.

"You can thank Dahlia for that. She's changed my life. She's helped me so much."

His declaration makes her blush, and she drops her chin to hide her features, but the pins in her hair keep it from shielding her face.

The room falls silent until the oven dings.

"I'll get it," Dahlia says hurriedly, needing an escape from the tense room. The familiar sound of Hunter's limp comes into the kitchen behind her and he wraps his arms around her waist, Zip right behind him.

"I meant what I said, Little Flower. Don't let anything she says make you think otherwise. In her mind I left and came back the same person. She doesn't understand and honestly, I wouldn't be surprised if Melanie has been over to family dinner every Sunday since."

Dahlia pulls the lasagna out and sets it on the counter. "Remind me to never let you go back to Tennessee alone."

Hunter nuzzles her neck and she giggles. He was so worried about how she'd react to his mom bringing up his past. But just like she does with everything, she's the definition of elegance and grace. Taking everything in stride and not faltering. At least not from the outside looking in.

"Do you regret it?" she asks.

He sighs, his breath is hot against her sensitive skin. "No. If nothing else, this is the closure Mom needed that I've changed. I'm happy, safe, and have made something of myself here."

"And they're going to stay here for one week...?" Dahlia lets her voice trail off and spins in his arms. "Also, *friend*?"

"How did you want me to introduce you? Girlfriend? Lover?" He squeezes her hips like she loves and her lips part. "Future Mrs. Haynes?" There's a hint of mischief in his blue iris'.

"Hunter," Dahlia breathes out. They haven't even said the four-letter word yet. She's never let a man into her life as much as Hunter is. To be a part of her business and open herself like this—after Peter, she told herself she'd never let herself be this vulnerable again.

"Dahlia," he says in the same tone. He kisses her forehead and stands to his full height. "Dinner's ready!" he shouts and her mouth hangs open as he winks and turns to the table already set for four people.

Yes, because she can totally eat and act normal after that conversation.

Surprisingly, Lydia doesn't mention the woman from Hunter's past the rest of the night. Were they a tragic high school sweethearts tale? Dahlia feels pity for the love-struck teenager who clung to the promise her boyfriend would return from the war. It's the kind of stuff they make movies about, but Melanie didn't get her happy ending. Dahlia took her place.

After dinner and two more bottles of wine, Hunter shows his parents to the room they'll be staying in and then leads Dahlia to the front porch swing, grabbing a blanket off the couch as he walks by.

They sway slowly, staring at the stars decorating the sky like a million Christmas lights. Zip runs around the yard, nose to the ground as he stretches his legs from the tense evening.

"Will you stay?" Hunter asks.

"I stay all the time." Dahlia rolls her eyes.

He rubs his hand along his thigh. A tale she's learned means he's uncomfortable. She'll be the person he needs right now. Not out of guilt, but because, honestly, there isn't anywhere else she wants to be.

"I'll stay," she assures him and snuggles into his side. They'll have to talk about what he said earlier.

*Mrs. Dahlia Haynes.*

She chews on her lip, unsure if she likes the sound of that or not.

# Chapter Twenty-Three

HUNTER WAVES AT DAHLIA'S taillights down the driveway. He knew this was going to happen. She'd have to go to work, and he'd be alone with his parents.

No buffer.

"It's just us now, Zip." His dog whines as if he doesn't like the idea of it either.

The cabin door closes and Hunter braces himself for his mother. Wildly enough she was on her best behavior at dinner. Now he expects it's going to get worse.

"A girlfriend? You move halfway across the country and you get a girl-friend, a *ranch*, and just start over?" Her shrill voice skates down his spine and he clenches his jaw.

His dad leans in and whispers something in Lydia's ear, but she shrugs away from him and gives him a glare that seems to have a hidden meaning. Changing the subject, Jared says, "It's beautiful out here, son. I see why you chose this place."

Hunter beams with pride because if his parents had seen it when he first bought it, they would be singing a different tune.

"Thanks, Dad. Do you want to see the rest of the property?" he offers. At least it'll be something to kill time.

"I have some calls to make," Lydia announces and goes inside, leaving Jared behind.

Hunter rolls his lips between his teeth and looks away from his mother. He hoped she would have lasted a couple of days before she laid into him like this. Maybe even be happy for him.

Jared walks down the stairs and clasps a hand on his son's shoulder. "She has a lot going on at home," he says, trying to salvage the situation.

Hunter nods. "She always has something going on. Always trying to fix someone else's problems." He sucks on his teeth and jerks his head toward his truck. "Want to look around?"

"Absolutely! I want to know all about how you turned a ranch into a profiting wedding venue. How does someone even come up with that idea?"

Hunter shrugs. "Cattle seemed like too much work for one man."

Jared laughs, nodding his head. "You are right about that."

They climb in his truck and Zip hops in the backseat. Hunter drives around his ranch, showing Jared the four other wedding venues aside from the cabin. He even shows him the working barn and tells him about his plan to add cattle, eventually.

They park by the lake, and Hunter feels the weight of all the things his father isn't saying—or asking.

"This is my home, Dad."

Jared inhales deeply. "Anyone with eyes can see that. You're in love, son...with more than just Wyoming."

Hunter's chest tightens and he can't bring himself to look at his father. "How did you—?"

"As if the ranch wasn't enough, I saw the way you looked at Dahlia. It was exactly how I looked at your mom when I first saw her."

Hunter knew how he felt, sure. But he hadn't said it out loud. Will she feel this is all too soon? The last guy broke her heart. Is she ready to hear another man say he loves her? Would she even believe him? He knows he'll have his answer soon enough.

By the time they get back to the cabin, Lydia is swinging on the porch swing, her expression a mix of annoyance and impatience. Hunter sighs.

"Lydia, you should see what this son of ours accomplished with this place. What you see here is only a fraction of the ranch. It's beautiful, sweetheart!" Jared smiles proudly and kisses his wife on the cheek as he sits beside her.

Lydia manages a small smile at Hunter. "Maybe you can show me before we leave."

"I'd like that," Hunter responds.

His dad may accept the change, but his mother will be a different story. Maybe she'll accept it by the end of the week.

***

"You have to let me come!" Carly whines as she and Dahlia lock the front doors of the shop.

"I don't have to do anything and besides, it could be a total shit-show. Honestly, I don't even want to go. If that woman looks at me sideways one more time, I might blow."

"All the more reason I need to be there," Carly insists. "Come on, D. My life is so boring, I need a little action."

Dahlia rolls her eyes and spots Peter down the street, leaning on the hood of his truck.

"Fine," she says, absentmindedly. "But you have to be on your best behavior. No snide remarks or crazy looks. Got it? His parents are leaving tomorrow. Just one more day to show them I'm good enough for their son."

"Cross my heart. I'll be on my *best* behavior."

Dahlia shakes her head and walks out the back of the shop. "Just get in before I change my mind."

They get to Dahlia's parents before Hunter. Bonnie has two long tables set out in the front yard with fabric table cloths and Walt and Pa are supervising Tripp on the grill.

Carly is quick to open the door and inhale deeply. "There ain't nothing like Momma Bonnie's home cooking!" she shouts, and Bonnie lifts her head with a delighted smile.

"Carly! Get over here and give me a hug! Did Dahlia finally let you have a night off work?"

"Ha-Ha," Dahlia mocks and hugs her mother. "This all looks great, Momma. Really. Now, what do you need help with?"

Bonnie fusses over her dress and glances at the house. "There's salad and deviled eggs that need to be sat out. Keep em' covered though. We don't need the flies having a field day. Carly, can you check on Ma? She was working on potato salad when I last saw her."

"Sure thing," Carly says before disappearing, waving at the guys all around the grill.

"It takes three guys to man a grill while the women do all the rest," Dahlia teases as she links arms with her mom.

Bonnie tries to stifle her laugh as they head back inside.

It isn't long before the familiar roar of Hunter's truck arrives outside and Dahlia freezes in the kitchen, her palms sweating. Carly moves to stand beside her with a pie in each hand. "What are you waiting for? Go greet your *boyfriend*," she whispers, and Dahlia rolls her eyes.

This is it. This is the last evening with Hunter's parents. Then she'll be in the clear. They'll go back to Tennessee and she and Hunter will be left here. Back to long nights in the hunting shack and away from prying eyes. It's only been a week, and she misses the sex. One more reason she can't wait for Mr. And Mrs. Haynes to leave.

"Dahlia," Carly urges, and Dahlia smiles.

"I'm going," she hisses. The screen door bounces closed behind her as Hunter opens the passenger door for his mother. Zip is less patient and hops over the front seat, making a beeline for the opening, and rushes over to Dahlia.

Hunter whistles, signaling to Zip, and the dog stops and sits, looking back at his owner. Dahlia laughs and readies herself before walking across the yard to greet him.

"Hey," she says, feeling shy in front of everyone.

"Hey," he parrots, leaning in and kissing her softly on the lips. "You look beautiful."

Dahlia rolls her eyes. "I came straight from work. I probably have pieces of flowers still in my hair."

"Just one." He pulls a piece free, and a throat clears nearby, pulling them from the moment.

"It's wonderful to see you again, Jared. Lydia," Dahlia says. "I want to introduce you to my parents. This is Bonnie," she says as her mother walks up.

"Oh, it's lovely to meet the ones responsible for raising such an amazing son for my Dahlia," she praises and Jared pulls her in for a hug. "Walt!" Bonnie shouts, waving her husband over.

"We could say the same about Dahlia. Couldn't we, Lydia?"

Hunter's mother smiles, but it looks like her face will crack if you touch it. "Of course. It's a pleasure to meet you, Bonnie."

Walt offers his hand to Jared. "Nice to meet you, fine folks. Hope you brought your appetite. Bon doesn't know how to do *small*, so there is more than enough food."

"Well, it's a special occasion," Bonnie remarks and playfully swats at her husband. He grabs her hand and pulls her in for an embrace and Bonnie squeals. Jared laughs, but Lydia wears a guarded expression. "My parents, Marvin and Mildred are on the porch, then our youngest son, Tripp, is on the grill. That leaves Carly. She works for Dahlia and they've been best friends since they were children."

Dahlia tenses and Hunter threads his fingers through hers, acting as her anchor and keeping her from bolting like she wants.

"Foods ready!" Tripp shouts and Bonnie leads everyone to the table. Carly carries the pitchers of tea and lemonade and sets them on the table before she finds a seat.

Dahlia is thankful for the idle chatter everyone keeps going during the meal. Hunter runs a hand up and down her leg and she moves the food around her plate, pretending to eat, but really she's counting down the minutes to when it's over.

So far everything is going great. Even Tripp has been on his best behavior and hasn't said anything embarrassing. She glances at Carly, who has a mischievous grin on her lips.

Dahlia gives her a look to decipher what she's thinking, but Carly turns her attention back to the conversation that Dahlia hasn't kept up with.

Bonnie winks at Carly, and she excuses herself from the table. Dahlia gets up to go ask her what that was about, but Hunter squeezes her leg and keeps her in her seat.

"Do you know something I don't?" she whispers.

Hunter shakes his head and takes another bite. Dahlia looks at her brother, who has always been a terrible liar. He avoids her gaze, and she knows something is up. Each of her family members appears oddly suspicious. The only ones whose demeanor hasn't changed are Jared and Lydia.

Simultaneously, the warmth of Hunter's hand disappears and Carly steps out of the house, carrying a cake with lit candles on it. Dahlia's family sings '*Happy Birthday*' and she looks around, shocked.

It's her birthday. With everything going on, she totally forgot. When the song ends, she turns to ask Hunter if he knew. But he's not sitting beside her anymore. She spins around and drops her gaze, her heart nearly jumping from her chest.

The singing fades behind her.

Her hands shoot to her face, covering her mouth, and her eyes burn.

Hunter kneels on one knee with a box in his hands. He looks absolutely terrified.

"Dahlia Brooks," he says, his voice thick, and he swallows. "No amount of time with you would ever be enough, but I'd love to start with the rest of our lives if you'll have me, even with the missing parts."

Dahlia chokes out a laugh and his body relaxes slightly.

"Hunter—"

He cuts her off. "I love you, Little Flower. Will you marry me?" He opens the box and a beautiful white gold band with a solitaire diamond in the middle and smaller ones creating a circle around it sits perfectly inside.

Her body shakes, and she nods, tears cascading down her cheeks. "Yes," she says, never more sure of anything in her life. "Yes, Hunter. I will marry you!"

Applause erupts behind her, but she doesn't care about the audience. Hunter slides the ring on her finger and she helps him stand. His eyes shine with unshed tears and he pulls her into him, kissing her with the passion he usually reserves for private occasions.

Once he releases her, they spin and they're greeted with hugs and congratulations. They all knew. They helped Hunter plan this, and Dahlia had no idea.

She wasn't the only one in the dark. By the look on Lydia's face, she had no idea either.

Jared approaches and he hastily wipes at his eyes. "I'm so proud of you, son," he says, but there's something hidden under his tone. "We're proud of you," he adds, reaching for his wife.

Lydia refuses to step forward.

"Mom," Hunter urges, hoping she'll accept Dahlia and that Wyoming is his home now.

"I can't." Her voice cracks and she shakes her head. Looking at Dahlia, she says, "It's not you, dear. You're wonderful and successful, but—" She looks at Jared who shakes his head and she clamps her mouth closed.

Without another word, Lydia walks to the truck and climbs inside.

"Can I ask one thing of you, son?" Jared asks.

Anger simmers under the surface of Hunter's skin at the way his mother ignored his engagement. "Sure," he remarks.

"Come to Tennessee for a visit. Let us celebrate with your family and friends. If not for them, then your mom. Think about it?"

Hunter glares at his mom, then back at Dahlia. Her heart breaks for the pain in his blue eyes and she squeezes his hand, her engagement ring a foreign pressure on her finger.

"I'll think about it. The keys are in the truck. Dahlia can bring me back later."

Jared pulls his son in for another hug before leaving.

"From friend, to girlfriend, to fiancé all in one week," Dahlia teases. "I'm surprised smoke didn't come out of her ears."

Hunter can't suppress his laughter and pulls Dahlia in for another passionate kiss. "Tonight, we're going back to your place and I'm having sex with my future wife. I've missed you," he murmurs against her lips.

"I love you, Hunter Haynes."

His body stills and his throat tightens at her words. She said it. She loves him and she said yes. The nerves that have been eating away at him since asking Walt for his blessing finally subside and he feels like he can breathe again.

He's settling down, growing roots, and hopefully one day, building a family. All of which will be with this woman he loves more than he ever thought possible.

# Chapter Twenty-Four

THE FAMILIAR SCENT OF coffee, spices, and sugar waft out the door as Dahlia steps into Malt and Toffee.

"There she is!" Susan squeals, waving a copy of the newspaper around like it's a flag. "Get over here! Let me see the big ring."

Dahlia's cheeks redden as everyone in the cafe stares at her. Some smile and the ones from out of town just look confused. It's been a month since Hunter proposed, but now the words got around since her mother had it put in the newspaper.

She lifts her hand to the top of the counter and Susan snatches it up, turning and angling it so the light dances off the diamonds.

"My, my, he did good, didn't he?" she coos.

"He really did." Dahlia beams with pride, knowing that Hunter Haynes is going to her future husband. "My mind is still reeling. I never thought—well, you know."

Susan flicks her gaze at the corner of the cafe, but Dahlia doesn't notice. She's too transfixed by the ring on her finger.

Peter sits across from Katherine at a table, his hand gripping the cup. When his wife isn't looking, his gaze lingers on Dahlia and the engagement ring that shines on her left hand.

Susan leans in closer, her eyes full of love and happiness. "I'm thrilled for you, Dahlia. You couldn't have picked a better man."

Dahlia sighs. "I love him more than I ever thought possible. It almost hurts—at times. Is that normal?"

Susan laughs. "Honey, I was terrified of Sammy. We were much younger than you when we started dating, but when he popped the question, I still remember the sheer terror. It's like your heart lives outside your body from that point on. It should be scary. You're trusting someone else with your heart."

Dahlia nods enthusiastically. "Exactly! I'm worried all the time and keep waiting for the other shoe to drop. Like this is too good to be true, isn't it?"

Susan lets go of Dahlia's hands and places them on the counter. "How about some caramel and cinnamon to calm the jitters?"

"Thanks, Susan. I'm waiting for Hunter, actually. Did you know he got a motorcycle? Well, he got it like months ago, but today is the first day he's taking me out for a ride."

Susan's eyes narrow as she mixes Dahlia's drink. "You better be careful. Those things terrify me, but I can see the appeal."

"Once again, I'm terrified," Dahlia says. Her body is a hum of jitters. Susan sets the drink in front of her and Dahlia thanks her before heading outside to sit.

As she turns, her gaze gets locked onto Peter in the corner. His stare makes Dahlia's skin crawl, and she retreats outside to a table while she waits for Hunter. The entire time she feels his stare on her back.

Finally, the rumble of a motorcycle approaches and Hunter backs into the empty spot in front of Dahlia. He's wearing a backward baseball cap and pops the kickstand down. Swinging his leg over the back of the motorcycle, he smiles at Dahlia.

Her heart leaps in her chest, just like it does every time she sees him. She is like one of those sickly in love bimbos that can't form a sentence without leading back to how much she loves her fiancé.

"There's my little flower," Hunter greets, wrapping an arm around her waist and dipping his perfectly sculpted lips down to kiss her.

"There's my adrenaline seeking soldier," she teases back.

"Are you ready?"

Dahlia looks from Hunter, then to the motorcycle. He added a backrest to it after he bought it, ensuring his girl will be comfortable and feel secure.

"Yes—no—maybe," Dahlia stammers, and Hunter lifts her hands to his lips, kissing the inside of her palm.

"I promise to go slow and be careful."

"I trust you," Dahlia quickly supplies. "It's all the other factors."

Hunter leads her to the left side of the bike and walks her through how to get on and where to put her feet. Once she's on the bike, Hunter fires the engine up and it rumbles underneath her.

He revs the engine and several people on the sidewalk stop and stare.

"Ready?" he shouts, excitement clear in his smile.

"As I'll ever be!"

Dahlia tightens her arms around his torso. The bike smoothly accelerates until it's just the two of them and everyone else and their opinions fade behind away.

The rush of the wind, the leaning of the motorcycle in the curves, it's a high she's never experienced. She holds her breath as they roll to their first stop sign and Hunter slides his hand across hers on his torso.

Dahlia tightens her hold and smiles against his back and his shoulders lift with his inhale before he takes off again.

Riding alone is its own special kind of peace. It quiets Hunter's mind, makes him feel free. But having Dahlia's arms tight around him with her thighs secure on either side of his body, it's something else entirely. She has to fully trust him to ride on the back of his motorcycle with him and she'll never know how much it means that she got on today.

He runs his hand from her knee, down her shin, then back up as they ride along the straight highway. A pronghorn grazes in the distance and Dahlia points it out.

She's his home. Wyoming is his home. He found his peace when he thought it would never be possible. Hopefully, one day he'll see Sergeant Brooks again so he can thank him.

Hunter parks at the back of Dreaming of Dahlias. He holds the bike steady while Dahlia climbs off, then puts down the kickstand and stretches as he stands.

"That was—" Dahlia's cheeks are sore from smiling so long during the ride. "I want to go again—not like now, but again."

Hunter adjusts his baseball cap and chuckles. "All you have to do is ask."

She steps forward, taking his hands in hers and he leans back into the motorcycle. "Why are we waiting?"

He furrows his brows. "To go riding again? I'm worried you'll get sore and—"

She places her fingers on his lips. "No. Why are we waiting to get married? I don't want a big white wedding and I definitely don't want flowers. I do enough of that. Just you and our family. I don't want to wait, Hunter."

He cups her cheek and brushes his thumb across her cheek. "I don't want to wait either, Little Flower. But—" He sucks in a deep breath and Dahlia's excitement plummets.

"But what?"

He pushes off the back and paces a few steps, removing his hat and rubbing the back of his neck. "I want to get things right with my parents. I want them to be there. I know it sounds dumb, considering Mom hasn't spoken to me since she left."

"No. It's not dumb. I couldn't imagine what that was like. Have you called her?"

Hunter shakes his head. "I just don't understand why she was so against this and why she reacted that way. I tried talking to her before she left, but she wouldn't listen. Literally she just stared, opening and closing her mouth like a fish."

Dahlia wraps her arms around herself, unsure of how to help in this situation. What if Lydia never accepts her?

"What are you going to do?"

Hunter stops pacing and puts his hands in his jean pockets. "I'm going back—to Tennessee—like Dad asked. And..." He watches Dahlia to gauge her reaction. "I want you to come with me."

"Me? But I have the shop—weddings, clients—I can't just...go." Hunter drops his chin and when his blue eyes land on her again, they're filled with pleading words Hunter doesn't say. He doesn't want to do this without her. He doesn't know if he can. But he can't force her to go. Perhaps this is something he's supposed to do on his own.

"Okay," he responds.

"What?"

He walks back over to his bike, swinging his leg over and turning on the engine. "I asked you to come and your answer was no. So, okay. I'll go, sort this out with my mother, then come back here and marry you."

"Hunter—" Dahlia starts, trying to get him to understand that her shop is her life. She's never left it unattended. She's never even been out of the state and to just up and leave her livelihood in the hands of someone else is terrifying.

Hunter revs the engine. "I'll call you when I get home," he says before he's lifting his feet onto the bike and driving away.

"Hunter!" she shouts, but it's no use. He's gone.

Guilt churns her stomach. Why couldn't she just say yes? Why did she hesitate? She stands there for several minutes, wishing by some miracle he'd come back and they could have a do over from the moment he asked her to go. But the sound of his motorcycle grows farther away until she can't hear it anymore.

She makes her way to her apartment, staring at the clock every five minutes, anxiously waiting for him to call. After showering, she tries to drown herself in her work like she used to when something bothered her, but it's useless. After an hour has passed and she still hasn't heard from him, she throws her pride out the window and grabs her phone.

It rings three times before he answers and she wants to hang up when she realizes he didn't call.

He didn't call her.

Silence comes from the other end before a voice she doesn't recognize speaks. "Hello?"

Dahlia pulls the phone away to look at the caller ID, then brings it back again. "Who is this? Why do you have my fiancé's phone?"

Dahlia pushes to her feet and clings to the phone.

"Who is this?" she asks again when they don't answer quick enough.

"Ma'am, I'm afraid your fiancé was in an accident. He's being rushed to the hospital. I'm the officer that arrived at the scene and found his phone."

The world tilts and Dahlia grabs at the kitchen table.

*Accident. Hospital. Accident. Hospital.*

The words bounce around her head and that's all she can hear.

"Ma'am? Hello? Ma'am, are you there?"

Dahlia gathers herself, grabbing her keys and purse. "Yes, I'm here. I'm on my way."

# Chapter Twenty-Five

EVERYTHING CAN CHANGE IN the blink of an eye. One moment you're telling someone you love them, the next they're gone.

Dahlia races down the highway, and the flashing lights of a tow truck force her to slow down.

She chokes out a sob at the sight of the mangled, burned orange metal.

Her car lurches as she puts it in park and jumps out, rushing past the blockade.

"No," she chokes out at the sight of Hunter's motorcycle being dragged up the ramp of the tow truck.

"Miss, you can't be here," a man says, and guides her back to the other side of the police car.

"What happened?!"

"We don't have those details, but it looks like a hit and run."

"Someone hit him? Why aren't you looking for them?! Who hit my fiancé?!"

The officer tries to wrestle her back away.

"No! Let go of me! Why aren't you looking for who hit him?!"

"You can't be here!" he says with more force, his fingers digging into her biceps as he hauls her back.

*Hunter. He has to be okay—he has to.* The metal of the bike scrapes against the tow truck bed, the sound making her want to crawl inside of herself. Another officer grabs Dahlia's arm and drags her back.

"Someone hit my fiancé! He—" she gags through the sobs, snot and tears smearing across her cheeks and chin. "Where is he? Where's Hunter?!"

The officers try to answer her, try to console her out of her hysterics to listen to reason, but it's no use. Dahlia is so far into the depths of her panic, she can't hear anything, can't feel the bruises forming under their grip.

"He's gone," she whispers, because how can anyone survive that pile of scrap? How can a motorcycle compete with a vehicle? "I've lost him. He's gone. I've lost him...he's—"

"Hey! Get your hands off my sister!" Tripp shouts, grabbing Dahlia and shoving her behind him.

"Dahlia, get in my truck, now," Tripp orders. "I'm taking you to the hospital, then we'll figure this out."

She grabs her head, trying to steady the nausea twisting her stomach. "He—he can't—Hunter's...Tripp, I can't breathe...I can't."

Tripp wraps his arms around his sister and guides her to the truck. "We don't know anything yet, D. Come on, I'll take you."

He straps her into the passenger seat and runs around the truck.

"Tripp—" Dahlia croaks out as he puts the truck in drive.

"We don't know anything, Sis. Alright? Don't go there."

*Too late.*

She stares at the passenger mirror, burning the image of the motorcycle into her mind. All she can think is, *how does anyone survive that*?

\*\*\*

DAHLIA SITS IN THE waiting room, her cheeks caked with dried tears as she waits...and waits...and waits. When they arrived, she was informed the doctors were doing everything they can—nothing more. No details on how he is doing or how extensive his injuries are.

Tripp called her parents and they've been waiting with her. The obnoxious ticking of the clock on the wall marks the minutes.

"Tripp," she says, breaking the silence. Her voice is gravel, her throat raw. "I need you to go get Zip. Hunter will need him when he wakes up.

"Okay," Tripp says, pushing to his feet and kissing the top of his sister's head.

"Mom, Dad, you guys should go. There isn't anything you can do here and I—"

Bonnie shakes her head with her hands folded in her lap. "I'm not leaving my baby alone to wait."

"Mom," Dahlia says, her voice stronger now. "I'd feel better if you were at home. I'll call you as soon as I hear something."

Bonnie opens her mouth to argue, but Walt places a hand on her shoulder. "Dahlia has always been our independent one. Let's give her some privacy." He faces his daughter. "And you call us as soon as you hear something. I don't care what time it is."

Dahlia nods, standing to hug both her parents. "I promise I'll call."

She waves once more at her mother's worried expression as Walt leads her out of the emergency room doors. Pacing the length of the waiting room, she stops when the bay doors open and spins.

It's not a doctor or a nurse that steps out and Dahlia exhales.

She alternates between pacing and sitting, then staring at the vending machine like it'll magically produce mini liquor bottles.

"Sir, you can't have that in here! Sir!" the receptionist shouts and Dahlia startles at the loud noise.

She steps back into the waiting room and Zip pulls on his leash, eager to get to Dahlia. Tripp lets go and Dahlia drops to her knees, burying her face into his white fur.

"Ma'am, we don't allow pets—" the receptionist huffs and Dahlia lifts her head.

"He's a service dog. My military veteran fiancé's, service dog," she snaps and the woman's eyes soften. "He has every right to be here for him."

She relents and leaves the waiting room with Dahlia sitting on the floor, clinging to Zip while her brother takes a seat.

"You should go too," Dahlia mutters. "Who knows how long it'll take if he—if—"

"When he wakes up," Tripp supplies, and Dahlia wipes her nose.

"How does this happen? Why me? I finally, finally find happiness with someone, trust someone, let myself fall in love and then—" She waves her arm around the waiting room. "What did I do that was so awful to deserve this?"

Tripp sighs. "You didn't do anything, Sis. This is—it's fucked up. That's all I got."

Dahlia snorts and leans back against the wall. "Yeah," she agrees.

The clock on the wall ticks by the minutes. Zip grows anxious, sensing something isn't right, and Dahlia does her best to calm him.

"How did you know where I was?" she asks.

"I was at Harrington's waiting to get the oil changed and it came across the scanner about a hit and run involving an orange motorcycle." He drops his gaze to his hands. "I went to see for myself before I called you."

Dahlia stares off into the white ceiling. "Thank you," she whispers and Tripp sighs, not knowing what else to say.

A doctor steps into the waiting room and Dahlia immediately stands.

"Are you the family of Hunter Haynes?" he asks.

"Yes," she answers quickly. "How is he? Is he—?" She can't bring herself to finish that sentence.

"He's stable. We have him in the ICU for observation for the next forty-eight hours. He was very lucky. Most cases we see involving a motorcycle and a vehicle collision don't end this well."

"But you're saying he's going to be okay? He's alive?" Dahlia clutches her chest and Zip whines at her feet.

"He has some broken ribs, one punctured a lung that should heal on its own over time, and a compound fracture of his left arm we had to operate on. Road rash is on his side, back, arms...again, he is very lucky it wasn't worse. But he should make a full recovery."

Tripp steps forward, placing a hand on Dahlia's shoulder. "When can she see him?"

"I can take you back now. The anesthesia should wear off and he'll be waking up soon."

She grabs Zip's leash and looks back at her brother. "Call me if you need anything, Sis."

"Thank you. Call Mom and Dad for me. And Tripp," she stops, fully facing him. "Thank you...for being here."

He nods, rocking on his heels. "Anytime."

Dahlia takes shallow breaths as she walks deeper into the hospital. Zip pulls slightly on the leash, like he senses his owner is close. The doctor stops at a cracked door and pushes it open. "Let us know if you need anything. He'll have nurses coming in to check his vitals, too."

"Thank you."

Dahlia steps inside and Zip pulls the leash free from her grip. He bolts for the bed and she reaches for him.

"Zip, no," she hisses, worried that he will hurt Hunter more if he jumps on the bed. The dog doesn't listen and plants himself on Hunter's chest, careful to avoid the arm in a brace.

Hunter grunts under his weight and Zip licks at his cheeks and chin.

"Zip," he says, his voice deep and husky.

Dahlia gasps and hesitantly walks over to his bedside. His eyes flutter open and he winces against the overhead lights. He looks wildly around the room, and Dahlia steps forward.

"Hi," she says, like she doesn't believe this is real.

Hunter immediately relaxes into the bed and puts all his focus on his little flower.

"What happened? Where am I?"

She swallows and tries to be as delicate as possible. "You're in the hospital. There was an accident—after you dropped me off—someone, uh, hit you." Her hands shake and tears form in her eyes. She spins her engagement ring on her finger.

When she looks back at Hunter, tears stream down her cheeks and her jaw aches from holding back the sobs. "I thought I lost you. I'm so sorry about Tennessee. I'll go with you—I'll go everywhere with you because the thought of being here without you—I never want to feel that way again."

Hunter tries to sit up, but he hisses at the pain in his ribs. Dahlia closes the distance between them and places a hand on his collarbone, encouraging him to lie back. Hunter sags into the bad, the mattress cover crunching under his weight.

"I shouldn't have left like that. I should have stayed and talked it out with you. Of course, you'd be hesitant to travel a full day's time to somewhere you've never been to see people who haven't been exactly welcoming."

She sniffs, wiping her face, and then her mouth falls open. "Oh, my god! I didn't call your parents. I—I'm so sorry." Hunter clings to her hand as she tries to pull away.

"Don't. I'd rather have you all to myself for a while. Besides, I'm fine. Just beat and banged up. I've had worse."

Dahlia leans down, resting her head on his chest. Sobs of relief wrack through her body. The war of emotions she's had over the past eight hours hits in one giant wave and she can't stand tall and hold them back anymore.

"Shhh," Hunter comforts, pulling her against him until she's in the bed on her side and he's petting her hair. "I'm not going anywhere, Little Flower. I'm right here and I love you so much."

There's still the mystery of how he wrecked. There're flashes and pieces as he came too, lying on his back with tires squealing in the background. The sun was blinding overhead, and he tried to blink everything into focus, but he couldn't move.

As Dahlia lies beside him, her deep even breaths telling him she'd fallen asleep, he keeps trying to replay the accident. Dahlia mentioned someone hit him. If he could just remember something.

With Zip nestled between his legs and Dahlia's delicate hand splayed on his chest, he succumbs to exhaustion. He's lucky, he knows that. As soon as he's well enough, he's going to Tennessee and settling whatever is going on with his mother, then marrying the amazing woman who he can't imagine life without.

Officer Quinn wakes them up, wanting to ask Hunter some questions, to see if he can remember anything leading up to the crash. The doctor told Hunter his memory could come back, but there is never anyway to tell when the body has endured trauma.

Hunter scoffs. He knows plenty about trauma.

"If you remember anything, call us." Officer Quinn hands him his card and nods at Dahlia before leaving.

His breakfast sits untouched as he stares a hole into the wall.

"You need to eat," Dahlia says, running her hand up and down his uninjured arm.

"I need to remember." He squeezes his eyes closed and clenches his jaw. "I left your apartment—driving down the road—then...ugh," he groans, jerking his arm from her touch and running a hand over his face.

"Hey, it's okay. They'll find them. Your memory could still come back. Just...don't push yourself, Soldier." She leans down and kisses his forehead. Hunter grabs her ass and pulls her closer, angling his head to take her mouth with his. Her tongue dances with his and he moans against her lips.

"Don't ever scare me like that again," Dahlia murmurs.

"As soon as I'm out of here, we're going to Tennessee. Then I'm marrying you, Dahlia Brooks."

She nods and presses her forehead to his. "Okay, Hunter Haynes."

# Chapter Twenty-Six

"Mom," Dahlia says with an exasperated sigh. "Mom, we don't need all of this." She takes another casserole dish from Bonnie and tries to find room for it in the cabin refrigerator.

"What Dahlia is trying to say," Hunter says with a wince as he shuffles into the kitchen. His spare prosthetic doesn't fit as well as the one mangled in the crash. "We appreciate everything you're doing."

Bonnie arches a brow at Dahlia. "I knew I liked this one. Now, son, are you sure you don't want to call your parents? I'm sure they'd want to know."

Hunter forces a smile. "I don't want to worry them over nothing. I'll tell them about when we go down in a couple of weeks."

Bonnie wipes her hands on her pants. "Okay, sweetie. Well, if you two need anything, you call us. Okay?"

"Thank you, Mrs. Brooks," Hunter says.

"Thanks, Mom. I love you." Dahlia hugs Bonnie.

"I love you. *Both* of you."

Dahlia helps Hunter back to the couch after Bonnie leaves. "So," she says, carefully sitting down next to him. "What do you want for dinner? You name it, I'm pretty sure it's in that fridge."

Hunter chuckles, then sucks in a pained breath.

"You're hurting," she states. "It's time for your medicine—"

"No," Hunter interrupts. "I don't want that stuff. Over-the-counter medicine will be fine."

"You were run down on a motorcycle a week ago. You have broken ribs, and an arm held together by rods and screws," Dahlia deadpans. "I think that calls for more than something over-the-counter."

He leans back on the couch, his hair a tousled mess on top of his head. "Don't worry about me, Little Flower."

She huffs and crosses her arms. "Well, since you feel *fine*, you need a shower."

Hunter points at his arm in a brace. "Can't get it wet."

"Which is why I'm going to tape a trash bag around it. Come on, Soldier. I'll rub you down from your head to your toes."

A fire ignites in Hunter's eyes and he curses himself for being in this shape and not being able to do something about the way Dahlia is making him feel.

"You're undressing me with your eyes," she teases and helps him to his feet.

"It's my favorite past-time."

She snorts and walks beside him to the guest shower on the first floor.

The hot water runs over Hunter's body and he hums deep in his chest at how amazing it feels. Dahlia rubs her hands over his muscles and her stomach twists at the bright purple bruise going around his ribcage and the scabbed and swollen skin from the road rash.

"Little Flower," Hunter says, his voice thick and deep.

"You can't look at me like that," Dahlia whispers, trying her best to not look at his hardening cock.

"I can't help it." The water beads across her body, over her pebbled nipples and down the apex of her thighs.

"Hunter," she whines, an ache forming where she wishes his cock was. "You're hurt. *I'll hurt you.* We can't."

He clings to the handle to keep his balance, pissed he can't touch her like he wants. "Kiss me then. At least give a starving man a taste."

She hesitates, knowing that if she kisses him, she'll only want it to go farther.

"Don't make me beg, Little Flower."

Pushing to her toes, she's careful to not brush her body against him, and gently presses her lips across his. She retreats and Hunter's blue eyes darken, and Dahlia drops her chin.

Grabbing a cloth with soap, she slowly cleans his skin. The sponge bathes at the hospital are nothing compared to having Dahlia rub down every inch of his body. Once the last of the suds have gone down the drain, she has him turn so she can wash his grown-out blond hair.

"You need a haircut," she states as her fingertips massage his scalp.

"I need you," he remarks, his resolve slipping.

Dahlia laughs and tips his head back to rinse the shampoo from his hair. His body sags, his limbs growing heavy from exhaustion. "You need rest, Soldier. There will be plenty of time once you're better. Stay here while I get towels."

\*\*\*

THE SUN HAS BARELY crested the mountains around Hunter's ranch when Dahlia's phone rings, interrupting their sleep. She rolls to the side, answering it without looking at the screen.

"Hello?"

"Dahlia, it's Susan. How's Hunter? I've been so worried."

Hunter flicks on a light and gasps when he tries to get himself up, his injuries screaming at him from growing stiff overnight.

"Oh, Susan. Hi...he's fine. Just tired. He's healing and getting around on his own now. Doctor said his lung has fully healed and most of the bruising is gone."

"Good. That's good. Listen, I—" A door clicks closed on the other end before Susan continues. "Did they ever find out what happened?"

Dahlia flings back the blankets and shivers as she places her feet on the cool hardwood floor. "No—he still doesn't remember." She retreats to the bathroom. "The cops are ruling it a hit and run, but Hunter can't remember anything about the vehicle."

There's a long stretch of silence, and Dahlia wonders if the line got disconnected. "Dahlia...?" Susan says, and Dahlia stares in the mirror.

"You know something, Susan."

"I have a hunch. But it's literally insane. Keegan is working at Harrington's now and he was just in here this morning, going on about a truck with a busted fender from a month ago. Something about having trouble getting the parts he needs and everything being on backorder."

"Okay? Are they local? Do we know them?"

"He didn't say...but..." Susan pauses and Dahlia leans against the vanity.

"Susan, please. Your hunches are never wrong."

"Okay," Susan sighs. "Peter came into the cafe with a new truck. When I asked him what happened, he didn't really answer. Maybe it's nothing..."

Dahlia doesn't hear the rest of her sentence over the roaring in her ears. Peter. Hunter warned her about the insane gleam in his eyes.

"He hit Hunter," Dahlia whispers.

"We don't know anything for certain—"

"No," Dahlia says louder. "I do. I know it in my gut. He—" She paces the floor, her body full of rage and vengeance. It burns through all logical reasons. Hunter warned her. He saw what kind of man Peter could be and she blew it off.

"What are you going to do, sweetie?" Susan asks.

"I don't know yet, but he isn't getting away with this. Thanks, Susan."

Dahlia chews on her bottom lip and stares at her phone. Does she tell Hunter? Or does she handle this herself first? Hunter is in no shape to be getting into a fight, and she knows that's exactly how it would happen.

She walks back into the bedroom, shoving her emotions aside, and smiles at Hunter, who is still lying in bed.

"Morning," she says, walking to his side. "How did you sleep?"

"Like shit," he grumbles. "What did Susan want?"

"Just checking on you. You're the talk of the town right now."

Hunter studies her features. "There's more. Something you aren't telling me."

Dahlia drops her chin and splays her hand on his chest. "Let's get you up, then I'll fix breakfast, okay?"

She promises herself she'll tell him—just later, when she doesn't have to worry about him hurting himself worse.

\*\*\*

Dahlia pulls her car into Harrington's and takes a deep breath before getting out. Keegan, Chris Harrington's son, greets her as he walks out of the bay with a smile on his face.

"Can I help you?"

"I'm due for an oil change. Was wondering if you had time today?"

"Let me check the schedule. If you want to wait inside, I'll be right there after I finish up."

Dahlia nods and waits for Keegan to disappear inside the garage bay. She nervously drums her fingers on her thigh.

*Now or never.*

She walks toward the front office, then past the doorway to the lot behind the garage. She just needs proof, then she can go to the cops and they'll file charges.

Her heart hammers in her chest and she checks behind her to make sure she wasn't being followed. Lucky for her, there aren't that many vehicles. But she doesn't see Peter's truck either.

"Shit," she mutters.

At the far back of the lot, tucked between two trucks, is a vehicle covered in a tarp. Dahlia rushes over and grabs a corner of the nylon material.

She recognizes Peter's blue truck immediately. The bumper and right fender are busted up. Crouching, she takes a closer look, running her fingers over the metal.

Having a busted truck around the same time as Hunter's accident won't prove anything. She needs proof.

"Dahlia?"

She freezes at the sound of her name. Her palms sweat and she spins on the balls of her feet, staring at Peter, who stands a few feet away.

"Don't come near me," she states, pushing to her feet and adding distance between them.

He raises his hands. "What is wrong? You act like you've seen a ghost or something."

"You did it," she states. "You hit him, didn't you? Why, Peter? You could have killed him!" she shouts.

He closes the distance between them in three long strides and clamps a hand over her mouth, pinning her to his busted truck. "I don't know what you think you know, but you're wrong. I didn't hit anybody. There was a deer on 502 that jumped out in front of me. There's hair and blood on my bumper to prove it."

Dahlia shakes under him, and his dark green eyes flick between hers.

"If I hit your precious *fiancé*," he says the word with disdain. "Then there would be orange paint transfer on my truck. Do you see any orange?"

He grips her jaw and angles her toward the truck.

"No," she whimpers.

"No? Exactly. I didn't hit him and I'm appalled that you would think so." He lets her go and straightens. "What kind of man do you think I am, D? To think you came all the way down here to accuse me of purposefully hitting someone with my truck and leaving them on the side of the road? Jesus, Dahlia! Do you know how insane that sounds?"

She shakes her head, glancing at the exit, but Peter blocks her path. The tufts of deer hair are clear in the busted bumper. How could she think so horribly about someone she's known her whole life? Clearly she let her imagination get the best of her and it drove her to do something as stupid as sneak into the car lot and accuse her ex-boyfriend of trying to kill her fiancé.

"I'm sorry, Peter—I know that doesn't make up for me snooping around. I'll just go—"

He steps in front of her and stares her down.

"You're sorry," he snorts and sucks on his teeth. "You just can't get over me, can you? Dahlia, it's been six years—I think it's time you need to accept that I *left* you. I got *bored* with you and chose Katherine. It's sad really, seeing you try to make me jealous with the out-of-town-wanna-be. You're better than this, D."

Her blood rushes to her cheeks and ears. "I am so over you. From the moment you walked out on me—I was done. Hunter loves me and I choose him. This has nothing to do with you," she says through gritted teeth.

"Well honey, then why are you here?"

She doesn't answer him. Squeezing between him and his truck, she sprints out of the garage lot without turning giving him her back. Keegan steps out of the office with a hand raised as she pulls out of Harrington's.

# Chapter Twenty-Seven

Hunter paces along the porch, his arm aches, but it's nothing compared to the anxiety coursing through his system. Zip whines at his feet, sensing the unease. He calls Dahlia's phone again, and it goes straight to voicemail.

He calls the shop...nothing.

He's nearly ready to call her parents when headlights shine up the driveway and her vehicle comes into view. Clinging to the railing, he makes his way down the steps and pulls her door open the moment she puts the car in park.

"Hey, what's—"

"Where have you been? I've been stuck here worried sick! I tried calling your cell, and it went straight to voicemail, then the phone at the shop just rang through."

Guilt washes through her.

"My phone died. I'm sorry, I didn't mean to worry you...and I wasn't at the shop."

He exhales and leans on the driver's door. "Where were you?"

She chews on her bottom lip and steps out of the vehicle. "I think we should talk about this inside...with rum. Lots of rum."

Hunter stiffens, but he moves to the side and closes her door. Inside, Dahlia pours two glasses of rum and coke and they sit by the unlit fireplace.

"Okay," she says, preparing herself for his reaction. She tells him about Susan's hunch and going to Harrington's to see for herself.

"Are you fucking insane?! You confronted him? Alone? Did he hurt you? Dammit, Dahlia!" Hunter stands and slams his hand against the fireplace.

"I'm fine! I'm sorry I didn't tell you, but this is *exactly* why. I didn't want you to hurt yourself or make things worse by hurting him. It's his word against yours and you can't remember anything. There aren't any other witnesses and I did the only thing I could to get evidence."

Hunter scoffs. "But you went *alone*! Nobody knew where you were. What would have happened if you never came back? Or heaven help me he put his hands on you?!"

Dahlia pushes to her feet and plants her hands on her hips. "I'm fine. Besides, there wasn't any paint from your bike on his truck. It wasn't him. I was so sure—it made sense. He said he hit a deer on 502. There was hair to prove it."

Hunter sits back on the couch, the adrenaline rushing through his body, making him anxious. "Dahlia, you can't—don't you *ever* do something like that again. Not without talking to me and letting me know where you are. Got it? He could have seriously hurt you. I still don't trust him and the way he looks at you. Dammit, woman."

"I'm sorry. Susan said she had a hunch and they're never wrong. I was trying to get closure for you—for us. I know it's driving you crazy not being able to remember, and I wanted to help."

Hunter lays his uninjured arm over the back of the couch. "Come here, Little Flower." Dahlia snuggles into his side. "You scare the hell out of me...loving you scares the fucking hell out of me."

"Who are you telling? I thought I lost you, remember?"

He chuckles and Zip jumps onto the recliner. "We need to come to terms with the fact that we may never know who did this. It fucking sucks, but I'm not living my life trying to find retribution when I have all I need right here." He kisses the top of her head.

"So, we let it go?"

"We let it go," Hunter states with a long exhale. "And we focus on us and surviving the next week."

Dahlia groans. "Right. Your mother." It'll be the first time she's ever left her shop since she opened. Dahlia's never even taken a vacation, but next week she'll be going to Tennessee to where Hunter grew up and Carly will be in charge of the shop.

"Yup," he says, popping the *p*.

***

Dahlia didn't know what to expect when going to Hunter's childhood home, but a house in the suburbs with a wood plank fence for privacy, was not it. No wonder he felt like he couldn't breathe when he came back. She's antsy and doesn't have a reason aside from the fact that she's used to her closest neighbor being a minimum one hundred acres away.

Lydia steps out of the two-story brick house that looks identical to the one next to it. Hunter barely has time to put the truck in park before she's reaching for the driver's door. Her eyes land on Dahlia in the passenger seat and Dahlia ignores the way her smile falls and opens the backdoor for Zip. The grass is so well maintained; it looks fake. Zip sniffs hesitantly with one paw off the ground like he has the same thought.

"What a surprise. I see you brought Dahlia with you—oh my gosh! What on earth happened to your arm?" Lydia gasps and practically pulls her son from the truck. He still has a brace he's supposed to wear to keep his arm stabilized.

"Yes, I brought my fiancé. I want to introduce her to everyone. My arm is fine, just a scratch."

Lydia reaches for the brace, but Hunter pivots out of her path. "It's fine, Mom. Can we please get inside the house before you start fussing?"

His mother huffs her annoyance and closes the door. A ramp leads up to the porch. Lydia steps toward it while Hunter stays on course for the steps.

Dahlia rolls her eyes in disbelief and Lydia stares as her son walks past her.

"I'm excited to show her around," he says, not missing a beat.

Did they really build a ramp because of his leg? She fights the urge to snap at Lydia for making Hunter feel less-than, but she bites her tongue for her soldier's benefit.

Inside, the house is set up like the front page of a magazine. Dahlia glances at her shoes and debates if she should take them off or not.

"Dad! We made it!" Hunter shouts, and Jared steps into view from the end of the hallway. Surprisingly, he bypasses Hunter and pulls Dahlia into a hug and takes her suitcase from her.

"Hunter didn't say you were coming! I hope the drive wasn't too much for you." He turns his attention to his son with a disapproving look. "You made her ride straight through?"

Hunter's brows raise and he glances at Dahlia. "Well—I—"

"It was fine," Dahlia says with a yawn and Zip whines at Hunter's feet.

"Hunter, we raised you better than that, son. You should have gotten a hotel. Poor thing." Dahlia manages a smile for Jared's sympathy.

"I'm okay, really. I didn't want to stop either. We were both excited to get here." She prays she isn't laying it on too thick, but a part of her hopes that by the end of the week, Lydia will accept her son's new life and choices.

"It's late. Why don't I show you your rooms and we can talk tomorrow? She looks exhausted," Lydia chimes in.

Dahlia doesn't know if she should be offended about looking *exhausted*, but she's right.

Hunter groans and reaches for Dahlia. "Mom, I'm not a horny teenager. We're not staying in separate rooms. If that's the case, then I'll get a hotel and we'll come over tomorrow."

Dahlia rolls her lips between her teeth to hide her smile. She hadn't even caught that his mom said *rooms*. Thankfully, he was quick to shut that down.

"That's—" Lydia tries to say. She glances at her son's prosthetic leg hidden under his jeans. "We just thought you'd want to stay downstairs, but with that bed being a twin..."

Dahlia watches Hunter for his reaction. First the ramp, and now this. Dahlia has never once second guessed if Hunter could do anything. He lives alone, for Christ's sake—well, most of the time. But she doesn't help him do anything day to day. Did they see a fucking ramp in Wyoming?

No.

She has to school her features to keep from showing her annoyance that's growing for this southern woman.

The house goes silent and Zip pushes against Hunter's leg. Dahlia takes her bag from Jared with a sympathetic hand on his shoulder. "We'll take the room upstairs."

Hunter doesn't wait for his mother's approval or other remarks.

"We'll see you at breakfast," Jared says as he wraps a hand around his wife's waist.

Hunter leads the way up the stairs that start by the front door. They're carpeted and again, Dahlia's politeness screams to remove her shoes, but she does the same as Hunter. The only room on the second floor is a loft style guest room with an attached bathroom. He drops his luggage on top of the chest at the foot of the bed and Dahlia sits hers beside the chest of drawers.

"You should shower," he says, his voice hollow and empty. "I'll take Zip out."

She notices the slight wince around his eye when he steps on his left leg. "Hunter, it's me. Look at me," she urges, desperate to ease some of the strain rippling across his muscles.

"Don't, Little Flower. I'm okay."

"I know," she says and walks over to lay her head on his chest. "I was just *suggesting*..." He glances down at her, looking up at him through her eyelashes.

He smirks. "And what is that?"

"I'll take Zip out; you get *our* shower ready and we can act like those horny teenagers you were talking about."

He sighs and kisses her forehead. "I'm fine, really."

"I never said you weren't, Soldier. But you drove the entire way and I know it's because you're scared of my driving. So, I'm taking Zip out as payback."

She pulls away and Zip eagerly prances to the door. "I don't think that's how punishments work."

Dahlia pushes her hair behind her ear and smiles over her shoulder. "How about I don't let you come until I say so?"

Hunter reaches for her, his eyes darkening with desire. Her stomach flips, but she jumps back before he catches her and jogs down the steps, a ridiculous grin on her face.

"Take him out back!" Hunter shouts, and Dahlia takes a turn at the bottom of the stairs in search of a back door.

Once on the back deck, she's able to breathe easier. It may look like all suburbs from the front, but there are wide open fields and woods at the back. She sits on the steps while Zip runs around, stirring up quail and occasionally checking that Dahlia is where he left her.

The screen door opens and Dahlia spins. Jared smiles down at her and gently closes the door behind him. "I thought you were Hunter," he admits.

"He's taking a shower. I offered to let Zip stretch his legs."

He nods and wipes his palms on his jeans.

"Lydia is one tore up mess in there. She's worried she's offended Hunter and I've had to talk her down several times to keep her from climbing those stairs."

Dahlia doesn't say anything. She can't help but suspect it's *her* Lydia is trying to purposefully offend. But that could be her imagination getting the best of her, too. At least that's what she keeps telling herself.

"It's hard. Our son left for the war and the person who came back...his face is the same, he sounds the same, but—" Jared leans on the porch railing and stares out at the painted sunset sky.

"He's still Hunter," Dahlia says. Running her hands up her arms to knock off the chill.

"It's like I don't know how to talk to him. And Lydia," he blows out a breath. "I told her insinuating the stairs were too much was a bad idea."

Dahlia stands and Zip quickly races across the field, tongue hanging out and panting. "He's still your son. Just don't treat him any differently than you did before."

Jared smiles at her advice.

"I'm glad he found you up there in Wyoming. Thank you for coming with him. It's about time everything's out in the open."

Dahlia tilts her head, wondering what that could mean. Do they mean her?

Jared sighs and heads back inside before she can ask.

# Chapter Twenty-Eight

HUNTER SHIFTS IN THE bed while Dahlia lays with her leg draped over his waist and her head on his chest. But it's not enough. The cars outside, the sirens in the distance, the sound of someone closing a car door nearby—it's all too much. He closes his eyes, and those sounds morph into something more. His body screams he's not safe. He's vulnerable—exposed—and he needs to be ready.

Zip crawls up his torso from the end of the bed and licks his chin. His movement makes Dahlia stir, and she blinks up sleepily at Hunter with his eyes squeezed closed and breathing rapidly. Sweat beads across his forehead and she pushes herself up.

"Hey," she whispers. "Hunter," she says with more authority, and his eyes spring open. Her heart breaks at the pain etched in his features. His blue eyes are full of terror. "I'm here. What can I do?"

Zip inches up closer, completely laying on Hunter's chest. "It's all so loud," he says, his throat tight.

Dahlia brushes a hand down his arm and orders Zip to move by snapping her fingers. She swings the blankets off and pulls on a pair of jeans and a shirt. "Get up," she tells Hunter.

"Dahlia," he sighs. "There isn't anything you can do. It's me."

She grabs his jeans and a shirt and throws them at him. "Get up. That's an order."

Hunter reluctantly does as she asks. Once they're both dressed, they quietly creep down the stairs. "It's three in the morning. What are you—"

She cuts him off by placing a finger to his lips and hands him the blankets she carried from upstairs. "I'll meet you out back." When he doesn't move and just stares, she gently pushes his shoulder. "Go. I just need to grab something from the truck."

He arches a brow, and Dahlia gives him one more push before he listens. After she learned about why he moved to Wyoming, Carly mentioned stories of things one of cousins went through when her husband came back in a similar state as Hunter. Sleeping outside seemed to help him. Dahlia knows it's a long shot, but she wanted to be as helpful as she could this weekend.

She pulls the hidden bag from under the backseat and walks around the house through the side gate. Hunter stares at the stars in the middle of the open field. His shoulders look relaxed, and she's hopeful he won't take this next gesture as her trying to treat him like he's broken. Not like his mom keeps doing.

"Hey, Soldier."

He turns and holds a hand out to take hers and pulls her into his side. "Hey, my little flower."

Dahlia's cheeks heat and she hopes she never grows immune to his nickname for her. "I kind of have a surprise and I really hope you don't get mad."

She doesn't wait for his response, instead she leads him to the trees, further from the house and the noises of the busy street. Surprisingly, the brick houses and fences block out a lot of the suburbia sounds. Dahlia walks until she finds two trees that are perfect and she holds the bag out between her and Hunter.

"What is it?"

"It's a hammock. Well, a two-person hammock. I thought—" she huffs and lies it all out there. "I know your mom has been treating you like you're incompetent and I'm not trying to do that. Carly has a cousin and well—none of that matters. I thought maybe sleeping out here would help, with you know..."

Hunter steps closer and tucks one of her wild curls behind her ear. "You packed us a two-person hammock because you thought this would happen?"

She stares up at him. How does she respond to that? What response is he wanting from her? She doesn't want to make him feel less than anything because, to her, he's everything.

"Would it help if I said that the guest bed is hard as a rock and this will be way more comfortable...possibly?" She holds it up like a child who just found the coolest rock.

"Are you afraid of me, Little Flower?" His voice drops lower, and he grips her chin between his thumb and finger. "Do I scare you?"

"No," Dahlia says, but it comes out breathy for a whole other set of reasons.

"Don't ever hold back from telling me what you're thinking because you're worried about how I'll react. It is my job to make you feel safe and secure in this relationship and if I've done something to make you feel otherwise—"

"You haven't," she says quickly. "I saw the way you responded to your mom's assumptions. I don't ever want to be the reason you get that distant look in your eyes. That's all." She drops the hammock bag in one hand and grips his forearm that's still holding her chin.

"Let's put up the hammock, Little Flower. How is it you know me better than the people who raised me?" he mumbles, almost like to himself.

"Because I listen. I'm always listening, Soldier."

His gaze flicks between her eyes, then down to her lips. Her breasts rise and fall with her deep breaths.

"Then I want you to listen very, very closely. Okay?"

She wets her lips and nods. Her body hums in anticipation at what he is going to say.

"Dahlia, I love you."

She gets lost in the way his deep blue eyes look down at her, like he's baring his soul to her and he's utterly at her mercy. It's not the words, but how he says them. His voice is laced with all the emotions he's fighting with. He's making himself vulnerable, something that his entire body fights against, but he's doing it to prove himself to her.

"I know you do, Hunter. I think I've loved you since you helped with that first wedding. I was just too scared to listen to my heart."

His grip on her chin waivers and she steps closer to him so her chest brushes his. He lets out a long breath and kisses her fervently. It's pure passion, acceptance, and one hundred percent commitment.

His hand travels down her shoulders, her ribs, those curvy hips he loves so damn much and grabs her ass. Dahlia gasps at the sensation and grips his T-shirt.

"Your arm."

"It's cute that you think you can hurt steel and rods," Hunter jokes.

"I'm scared it'll hurt you, jerk."

He shoves her back until she is pinned between him and a tree. "Little Flower, I have you in the woods, alone, away from everyone. I fucking want you right here and I want you now. Understand?"

"Then take me, Soldier," Dahlia challenges and Hunter grabs the collar of her shirt and rips it down the front. The cool night air brushes against her nipples and they pebble.

He hungrily pulls one into his mouth and swirls his tongue around the sensitive skin before moving to the next. Dahlia's center tightens, and she digs her fingertips into the bark of the tree, already wet and ready to have him inside of her.

Hunter grabs her ass and groans, his blue eyes finding hers. His arm won't let him lift her and take her like he wants, with this bark scratching down her bare back and ass.

"I think it's my turn to be on top." Dahlia's voice comes out breathy, and Hunter's blue eyes fill with heated desire. She doesn't give him time to argue, she knows his arm isn't one hundred percent, and she is not letting him push himself and possibly prolonging the healing process.

She pulls his shirt over his head and skims her fingers across his muscles and scars. Her hand hovers over his arm in the brace and her mind tries to trap her in the memory of Peter, but like Hunter asks, she's letting all those emotions go. Hunter's still here. She can touch him, hold him, feel him—her ex doesn't deserve a place in her mind.

Hunter cups her cheek, his fingers pressing into the base of her skull, and he pulls her into him. His tongue dances with hers and heat builds between them, the chill of night forgotten. She takes his hand and leads him to a clear spot on the ground and he lies on his back.

On her knees, Dahlia unbuttons his jeans and slides them down his legs, over his knees, and to his ankle and base of his prosthetic. She palms his erection through his boxers and Hunter's muscles flex under her touch.

"I've never—" she whispers and Hunter takes her hand, guiding her to grip his balls. "What if I'm too big?"

Hunter's movements freeze and Dahlia worries her bottom lip, too afraid to see the look on his face.

"If you ever talk about yourself like that around me, I will make sure you'll be so sore you can't sit. Got it, Little Flower? You're perfect—fuck, you're beyond perfect. You're going to straddle me and I may nearly come from having you on top of me. That's what you do to me. Don't ever second guess that."

She lifts her brown eyes, and they shine in the moonlight. His words give her confidence and she leans down, her breasts brushing against his chest, and kisses him. He nips her bottom lip, and she moans against the pressure.

"Ride me, Little Flower. Take everything from me," he whispers and she kisses down his neck, his sternum, below his belly button. He sucks in a breath as his cock springs free and Dahlia wraps her mouth around the tip. She licks from the base to the cum coating the pink skin, then takes him to the back of her throat.

Fisting her hair, his hips buck. Her tongue swirls as her mouth glides up and down his cock. "If you keep doing that, I'm going to come," he warns through panting breaths.

Dahlia pulls back, wiping her mouth with the back of her hand and she pushes to her feet. Slowly, she slides her jeans down and kicks them off her feet. "Are you sure?" she asks, and Hunter's features morph.

"If you don't get your pussy around my cock, I'm going to make you wish you'd listened the first time."

She blushes and her lips part at his tone.

"I'm not kidding, Dahlia."

Stepping over Hunter, she braces herself on his chest and lowers down. Hunter guides his cock to line up with her center and she stops shy of being fully seated.

"Little Flower, take it all," he says with a bite to his tone. He grabs her hips and shoves her down the rest of the way. Dahlia cries out and her head falls back as her body relaxes at the size of him shoved up inside of her. She feels so full, it's euphoric. Her hips rock and Hunter's grip loosens as she finds her movement.

"Hunter," she pants, his thrusts hit places she's never felt before.

"You're fucking beautiful and all mine," he responds. Dahlia lifts her head and looks down at the man underneath her. She's in control. She's taking his cock and riding him to her orgasm.

A smile lifts the corner of her lips and she runs a hand through her hair, tossing it to the side before leaning down. "I'll always be yours, Hunter Haynes." Her lips crash into his while he thrusts into her hips.

She's panting and Hunter slaps her ass, causing her to jump. "Lean back and play with your clit. Use me. Use my dick to get your pleasure, love."

Palming her breast, she drops her hand between her thighs. She shudders as her fingers roll across her sensitive bundle of nerves and her thighs squeeze around Hunter.

"That's it," he encourages, bracing his legs on the ground and lifting to get deeper into Dahlia. Her fingers work faster and her labored breaths become something more. Something deeper and passionate.

"Come for me, Little Flower," Hunter moans, her pussy tightening around his dick.

Her breasts bounce with her movements, her wild brown curls swaying around her body. "I'm—" her words get cut off as she cries out, her pleasure stealing her voice and ability to think. Hunter bucks his hips up, meeting her cries with a moan of his own. Her name is the only thing slipping between his lips.

She collapses on his body.

"I can't wait to marry you," he whispers, wrapping his arms around her, clinging to his gravity.

His home.

# Chapter Twenty-Nine

"NANCY SAYS HE SNEAKS out every night to sleep outside in the woods. It's so sad."

Dahlia squeezes between the woman gossiping by the punch bowl. She has half a mind to spike it just to make today more interesting. Lydia insisted on hosting a party for the small-town hero back home. Apparently, that meant not just the neighbors, but an open invitation to the entire town. The rumors have been flying about who the mystery woman Hunter brought back from wherever he's been hiding and apparently Nancy is a peeping tom since she knows about Dahlia and Hunter's nightly routine.

Dahlia leans in the doorway with her cup against her lips. Hunter laughs, a genuine belly laugh, surrounded by guys he went to school with. She can't fight her smile at the sight and decides to hang back for a bit. Every once in a while he gets the wild look in his eye and that's when she steps in to give him an excuse to take a moment and walk away with her.

"Isn't this nice," Lydia chimes. "He's back to his old self. I knew if he would just come home and give it a chance, it would work."

Dahlia bites the edge of her cup to keep from spewing the truth. If his mom wants to live in this delusional land while they're here to visit, she can. The doorbell rings and Lydia scurries away to be the picture-perfect host.

Hunter looks around, and when he spots Dahlia, he winks before nodding at something one of the guys say.

A woman walks up beside her and says, "He looks so happy."

Dahlia hums, not looking over at the woman. She's had people coming up to her all day, complimenting how Hunter is doing and telling her childhood stories. What's one more person?

"It's sad really," the woman continues. "He clearly belongs here. Look at him. Surrounded by friends and people who love him."

Dahlia pivots to face the newcomer. She holds a pie dish in her manicured hands. Her hair lays in perfect blond waves down to her mid-back. Bright red painted bow lips complete her look of innocence with her big doll eyes.

"I'm sorry—who are you?" Dahlia asks, already suspicious that she knows the answer.

Her lips spread into a sweet smile. "I feel sorry for the woman who drove all the way down here with him, just for him to realize this is where he belongs. He'll regret ever leaving this place. I've even heard they're engaged."

Hunter looks past his friends to check in with Dahlia again. She's been so patient with him today. He knows what his mom is doing. It's obvious. But he isn't going to stay. He's found something in the mountains of Wyoming that Tennessee will never be able to offer him.

His little flower is no longer standing relaxed in the doorway. Instead, she's facing Melanie and, from the look on Dahlia's face, whatever his ex is saying...isn't good.

"Zip," Hunter commands and his dog falls into step beside him as he pushes past his high school friends. As he gets closer, he can make out the tail end of Melanie's speech.

"...he's back now, and that means something. Don't get it twisted that you're his savior. I've known him my whole life and better than you ever could."

"Hey, Little Flower," Hunter draws and plants a kiss on her temple. Her body is rigid with rage, an emotion Hunter isn't used to seeing her show.

"Hunter!" Melanie coos and holds her hands out with the pie. "I brought your favorite. Peanut Butter, remember?"

Zip moves to stand between Dahlia and Hunter, licking her hands, and pulls her out of her trance.

"Melanie. What are you doing here?" Hunter asks, his hand snaking around Dahlia's waist, pulling her close.

"Oh, don't be silly!" Lydia breaks in as she steps through the back door. "I invited her. Ya'll have been friends for years and this thing between you shouldn't stop that."

Dahlia arches a brow, but the way Hunter's fingers dig into her hip keeps her from saying anything.

"This *thing*? You mean our engagement? This is crossing a line, Mom." His voice comes out strained and low. Zip's ears perk at his owner's tone and looks around for what has him on edge.

"Lydia," Jared says as he steps into the group that's forming. "Let's not make a scene, dear. Come on. Melanie, it was nice of you to come, but perhaps you should..."

"Jared!" Lydia snaps. "She's my guest, and she's staying. Hunter has to understand—"

Hunter chuckles, but there is no humor in his voice. "Don't worry, Dad. I was going to take Dahlia to show her the lake. Mom can keep *her* company. Come on, love." He moves his hand from Dahlia's waist to her hand and leads her past his mom and ex-girlfriend. Dahlia sets her cup down on a table as they pass it while Lydia shouts after them. Dahlia looks over her shoulder to see Melanie with tears in her eyes. She pities the woman who is clearly stuck on someone she can never have.

"Are you—?" she starts to ask Hunter once they're in the truck, but he sits staring at the windshield with shaking hands on the steering wheel.

***

THE WATER LAPS ON the shore, and Hunter throws another stick for Zip to jump in after. "I'm sorry."

"Don't. You didn't—"

Hunter shakes his head. "No. I brought you here. I put you through *that*. I never believed Mom would—fuck!" he shouts.

Dahlia places a hand on his forearm and forces him to face her. "Do you really think I'm going to let what some dolled-up-southern-barbie said get to me? She may have known you from way back, but I *know* you. The real you. The one standing right here. The one who told me he loved me and let me in. I have the parts of you she'll *never* be privy to. And nothing she says will ever change that."

She moves her hands up his chest and lightly grips his T-shirt.

He breathes in the smell of her shampoo and buries his face in the crook of her neck. "I thought—I was worried she had said something to make you hate me."

"The only thing that could do that is if you tell me her pie is better than mine."

Hunter chokes out a laugh and between kisses he says, "Little flower, everything about you is better. Your laugh. Your love. The way you look at me when I test your patience. Nothing compares to this."

"Why don't you let me show you how much better I am?"

Hunter braces himself on the open tailgate of his truck. Dahlia steps between his legs and pulls his shirt up over his head, tossing it to the ground. She grazes her fingertips down the muscles along his ribs and down the V that disappears under the belt of his jeans.

"Anyone could walk up here, Little Flower." His voice is low and thick.

"I don't care." She unbuckles his belt and quickly pulls it free from the loops. Hunter grabs it before she can toss it aside too.

"Good, because the entire county is about to hear you."

"Are you sure it's me they'll be hearing?" she remarks. Her stomach tightens, and she squeezes her thighs together for relief. Hunter runs his thumb across her bottom lip and pulls it down. He lifts the belt laying in his other hand and a mischievous smirk spreads on his lips.

"I'm going to put this around your neck and fuck you. Then we're going back to Wyoming and you're moving into the cabin with me. The main cabin, Dahlia."

It wasn't a question, or even an offer. It was a demand—an order—and he doesn't wait for her to say okay. He cinches the belt tightly around her throat and gives it a firm tug, bringing her closer to him.

"I want your hot mouth wrapped around my cock and for you to stare up at me so I can watch as I fuck your mouth."

She licks her lips in anticipation. The tightness of the leather around her throat as he pulls on it makes her clit ache for friction. Hunter angles his head, his nose grazing her jawline.

"Do you like that, Little Flower?" He pulls it tighter and a small gasp escapes her parted lips. "You look so damn sexy with that fire burning in your eyes." He grips her hand and moves it to cup his erection through his jeans. "This...this is what you do to me. I want you every damn day and feel like I will never have enough. I wake up starving for your touch, your kiss, the burning of your skin. I don't want you to ever doubt how I feel about you."

Dahlia moves her hand along his cock and it pushes against the restraint of his jeans. She drops to her knees, keeping eye contact as she unbuttons his pants, sliding them down his legs and to his ankles. She rests her hand above where the prosthetic connects and massages the muscle there.

Hunter groans in relief and his hand tightens around the belt. His cock jumps and cum beads at the tip.

"How does that feel?" she asks, digging deeper into the muscle.

Hunter's head falls back, and he shudders under her touch. He bites on his bottom lip and Dahlia moves one hand, wrapping it around his cock and licks across the head. Hunter thrusts his hips forward, forcing his cock to the back of her throat. He pulls the belt tight, keeping her from moving away from him.

Her cheeks hollow and she twists her hand at the base of his cock as he fucks her mouth with urgency. A need that only Dahlia can fulfill.

"Eyes open," he orders. She looks up through her eyelashes and a tear escapes down her cheek. Hunter eases, worried he's hurting her. She moves her hand to cover his on the belt and pulls it tighter up. The last thing she wants is for him to take it easy on her.

A car door closes nearby and Hunter stills, listening for the intruder. Someone is at his back and he fights the impulse to find cover and wait. Dahlia squeezes her fingers, forcing his attention to stay on her.

*Don't stop*, she says with her eyes and body. The last thing she wants is for him to let up because he's worried she can't handle it and she doesn't want to lose him to his memories. Not here. Not at this moment.

The thrill of knowing there are people nearby intensifies everything. Let them find her on her knees, devouring this man. The only man she'd ever let take her like this. In the back of her mind, she hopes it's Melanie coming to see if she can find Hunter. Wouldn't it be a sight for her to see Dahlia on her knees with a belt around her throat?

Hunter fists his hand in her hair, the pain of him pulling the strands turning into pleasure as he fights his training. He rocks his hips faster. Her jaws ache and she squeezes his balls as they tighten. He comes down her throat, moaning *little flower* as he does. He doesn't care about who hears because in less than twenty-four hours, this place will be in his rear-view mirror and he'll be going home with the woman he loves.

She slides his cock out of her mouth and wipes her chin with the back of her hand. As she stands, she pulls his jeans up his legs and buttons them. He loosens the belt and helps Dahlia to her feet.

Her hair is a wild mane of curls and smudges of makeup surround her eyes.

Laughter gets closer and Hunter removes the belt, tossing it into the truck bed behind him. A couple holding hands steps into view from the tree line and balks at the sight of Hunter's naked torso and Dahlia's rustled state.

Zip jumps up and lets out a warning growl at the newcomers.

"Zip," Hunter states and the dog sits, but doesn't take his eyes off the couple.

"Everything okay here?" the man asks as he studies Dahlia. The woman with him stands back, reaching for her pocket.

Dahlia gives a sheepish smile and Hunter glances up at the man, revealing who he is under his cowboy hat. The stranger's eyes go wide. "Oh shit, Hunter. I thought—we'll go this way." He stumbles over the rocks and Dahlia giggles into her hand at their quick retreat.

"Shit," Hunter grumbles.

"What?" Dahlia asks, not understanding where his tone is coming from.

"That was Melanie's older brother."

Dahlia's giggles turn into full laughter as she imagines how that conversation will go when Melanie finds out exactly what happened on this lake shore. Or rather, what her brother assumes happened.

Hunter's scowl softens, and he laughs, pulling Dahlia against him and feverishly kissing her soft slips. "Are you ready to go home?"

*Home.* To his cabin. With him. Back to Wyoming.

Her laughter quiets, but her cheeks ache not only from sucking on his cock, but from the smile stretching across her face.

"Yes. I am so ready to go home."

# Chapter Thirty

By the time they get back to the house, the party is over and only one vehicle remains parked on the street.

"Shit," Hunter hisses, and Dahlia doesn't have to guess who the car belongs to. "We could just leave our stuff."

She sighs, wishing it was that easy. "This is what we came to Tennessee for, right? Closure? Prove to your mom this is your life now?"

Hunter takes her hand and kisses the engagement ring on her finger. "You're stubborn. Even after the stunt she pulled today, you're still willing to walk through those doors."

Dahlia shrugs. "I've been told that a time or two."

He takes a fortifying breath and walks around to open her door for her. Hand in hand, they climb the steps to his childhood home and prepare for the worst.

Lydia comes down the hallway the moment the door opens. "I can't believe you just left like that. Those people came to see you—to celebrate you and you just left. I'm disappointed in you."

Hunter squeezes Dahlia's hand. "Likewise, Mom. I brought my fiancé here to meet everyone, and you invited Melanie, who was horrible toward Dahlia. I won't stand for her to be treated like that."

Lydia's mouth falls open, and she looks from Dahlia back to her son. "You don't understand. I—Melanie—"

Jared steps into the hallway, his expression grim and tormented.

"What your mom is failing to say is we need to talk, son. Alone." He looks at Dahlia, the normal joyous man looks sad, and she gets the sense that something big is about to happen. "Dahlia, will you please give us a moment alone with our son?"

"No—" Hunter immediately responds, but she places a hand on his chest. There isn't any sign of Melanie, but whatever happens, he knows where Hunter's heart is and trusts him to take up for her, even if she isn't in the room.

"It's fine. I'll start packing."

"Dahlia," His voice soft and low. He doesn't want her to go. He doesn't want to listen to anything his parents have to say, especially knowing Melanie is somewhere still in the house.

"Twenty-four hours," she reminds him and he nods, kissing her once before letting her go.

"Let's get this over with," he tells his mom, and her eyes narrow.

She leads Hunter down the hallway and Dahlia climbs the stairs until she reaches the guest room. Using the excuse to pack sounded good downstairs, but they've been living out of their suitcases since they've arrived and it takes no time to pack the bathroom up. She sits on the bed, her legs bouncing in anticipation over what's going on downstairs, and she clings for something to do to pass the time.

She texts Carly, checking on the shop, and she receives her classic response that she's on vacation and shouldn't be thinking about work at all.

Some vacation this is cracking up to be. Laying back on the bed, she twirls the ends of her hair in her fingers.

Downstairs, Hunter paces around the kitchen while Lydia and Jared sit at the kitchen table. "Well?" he asks, wondering what was so private Dahlia had to go upstairs for.

His parents can't meet his eyes, and he knows this is all about Dahlia and the fact he isn't staying in Tennessee. Their little plan didn't work, and this is one last ditch effort to convince him to stay.

"I'm not staying, Mom. So, if there isn't anything else, I'm going to help my fiancé pack."

He moves to walk out of the room and Jared grabs his arm. Melanie steps into the doorway of the kitchen and Hunter rolls his eyes.

"Seriously?"

"You need to hear this," Jared states evenly, a begging tone in his voice.

"It's not going to change anything," Hunter responds and Melanie smirks.

"Everyone, sit down, please," Lydia says.

Melanie saunters over next to his mother and sits. Lydia takes her hand in hers like she needs comforting and Hunter snorts. They're laying it on thick.

Jared motions for Hunter to sit beside him.

He scoffs and plops down.

"So?" he asks.

Lydia and Jared look at Melanie and she wipes at a tear welling in her eyes. Hunter waits for the sob story, mentally counting down the minutes to when he can get Dahlia and go back to Wyoming.

"Go on, honey," Lydia urges and Melanie nods.

"Hunter," his ex-girlfriend says. "After you left, I found out I was pregnant. We didn't have a way to contact you. My parents kicked me out when I started showing, and your parents took me in." Her voice cracks and Lydia rubs her back.

"What about the father?" Hunter asks, clueless about what this has to do with him.

"Today was the first day I've seen him in three years," Melanie says with a shy smile. "You have a daughter, Hunter. Her name is Faith."

The air whooshes from his lungs. "That's not possible," he rasps. He would know if he had a kid.

"It is," Melanie assures him. "Remember the night in your truck after your welcome home party?"

Hunter barely hears her over the roaring in his ears. He doesn't remember because he was drunk just to get through the day. It all comes in flashes and fragmented memories.

He can't have a daughter—he can't. He jumps up from the table, his heart racing and palms sweating. Bracing his hands over his head, he tries to breathe.

This can't be happening.

"Hunter," Lydia says, slowly pushing to her feet and trying to calm her son.

Downstairs, a door slams and Dahlia springs up from the bed.

"Hunter!" Lydia shouts and Dahlia races down the stairs until she finds Jared, Lydia, and Melanie chasing Hunter onto the back porch.

"You're lying," he shouts, pointing at Melanie. "You—And you knew?!" he roars, pointing at his parents.

"We didn't know how to tell you. It's not like you left us a phone number to call you," Lydia snaps.

"No," Hunter scoffs. "You just spent a week at my house and said nothing about me having a fucking kid!"

Dahlia's eyes widen, and she makes a squeaking sound. All eyes turn on her and she takes a step backward.

"This doesn't concern you," Melanie snaps, stepping toe-to-toe with Dahlia. "This is a family matter which doesn't include you."

"She's my fiancé," Hunter interrupts. "This sure as hell concerns her." He steps onto the porch and positions himself beside Dahlia.

"I don't want her anywhere near my daughter," Melanie seethes, and Dahlia takes another step back.

Hunter removes his hat and runs his fingers through his hair. "How do I even know it's mine?"

"Are you calling me a whore? Saying I slept around?" Melanie screams, stepping closer.

"That's not what he's saying," Lydia interjects.

"Let's all just take it down a notch and have a conversation without waking the entire neighborhood," Jared steps forward, placing a hand on Melanie's shoulder to urge her back.

Hunter is a father? And his parents have been keeping this a secret since he called months ago? This is why they wanted him to come to Tennessee. This is why Lydia was distraught over Dahlia and the engagement.

Dahlia's shell-shocked expression jerks from Hunter, to his parents, to Melanie and back.

He has a daughter in Tennessee.

"Grandma!" a child cries from inside and Lydia glances at Melanie, who runs a tired hand over her eyes. Dahlia tracks her movements as Melanie goes inside the house and disappears into the downstairs bedroom.

"How could you?" Hunter grits out, his body feeling like he's going to explode.

"Son—" Jared starts, but Hunter shoves his shoulder into him as he stalks past toward the open field.

Lydia sighs, suddenly looking frail and less like the judgmental woman Dahlia knows.

"You knew? And you never told him?" Dahlia asks.

She scoffs. "I don't answer to you. What do you know about raising children? Everything you do, every decision you make, is with their best interest in mind. It's all a gamble. Sometimes it pays off and sometimes it doesn't."

"This isn't a fucking career choice or buying a new car. He had a fucking kid, and you didn't tell him?"

"Dahlia," Jared scolds and Dahlia moves her attention to him.

"And you," she points. "You went along with it. Lied to your son and made him think that you simply didn't approve of his decisions. You're—I don't even have the words to describe how fucked up this is."

Dahlia throws her hands up in the air and pushes past Hunter's parents to chase after her soldier.

He's staring out at the night sky, his hands shoved in his pocket to hide how bad he's shaking.

It can't be true.

He'll demand a paternity test. He'd know if he had a child—a daughter. He wouldn't have abandoned her because he would've known. This isn't how he imagined this chapter of his life. He was supposed to marry Dahlia and then discuss having children and growing a family. Now what? How can he be there for his daughter that is twenty-four hours away?

How does this work?

What does he do?

As Dahlia gets closer, Hunter is mumbling over and over. *What do I do?*

Her heart breaks for him in a way she never thought it could. Her mind races to find solutions, to find answers to help him. His body visibly shakes, and she stands several feet away, worried about how reactive he is right now in the fight-or-flight state and how he'll respond to being touched.

"Hunter," she tentatively whispers.

"I don't know what to do. I don't—" his voice cracks and he drops his chin. "I abandoned her. I left her. What—what am I supposed to do? Her parents kicked her out when they learned she was pregnant and she's been living with mine ever since." When he turns, tears run down his face. Dahlia's eyes burn at the sight and her bottom lip trembles. He looks so young, lost—and she doesn't know how to help him. "Tell me what to do, Dahlia."

She shakes her head, her throat constricting and jaw aching at the sobs she's breathing through. "Hunter—" her voice breaks and a sob escapes her soldier. She doesn't hold back as she steps forward and wraps her arms around him. His body sags against her and he grips to her like she's the only thing holding him together.

"I left her. I left, and she doesn't know me. What kind of man abandons his daughter?"

Dahlia clings to his shirt at his back. "You didn't know. It's not your fault. You didn't know."

"That's no excuse. I should've called."

Dahlia rests her chin on the crook of his neck. Her tears absorb into the collar of his shirt.

"You have the chance to fix it now." The words barely escape her tightening throat as sobs threaten to overtake her. "Go meet your daughter, Hunter. You can't go back in time, but you can do something about it now."

He sniffs and pulls back, keeps his hands firmly on Dahlia, terrified to let her go. He looks past her at the porch where his parents stand and Melanie holds a blonde toddler on her hip. His blue eyes are unsure as he glances down at Dahlia. She nods, and he lets go, taking slow steps toward the porch.

Dahlia wraps her arms around her body. She has to keep herself together to get through this next part. She can break down after. But first she has to do what is right—what is best for Hunter—the man she loves above all else. She has to do what needs to be done, and it's going to be the hardest thing she's ever had to do.

Hunter stands beside Melanie and the little girl gazes up at him with his blue eyes. Lydia places a hand over her mouth, tears forming in her eyes, and Jared places his hand on her shoulder.

Hunter's daughter reaches for him and Dahlia lets the tears fall as he takes his daughter for the first time, surrounded by his parents.

"This is your daddy, Faith," Melanie says, her eyes beaming at Hunter and the little girl smiles.

Nobody glances at Dahlia as she slips around to the front of the house. She focuses on the task ahead of her, placing one foot in front of the other.

Once she's in the guest room, she pulls her phone out and types before locking the screen and dropping it to the bed.

It was all too good to be true. And even now, Hunter is the perfect man, but she can't make him choose. He was so distraught about abandoning his daughter that Dahlia will do the right thing, even though it's going to hurt like hell.

She's only able to take shallow breaths as she zips her bag and makes her way back down the stairs. She's seen this movie before, and even though it may work for a while, the wear and tear of distance will be too much and she refuses to put the man she loves through more pain. She'll do this. For him. For his future and his daughter's.

She reaches for the front door knob and a voice stops her.

"Dahlia," Hunter says with disbelief in his tone.

She's about to crumble and second guess her decision. Shoving her emotions aside, she turns with her suitcase firmly held in her hand.

"It's the right thing to do," she whispers, worried that if he gets too close, she'll change her mind.

"What is?" he asks, stepping closer and Dahlia opens the door, but Hunter places an arm against the door frame, blocking her exit.

"You have a daughter," she says, not meeting his gaze. "She's here and I'm there. You need to be here, Hunter."

"What are you—? No, that's not what I want. I love you. We're getting married. You said yes. You can't just leave."

Tears well in her eyes and she sits her bag down by her feet. Lifting her left hand, she admires her engagement ring gleaming. All the promises of their future and happiness. Her chest cracks apart as she pulls it from her finger and sets it on the table beside the door.

"I love you, Hunter Haynes—more than anything."

He stares at the ring, jaw clenched and features turning red. "No, you don't. If you did, you wouldn't be doing this. You don't destroy what you love. Why are you doing this?!" he shouts and his features morph into pain.

Dahlia lifts her suitcase. "I can't make you choose between me and what all you've missed out on. I won't."

He drops his arm, clenching his fist at his side. She's choosing to leave him. She's breaking her promise of their engagement all because of something he did three years ago. Back when he was a lost and totally different person. "You want to leave me? Fine. Go. But don't pretend you're doing it for anyone but yourself."

"I'm not—"

"What? So, things aren't perfect and it got hard? You're bailing. You're so scared of getting hurt that you don't trust anyone—not even me. So go, Dahlia. Go back to Wyoming and tell yourself you're doing this for me, if that's what it takes for you to sleep at night. I'm not begging you to stay."

To prove his point, he steps back, the open door a line she's about to cross. Tears spill down her cheeks and she adjusts the suitcase in her grip.

Down the hall Lydia and Jared stand, both with solemn expressions. Zip sits at Hunter's feet, his brown eyes gazing up at Dahlia with a plea of his own.

She allows herself one last look at her soldier before stepping across the threshold to the waiting car to take her to the airport and back to Wyoming.

# Chapter Thirty-One

THE DOOR SLAMMING BEHIND her signifies the clean break. By the time she gets into the back of the cab, she can barely breathe through the sobs. Every time he's called her little flower, those moments he lets her in to see his haunted nightmares, lying next to him in bed right before the sun rises and he's at complete peace—it all plays across her mind.

It hurts to breathe, to exist, to think of continuing life without him. Her heart isn't beating in rhythm anymore. It's like she left it with Hunter and she knows she'll never get it back.

Pulling out her phone, she wipes the snot and tears from her face.

"Momma?" she says when Bonnie answers, her voice breaking and barely audible. "I'm coming home."

"Oh baby," she says, and Dahlia sobs, wishing she was already home and in her mom's arms.

"It hurts," she whispers through the tears.

"I know, baby. I know."

Dahlia moves the phone away and tries to swallow the sobs, to pull herself together.

"We'll pick you up at the airport. You just let us know what time and we'll be there. We love you so much, baby."

"I love you, too," she squeaks.

Dahlia drops her phone to her lap and the smiling picture of her and Hunter in his cabin stares back at her. She'll never forget the haunted look he wore as she walked out the door. He may hate her—hell, she knows he does right now. She nearly hates herself, but when you love someone as much as she loves Hunter, you spare them from what pain you can.

Locking her phone, the screen turns black, and she lifts her hand to her mouth as she gazes at the woods of Tennessee flying by outside the car. Tomorrow it'll hurt more, and the next day, until one day the pain will be manageable. She just keeps looking forward to that day.

Inside the house, Hunter grabs onto the stair railing, his world spinning and heart aching in his chest

"Son?" Jared asks, and Hunter raises a hand.

She left him. Just like that. His parents knew he had a daughter and never mentioned it. Now the woman he loves above all else left him behind with her ring that signified his promise to love her forever.

"You knew," Hunter says in disbelief. "You and mom knew all this time. You've watched her grow up over the past three years. They live here."

Jared hangs his head. "Melanie didn't want us to tell you. She wanted to be the one to do it."

Hunter doesn't say anything as he picks up Dahlia's engagement ring.

"What are you going to do?" his father asks.

"I have no idea now."

He clenches his fist around the ring and grabs his keys.

"Hunter," Lydia shouts down the hallway. "Where are you going?"

"I can't stay here—I—"

"What about Faith?" Melanie asks as she steps into view, holding the toddler on her hip. Hunter drops his gaze and turns the doorknob. He doesn't want his daughter's first memories of him to be a broken man who feels like he just lost everything.

His mother continues to shout after him, even as he pulls out of the driveway with Zip.

Sitting at the lake in the exact spot he was merely hours ago, he stares out at the placid water. How did everything go south so fast? He was just planning his courthouse wedding and counting down the hours to when he would be back in Wyoming. Dahlia was supposed to be at his side through every obstacle in life—every hardship—not just walk away when it got...complicated.

Tears burn in his eyes and trickle down his cheek. He thought he finally found happiness. He found a home. And in a blink, it was all ripped away. Once again, he feels lost and doesn't know which way is up and which way is down. Dahlia was his gravity and now he's spinning out of control.

When Hunter pulls his truck back into his parents' driveway, Melanie's car is still there. Jared sits on the porch steps and pushes to his feet, his eyes heavy and shoulders slumped.

"Your mother and I should have told you," he admits as Hunter approaches.

"It is what it is. Can't go back and change it now," he says, void of emotion.

Jared nods and neither of them moves. "Did you make a decision?"

"I'm going to get a hotel—at least until I figure some stuff out. I'd like to get to know my daughter and spend the time I have here with her."

"Why don't you stay here—"

"No," Hunter says, cutting him off. "It's too soon."

His father deflates and steps aside. Hunter gets his bags and Lydia stands with Melanie at the bottom of the stairs when he comes down. Jared pulls her aside and Hunter doesn't have anything left to say to any of them as he leaves.

***

BY THE TIME DAHLIA reaches the airport, her eyes are dry and she feels like a zombie. She goes through the motions, boards the plane and stares out the window.

As promised, her parents are waiting for her in Wyoming and the sight of her mother's red-rimmed eyes has Dahlia running to her waiting arms. With her mom supporting her weight, she grieves all the could-have-beens and what-ifs in the middle of the airport. She doesn't care who sees or what people think. Her world—everything she knows is crashing down around her and she's drowning.

"Come on, sweetie." Walt places a hand on her back, tears falling down his wrinkled cheeks at the sight of his daughter breaking.

In the car, Bonnie rides in the back, running her hand over Dahlia's hair as she lays in her lap.

It's night by the time they arrive at the farmhouse. Getting to the guest room and settling under the covers goes by in a blurry haze. She doesn't fall asleep until she's too exhausted to blink. Even once her eyes are closed, her mind replays her favorite memories with Hunter and that betrayed look when he told her to go.

Bonnie switches out Dahlia's meals on a tray. Time and time again they go untouched.

"Honey, what happened in Tennessee?" Bonnie asks when bringing her dinner. "You need to talk to us."

Dahlia lays there motionless, staring at the wall. Her mother sighs in defeat and pulls the door closed to a crack behind her as she leaves. Concerned whispers echo down the hallway, but she can't make them out. She rolls, giving the door her back and waits for her body to give up the fight and let her succumb to sleep again.

***

THE BLINDS ARE WRETCHED open, light flooding the guest room and Dahlia groans, pulling the blanket over her head.

"That's about enough of this," Carly states, pulling the blankets off Dahlia.

"Go away, Carly," she groans and places the pillow over her head.

"No. Not until you talk to me and tell me what happened." When Dahlia doesn't move, Carly plants her hands on her hips. "I am not above dousing you with a cold bucket of water, you know."

"Ugh!" Dahlia throws her pillow in the direction of her best friend's voice.

"She grunts! That's progress," Carly teases.

Dahlia rolls to her back, scowling at her standing in front of the bright window. Carly's expression softens at the dark circles under Dahlia's eyes.

"You look like shit," she states, and Dahlia scoffs.

"Thanks." She moves over as Carly sits on the edge of the bed and places a hand on her back.

"What happened, D? You guys were so happy."

Dahlia's eyes burn at the reminder and she tucks her hands under her head.

"He has a kid. He didn't know and when he found out—I couldn't make him choose between me and his daughter." Dahlia wipes at the new tears on her cheeks. "She's only three, and he was so distraught over abandoning her. So, I made the choice for him."

"Dahlia," Carly says, her voice soft and full of empathy.

"Don't." Dahlia pushes up in the bed to sit beside her friend. "You'll just make me cry again and I'm so tired of crying. My eyes physically hurt."

Carly wraps an arm around her and nods. "How about a shower? You smell like stale farts and sadness. Also, your hair is flat—like depressingly flat."

Dahlia shoves her friend and gasps. "Carly! That is so mean!"

"You're not friends with me for my pleasantries." Carly stands and holds her hand out to Dahlia. "Time to stand tall and push forward. Fake it till you make it, right?"

Dahlia offers the tiniest of smiles because that's all she has left and takes her best friend's hand. Bonnie leans against the hallway wall with towels when Dahlia steps out of her room and gives her a sad smile as she holds them out.

"Thanks, Momma."

Bonnie cups her cheek and Dahlia places her hand over her mother's. "I'm going to be okay," she lies.

She'll fake it every day of her life if she has to, because deep down, she knows she made the right decision and Hunter is where he should be.

# Chapter Thirty-Two

DAHLIA STARES AT THE clock in her apartment until it's nearly eight at night. Everyone in the shop will be gone, and she doesn't have to worry about facing a soul.

In a loose T-shirt and pajama shorts, she makes her way down to the back room of Dreaming of Dahlias and turns on the overhead light. It buzzes to life, and she takes in the familiar scent of fresh-cut flowers and floral glue. This is when she comes down to work. Carly runs the shop along with the high schoolers they hired and Dahlia works through the night when she wants to avoid sleep.

With sleep comes dreams of Hunter and she'd rather avoid those if she can. She pulls out the binder for the wedding this weekend and flips through the pages. She remembers the clients when they came in eight months ago. They were so happy, constantly smiling and clearly in love.

Like her and Hunter...

Dahlia sighs and shakes her head. There isn't room tonight for the memories to trickle in. Clicking away on her phone, she turns on her creative playlist and the first song comes through the overhead speaker.

Closing her eyes, she let the familiar song settle around her like the embrace of an old friend. She sways in a small circle in the middle of the room, then makes her way to the cooler. While envisioning the bouquet in her mind, she pulls the flowers and greenery she needs. In those few hours, she loses herself in her work. Her mind doesn't wander and her hands aren't idle.

She can pretend everything is fine, and she's whole, instead of the broken person living in a flawless complexion. Why can't she feel like this all the time? Her shop isn't enough during the day. With Carly and the interns, there isn't enough to do to keep her busy, and that's when she goes dark.

With each flower she adds to the bouquet, it's like a piece of tape on her heart—her soul. She's putting her pieces back together. Like she's the bouquet and the flowers are the remains of her heartbreak.

Hunter once asked her why she wanted to be a florist.

*"I wanted to be a part of something incredible and beautiful. I wanted to take a living thing and make it better than it ever thought possible. I feel the most like my true self when I get lost in an arrangement, trusting my instincts to see the whole picture while working on one tiny element. Isn't that what we all want? To be a part of something greater?"*

Perhaps she isn't meant to have a happily ever after. Instead, she is meant to be the person behind the scenes of everyone else's. Making sure no detail is missed, and the day is perfect with beautiful aisles and arches.

Nobody can deny the love when the bride smiles behind the most beautiful arrangement or when the newlyweds pose with a breathtaking aisle and decorated venue.

With each song that ends, a new one starts and Dahlia eventually hums along to the tune. This is what she needed. This is how she holds herself together.

This is how she copes until one day Hunter won't be the first thing she thinks of when she wakes up or the last thing she thinks of when she falls asleep.

Above all else, she has her work. She has her passion. She simply needs to nurture it and remind her of who she was before him.

Once she's done for the night, she sweeps the back room, straightens the shelves, organizes the checkout counter—anything she can to prolong sleep. Around midnight her stomach growls, and she sighs against the table, knowing there isn't a damn thing in her apartment to eat.

She runs a hand over her frizzy bun and accepts that the only way she is getting any food tonight is from Beau. She locks the shop up and pulls her jacket tighter around her chest. Hopefully, since it's a Wednesday, the bar and grill will be empty and she'll get by with minimal stares.

The night is nice, and she chooses to walk versus drive. She sighs in relief when the parking lot only has a handful of cars in it and she doesn't recognize a single vehicle. Music plays quietly overhead inside. It's a totally different vibe than Friday and Saturday with dancing and a live band. Dahlia used to think the people who went to the bar on week nights were low-lives or drunks. Look where she is now.

"What can I get you, honey? Something strong?" Christy, the blonde bartender, asks.

"Uh, is Beau here?"

Christy shakes her head. "Took the week off to take his family to the beach. Did you need something?"

Dahlia climbs onto one of the bar stools and leans on the counter. "A burger, I guess—and fries."

"Need a drink?"

She debates for a minute. "Just water, please."

When Christy disappears into the kitchen, someone else takes the bar stool beside Dahlia. She keeps her focus on the wood grain that's been worn over time, hoping the person gets the hint that she doesn't want to talk.

"Looks like the rumors are true," the man states. "What happened to that beautiful ring?"

Dahlia shoves her hand into her lap, hiding her bare ring finger, and clenches her teeth. "Go away, Peter. You're literally the last person I want to talk to. Actually, no. If we were the last two people left on earth, I'd rather go mad talking to myself than waste an ounce of my breath on you."

Her brown eyes burn with ire.

"That's not very nice, D. I just came over here to check on you and that's how you behave? You used to be so polite."

She snorts and braces her elbow on the counter.

"I also used to think you were hot. People change." She shrugs.

Peter downs his beer and raises it for another. Christy drops it off along with Dahlia's water, then disappears into the stockroom.

"Not like you to be out on a Wednesday. He must've really done a number on you," he murmurs. A finger trails down her spine and she swivels on the stool, batting him away.

"Don't touch me. Ever," she demands and the few people around them look up from their glasses.

Peter smirks, letting his hand fall to his pocket. "Jumpy. Anyway, I need your opinion on something."

She ignores him, but he pulls his phone out, anyway. "Katherine and I are thinking of moving and I—"

"Yes. That's a great idea. Move far, far away," Dahlia interrupts.

"I'm trying to have a civil conversation like two old friends and you're being mean. Just look at the pictures, please."

Dahlia leans her head back and looks at the ceiling. "Fine," she relents. She'll do anything to get him to shut up and go away.

He hands her the phone, and she turns it over to see whatever he is so intent on showing her. The first picture is a for sale sign at the base of a driveway with the realtor's information on it.

Dahlia swipes and white noise fills her head at the picture. Her knuckles go white and her hand shakes.

*He isn't coming back—ever.*

"What do you think?" Peter asks, leaning in. He swipes to the next picture of Hunter's ranch, an aerial view of the cabin and barn used for weddings. "You decorate for the weddings—I make money without lifting a finger. It's a solid investment, really."

*He isn't coming back.*

She's never going to see him again. This is real.

"Say something," Peter urges. "What do you think, Little Flower?"

Dahlia grabs his beer bottle and slams it across the side of his head. Peter staggers off the stool, cupping his hand to his head as blood trickles down his cheek.

"Don't *ever* call me that and stay the fuck away from me." She throws his phone at him and rushes out of Turnpike.

A wound she thought was healing rips wide open in her chest and she runs until she reaches her car and starts the engine. Her entire body shakes as she takes the curves too fast, squealing tires. She wipes at her eyes, trying to focus on the long stretch of road in front of her.

The curves up the mountain force her to slow down and when her headlights shine across the for-sale sign at the bottom of Hunter's driveway, she sobs. Leaning her head on the steering wheel, she collapses with the fact that Hunter Haynes will never be in Wyoming again.

She doesn't have anyone to blame. He didn't do something awful like Peter, where she can hate him. He didn't leave her or tell her he didn't love her.

She left.

She did this.

She doesn't have anyone to blame but herself.

Her phone rings, cutting through her choking tears and she blinks the screen into focus.

"What?" she asks, not caring how she sounds.

"Where are you? What happened at Turnpike? What did Peter say?" Tripp demands answers and Dahlia's sobs turn into hysterical laughter.

"Of course, everyone already knows. Once again, Dahlia Brook's shitty love life is the talk of the whole fucking town."

Tripp sighs and softens his tone. "Where are you, Sis? Tell me what happened."

"He's not coming back!" she screams, staring at the for-sale sign. "Peter said he's going to buy the ranch. It's for sale, Tripp. He's never coming back."

A part of her held on to hope and she didn't even realize it until the chance of her seeing Hunter again completely disappeared.

"I'm on my way," Tripp says, his truck roaring to life in the background. "I'll be right there, D. Just wait, okay?"

"No. I'm going home. I just—I needed to see if it was real. I'm fine. I'm going to be fine."

Tripp is quiet for several minutes. "They said you busted a bottle across Peter's head."

She chokes out a laugh. "God, I did! I can't believe I did that! I just snapped. He was being condescending, and I knew he was trying to get to me and I—I lost it."

"Why don't you come out to the ranch for a few days? Ride the horses. Breathe in the fresh air and get a reset."

Dahlia's eyes hang with exhaustion and she puts her car in drive. "Thanks, Tripp. I think I just need to get back to being me—back to my shop and taking control over the things I can again."

"The invite is always there, you know. And you can call me anytime you need."

Her headlights run across the sign until it's left in darkness in her rear-view mirror.

"I know. I love you, dork," she says, somehow feeling lighter.

"I love you too, turd. Be careful going home."

"I will."

The phone lights up against her cheek when Tripp disconnects the call. Instead of going home, Dahlia drives down back roads for hours. She cranks the music up and rolls the windows down while turning the heat on high.

The songs pass her lips in a sorrow-filled screech until she barely has a voice left at all. Just like that, a chapter of her life is over and it's time to move on.

She'll take it one day at a time. Waking up, doing her best, then going to sleep. Until one day she doesn't have to try, and she'll be healed.

With time.

# Chapter Thirty-Three

HUNTER FLIPS THROUGH THE ad of his ranch. The pictures are breath-taking and they truly captured the essence of his place.

Not his place—not anymore. At least it won't be once he accepts a bid.

He still hasn't heard from Dahlia and he's positive she's heard the news of him putting his ranch up for sale by now. How could she not? He thought maybe that would make her call.

Turns out he was wrong.

After a couple of weeks, he and his parents reconciled enough that he is staying with them until he commits to finding his own place in Tennessee. Melanie and Faith stay in the downstairs bedroom while Hunter avoids the guest room, choosing to sleep out here for as long as he can.

He swings in the hammock Dahlia left in the woods. The weather is growing colder with the Autumn months and soon he won't be able to seek solace out here. He hasn't been able to get enough of Faith since she reached for him that night. Even her tantrums are adorable and his heart nearly bursts at the sight of her smile and her laughter. He was shocked at how quickly she called him daddy, as if he'd been there her whole life. He thought for sure that was a title he'd have to earn, not one that was just handed to him. He hasn't been around to be a dad, certainly doesn't even know the first thing about raising a child.

But every day he tries.

He's been hanging out with his friends from high school on the weekends. It's like none of them have changed. Some are married, even have children of their own, but they're all still here. They still hang out at the same places, drinking or shooting guns, just like when they were in high school. It's a nice distraction—for a while—until he comes back to his parents'.

This is when it's the hardest. When Faith goes to sleep and he doesn't have her to keep the shadows from creeping in.

His phone is the only light under the moonless sky, and he flicks through pictures of him and Dahlia. He brushes his thumb across her cheek and opens her contact on his phone.

He hasn't called.

He told her she had a choice to make and he wouldn't beg her to stay. Then she just walked out, like it was easy. Too fucking easy.

Locking his screen, he tosses it to the bottom of the hammock and stares into the dark night.

It's been nearly two months since he watched half of his heart—no, not half—Dahlia has his whole fucking heart and she walked out with it, leaving him as this shell of a person.

He doesn't want to go to Wyoming where he'll see her living her life without him. It would wreck him. Instead, he likes to imagine that she's somewhere staring at the moonless sky, missing him as much as he's missing her. He thought he found what everyone in life looks for. Their love was something to test the trials of time. They'd already been through so much, he never thought it would simply end. He never thought there would be life after Dahlia...because there never was an after. She was his future.

Deciding to sell his ranch was the final break. It hurt to make that call—almost as much as watching Dahlia walk away.

It's the best choice. Maybe he'll find happiness somewhere else, like he had in those mountains with the snow and wide-open spaces. But he knows he'll never find anyone to come close to Dahlia Brooks.

It isn't until his body shakes that he realizes how cold he is. His arm is stiff as he straightens his elbow and flexes his fingers. Zip jumps to his feet as Hunter stands.

He misses his cabin, but he'd never be able to go back there with the memories of his and Dahlia's first time during the snowstorm or all the times after. She's everywhere...except Tennessee.

***

HUNTER SITS ON A wicker chair on his parents' back porch while Zip runs around the yard.

The door opens and closes behind him. A hand lands on his shoulder and he locks his phone. "Faith fell asleep on the couch," Melanie says. "I work tomorrow, but maybe after I get off we could go have dinner—talk about...us?"

Hunter jerks away from her touch and pushes to his feet. He retired the cowboy hat for a baseball cap since Dahlia left. The small bill doesn't offer the same shield he grew used to. "What are you talking about? There is no *us*."

"Well, not officially. But you're home now and Faith and I live here. She's your daughter and I'm her mom…" her voice dies off and Hunter moves to give her his back. "Is it *her*? The woman who left you the moment she found out you had a child?"

Hunter bristles, his muscles rippling under his jacket. "You don't know anything about her."

Melanie scoffs. "Just that she abandoned you like you meant nothing." She moves closer. "But I'm here and I—I love you, Hunter."

He steps farther away, turning to face her fully. "Nothing has changed for me, Melanie. I'm here because I have a daughter. I'm so sorry—but there isn't and won't be an *us*."

Her eyes well with tears and her bottom lip trembles. Hunter knows that trying to comfort her will only give her the wrong idea, so he pushes his hands in his pockets and stands firm.

Melanie lifts her chin, her gaze narrowing on Hunter. "Fine. If that's how you feel, I'm taking my daughter. You won't be seeing her again."

"Now wait a minute, you can't do that. Just because I don't want to be with you, you're going to keep me from seeing her?"

She moves toward the door and Hunter blocks her path.

"My daughter deserves to have a dad who *wants* to be with her and loves her mommy. Not someone who stays out of guilt."

Hunter's jaw clenches and he struggles to keep his composure. "Don't do this, Melanie. I have money and I will fight you on this. I'll take you to court if I have to and fight for my right to see my daughter. I'm not just going to give up on her and let you use her like a tool to get what you want. That isn't love, it's infatuation."

Her mouth falls open, and she shoves against his chest. "You can't take her from me! She doesn't even know you! You're a stranger. You aren't the man I fell in love with and gave my heart to. I don't recognize this monster you've become."

"I'm not trying to take her from you," he says softly, attempting to deescalate the situation. "I'm not letting you take her from me, either. I'm sorry that you wasted the past three years waiting on me, but I will be a part of Faith's life."

The fight in her eyes waivers and Hunter relaxes against the door.

"Fine," she states. "I'm going to bed."

Hunter nods and steps aside, letting her open the door. He takes a deep breath, taking off his hat and running a hand through his hair.

Jared cracks the door open and steps out onto the porch. "What are you doing, son?"

Hunter scoffs and raises both hands in the arm. "How the hell am I supposed to know? I'm stuck in a place I never wanted to be because of a mistake I made three years ago. And I love that little girl, I do, Dad. I can't explain it, but I fucking miss *her*."

Jared steps up beside him and they both stare at the open field. "Then why are you selling your place? Why are you giving up?"

"Because I don't see how any of this works if I'm in Wyoming. I won't be a dad that lives across the country and only sees his daughter during the summer or school breaks. I want to be a part of her life and I can't do that from there. The only way this works is if I stay."

"But you're miserable here," Jared states.

"I'm not—I'm just—"

"This isn't home to you. Not anymore. You've always been a shit liar and if you stay out of guilt, you'll grow to resent the person you stayed for."

Hunter places his hat backwards on his head and leans against the porch railing. "Home isn't a place, Dad."

Jared smiles and clasps his son's shoulder. "I told your mother that same thing when we were younger."

Hunter smirks. "So, what do I do?"

Jared inhales a sharp breath and whistles. "I wish I could tell you. Just listen to your heart, the rest will fall into place."

Jared leaves Hunter with his thoughts.

*Follow your heart? That sounds like some Lion King shit. All I need is a monkey with a staff to whack me across the head.*

Hunter flips through the pictures of his ranch once more—knowing what he needs to do before he can make any permanent decisions.

He wasn't bluffing when he told Melanie if she tries to keep his daughter from him, he'll fight her for rights to see her. He just hopes his ex-girlfriend is understanding, and it doesn't come to that.

# Chapter Thirty-Four

DREAMING OF DAHLIAS IS slow for a Saturday. Carly sucks on a piece of candy and Dahlia clicks through the pictures they took of inventory to update the website.

"Do you want to go on a trip?" Dahlia asks randomly.

"Um, sure? To where?"

Dahlia shuts down the computer and grabs her keys. "I need to run by the wholesaler in the city for some last-minute things for this weekend. We could grab lunch, have some drinks, and make a day of it."

"Look out world! Dahlia Brooks is closing early on a Saturday to have a girls' day! Who are you and what have you done with my workaholic best friend?"

Dahlia rolls her eyes. "Are you coming or not?"

Carly locks the front door and hooks her arm through Dahlia's. "Let's go. But we're getting food first. That one fancy restaurant with the delicious noodles."

The women eat their weight in creamy chicken pasta and rolls. Dahlia hasn't had that much fun in a long time, laughing and joking around with Carly. Maybe a trip out of town was exactly what she needed. A change of view. A new perspective.

"We should do this more often," Dahlia states as her and Carly lean back into the dimly lit booth. There are plants decorating the inside of the restaurant, with palm leaf style fans high above.

"When was the last time we had a girls' day out? It had to be before Dahlias," her best friend remarks.

Dahlia tries to recall the last time she did anything fun besides the occasional trip to Turnpike. "Has it really been six years?"

Carly nods. "Time flies when you're having fun."

*Fun*. Dahlia loves her job and her business, but she decides right there to take more time to enjoy and experience life.

"What is *he* doing here?" Carly sneers.

"Who?"

Carly nods her head toward the entrance through the broadleaf plants. Peter adjusts his tie at the hostess stand and searches the restaurant like he's looking for someone. A young, long blonde haired woman approaches him and his face lights up.

"No way," Carly gasps, and Dahlia's mouth falls open.

The woman wraps her arms around Peter's neck and he pulls her against him by her hips.

A camera shutters and Dahlia stares at Carly in disbelief. "I think it's time for you to get some payback," she says holding up Dahlia's phone with a sweet smile and photographed evidence of what they just witnessed.

"I couldn't—"

"You can and you're going to. Don't you wish someone had told you about Katherine?"

Dahlia takes the phone and studies the picture. The women duck their heads as Peter and his *date* walk past.

They sit and Dahlia peers around the edge of the booth. Peter holds the woman's hand across the table and runs his thumb across her skin.

Carly is right. He deserves this. She lifts her phone and takes several more pictures.

Him lifting her hand to his lips. The woman's foot caressing his leg under the table.

Carly wears an excited smile and nods her encouragement. "Do it."

Dahlia bites her lip and pulls up Katherine's direct message. Without hesitation, she sends the pictures over and tosses the phone back at Carly like it's a hot potato.

"Did she read them?" Dahlia asks, glancing at Peter's table.

He checks his phone, then places it back in his pocket.

"Oh, yes," Carly says.

Peter checks his phone again and excuses himself. He walks outside the doors and Dahlia quickly pays their bill on the table check out system.

Before they can leave, Peter comes back inside an image of irate and danger as he searches the booths and tables.

Carly grabs a server that walks by. "Can we sneak out the back? My friend's dangerous ex is here and we don't want to run into him."

She subtly points at Peter as he stalks across the restaurant, his hands clenched and veins popping from his neck.

"Absolutely. Wait right here," the waitress says and walks over to the hostess stand. She whispers something to the staff before coming back to Carly and Dahlia.

"Okay, follow me."

They keep their heads down as they follow the waitress until they reach Peter's date. Carly stops and places a hand on the table. "Just so you know, he's married and a total asshole. You can do better."

The young blonde's lips part, and she searches for her date. Dahlia grabs Carly's arm and pulls her along. The waitress takes them through the kitchen and out the back doors.

"Thank you!" Dahlia shouts as they make a rush for her SUV. Inside, she locks the doors and melts into her seat, hysterical laughter bubbling up in her chest until she can't contain it.

"Did you see the look on his face?! He was pissed!"

Carly leans forward, trying to spot Peter through the parking lot. "Let's sit here until he comes out."

Dahlia starts her car. "Let's not push it."

"Why? It's not like he's *dangerous*. It's Peter."

Dahlia runs her hands over the steering wheel, worrying her bottom lip.

"Hunter," she starts, her voice cracking at saying his name. "He, uh, always had an off feeling about Peter. Said there was this look in his eyes that he didn't trust. When Hunter was hit, Susan called me a couple of weeks later and said she had a hunch after Peter showed up with a new truck."

"She thinks it was Peter?" Carly's eyebrows shoot up to her hairline.

Dahlia nods. "I kind of sneaked into Harrington's to look at his truck. He caught me and the way he looked and his tone... It—he scared me."

Carly leans closer. "Well? Did you see his truck?"

"Yeah," Dahlia sighs. "He claims he hit a deer. There were tufts of fur in his bumper and no orange paint from Hunter's bike. Susan's hunches are never wrong, but there wasn't any proof and Hunter never remembered."

"Damn...that's a lot, D."

The restaurant door flies open and Peter chases after the blonde woman with smudged mascara.

"Yeah. Then he made a point to show me the ranch was up for sale and said he wanted to buy it. We all know how that went."

Carly goes through the motions of crashing a bottle against her head. "Boom."

"Yup."

The woman storms off and Peter screams before getting into his car.

"Well, looks like for once...he lost," Carly says, sitting back in her seat as Peter peels out of the parking lot.

Dahlia stares after his taillights. Something in her gut tells her she may have won this battle, but the war isn't over.

***

ZIP WHINES IN THE front seat of the Hunter's truck.

"We're almost there, boy. Just a little farther."

The white German shepherd huffs and lays down. It's nearly sunset and his nerves hum under his skin at being back. His phone rings and he rolls his eyes at the number of times his parents have called. It's like they're worried he's going to disappear again even though he promised a blonde-haired, blue-eyed girl he'd be back in a week.

His brows furrow at the unknown number.

"Hunter Haynes," he says in a way of greeting.

"Mr. Haynes, this is Sheriff Jones. We met several months ago when you were in your accident."

Hunter's headlights shine across the for sale sign at the end of his driveway as he turns. "Yeah, I remember—uh, what can I do for you, Sheriff?"

"There's been a development on your hit-and-run case. I was hoping you could come to the station and verify some new information for us."

Hunter puts his truck in park and runs his palm along his thigh. "A development? Like you think you found the person responsible?"

"We do," the sheriff responds.

"Yeah—I can be there first thing in the morning. I just got back into town, actually."

"Could you come tonight? We think this person might be a flight risk and we'd rather not wait."

He straightens in his seat, the edge to the sheriff's tone reminding him of when they'd receive sensitive orders in the war. Whatever is going on is dangerous and needs to be dealt with quickly.

"Of course," Hunter says, his truck throwing gravel as he backs up. "I'll be there as soon as I can."

\*\*\*

DAHLIA TURNS OFF THE overhead shop lights, leaving a few lamps on to light the space.

She holds her phone to her ear as she makes her nightly rounds, talking with Carly. "It doesn't make any sense. How has nothing happened? Nobody in town is even talking about it. I thought for sure she'd packed up her daughter and left," Carly says.

"I guess some people are more afraid of being alone than being lied to."

"Some life that would be," her best friend mutters, locking down the computers and register.

"At least we can say we didn't keep his secret. I was kind of hoping it would blow up in his face, though."

Dahlia smirks. "I was too," she admits.

"Guess I'll see you tomorrow? Are you sure you want to do it? Me and the girls can handle it."

Dahlia closes the open wedding binder on the counter. This will be her first job at Haynes Venues since she came back from Tennessee.

"No—no, it's fine. This is my business and my brand. I'll see you bright and early."

Dahlia turns off the back-room lights and locks the back door before going up to her apartment. She kicks her shoes off and pulls her hair free.

The music on her phone connects to the sound bar underneath her television and fills the space. Pouring herself a full glass of wine, she takes a generous drink and walks over to the window, admiring the sunset.

Thoughts of going back to Hunter's for the first time flood her mind and she shoves them down by belting the words to the music. As far as she knows, the ranch is still for sale, which means Peter was trying to get under her skin or Hunter refused to sell it to him.

She chuckles at the latter. That would have been something to see.

A reflection dances across the window and she spins, her wine splashing onto the floor.

"What the hell are you doing here? Get out!" she screams, her flight response kicking in as she searches for a way past Peter to reach the door.

"You just couldn't keep your nose out of my business, could you?" he slurs with bloodshot eyes. His hair is a greasy mess hanging down his forehead. "Just couldn't leave well enough alone. You saw an opportunity to ruin my life, and you took it."

"Peter," Dahlia says softly, trying to calm him down. "I need you to leave...you're drunk and not thinking clearly."

He pushes the heel of his hand to his forehead and mutters something to himself, then slams his hand down onto the counter. Dahlia jumps, her couch the only thing separating them.

"Don't you dare tell me what to do! You—you did this! This is your fault. Flaunting around here with that cowboy wanna-be—trying to make me jealous—"

Dahlia takes a step to the side, trying to make her way around the couch. "It's been years and you left me. You have Katherine and a beautiful daughter. Don't do this. You still have a chance to do the right thing and leave."

"Stop! Just stop! There is no going back. She knows—she knew all along and she's going to make sure I am punished for going out on her. Yeah," He chuckles, but it's void of humor. "She's going to make sure I get what's coming to me. I can't go to jail, D. I can't—"

"Peter," she gasps. "What did you do?"

# Chapter Thirty-Five

HUNTER PULLS INTO THE police station and Zip jumps out behind him. He rolls his shoulders, pulling his jacket higher around his neck to block the wind.

The door jingles as he steps inside and the woman behind the desk looks up over her glasses.

"Can I help you?" she asks.

"Sheriff Jones asked for me to come in. I'm Hunter Haynes."

Her eyes widen slightly and her hands tremble as she stands. She wipes them down the front of her shirt and steps out from behind the desk.

"You need to follow me, quickly."

Her heels clack down the hallway until they reach the sheriff's office. Hunter steps in and scans the room. There are four deputies standing against the wall and Sheriff Jones braces himself on his desk with a laptop sitting beside him.

"Haynes," he states, and Hunter tips his hat.

"Sheriff. What's all this?"

Sheriff Jones runs a hand across the back of his neck and sighs. He lifts a small black camera. "This was dropped off a couple of hours ago and well—" He clicks a button on the laptop and the recorded footage plays.

Hunter steps closer for a better look. At first, nothing happens. It's a view across an empty highway into an open field. He leans in, looking for whatever he's supposed to see when an orange motorcycle passes across the camera. Hunter's chest tightens and his breath hitches. The camera moves until it's facing the highway and gains speed down the road. It gets closer to the orange motorcycle, Hunter's familiar hat sitting backward on his head. He's rammed from the back and Sheriff Jones pauses the video.

It's a dash cam...and that's him. That's how he wrecked. Someone ran him down.

"Who is this?" Hunter asks, but he already knows. Since Dahlia told him about the garage lot, he knew she was right, but he couldn't risk putting her in danger and pursuing answers. He chose her over getting even.

"Keep watching," Sheriff Jones says.

Hunter grinds his teeth, and the sheriff starts the video again, but it's from a different angle. It's in the woods and nothing happens for several seconds. Then Peter comes into view, running his hands through his hair and looking at his busted bumper. His crazed gaze darts directly to the dash cam and the video stops.

"He turned it off here. We called Harringtons where he took the truck and they said he claimed he—"

"Hit a deer."

The sheriff nods. "Do you want to press charges?"

"Yes." Hunter stands tall and holds the sheriff's stare.

Sheriff Jones nods and the officers ready themselves.

"Sheriff?" the receptionist says loudly, her heels clacking down the hallway. She steps to the side and reveals a woman that Hunter has seen around town with a bruise forming on her right eye.

"Mrs. Rollins, what happened?"

"He's gone. Peter—he found out I brought the dash cam and he—" she hiccups through her tears.

"Put an APB on Peter Rollins. I want this town locked down." He steps toward Katherine. "We'll find him."

She nods and turns to watch the officers disappear down the hallway. Hunter stays back, missing one piece of the puzzle.

"Why'd you do it? Why'd you turn him in?" he asks.

Katherine huffs and rolls her eyes. "Because he lied. I caught him cheating on me—well, your girlfriend caught him and sent me pictures."

"Girlfriend—Dahlia?"

"Looks like she got even after all these years." Katherine sniffles. "Peter was pissed when he found out that's who told me."

"He knows Dahlia is the one that sent you the picture?" He nearly shouts.

"Yeah. He went through my phone and saw the messages."

Hunter removes his baseball cap and runs his fingers through his hair. He knows where he went. His gut has never been wrong and from the moment he met Peter Rollins, he knew he was a danger to his little flower.

"Zip," he shouts, before running down out of the police station and hopping into his truck. The sheriff and squad cars are already gone, but he doesn't have time to find someone to tell them what he knows. Peter is unhinged enough to run him down on a motorcycle, there is no telling what he is capable of.

\*\*\*

Dahlia faces Peter, trying to work through the possibilities of getting away from her ex.

"Peter," she tries to placate him. "I'm sure Katherine will forgive you—just go home, talk to her. She loves you—"

"No! No, not after this. She—I can't go back. I can't go home. They'll find me and then—I have nowhere to go and nothing left." He waves his hands around her tiny apartment.

The music cuts off as her phone rings and Peter jerks his head to the counter where it lights up. He snatches it and scowls while it continues to ring.

"I thought you two broke up? You know, you went out of town and came back without him? Why is he calling you?" Peter shoves the phone toward Dahlia and she shakes her head.

*It's Hunter.*

"I-I don't know. I haven't talked to him. I swear."

He pinches the bridge of his nose and shakes his head.

"He knows. They know. It's over. She betrayed me—turned me in—there's no way out."

Dahlia takes slow steps toward the door, pausing when Peter's red eyes land on her. "What are you talking about, Peter? What did Katherine do? What does Hunter know?"

He points a finger at her and she freezes. "You already know. You knew before anyone. She knew too—but she swore to keep my secret. Then you." His eyes flare and he closes the distance between them, wrapping a hand around Dahlia's throat. Liquor is heavy on his breath and he leans into her. "You ruined everything. You took my family. My life. You took *everything* from me!"

She squeezes her eyes closed and her phone rings again in Peter's hand. The pressure of his finger disappears, and she cracks her eyes open. Peter presses ignore.

"You ran him down," she whispers. "You tried to kill him."

Peter sucks on his teeth and nods. "I had you. You were here, working every day. Lived in town. Didn't date. Never had anyone over. You were still mine. Then he showed up and slowly you slipped away. I was losing you piece by piece. Then you got engaged and there was talk of you going to Tennessee—I had you until he showed up."

Dahlia grips her glass, tears burning her eyes at his admission and delusions. "The day you chose Katherine over us is the day you lost me, Peter. That was long before Hunter arrived."

"No," he hisses, tossing her phone and tightening his hand around her throat. "You're wrong. I know how you felt. We could've had something great—continuing the game we've been playing for years, but you had to choose him."

"There was never a choice because you didn't exist to me. There was no game!" she screams, and his fingers squeeze into her windpipe. "Now the whole world will know what you did and the kind of monster you are." His grip makes it hard to swallow. "He was right about you."

Peter's face reddens, and he presses Dahlia into the wall. "I should've backed up and made sure he was dead. At least I can take you with me."

*With him?*

Dahlia can't say anything more when he grabs her arm and drags her toward the door. She claws at his arm and the wine glass shatters at her feet. He bares his teeth as his body shakes, grunting against her fight.

Hunter fumbles with the spare key Dahlia hides out back. It slips, and he curses, trying like hell to get it to line up. The lock releases and he races up the steps and Zip rushes past him into Dahlia's apartment. His dog's growls are followed by a scream of pain. He finds Dahlia laying on the floor, her hand clutching her throat and tears falling down her cheeks. She glances up at her soldier and relief washes over her features.

Hunter doesn't let his attention linger on her. He fights the urge to rush to her side until he isolates the threat. Zip sinks his teeth into Peter's leg and he kicks out at the dog. Hunter rushes the man who tried to kill him. God knows what he did to Dahlia.

They fall to the floor and Zip keeps his jaw locked, growling around the blood dripping from Peter's muscle.

Dahlia crawls on her hands and knees to her phone and calls for help. She doesn't know why Hunter is here or how he knew she needed him, but she's never been happier to see him. She gets to her feet, resting a hand around her throat as she staggers over to him.

Blind rage clouds his vision as he wrenches Peter's arm behind his back. It makes a horrible cracking sound and Peter cries out. He tried to kill him, then he came after the woman he loves. The world would be better off without someone like him.

The room around him goes dark. What would have happened if he hadn't come back to Wyoming? He never would have seen Dahlia's brown eyes light up as she stood back to admire her work. She never would have laughed again or smiled when the sun kissed her skin.

He knew the danger this man posed from the first day he met him and he wasn't here to protect her. He should've been here. This is where he belongs with the woman he loves...his home. He belongs with her.

"Hunter," a soft voice calls out to him, pulling him from the dark thoughts, but it sounds too far away. "Hunter, look at me."

A hand lands on his shoulder and he spins, ready to face the next threat.

"Come back, Soldier," Dahlia urges, her brown eyes pleading for Hunter to snap out of it. The sheriff stands behind her, his gun drawn and aimed at Peter. "It's over, Hunter. I'm okay," she croaks, lifting her hand to her sore throat.

The sheriff nods, stepping closer. Hunter shudders, then slowly pushes himself up. "Zip," he commands, and the dog releases his grip, backing slowly, but keeping his eyes trained on the man who tried to hurt Dahlia.

Officers rush in behind the sheriff, and Hunter gently places a hand on Dahlia's elbow to guide her out of the way. She wraps her arms around her body and he shrugs out of his jacket, placing it around her. Dahlia pulls it tighter and Hunter leads her toward her bedroom while officers bark orders at Peter and read him his rights.

"Let me see," Hunter demands, stepping into Dahlia's bedroom with her and gently lifting her chin. Bruises are already forming from Peter's grip and Hunter hates that he let this happen. "I'm so sorry. I should have been here—I—"

"I'm okay." She takes his hand from her chin and quickly lets go when she realizes she weaved her fingers with his. "I'm going to freshen up and I'll be right out." She studies Hunter expectantly, waiting for him to step out of her room to give her privacy.

He hates the idea of letting her out of his sight.

"I'll be right outside if you need anything. Then I'm taking you to the hospital."

"Hunter—" Dahlia protests, but he closes the door, not listening to her excuses as to why she doesn't need to go.

She stares at the physical barrier between them.

*Why is he here?*

*How did he know about Peter?*

Her heart flips at the sight of him again. But she doesn't let herself linger on that fact. His ranch is still for sale—he probably was here by chance to sign papers or he could have sold it and needed to get some last-minute things from the ranch.

Lifting his jacket, she inhales the pine and cedar smell that takes her back to their first night at the cabin.

He can't be here to stay, not with his daughter back in Tennessee. She can't let herself build up hope, only for it to get ripped away again. Dahlia shrugs out of the jacket and tosses it onto her bed. After pulling on a clean shirt and pants, she goes to the bathroom and studies herself in the mirror. Mascara runs down her cheeks and her hair is a wild mess around her face.

She cleans the smudged makeup from her eyes and pulls her curls into a bun on top of her head. Hunter was right about Peter.

He tried to kill her fiancé—over what—her? It's insane, but she can't deny it after everything her ex said.

# Chapter Thirty-Six

A SOFT KNOCK SOUNDS at Dahlia's bedroom door before it opens.

"Dahlia?" Hunter asks and the tapping of Zip's toenails on the floor gets closer. "Zip," he hisses right before the familiar wet nose nuzzles the palm of her hand.

The dog stares up at her with his big brown eyes and Dahlia crouches, running her hands over his white fur.

"There's my hero," she coos and Zip places a paw on her knee. "You are such a good boy, Zip."

Wood creaks beside her and she startles. Hunter leans against the door frame, his jacket gripped in one hand and the other in his pocket. "He's gone. Someone will come in and take pictures for the report."

Dahlia nods and pushes to her feet, avoiding his gaze. "What now?"

He sighs. "We have to go to the police station for you to file a report, but I'm taking you to the hospital first."

"Hunter," she says with an exasperated sigh. "I'm fine. He didn't hurt me. He just—" her voice cracks, and she squeezes her hands together to stop them from shaking.

He fucking terrified her.

She squeezes her eyes closed, clinging to her composure.

*I'm fine. I'm fine. I'm fine,* she repeats to herself. Physically, she is, but mentally she's on the verge of a panic attack.

"Can I...hold you?" Hunter asks, his voice so small and tentative it causes a new tear to escape Dahlia.

Her throat tightens, preventing her from answering. She nods and Hunter drops his jacket, pulling her into his chest. His body shakes as she leans against him. She hadn't noticed it when he was standing there, all calm and collected.

"I was fucking terrified I was too late," he murmurs into her temple.

Dahlia tentatively places her hands on his back. She should ask what he's doing back in Wyoming, but she's too terrified of his answer.

"But you weren't," she says instead, choosing to live in a fantasy where the past two months never happened. She never walked away from him, never learned about his daughter, and never went to Tennessee. He's still her soldier, and she's still his little flower.

"We should go," he says, his voice deep and raspy. Dahlia lifts her head and looks up at him. His familiar blue eyes pull at her soul and her chest tightens.

Hunter lightly brushes his thumb across her cheek. Every cell in his body screams at him to kiss her, to latch onto her and never let go. But he fights it, because he can't pretend that he didn't watch her walk away. He drops his hand and backs up a step, picking up his jacket and clears his throat.

"Are you ready?"

Dahlia swallows everything she wants to say. She was strong enough to do the right thing in Tennessee, but having him here, in her apartment—she doesn't know if she is strong enough to do it a second time.

She wants him to stay. She still loves him more than anything. But nothing has changed.

"Yeah," she whispers, brushing past Hunter to the kitchen. She grabs her keys, but Hunter plucks them from her hand.

"Absolutely not. I'm driving until I know you're okay."

"He didn't hit me or anything. Just roughed me up, I guess—but I am perfectly capable of driving."

Hunter doesn't offer her keys back. He just stands there with a bored expression on his face.

Dahlia huffs. "Fine. Whatever. Let's just get this over with."

Grabbing her jacket, she walks ahead of Hunter down the stairs, her body fully aware of his gaze on her every movement. It's like there's a charge between them and her skin tingles with him being so close. The hair on her neck rises and chills dance across her arms. Each footstep thumps at the sound of her heart.

Her hand slides down the stair's railing and she glances over her shoulder, her breath stuttering.

Hunter clenches his fist in his pocket. It's torture being this close to her and not touching her—not knowing if she is his or not. He came back to talk to her. That was the whole point of this trip. Then Peter had to go and show his true colors. He knows now isn't the time to have the, *what are we*, discussion, but having her literally just out of reach is killing him.

The stairs seem to go on forever as he places one foot at a time. Once they reach the landing, Dahlia's cheeks burn and she can't force herself to take one more step toward the door until she knows why Hunter is here.

She stops, angling her head so she can see him out of her periphery, but not fulling turning around.

"Why are you here, Hunter?"

He steps closer, brushing his chest to her back. "When we have that conversation, we'll fuck or fight, and I can't do either of those things until I know he didn't hurt you."

She huffs. "I told you, I'm fine."

"I promise we'll talk. Humor me, Little Flower." The words slip from his lips before he can stop them and she gasps.

He waits for her to say something or rage that she isn't his anymore. But she opens the door and steps into the night.

Blue and red flashing lights surround the back entrance of her shop. She shields her eyes and Hunter wraps an arm around her shoulders and leads her to his truck. People stand with just the police tape separating them with horrified expressions.

"Dahlia!"

Hunter tenses and readies himself to shove them away.

"Mom! Dad! She's here! She's with—" Hunter lifts his eyes to Tripp. "What the hell are you doing here?" he asks.

"Tripp, I'm fine. Quiet down before you give Momma and Daddy a heart attack." Tripp steps toward his sister and dares Hunter to try and stop him. Hunter relents and moves away from the passenger door.

"Oh, my baby," Bonnie sobs as she runs across the parking lot with Walt on her heels.

"Momma, I'm fine. See? Please don't cry."

Her mother tries to console herself as her hands hover over Dahlia's body.

"What the hell happened? Someone said Peter had a gun. Someone else said he killed Katherine!" Walt demands.

"There wasn't a gun. Katherine is bruised up, but alive. Peter was drunk and things got out of hand," Hunter supplies and Bonnie and Walt jerk their attention in his direction as if they didn't notice him.

"You're...here?" Bonnie asks and looks back to her daughter.

"It's a long story, Momma," Dahlia sighs. "I promise I'll call you—"

Tripp chuckles. "Yeah, because you think they're going to go home? We'll meet you guys at the hospital unless..." He flicks his gaze to Hunter out of the corner of his eye. "You want to ride with us, Sis?"

Bonnie waves her hands. "She's already in his truck. He might as well take her. We'll meet you there, sweetie."

Her mother kisses her cheek before she can get two words in and Tripp closes her door. He grabs Hunter's elbow before he gets out of reach.

"What are you doing here? You broke her, and she just started being able to work again. If this is some kind of fucked up game to you—"

"It's not," Hunter states evenly.

Tripp chews on his cheek and releases his grip. "It better not be."

As Hunter gets in the truck, Dahlia's gaze burns into his skin. He keeps his focus straight ahead, because if he looks at her, he won't make it to the hospital before he tells her why he's back in Wyoming.

***

DAHLIA HUFFS AT BEING forced to lie in the hospital bed. "This is ridiculous. My throat barely hurts anymore."

Hunter grunts as he leans against the window. It may not hurt, but it's bruised and makes it hard for him to look at.

Her parents and brother rush into the room and she just wants to disappear. Through the chaos, she keeps her gaze locked on Hunter. A million questions circulating around her mind and each one just leads to more questions.

His phone rings and his brows furrowed as he looks at the screen. "I gotta take this."

Dahlia watches as he goes, wishing she knew what had him looking so flustered and who was on the other end of the line. What happened between him and Melanie after she left? They have a kid together. That would be enough to rekindle old feelings.

Burned-out flames relight all the time.

Did he come all the way here to tell her he's moved on?

No. Hunter wouldn't be that cruel...but then why? Why show up randomly at night?

Hunter paces the hallway outside. "How high is the fever?" he asks, pinching the bridge of her nose. The doctor walks past him into Dahlia's room and he lingers at the edge of the door to hear what is said.

"I don't know," Melanie responds.

"Well, how do you know she has one if you didn't check it?" he snaps, immediately regretting the tone.

"Don't yell at me! I'll just let you go. Clearly I'm bothering you and you aren't concerned about your daughter's well-being."

"Melanie, that's not—" he sighs. "Is my mom there?"

"Yes—"

"Will you give her the phone?"

Dahlia's doctor leaves and Hunter internally curses himself for missing what was said.

"Hunter?" Lydia says and Hunter takes a deep breath. "Is she okay? Do I need to be worried or—?"

"She has a cough, but I think she's fine. Feels like she has a low-grade fever, but nothing a lukewarm bath won't fix."

Hunter lets out a long sigh. "Look, I know we've not really been on speaking terms since...everything, but Dahlia was attacked tonight. She's fine and I don't have time to explain, but I can't answer the phone every five minutes because Melanie is calling. Can you—do something? I don't know."

There's a shuffle from her end and Hunter waits, the toe of his boot tapping on the floor. "You're my son and I will do whatever I can to help you. Promise me you'll call and tell me what is going on?"

Thankful for his mother's intervention, Hunter nods. "I'll tell you everything as soon as I can. And...thank you."

Hunter steps into Dahlia's room and finds her out of the bed and grabbing her clothes.

"What did they say?" he asks.

Bonnie and Walt wear exhausted expressions and Tripp stares daggers into Hunter.

"I'm fine. Clean bill of health," Dahlia says, her tone short. "I'm actually going to stay with my parents for the night, so you can go."

"Dahlia," Bonnie hisses. "You could at least thank him for stopping Peter and looking after you."

"Thanks," Dahlia chirps without glancing up.

Hunter stares at her, puzzled by where her attitude change has come from.

"Mr. and Mrs. Brooks," Hunter says. "Can I have a moment to talk to Dahlia before you go?"

Her parents stand and Walt slaps Tripp on the leg when he doesn't follow.

"What? He asked you two. Not me." Bonnie mutters under her breath and pulls him after her.

Hunter pushes the door closed and prepares himself to have a discussion that he hoped to have at his place with his bed for the aftermath.

# Chapter Thirty-Seven

"I GUESS WE'RE DOING this here," Hunter mutters to himself, turning his baseball cap around on his head.

Dahlia huffs and spins to face him. "Doing what? What is there for us *to do*? We're not a thing. There is no us. Why are you even here, Hunter?"

"Now hold on a minute. Can we rewind to before whatever the fuck changed since we left the apartment? What happened to the Dahlia that wanted to know why I was here and wanted to have a conversation?"

*Fighting it is*, Hunter sighs and rolls his shoulders.

"Perhaps I do have a concussion and I need to be reevaluated," she snaps and grabs her belongings.

"Dammit, Dahlia. What the hell is wrong with you?"

She drops her bag and balls her fist. "What's wrong with me? Oh, I can't believe you! I heard you on the phone—with your mom. How's Melanie, by the way? Seems like ya'll are really close now for her to be calling you constantly. Is she asking when you'll be home? I mean, it only makes sense since you've been living under the same roof for two months."

His ears burn and he narrows his gaze. Is that what she thinks? That he just moved on and went back to Melanie after she walked out.

"So, what if we are?" he asks. If she wants to act like she knows exactly what is going on and she wants him to leave, clearly his reason for staying is gone.

Dahlia rushes toward Hunter. "Why come back? What the hell are you doing here?"

"Because of you!" he shouts, and Dahlia backs up a step. Hunter rips his ball cap off and runs his fingers through his hair.

"What?" Dahlia asks, her lips parted.

He shakes his head and steps further into the room, bracing himself on the end of the bed.

"I had to see if there was anything left for me in Wyoming."

Dahlia scoffs and bites the inside of her cheek. "Well, you put your ranch up for sale, so I guess not." The words taste like acid coming out of her mouth and Hunter bristles.

"Yeah...I guess not." He puts his hat back on his head and whistles for Zip. Tripp is standing right outside, and he stands eye level with Hunter.

"Not a fucked-up game, huh?" Tripp snorts. "You should've stayed in Tennessee."

Hunter shoves past him. He's right. He never should have come back. It's clear she doesn't want him here.

Dahlia breathes heavily through the tears threatening to spill over her cheeks.

She rushes out of the hospital, Tripp following behind her. She rounds a corner and nearly collides with a bruised and beaten Katherine in a hospital gown.

Dahlia skids to a stop, her mouth falling open at the bright bruise around her eye.

"I heard they arrested him," Katherine says, her voice monotone and hollow.

"Yes," Dahlia responds. Old bruises peek out from under the hospital gown and Dahlia regrets every bad thought she's had of her. "I'm sorry—"

"No. You don't apologize to me and I won't apologize to you. You won the day Peter left you and I lost the day he chose me. It took me way too long to realize that."

"What will you do now?" Dahlia asks, genuinely concerned about her well-being.

"I'm taking my girl and we're going back to South Dakota. Did you know she's never seen where I grew up? Peter always had some reason why we couldn't go. I think it's the fresh start we need."

"I wish you the best, truly." Dahlia offers her a smile and Katherine gives her a small one in return before walking past and disappearing down the hallway.

"Damn, you really don't know what goes on behind closed doors, do you?" Tripp remarks, and Dahlia shakes her head. She can't believe all these years she was oblivious to the abuse and life that Katherine lived.

She was right though, Dahlia won when Peter chose someone else. She couldn't imagine that being her future.

***

CARLY LOADS THE LAST of the flowers into the back of the SUV. "Are you sure you are up for this? It's not too late to call one of the girls."

"Leave it alone. I'm fine. Let's just get this over with."

Dahlia avoids looking at the for-sale sign as they pull into Haynes Venues. There isn't any sign of Hunter or his truck when they park between the cabin and the barn.

"Coast seems clear," Carly sighs as she opens the trunk.

"I'll take the barn; you decorate the cabin. If you have questions—"

"I've got this, D. Just don't overdo it, okay?"

Dahlia nods and grabs the arch decorations. Being inside the barn brings back memories of her and Hunter. She barely slept last night after her parents took her back to their house.

She wanted to go to Hunter's and force him to say exactly why he was here, no matter how painful it'll be to hear.

Maybe he's already left.

She doesn't bother turning her music on today. After Peter last night, then her fight with Hunter, she doesn't even want to be out of bed.

But she can't let herself crumble every time things get hard.

Working in silence, she gets stuck in her head, lost in what-ifs and could-have-beens with Hunter. Why does her mind continue to torture her? What's done is done, and she needs to accept it.

On the other side of the ranch, Hunter stands on the edge of the porch and leans on the column. His exhale comes out in soft plumes between his lips. It'll start snowing within a couple of weeks.

Everything was just as he left it when he arrived last night. He sat by the lit fire until the sun rose over the mountains. He wonders if Dahlia would be the one setting up today or if she will let Carly take the reins.

He could call her. Check on her, but after what was said between them...he's the last person she'd want to talk to.

His phone rings and an unknown number appears.

"Hunter Haynes," he answers.

"Hey, it's Carly—Dahlia's friend."

"I know who you are, Carly," Hunter says. "Is everything okay?" He steps back into the cabin and pours his remaining coffee down the sink.

"Sorry, I didn't know who else to call. I'm setting up at the cabin and all the lights just went out. Where is your breaker box?"

He grabs his truck keys off the table and Zip rushes to the driver's door. "I'll be right there."

"Oh. You're here—like here, here. That's—um—that's not necessary. If you just tell me where it is, I can handle it."

Hunter smirks into the phone. Dahlia did come. That's the only reason why Carly would act this way. "Thanks, Carly."

"Thanks? For what? I—"

He hangs up and his truck bumps along the unpaved driveway to the main cabin. Maybe he has one more chance to talk to her.

Carly stands with her hands on her hips at the entrance, her expression less than appreciative. "Well?"

"It's right this way," Hunter says as he steps inside looking for familiar curly hair. Soft music plays, but it isn't the songs he's nearly memorized that Dahlia uses.

Carly notices how he looks around as he makes his way through the house, lingering at each open door like he's waiting for someone to jump out.

"She's not here."

Hunter drops his chin. She didn't come.

"I know where she is, though," Carly supplies and places her hands behind her back. "But first, you have to answer one thing."

Hunter pulls open a hidden door under the stairs and runs his fingers down the breakers.

"What's that?" he asks.

"Why are you here? Is it to break her heart? Or do you really love her?"

Hunter flicks the breaker and the lights flash on. He closes the door and rests his palm on the wood. "I'm here for her...but I'm worried she doesn't want me here."

Carly crosses her arms and purses her lips. "Fine. She's in the barn."

He jerks his eyes toward her and Carly smirks.

"Tell her she can thank me later."

He smiles and whistles for Zip to follow him. Standing outside the barn, his nerves get the best of him. He cracks the door and slips inside, rehearsing what he's going to say to make her at least listen before she storms out.

The barn is silent, and it makes him uneasy. If Dahlia is working, where is the music she always swayed and got lost singing to? He walks into the open space and she's softly humming as she stands on the top of the ladder, reaching for the exposed beam above her.

The same ladder he saved her from last time.

Too worried about causing her to lose her balance, he leans against the wall and watches her from the back of the barn. He recognizes the tune she is humming. He's heard it from her playlist enough he can almost recall the lyrics.

Something about being sad in the summer, but the tune is upbeat which never made sense to him. Even as she climbs down the ladder, he can't bring himself to break her trance. He's always loved watching her work, but today it's robotic and less passionate.

She starts picking up the cut stems and left over flowers without even stepping back to admire her finished product.

"Dahlia," he finally says when it's clear she is packing up to leave. Her movements stop and she slowly lifts her wide brown eyes to him.

"Hunter," she states, her voice full of shock and sadness. "I was just leaving." Quickly, she grabs as much as she can and moves toward the door. Hunter steps in her way, blocking her from leaving.

"Wait, just give me five minutes, please."

She swallows, straightening her spine. "My clients will be here soon and I make it a habit to be gone by the time they arrive."

"I know—I just—I came back for you. I'm in Wyoming to see you. I'd really appreciate it if you'd give me a chance to talk to you."

Dahlia's stance falters. He came back for her? To see her?

"I don't have time to do this here," she says.

"Then come to my cabin with me. Carly can take your car. If you want nothing to do with me after we talk, I'll drive you into town and you'll never see me again."

She hesitates, terrified of hearing what he has to say. Terrified that all the pain she's tried to overcome will rush to the surface and she'll have to start the process all over again.

"Please," Hunter adds, his tone full of the same vulnerability as when he let her in for the first time.

Dahlia huffs, knowing she's a glutton for punishment. "Okay. I have to load this stuff, then tell Carly."

Hunter takes the stuff from her hands and tries to suppress his smile, hoping beyond hope that she chooses him.

# Chapter Thirty-Eight

THERE'S AN AWKWARD ENERGY between them as Hunter parks his truck at his cabin. Dahlia doesn't wait for him to get out before she shoves her door open and slams it. She stops on the porch, taking in one of her favorite views of the woods.

Hunter's boots tap on the porch behind her and she takes a deep breath. "How's your daughter?"

He stops beside her, keeping distance between them. "Faith's amazing. I still have no idea what I'm doing, but she doesn't seem to care. She's just a happy kid."

"That's great, Hunter. I'm happy for you. Seems like you are doing well."

He pivots to stand in front of her, forcing her to look at him. "I must have one hell of a poker face if you think I'm doing well."

Her brows furrow, and she tries to take a step back, but he grasps her hand and places it on his chest.

"What are you doing?" she asks.

"Making sure you're listening when I say this." He takes a deep breath and revels at how her simple touch makes him feel lighter. "I had to come back—I had to see if I had a reason to stay before I made any final decisions.

I love you, Little Flower. I haven't stopped and this ache inside my chest has hurt every damn day since you left."

"Hunter—" Dahlia tries to interject, but he grabs her other hand and places it on his chest. His heart pounds under her palms.

"If you don't love me—if you never want to see me again—tell me and I'll go. I'll leave you alone and you'll never hear from me. But I need you to understand that there won't be anyone else for me in this life. I'm completely and utterly in love with you, Dahlia Brooks, and if there is even a sliver of a chance that you feel the same way, I'll stay. I'll stay and we'll work through this and figure this out together."

His eyes well with tears and Dahlia's heart jumps from her chest at his confession. "How? How can you be here and be with your daughter? And what about Melanie? She lives with your parents and I heard you on the phone."

"There is *nothing* between Melanie and me. She tried," he says with a wince. "I don't know how it'll all work. All I know is I need you. I want you. I fucking miss you, Little Flower."

She grips his jacket, a curl falling in front of her face. She wants more than anything to kiss him, to have him touch her and remind her of what it feels like to have his skin against hers. "What if you change your mind? What if the distance becomes too hard and you go back? What if it strains your and Faith's relationship and you hate me for keeping you here?"

He brushes his fingers across her cheek and tucks the curl behind her ear. "I'll always choose you. But this only works if you choose to love me, even with my baggage. I'm no good to Faith if I'm miserable and living in Tennessee."

"I thought you weren't going to beg?" she remarks with a twinkle in her eye that turns to tears. Her throat tightens, and she drops her chin. "I was trying to do the right thing, to take the weight of making a choice off your shoulders. I never stopped loving you and I've missed the hell out of you."

He takes her chin between his finger and thumb and lifts her head. "Say you choose me, Dahlia. Tell me you'll be here through every decision and every good and bad time. Love me with your whole heart and never stop."

Her bottom lip quivers, and she pulls it between her teeth. "I'm scared," her voice cracks. Hunter brushes the tears from her cheeks.

"Then let me be your comfort. Let me love you and I promise I'll never let you go again. I'll beg, get on my knees, whatever it takes, but I'm never going to stand by and watch you walk out a door without fighting for us. I'll prove it to you every day that I choose you."

A sob escapes her, and she buries her face into his chest, inhaling the pine and cedar scent she loves. He wraps his arms around her and rests his chin atop her head.

"I missed you so damn much, my little flower."

She sniffles into his jacket and pulls back. "I never stopped loving you. You were right, things got complicated, and I bailed. In the past, I'm not the one who gets chosen and I could never expect you to pick me over, Faith. I really don't want to live without you, Hunter. I love you."

A smile lifts the corner of his lips and he cups her cheek. "Can I kiss you and take you to bed, Dahlia?"

"Yes." With her exhale, she lets go of every doubt she has about this man. He leans down, molding his mouth to hers with fervent need. She clings to his jacket as he grips her ass, pulling her as close as possible. His muscles shudder across his back as if he's never had her before, and she moans as his tongue parts her lips.

"I need you now, Little Flower. So, I know this is real," he says between panting breaths.

"Take whatever you need, Soldier." A deep rumble of approval vibrates through his chest. Dahlia wraps her legs around his waist as he carries her inside the cabin. It still smells of smoldering embers from the fire earlier and the only light is the sun's rays shining through the windows.

He places Dahlia at the edge of the bed, and her hands quickly fumble for his belt while he shoves out of his coat.

He came back for her. She gazes up at him and knows that without a doubt, he would fight for her. He loves her and knows he'll prove it every day for the rest of their lives.

"Ask me again," she pants as he pulls his shirt over his head.

"What?" Her fingers trace the lines of his muscles and skim across his low abdomen.

"Ask me to marry you again," she states, never surer of anything in her life. She can't live in fear that she'll get hurt or lose him. To live like that wouldn't be living at all. He sucks in a breath and takes her face in hands.

"Are you sure? Like really sure, because I can't handle you leaving me again."

Dahlia pushes to her feet, pressing her chest flush against him, and runs her thumb across his bottom lip. "Ask me again," she repeats.

Hunter's hands slide down her body as he lowers himself to the floor on one knee. His fingertips brush under her shirt and dig into her hips. "Dahlia Cheyenne Brooks, will you marry me? Monday morning on the courthouse steps? I don't want to wait another day for you."

Threading her fingers through his head, she nods. "Yes. Monday. Yes, I want to spend the rest of my life with you. And I promise to love you till death do us part, Hunter Haynes."

He grabs the elastics of her leggings and pulls them down her legs and Dahlia giggles.

"Till death do us part." He kisses her stomach, then tugs her panties down and kisses just above her slit. "Lay back on the bed, Little Flower. I've been a starving man without you."

Heat rushes to her cheeks, and she does as he orders. Looping his arms under her thighs, he grips her legs and pulls her to the edge of the bed. A small gasp escapes her and Hunter grins as he grabs her panties with his teeth and slides them down her legs.

"With moves like those, I'll have to find a garter for Monday," Dahlia rasps, her hand fisting the blanket at how much her center aches for a release.

"I require that. Along with something thin and lace covering your delicious breasts and pussy. I want to unwrap you like a present." His hot breath ghosts the apex of her thighs and she nods.

"Whatever you want, Husband."

"That's right, Little Flower. I'm going to be your husband and you're my wife. You're mine and I'm yours."

Hunter buries his face between her legs and pulls her clit between his teeth. Dahlia cries out and her back presses into the mattress. His fingers dig deeper into her flesh while he licks, bites, and sucks like it's his dying wish.

She's his. He has her back and he'll be damned if he ever lets her go again. He doesn't know what his future looks like, but he knows she'll be by his side every step of the way.

She's his home.

Dahlia's legs tense around his head and her body shudders as she cries out his name.

His name.

That's his favorite sound in the world. He swallows her orgasm and kisses the inside of each of her thighs before lifting his glistening smile to Dahlia.

"There are two things, before we get married," she pants, her chest rising and falling with heavy breaths.

"What's that?"

Laying back, she drapes a hand over her forehead. "Get rid of that fucking sign at the end of your driveway."

Hunter chuckles and pushes to his feet, offering a hand to Dahlia.

"And I want to live here with you, Hunter."

"This tiny cabin?" he asks, surprised.

"It's all I've ever envisioned with you. Our home."

He brings her finger to his lips and kisses them one by one. "Your wish is my command, Wife. This will be our home and I'll wake up to you at my side and Zip at our feet. Then we'll sit on the porch with coffee and watch the storms roll in. When the snow gets too deep to leave, we'll keep each other warm and stay in this bed."

Dahlia slides her hand across the bulge in his boxers. "And we'll watch the sunsets and sunrises together."

He nods. "And number two?"

"I prefer the cowboy hat," she whispers shyly.

He steps closer. "Done. I'm going to fuck you now, Little Flower, and it's not going to be easy. I lived thinking I'd never have you under me again and that kind of loss does things to a man. Are you ready for me?"

Her eyes burn, and she squeezes her hand, causing him to hiss. "Do your worst."

# Chapter Thirty-Nine

HUNTER WEAVES HIS FINGERS with Dahlia's before she can get out of the truck. "Tomorrow," he states, hating letting her go.

"I'll be the one in white," she remarks, exhausted from the long day of shopping with Carly.

"I can't wait, Mrs. Haynes." Heat fills her cheeks and at the sound of her future name. She rubs her thumb across his hand and shifts in the seat.

"Have you...called them yet? Jared and Lydia?"

Hunter inhales loudly. "I guess that's another reason I don't want to let you go." He squints at her with a sideways grin. "Do I have to? I mean, they kept Faith a secret."

Dahlia levels him with a look. "Yes, you do, because we are not them."

"Fine," Hunter grumbles. "One last kiss as Dahlia Brooks?"

She rolls her eyes and leans across the center console, pressing her lips to his. When she tries to pull away, Hunter places a hand at the base of her neck and deepens the kiss.

"How about one last fuck as Dahlia Brooks, too?"

"Hunter," Dahlia scoffs and pushes him back. "Unlike you, I have to get ready early tomorrow morning. I may not want a big white wedding, but I want to look the part. Then, you can undress me any way you like after we say I do."

He groans and bites his bottom lip. "You are just torturing me at this point."

"I have to keep you on your toes. We have forever to go and I can't have you getting bored." She kisses his cheek and hops out of the truck.

"I don't think that is possible!" he shouts as she closes the door and sashays to her apartment. Hunter breathes through the anxiety that curls his stomach of her staying in her apartment tonight...alone. He knows Peter is gone and there aren't any dangers to his little flower, but it's all too fresh in his mind for him to think logically.

His phone chimes and he pulls up the message from Dahlia.

**Go home, Hunter.**

He glances out his windshield at the second-story windows. Dahlia waves her hands for him to shoo and he smirks. He knows Carly and her mom are coming to stay with her, and he has no reason to be this worried.

Maybe it's his way of postponing his dreaded phone call.

Reluctantly, he heads to Turnpike to get a famous Beau burger before heading home. As he runs his hands around his steering wheel, his stomach twists and he lifts his phone.

"This is going to suck, or it's really going to suck," he says to Zip. With a deep breath, he calls his parents and sets the phone on speaker.

"Hunter? Thank goodness. You had us worried. The last thing we hear is Dahlia was attacked, then nothing," Lydia answers.

"Hey, uh, sorry. It's been a crazy forty-eight hours. How's Faith? Is her cough better?"

"Yes, she's fine. Nothing a bath and some sleep didn't cure. You just missed Melanie. She went to work."

"Good, I'm glad she's better. Is Dad around? There's something I want to talk to you both about." He runs his hands down his jeans. Three months ago, he didn't care what his parents thought about him marrying Dahlia. But since he's been home and they've mended some of their relationship, he can't in good conscience not tell them.

"Yeah, he's out back. Is everything okay? Is Dahlia okay?"

Hunter takes a deep breath. He should've known this wasn't going to be a quick call. "Yes, everything is fine. Dahlia was attacked in her apartment, but they got the man and he's going to jail."

"Attacked in her apartment?" his moms squawks. "Who was it? Why would they do that?"

He pinches the bridge of his nose. "Because he was her ex-boyfriend and his wife turned him in for—" his voice cuts off. He realizes he never told his parents about his wreck and that's a conversation he doesn't want to start. "His wife caught him cheating, and he blamed Dahlia—but that's not why I called. I need to tell you and Dad something."

"Jared," Lydia says over the phone. "The man who attacked Dahlia was arrested!"

Hunter can't hear his dad's response and it sounds like Lydia left the phone sitting while they have a full conversation.

"Mom? Dad?" He says, trying to get their attention.

"Yeah, yeah. Okay, we're both here."

"Are you okay, son? Did he hurt you?" Jared asks.

"No, Dad. I'm fine. Look, I want to talk to you guys about something, okay?" He's met with silence. His heart hammers in his chest and he runs his hand across the back of his neck. "Dahlia and I...uh we're getting married...in the morning."

He stares at the phone sitting on his dash, waiting for screams or a lecture about why this is a terrible idea.

"Hunter," his mother starts, her voice carrying a heavy weight of disappointment. "What about Melanie?"

"What about her? I don't love her and told her time and time again there isn't going to be anything between us," he snaps, annoyed that is the first thing his mother has to say.

"Easy son, that's not what she's getting at. It's just—she lives here with us and Faith..." Jared tries to interject.

"What if she tries to take her?" Lydia asks, her voice small, and she actually sounds scared.

Hunter clenches his fist. "She won't. I already told her if she did, I'd hire the best lawyer and fight her for my rights. Mom, Dad, this is a good thing. I love Dahlia and she loves me. I just wanted to let you know before tomorrow."

"And you're happy? Truly happy?" Lydia asks, her voice thick with unshed tears.

"I am, Mom." He swallows. "I don't want to live without her."

"I hear you, son, but what about Faith? Are you staying in Wyoming, then?"

He runs his hand over Zip's head as he says, "This is my home and I know that's not what you want to hear, but it's true. Don't tell Melanie yet. I'll talk to her when I come back, like we planned, and we'll work something out."

"I can't believe you're getting married and we won't be there," Lydia says and guilt tightens in Hunter's chest.

"I don't want to wait another day. I thought I lost her for good once and I'm not doing that again. Whatever happens, we'll face it together. Please don't make me feel bad about finding my happiness."

Lydia sniffs and Hunter lays his head back. "I'm not. You can't tell me that then expect me to not get choked up. It's a mom's dream to watch their baby fall in love and get married and I've missed both of those."

"I know—and I'm sorry for that, but I can't fix it now."

Jared murmurs something and Hunter stares at the phone, his shoulders slumping at how much pain he has caused his parents.

"Just promise you'll take pictures. We love you, Hunter," Jared says.

"I will. Love you guys, too."

His phone lights up with the disconnected call and he sighs. Honestly, if he could go back and do it all over, he wouldn't. Leaving his parents, breaking away from his old life, all the pain, the hurt, the haunted nights, they led them to Dahlia. He'd go through all the hell for it to lead him right back here.

He still plans to thank Sergeant Brooks one day. He's hopeful he'll find his peace and make his way back to his family, too. Hunter pockets his phone and Zip follows him out of the car.

Hunter steps through the door and Beau claps loudly and whistles, causing the rest of the crowd to join in.

"There's the man of the hour! From a small-town hero to getting hitched tomorrow. Get over here! Your first drink is on me."

The tip of Hunter's ears burn and he drops his chin to hide under the brim of his cowboy hat. He nods at the congratulations shouted his way as he sits on the barstool.

"Does the whole town know?" he asks Beau.

The bar owner chuckles. "Haven't you learned anything now while you lived here? I know you took down the for-sale sign at your ranch, too."

Hunter smirks and takes the offered beer. "Yeah, I put too much work into that place to sell it."

Beau winks. "And I'm sure a certain curly-haired flower shop owner didn't have anything to do with that decision?"

They laugh and Hunter orders his food.

"There are a few here in town not too thrilled about Peter getting arrested. He was the golden child according to his parents, but honestly, with enough money, you can buy anyone off. Except they can't push this under the rug. Don't take it personally if you get some hateful looks. What you did was a good thing, and the town is better for it."

Beau taps the bar top before disappearing back into the kitchen. At some point, Hunter got comfortable in the small town. He no longer counts the seconds to when he can leave and go back to his ranch. He'd go as far to say he's made friends here. Even if it is the bar owner.

"There he is," a voice shouts, and Hunter glances over his shoulder as the door closes. "My future brother-in-law."

Tripp smiles wide and saunters over to the barstool beside Hunter.

He bristles, not sure where this conversation is going to go.

"Tripp."

"Relax. I'm not here to bust your balls. Dahlia already threatened me. But it is your wedding night, which calls for a bachelor party and I figured since you're here, we can shoot some pool, sling some darts, and drink some beers."

Hunter shrugs and salutes his drink at Beau. "We're going to need more beer."

318

# *Chapter Forty*

"WHAT IF HE DOESN'T show?" Dahlia chews on her bottom lip and Carly flicks her head.

"If you mess up those lips, I will do more than flick you. Besides, I'm sure he didn't get drunk. It's Hunter we're talking about...he's like...not fun."

Dahlia scoffs and turns in the chair her butt has been glued to for the past two hours while Carly does her hair and makeup. "He is too fun."

Her best friend shoves her back around so she can't get a peek at herself in the mirror. "He's not one to *let loose,* is all I'm saying. I don't think he's capable of getting drunk and losing control. He'll be here."

Dahlia sighs, squeezing her fingertips. "If Tripp ruined this, I'll seriously hurt him. He was supposed to call his parents last night and let them know the news. It's killing me not talking to him to find out how it went. What if he hasn't slept? Or if his mom and ex wouldn't let him sleep for being overbearing? What if they refuse to support him and I wasn't there to give him someone to talk to?"

"I'm sure he's fine. He came back for you. He isn't going to let anything his parents say deter him, I'm sure of it."

"But it's not just his parents. What about his daughter? I mean, he says we can work this out, but how far has he actually thought this through? I don't want to ruin his life."

Carly flicks her head again.

"Ow!" Dahlia squawks.

"This is the type of thinking that brought you back from Tennessee. It is okay to put yourself and your feelings first, D. And you ain't ruining his life." Carly's phone chimes and she smiles over Dahlia's shoulder. "Besides, he's on his way. So, can you stop fretting and let me finish getting your veil in this masterpiece I've created?"

Dahlia's shoulders relax with her exhaled breath, and she flattens her hands on her thighs. "Okay, okay. Sorry. I'll stop moving."

"This is your *something old and something borrowed*," Carly says as she places the veil perfectly in her hair. "I'm surprised your parents agreed to let you do this alone."

"But I won't be alone. I have you. And with Hunter's parents not here, it just made sense. Besides, we're going straight to their house afterward to celebrate."

"Hell yeah we are!" Carly pumps her fist and howls, and Dahlia laughs.

Once Carly has Dahlia's hair scared to move out of place, she helps her best friend slip on her wedding dress. It was hard to find something on short notice, but Dahlia found the perfect mid-thigh white long sleeve dress that accents her curves.

"Ready?" Carly asks and Dahlia nods.

She slowly turns to face the floor-length mirror in her bedroom. Her breath stutters in her chest. The woman staring back at her is beyond gorgeous. Her brown curls are perfectly defined and pulled up atop her head with small ringlets framing her cheek bones. Her brown eyes pop against her flawless skin and she lifts a hand to make sure it's real.

Carly slaps her hand down. "Absolutely not. You look beautiful, Dahlia."

Tears burn at the back of Dahlia's eyes and she tilts her head, breathing through emotion. She refuses to ruin all the hard work her best friend did.

"I'm really doing this. I'm getting married," she whispers.

"I've never been happier for someone in my life, D. This is your happily ever after and you deserve it. Let yourself be happy."

Dahlia takes her best friend's hands and tilts her head to the side. "I'm ready."

When they make it to the shop floor, Carly disappears into the cooler. "Just one more thing."

Dahlia shifts her weight in her heels and checks the time on the wall since her best friend refuses to let her have her phone. Even though the superstition is that the groom shouldn't *see* the bride before the wedding, her best friend isn't taking any chances on them talking either.

Carly steps out of the cooler with a sheepish expression. "I know you didn't want flowers and a big white wedding...but, every bride should have a bouquet."

Dahlia forgets how to breathe as her best friend reveals the bouquet of different pinks and varieties of dahlias with greenery and other plants to add texture throughout.

"I know I'm not as good as you, but I know how much you love dahlias."

Her eyes burn and she can't stop the tear that escapes. "Carly! It's perfect. Oh, my gosh! You are truly an amazing friend and I'm so lucky to have you."

"Something new and," Carly points at the blue ribbon pinned around the flower stems. "Something blue. You're all set."

Dahlia pats the tear, careful to not smudge her makeup and wraps her fingers around the bouquet.

***

HUNTER ADJUSTS HIS DARK blue vest over his white long sleeve button down for the fifth time while he paces the courthouse steps. His cowboy boots are shining and blue jeans have a sharp crease down the front.

"Would you stop moving? You're making me dizzy," Tripp groans with sunglasses covering his eyes. Zip sits at his side.

"What if she doesn't show up? What if, last night when she got alone with her thoughts, she realized just how insanely crazy this is and got cold feet?"

"Dude!" Tripp cradles his head as he sits on one of the steps. "My sister doesn't do anything without analyzing every possible outcome. She is well aware of how insane this is and she said yes. She'll be here."

Hunter checks his phone again.

Nothing.

He's about to cave and call her when her white SUV rounds the corner of the courthouse and pulls into the parking spot next to his truck.

Carly pops open the driver's door and points her finger at the cowboy. "You better turn around and close your eyes. You're not ruining this photo op!"

Hunter smiles wide and turns, more than ready to have Dahlia in his arms again, only this time it'll be as his wife. Two car doors close and Tripp peels himself off the concrete and smooths down his shirt and adjusts his hat. He removes his sunglasses and stares, shocked at the sight of his sister.

"Tripp!" Carly hisses, lifting her phone.

"Oh, right." He pulls his phone from his pocket and snaps pictures of Dahlia climbing the steps to meet Hunter at the top.

"I almost didn't recognize you, Sis," Tripp teases, and Dahlia rolls her eyes. She stands at Hunter's back and Carly positions herself to capture his first look at his bride.

His button down and vest tailor perfectly to his body, and he fills out his jeans deliciously.

"You clean up nice," she teases.

"You came," he says quietly. His fingers itching to reach behind him and take her hand.

"So did you."

He takes a deep breath.

"Okay, when you're ready," Carly announces, and Dahlia's heart races as Hunter slowly takes a step away from her and turns.

The clicking of Carly and Tripp's phones fades into the background as he gets lost in the way Dahlia stares at him.

His gaze doesn't roam down her body. He doesn't glance at the bouquet between them or the heels on her feet.

Her lips part from his intense stare that doesn't leave her eyes.

"What do you think?" she asks, her voice coming out meek and timid. "Do you like the dress?"

Hunter's eyes shine and he rolls his lips between his teeth. "I've never seen anyone more beautiful, Little Flower. And you're here to marry me." His voice cracks and he drops his head to will the tears away.

"You could've showed up in leggings and a ratty T-shirt and I'd feel the same way I do right now. You always take my breath away." He lifts his head, the brim of his cowboy hat revealing the single tear that rolls down his cheek. "But today, you've made me the luckiest man alive, and I promise to never take what we have for granted."

Dahlia's bottom lip trembles, and she pulls it between her teeth.

"Ah-ah. Don't do it, Dahlia. The makeup, think of the makeup," Carly warns, and Dahlia laughs.

Hunter props his elbow out and turns to the side. "Shall we?"

Dahlia's eyes sparkle as she loops her arm through his. "Yes. Let's get married."

It feels like a dream as she walks through the courthouse on Hunter's arm. They sign the required paperwork and approach Judge Marshall with Tripp and Carly standing off to the side behind them.

"Dahlia Brooks," the judge says. "Does your momma know you're here? I didn't think I'd be seeing the two of you until the Rollins case."

Tripp chuckles and the judge eyes him over the top of his glasses, his bushy gray eyebrows narrowing slightly.

"She does. We're headed to their house right after." Dahlia ignores the mention of Peter and everything he did. He doesn't deserve an acknowledgment on the happiest day of her life.

The judge rolls his tongue behind his teeth and straightens the documents on this desk with a light tap.

"Very well. Do you two have vows, or are we doing this the standard way?"

"We don't—" Dahlia starts.

"Actually," Hunter cuts her off. He places his hand over hers on his arm, and turns. Zip sits at his side, volleying his attention between Dahlia and Hunter.

"What are you doing? I didn't prepare anything." Her eyes widen. She just assumed they would repeat after Judge Marshall.

"Relax. Just...listen."

Dahlia hands her wedding bouquet off to Carly and takes Hunter's hand.

"Dahlia Brooks. I was a lost and broken man when I came to Wyoming. I had no idea what I was looking for or hoped to get out of this place, but I never dreamed buying my ranch would lead me to you. When I first saw you, with a stain on your shirt—you turned it inside out and thought nobody noticed—" He chuckles and Dahlia scoffs, her cheeks heating. "I noticed. I noticed every time you got lost in your music while creating something beautiful. The way you eat granola bars like they hold all the important food groups. The way your eyes light up and you stand back to admire your work. But mostly, I notice the way you try to make sure everyone else is happy and taken care of before yourself. I'm here today, to promise you I will always be here to make sure you have everything you need. I'll be your rock, the person beside you through every trial of life. I'll be your home, Little Flower."

Her lips part and her body trembles. She grips his hands harder to keep from swaying. She knows with him; she'll never have to worry about not being loved. He'll pick her first, choose *them* over everything life will throw at them. Even after she broke his heart and made him feel unwanted, he came back for her. He gave her a second chance because he wasn't ready to give up on them. The brim of his cowboy hat shadows his blue eyes and she lifts her hand to brush her fingers across his cheek. The moment she was in trouble, he was there. He let her see his insecurities, and trusted her with his heart. And he's her forever.

Judge Marshall clears his throat, snapping Dahlia from her thoughts, and she blinks from Hunter to the Judge.

"It's your turn, Miss Brooks. Or are you going to repeat after me?"

"Oh," she says with a nervous laugh, dropping her hand to take Hunter's. "Right."

Hunter lifts her hand and kisses her knuckles.

"Hunter Haynes. I'd given up on the idea of falling in love and accepted that my shop would be my one true love in life. And I was okay with that. I had my work, my passion, my friends and family." She pauses, her throat tightening. "Then I met you that first day at your ranch and I thought you were the biggest asshole there was."

Hunter laughs and wets his bottom lip. "I thought you were stubborn and too good to talk to someone like me."

"You refused to let me climb a ladder and caught me when I fell. You've been catching me ever since. I fell for you from the moment you showed up at Turnpike that first night and decked my brother."

Tripp scoffs from beside Carly, and Dahlia smiles while she continues. "I was convinced I didn't need anyone to make me happy. I was ready to live the rest of my life alone and maybe get a cat or two. But you changed everything for me. You enhanced everything in my life and became a place I could let myself be vulnerable. You're everything I didn't know I could have in life, and I love you for it. With you, I'll always be home."

Hunter kisses her other hand and cups her cheeks to pull her close.

"Not so fast," Judge Marshall warns, holding a hand up. His wrinkled lips curve into a smile. "By the power vested in me, by the state of Wyoming and the court of law, surrounded by these friends who love you, I pronounce you as husband and wife. You may kiss your bride."

Hunter takes Dahlia's hand and pulls her into him, dipping her back slightly and kissing his wife. Tripp and Carly shout and clap while Zip barks excitedly.

"My wife," Hunter mumbles against her lips, and Dahlia wraps her arms around his neck.

"My husband."

# Chapter Forty-One

DAHLIA'S BODY FEELS HEAVY as she leans back in the passenger seat of the truck. Hunter pulls her hand to his lips and kisses the back of it.

"Are you tired, Little Flower?" he asks, his voice husky and insinuating more than his question.

A lazy smile curves across her lips. "I recall you were going to unwrap me like a present?"

He nips the back of her hand and a chuckle rumbles through his chest. "I thought your family might have wiped you out with their dancing and celebrating."

"Oh, I will pass out and sleep like a rock...after I get to fuck my husband."

Hunter puts the truck in park outside his cabin, his blue eyes holding the promise of what is to come. Her body hums with anticipation as he walks around to her door and opens it. Running his hand over her thighs, he steps closer, leaning in to brush his nose against her cheek.

"I can't wait to see what you have hiding underneath this wedding dress," he says, his fingers brushing the skin under the hem.

"Take me to bed, Soldier." She swings her legs around and Hunter takes her hand, helping her step down while Zip hops out behind her.

"It's cute that you think we'll make it to the bed before I'm ripping this off of you." He sweeps his arm behind her knees and scoops her up against his chest.

Dahlia squeals and wraps her arms around his neck, clinging to him.

"God, you make the most adorable sounds," he groans and nuzzles into her neck.

She knows better than arguing that she can walk or complain about her size to Hunter. Then again, his punishment for saying it out loud might be worth it. Dahlia chuckles, and Hunter pauses at the door.

"What?" he asks.

"Nothing, just thinking about how you'll react when you see what I'm wearing." His hold on her tightens as he twists the door knob open. The cabin is dark without a fire going, and Hunter sets Dahlia down on the couch and grabs a blanket.

"I can either start a fire before and it'll be warm when we're done, or I can put it off, then we'll be freezing after you're thoroughly fucked," he says with a grin.

"I've waited this long. A few more minutes won't kill me," she teases and pulls the blanket tighter around her. Hunter gently kisses her lips before straightening and leaves to get firewood.

In no time, he has a blazing, crackling fire going, and Dahlia moves closer for the warmth. Hunter sheds out of his winter coat and hangs it by the door.

"We'll be getting snow soon," he states as he walks up behind her and hugs her back against his chest.

Dahlia whines and leans her head back into him. "My least favorite time of the year."

Hunter nuzzles her neck, his hot breath skating down her spine. "I don't know. The idea of getting snowed in again seems good enough to me."

She laughs and places her hands over his, moving one over the apex of her thighs and the other to palm her breast. "Show me what I have to look forward to."

"Anything for my wife," Hunter whispers softly. He takes a step back and pulls the zipper down her back slowly, savoring every second of their first time as husband and wife. Gently, he presses his lips to the base of her neck and goose bumps trail down her arms.

"I keep waiting to wake up and this all be a dream," he murmurs, sliding her dress off her shoulders, kissing the crook of her neck tenderly. She shudders and sucks in a breath. "I can't believe you're mine."

He slides her arms free and the dress pools around her feet, revealing the cream lace material covering her breast that straps to a thong dipping between the apex of her thighs. His fingers travel into her hair and she sighs when he pulls the first pin free. One by one, her curls cascade down around her shoulders and she moans when he massages her scalp.

"That feels amazing," she sighs, her head angling to the side and Hunter leans down, biting and sucking on her throat. Dahlia's sighs turn to soft gasps with each touch of his lips. Fisting her hair, he guides her around to face him, her breasts barely concealed by the intricate design in the lace material. He releases the hold on her and palms her breast, rubbing his thumb across her nipples. Dahlia plucks his hat off his head and places it on hers, smiling at him like she just won the lottery.

"Like what you see?" she teases.

"Fuck yes," Hunter groans, grabbing her sides and pulling her toward him, his dick pushing against the zipper of his jeans. "This," he rasps, studying every inch of her curves and lace lingerie, leaving him a road map to his pleasure. "Is definitely doing it for me."

Dahlia chuckles, her nerves settling now that they are finally back at the cabin. She tips his hat and tosses it to the chair. "Your turn, Soldier. Undress." The top button of his shirt already sits open.

Hunter pulls his shirt from his jeans and lifts it over his head. Dahlia stands back, her nipples pebbled at the sight of him in nothing but blue jeans and boots.

His tongue darts out, licking his bottom lip, and Dahlia wants to taste him. His hands travel down to his belt and he pops it free, sliding it out of his belt loops with a snap. The sound causes Dahlia to squeeze her thighs together and her pupils dilate.

"Does my little flower like the sound of that?"

She doesn't know how to answer, her brain short circuiting at the mere idea of that belt slapping against her skin. Hunter cracks the belt once more and Dahlia's pussy clenches. She swallows, her gaze flickering from the leather in his hands to his blue eyes. His cock aches and his hands twist around his belt.

"Dahlia," he says, his voice serious. "You're in control. What do you want?"

"I don't know—" She grows self-conscious with the passing seconds.

Hunter places the belt across the back of the couch. He unbuttons his jeans and slides them down to the sleeve on his thigh and over his knee. "Just give me a second. I know this isn't the most romantic strip tease." He winces at his joke as he sits on the couch.

Dahlia steps forward, dropping to her knees between his legs. "Wait," she says as he reaches for his boots. "Let me."

Hunter squeezes his eyes closed and swallows the emotion of having her on his knees and not being able to take her like a whole man could.

"It's just," he mutters, and Dahlia cups his cheeks.

"It's your wedding night too, Hunter. Let me take care of you like I know you'll take care of me."

She lifts his first boot and unlaces it, sliding it free.

"Here, just slide the sleeve down and I'll unfasten it."

Dahlia swats his hand away and forces him to lean back. "You're going to sit there and let me do this. Got it?" She challenges and Hunter squirms on the couch, clenching his fists at his sides. "Good," Dahlia says with a smirk and slips his jeans free, followed by his boxers. She stands and holds her hand out for him to help him up.

"Now," she whispers, growing more nervous by the second. "Use the belt, Hunter."

His pupils dilate and lips part in shock. "You want me to use the belt...like before?" He has vivid memories of having it wrapped around Dahlia's throat at the lake.

Dahlia shakes her head and nibbles on her lip. She moves to stand beside him on the couch and bends down, raising her ass in the air, the cream-colored fabric of her thong stretching around her hips.

Hunter sucks in a breath and runs a hand down her back and over her ass cheek. "You want to be spanked, Little Flower?"

Dahlia nods, grabbing the belt from behind the couch and handing it to her husband. "Yes."

Hunter takes it and folds it over in his hands. "You tell me if it's too much. Promise? I don't want to hurt you, and this is new to me."

Arching her back, she glances at him over her shoulder, her cheeks tinged pink. "It's new to me, too."

Hunter's dick jumps in the air as he stands beside her. He rubs a hand over her delicate skin, then brings the belt down with a light smack.

Dahlia grips the couch cushions, and she sucks in a shocked breath. "More," she breathes out when he doesn't do it again.

Hunter's cock jumps when his belt hits her bare ass again. Her soft skin reddening from the sting.

"Fuck, Little Flower," he groans, bending over her back and biting on her shoulder. "You've got me so fucking whipped. Anything you want. It's yours. Honestly, I don't think I could ever tell you no."

Dahlia smiles and pushes to stand, but Hunter grabs her neck and keeps her from moving. "What are you doing?" she asks.

"I'm going to take you...right. Like. This."

He slaps the belt against her skin harder and she whimpers. "Yes."

Hunter pulls her thong to the side and runs his fingers across her center. "So wet for me, Little Flower." He tosses the belt aside as he moves to stand behind her and grips her hips. He runs his hands over the red marks.

Dahlia's skin burns and her body is wound tightly as Hunter's fingers skim across her body. He spreads her legs and the tip of his cock teases across her wet center, up to her clit.

"Are you ready for me, Little Wife?"

She pushes her ass against him, eager to have him filling her as her husband. "Yes, please." She grips onto the cushions as he thrusts his hips, stretching her wide and filling her until she can't take anymore.

Hunter's fingers thread in her hair, and he clenches his fist, pulling her head back. A whimper escapes her parted lips as Hunter slides his dick out and thrusts into her, her ass smacking against his abdomen. He pauses and peppers kisses across her shoulder and back, rolling his hips.

Dahlia moves her hand to find her clit through the lace and Hunter shoves it away. "Allow me," he whispers across her back. He presses down on her clit and Dahlia's ass pushes hard into him, moaning against the pain as he pulls her hair.

Hunter rolls his finger back and forth across her sensitive bundle of nerves, and Dahlia's legs tremble as she chases the high of her orgasm. Her muscles tense as he slides out and buries his cock completely, again and again.

"Come for me, Little Flower. I want to hear you cry out the name of your husband."

"Hunter!" she mewls as Hunter tends to her needy clit again. Her center tightens around his cock and he groans as she comes, rubbing her clit to ride out every wave crashing through her body.

He smiles and moves his hands to grip her hips, pulling her into him as he slams his pelvis against her. She gasps with each one and Hunter grinds his teeth, chasing his own release inside his beautiful wife.

He stills, nipping and sucking on her skin as he fills her with his cum. By the time he pulls out, they're both panting and sweating, with the flames casting shadows across their skin.

Hunter pulls her up from the bent position and spins her around. He crashes his mouth against hers, fisting his hand in her curls and pressing her lace covered breasts against his chest.

"How did I get so lucky to have you as my wife?" Hunter's blue eyes fill with love and passion.

She smiles, her gaze heavy from her orgasm. "How did I get so lucky to have you?"

Hunter chuckles and kisses her again. "Is it luck or a curse because—"

She playfully shoves him back and guides him until his calve and prosthetic hit the couch.

"Sit down and let me show you how lucky you are." Dahlia straddles him in her lace lingerie, and places her hands on his shoulders. "Hold on, cowboy."

# Chapter Forty-Two

DAHLIA LAYS BACK ON Hunter's bare chest, his arm wrapped around her body and tracing lines across her skin. A warm fire crackles in the hearth at the corner of the cabin and Zip snores softly on the couch.

Hunter breathes deeply in his sleep, and Dahlia feels restless. She rolls to her back and places a hand on her chest, trying to displace what has her feeling on edge. It's like her emotions are too much and her skin is tight and can't contain everything in her body. Her heart rapidly beats loudly in her ears.

She needs to run from the danger, but there is nothing here to run from. After all the sex, the shower, and eating until they passed out, she should feel...satisfied. At the least, too exhausted to feel like *this*.

Hunter rolls to his side and sighs deeply. Dahlia pushes up to sit and gazes down at him, her brows furrowed and a storm brewing underneath.

His eyes flutter open and he squints with one eye open and looks up at her. "What are you thinking, Little Flower?"

"I don't—" Her voice comes out as a squeak and Hunter immediately sits up, gently taking her chin and lifting her brown eyes to meet his.

"What's wrong? Are you hurting? Sick? What happened?"

She shakes her head, her bottom lip trembling and body shaking.

"I don't know, I—my chest hurts and I can't breathe." She goes to get up, fear guiding her as she pulls a sheet around her. She's not trapped or stuck. Why is she feeling like this?

Hunter takes her hand. "Hey. Look at me. Take a deep breath, okay? Watch me." He inhales a deep breath and lets it out slowly. Dahlia struggles to take anything more than a shallow breath.

Flashes of Peter in her apartment, Hunter's wrecked motorcycle, the day Graves left and never came back—everything seems to crash around her at once and she wants the images to stop.

"Dahlia!" Hunter shouts, moving around in the bed until he's on his knees in front of her. Her eyes spring open and she's rocking back and forth in the center of the bed. "You're having a panic attack, Little Flower. You're okay. You're safe. I'm right here. I have you." He lifts her palms to the scruff on his face and rubs them across his chin. "Focus on how this feels on your palms, what the fire sounds like in the stove. Zip," he orders, and the dog jumps on the bed, laying his head on Dahlia's lap.

"You're in our cabin. You're okay. Just talk to me, Little Flower."

She nods through his instructions, her breaths getting deeper with each one. Tears stream down her cheeks and she strokes Zip's white fur. She's never had a panic attack out of the blue like this, but with Hunter and her getting married, she kept everything that happened with Peter stuffed down and now that the weekend is over and she is safe in her husband's arms, her body lets it all go.

"A panic attack," she mutters, frantically wiping at her cheeks.

"Yes," Hunter says. His doubts immediately come to the surface. Was the wedding too much? Too soon? She hasn't talked about what happened with Peter and they've barely had five minutes to talk since he got arrested.

"Maybe this was all too much. I can go stay at the main cabin if that'll help or—"

"No!" Dahlia squawks. "Why would you say that?"

"Because you're having a panic attack in our bed on our wedding night. What do you need? What can I do? Is it the wedding or—"

Dahlia places both hands over his mouth. They tremble against him and his heart cracks at seeing her like this.

"Don't leave. *Never* leave. That's not—"

Hunter takes her hands and kisses the inside of each palm. "I'm going to hug you," he tells her, then pulls her against him.

"He broke into my fucking apartment," she chokes out. She's tired of being strong and pushing through. If Hunter isn't a safe place for her to break down and let her emotions to the surface, then where is?

"I know."

She grips onto his arm, needing the compression of his hold to keep her together. "He ran you down—he—" she hiccups and Hunter squeezes until he's sure he's hurting her. With all the shit he's seen and experienced that would send some men spiraling, finding Peter in her apartment makes the top of the list. He lets her say whatever she can. Rubs her arms, constantly reassures her that she is safe and nothing is going to happen like that *ever* again. They sit together, her settled between his legs, his muscular arms acting as her fortress until her body relaxes and her eyes grow heavy.

"I'm so sorry," she murmurs against her chest.

"No. You never apologize. This is love, marriage—we lean on each other and find solace in each other. Okay? Don't apologize for letting yourself be vulnerable with me."

She sniffles and nods, his chest hair tickling her eyelashes.

"Do you want to sleep? Or do you need to talk?"

She pushes up in his arms, her red, puffy eyes looking up at him. "I love you, Hunter Haynes. Just don't let go—ever."

He kisses her forehead and lays down to where he is flush against her back.

"Promise," he whispers into her ear. It isn't until her breaths are deep and even that he lets himself fall asleep.

*** 

DAHLIA PUTS HER SUV in park at the airport drop-off terminal and worries her bottom lip.

"I'll be back before—"

"If you say before I can miss you, then your trip would be like five minutes long. I'm already missing you and you haven't gotten out of my car yet," Dahlia says, cutting Hunter off.

He sighs and takes her hand. "We knew this wasn't going to be easy, but we're in it together, right?"

"Yeah. It doesn't make it suck any less."

He kisses the back of her hand and drops it back on the center console. "Three days. I'll be back in three days. Then next trip you'll be able to go with me and we won't be a part. I need to tell Melanie, and I told Faith I'd be back this week. I can't break a promise to a three-year-old."

Dahlia nods. "I know. I just wish I didn't have a wedding so I could go with you. And Melanie," she admits with a side-eye in Hunter's direction.

"Yeah," he sighs. "I know."

Dahlia hates the idea of them sleeping under the same roof. She trusts Hunter without a doubt, but her—she reminds Dahlia of a snake, waiting to strike all coiled up in the grass. She swallows her worry, determined to keep a brave face on as he walks into the airport. "At least with flying you'll get more time with Faith and be home sooner," she adds, managing a smile.

Hunter's deep blue eyes stare into her soul and he gives her a crooked grin. "I love you, Dahlia Haynes. My wife."

She blushes like she does every time his eyes take that hungry gaze that sets her skin on fire. "I love you, my husband."

He reluctantly drops her hand and opens the door. Zip hops out of the backseat wearing his service dog outfit and leash and Hunter holds onto it for show.

Dahlia grabs his bag from the back and closes the hatch.

She crouches by Zip and places the bag on the concrete. "You take care of him and bite anyone who tries to hurt him, got it?" The dog perks his ears and glances up at Hunter.

Dahlia stands, looping her thumbs in her blue jeans. "Be careful," she tells Hunter. "And call me when you get there or text—actually you don't have to, that sounds clingy and—"

Hunter steps forward and crashes his lips to hers. She melts into him, and opens her mouth. Their tongues clash as Hunter tips her back and deepens the kiss.

"I will call my wife as soon as I land."

"Okay," she says sheepishly and gives him one more quick peck for good measure.

He lifts his bag and tosses it over his shoulder.

She steps back to lean on her SUV and gives him a small wave. "I'll stay until I know you get boarded."

He walks backward, hating that he's already leaving her and they just got married. But he knew this would happen. He's had days to prepare for it, but it doesn't make it hurt any less. At least he can leave knowing Peter isn't a problem and there he's not leaving her to defend for herself.

When the automatic doors open behind him, he turns, fighting the urge to kiss her once more the entire way to the security station. Once he's sitting in the aisle seat with Zip between his legs, he texts her that he's on the plane and that he misses her already. He never knew his heart would be at war over two women. One just happened to be a three-year-old princess. If Hunter and Dahlia survived Peter and everything he tried to do to break them apart, Melanie will be no different.

Hunter only hopes she'll take the news of his marriage with grace and not make it all about her.

# Chapter Forty-Three

HUNTER'S UBER DROPS HIM off at his parents' just in time for dinner. The front door opens and Melanie smiles wide, holding Faith on her hip. "Daddy's home," Melanie coos to Faith, and she squeals at the sight of Hunter.

"Hey baby girl," he says, dropping his bag and taking her outstretched arms.

Hunter's mother steps up behind Melanie and places her hands on his ex's shoulders, guiding her back into the house. Lydia's gaze drops to the new wedding bed on his ring finger and she glances back inside, worry written all over her face.

"Hey Mom," he says, hoping for a '*congratulations*' or something.

"Did you have a nice flight?" she asks, ignoring the elephant in the room.

Hunter's demeanor grows cold, and he steps inside, not wasting his energy on a response. Jared beams at the sight of his son and pulls him into a side hug while tickling Faith's side. "Nice to have you back, son. How long are you staying?"

Melanie stops mid stride from carrying plates to the table and looks between Hunter and his dad.

"Did you close on a house down here?" she asks, and Hunter shifts his weight.

"We can talk about it after dinner," he states, putting his wedding band in his jeans pocket. He'd prefer to have the conversation after Faith is asleep, just in case things get ugly. He's not naïve. He saw how she responded to him coming back and saying *daddy's home* gave him an uneasy feeling. Telling himself she'll handle the news well doesn't mean she will.

Jared manages to keep conversation flowing throughout dinner as he talks about work at the construction company. They have some big job coming up that Hunter asks endless questions about to keep from talking about himself.

Afterward, Melanie helps Lydia in the kitchen while Hunter gives Faith a bath and settles her into her bed, reading her a bedtime story.

Her little eyes fall closed while she clings to a stuffed horse and Hunter kisses her forehead before exiting the bedroom, wishing this moment of complete bliss could last all night.

When he lifts his head, Melanie is leaning against the wall, her gaze skeptical as Hunter adjusts his cowboy hat.

"Do you wear that all the time?" she asks, pointing to his head.

Hunter sighs, remembering he's not in Wyoming anymore. "I do. Can we talk? Outside?"

He jerks his chin toward the back door, and Melanie follows him down the hall to the deck. The air is chilly, but not near as bad as Wyoming, with snow only days, maybe weeks away.

"Why did you need to bring me out here?" she asks when Hunter stops at the edge and doesn't turn to face her.

"We have some things we need to work out and discuss about Faith, and I prefer to not wake her up if we start yelling."

"Why would we yell?" she asks, totally clueless. "You're here. You came back, which means you choose to be here. We have time to figure this out between us and how to do what is best for Faith."

He nods and sucks on his teeth. "Exactly. What is best for Faith," he parrots. "I didn't come back because I chose Tennessee over Wyoming," he starts and her hope blooms because if he didn't come back for Tennessee, then he came back for another reason.

"Melanie," he says, and her lips part as he digs in his pocket. "While I was in Wyoming, I uh—" He slips the ring over his finger. "While I was there, I found Dahlia, and we got married Monday morning. I wanted to tell you in person."

Melanie's mouth opens and her hands fall to her sides. "What?" she snaps.

"I married Dahlia and I'm going back to Wyoming. I want to work something out, like a schedule for my time with Faith. Whether, that means I fly here or she can come stay with me—"

"Who the fuck do you think you are?! I'm not letting *my* daughter go anywhere with you!"

Hunter grits his teeth and his ears burn. "She's my daughter too and I have every right—"

"You have no rights! None! You weren't here. She doesn't even know you. This is to get back at me, isn't it? You only married her to hurt me. You don't love her—you—you can't!"

She backs up closer to the house and Hunter tries to keep his composure. "Melanie, I would never do anything to intentionally hurt you. I'm not that kind of man. You know that. And yes, I do love her. Otherwise, I wouldn't have done this. I'm sorry it's not what you wanted and I do have rights to my daughter. If we have to go to court, we will. I've told you that."

"So what? You and Dahlia can play family? No. Your money doesn't scare me. I'm not letting you take her anywhere, Hunter Haynes."

She reaches for the door and Hunter slams it closed. "I don't have to take her to Wyoming *tomorrow*. I just meant in the future. I am trying really hard to be reasonable here. I know I'll have to earn the right to take her. She barely knows me, but I'm willing to fly here and see her, spend time with her and work towards her coming to stay with me. I'm not going to just give up."

Her eyes mist over and her gaze narrows. She shoves him back and wrenches the door open. Lydia and Jared stand in the hallway, blocking Faith's door.

"Move," Melanie snaps.

"Honey, think about what you're doing. Just let her sleep then tomorrow we can all talk about this like adults."

Her wild eyes flit from Jared to Lydia, then she whirls on Hunter. "She better be here in the morning," she nearly growls.

"Where are you going?" Lydia asks, stepping forward, but Jared places a hand on her shoulder.

"Away from *him*," she seethes, pointing at Hunter.

The door slams and Lydia winces, clutching her throat. "What did you do?" she asks Hunter.

"Lydia," Jared warns. "You knew this was coming. We all did. Melanie is a grown woman, and you can't coddle her."

"I'm not coddling her, but if she leaves, where do you think Faith goes? Hm? She won't leave her here."

"It had to be done," Jared reminds her. "We aren't her parents. We're Hunter's."

"But I'm Faith's grandmother."

Hunter turns his back on his parents and steps out into the cool night air. There is only one person he wants to talk to right now, one person who he wishes more than anything was with him.

"Hey, Soldier," Dahlia answers, a smile in her tone.

"Gosh, it's good to hear your voice." Hunter leans on the porch railing and sighs.

"It went that good, huh?" Dahlia lays back on her bed in the apartment, her hand splayed out on the empty spot beside her.

"Well, the only way it could've gone worse is if she actually took Faith as she left."

Dahlia closes her eyes, her heart aching that she isn't there to help him through this. "I should be there," she mumbles. "I'm so sorry, Hunter."

"No, Little Flower. This was a long time coming. It's like we're in high school all over again with how she's acting. I hoped we could be adults. That doesn't seem to be an option. At least not right now."

"How are Lydia and Jared?" Dahlia asks.

Hunter glances through the back door at his parents hugging. "Mom is a nervous wreck about Faith and Dad is more tough love. Pretty much what I expected."

Dahlia pulls her cover up tighter and rolls to her side. "You say the words and I'll be on the next plane."

He smiles at the gesture and knows without a doubt she means it. "I'm okay. I promise. This is what I've been preparing for. We knew it was going to get ugly. I'm just glad Faith was asleep and didn't witness any of it. She didn't ask for this."

"Was she happy to see you?" Dahlia asks, changing the subject to happier things.

"She was. She reached for me and it nearly broke my heart. I swear that girl could ask me for anything and I'd do it. It's dangerous, the kind of power she has." He laughs and the weight that settled on his shoulders since he left the airport lessens with Dahlia's soft giggles.

"I can't wait to meet her. Maybe she can give me a few pointers."

"As if you need any help in that department."

Their laughter slowly fades into silence and Hunter rocks on his heels. "I miss you like crazy."

"I miss you too. Let me know if there is anything I can do."

He gazes out into the field at the rising moon. "I will. Sleep tight. I love you."

"I love you. Sweet dreams."

He stands in silence until the back door opens. "Hunter," Lydia says as she approaches.

"You couldn't even tell me congratulations? Or at least pretend you are happy for me?" he asks, his tone void of emotion.

"It's not that, honey. I just—I worry about Faith. Melanie has never been level-headed or reasonable."

Hunter scoffs and leans on the railing.

"I am happy for you, Hunter. I'm proud of the man you've grown to be. All every parent wants for their child is to find happiness and love and you've done that and more." Her hand tentatively lands on his back. "I'm worried about this next part, though."

He sighs and straightens, looking over at his mother. "I know. I am too. When she comes back, I'll try again."

She nods and pulls him in for a hug. "Do you have pictures of your wedding day? Your father and I would love to see them."

He smiles proudly and pulls out his phone. "Mom, she looked beautiful. I mean, she is always beautiful, but seeing her in her wedding dress and making a promise to be at my side for the rest of our lives was something else."

They walk back inside to meet Jared and sit around the kitchen table, flipping through each picture that was taken of his wedding day. His dad claps him on the back and tells him he couldn't be prouder.

"When will we get to see Dahlia again? She couldn't come back this time?" Lydia asks and Hunter is shocked the question came from her and not his dad.

"She had a wedding this weekend and with Melanie—we thought this first trip back would be best if it was just me."

Her eyes soften as she traces a picture on his phone. Hunter and Dahlia are dancing and she is mid-spin.

"Make sure she knows we are looking forward to her next visit. She's our daughter-in-law, after all."

"I will," Hunter says, thankful that at least something has gone right on this visit. Now if he can just get through to Melanie.

# Chapter Forty-Four

ZIP GROWLS SOFTLY ON the floor by the couch. Hunter rubs his eyes as he sits up in the chair where he fell asleep waiting for Melanie.

"Zip," he whispers, and the dog quiets but doesn't take his eyes off the front door.

The knob turns and Hunter jumps up, striding toward the door before it opens all the way.

"Jesus!" Melanie squawks, grabbing at her chest. "What are you doing?" she mumbles, shoving him to the side.

"What am I doing? Where the hell have you been? It's almost four in the morning." Hunter closes the door gently, careful to not wake his parents.

"Look, I'm really tired. Just leave me alone." Her words slur slightly and her eyes seem unfocused. Hunter grips her chin, getting a better look at her.

"You're fucking high?" He whisper-shouts and Melanie shoves his hand back.

"No, I'm not. Just move out of the way!" she shouts, and Hunter pinches the bridge of his nose.

"Don't lie to me, Melanie."

"I'm not lying! This is all your fault. I wasn't good enough—I'm never good enough. Not for you. Not for my parents. Not for my own daughter. You ruined everything!"

"Melanie," Lydia snaps from the end of the hallway. Her eyes hold a cold edge to them that Hunter thought was reserved for him. "Not like this. Think about Faith. You don't want to wake her up."

"It's all about Faith. Why doesn't anyone worry or care about me?!"

Hunter can't believe those words just came out of his ex-girlfriend's mouth. He starts to say something, but Lydia pushes her way past and wraps an arm around Melanie's shoulders. "We do care about you, sweetie. We love you and you know that. You're just tired. Go sleep it off and we'll talk in the morning."

Melanie starts to cry and Lydia guides her to the stairs for the guest room upstairs. Hunter stares after them in shock. Lydia seemed to know exactly what to say and how to handle his ex-girlfriend. Like she's done it before—enough times that her placating words of affirmation seemed repetitive.

When Lydia comes back down, Hunter stands with his arms crossed, waiting for an explanation. His mother can't bring herself to meet his gaze. She seems smaller, more tired than he's ever seen her.

"Mom," he says, needing to know exactly what is happening here. "How long?"

Lydia sighs, knowing she can't keep this a secret.

"She doesn't do it often. Only when she gets really upset or she loses a job."

"How long?" Hunter insists.

"After she had Faith. We tried to take her to the doctor, but she refused. Said she had it under control and just needed to take the edge off. Since you were here, she has gotten better. I thought she was finally getting her feet back under her."

"She's a drug addict," he states, revulsion rolling through him.

Lydia shakes her head. "No. She isn't always like this and she isn't like those others you see on the news."

"Mom," Hunter says, shaking his head. "Just because she's not tweaking, doesn't make it any less true. Does she get in the car with Faith like that?"

"No! Of course not!" Lydia scoffs. "Do you really think I'd let that happen? That's why she lives here. We can watch over Faith this way. I'm doing what is best for that little girl and nothing more."

"What would be best for Faith is having a sober mother who has her best interest at heart." Hunter paces a small line up and down the hallway. "Add this to the list of things you've kept from me. This changes everything," he grits out, running his hand through his hair.

"What do you mean?" Lydia asks.

"I can't in good conscience leave Faith here. Not when Melanie goes out and gets high when life is too much."

His mother's features fall. "You'd take her back to Wyoming?"

"I'll do what is best for Faith."

With that, he goes back to the living area, leaving his mother alone to process what he means. He was going to be cordial with Melanie, create a schedule of when he could visit, ease her into the idea of Faith coming to stay with him on certain holidays. But tonight, he saw the real her and she needs help. More than his parents can give her.

***

"Okay. Yes, yes, whatever you need to do. You know I'm on your side...yeah you, too." Dahlia hangs up, and Carly notes her worried expression.

"Who was that?" her best friend asks.

"Hunter—Melanie—she's uh, she came home last night high. Apparently, it's one more thing his parents have been keeping from him. He wants to file for emergency custody of Faith."

Carly gasps and moves around the counter until she's standing in front of Dahlia. "What does that mean? Is she coming here to live?"

Dahlia freezes at Carly's question. Obviously, she knew Hunter was a dad, but she never viewed herself as the mother figure. Those two aspects of his life are separate, and she still hasn't met Faith. But if he gets custody and brings her here...where will they live? They don't have anything in place to take care of a toddler. Not to mention Dahlia has no idea what she's doing and how to take care of a human.

"I—I don't know. I don't know what any of this means."

"You need to go. Be there for him—for your husband. I can take care of the Mitchells. It's nothing too crazy."

Dahlia stares at the open binder on her desk and the shop full of customers. "Okay—call the girls. Don't worry about payroll. I'll take care of it when I get back. I'll have my laptop and my phone if you need me."

"Don't worry about anything. Just go."

Dahlia nods, snatching her keys and phone, and rushes upstairs to pack a quick bag. She doesn't know anything about court or emergency custody, but Hunter had already called the lawyer's office this morning and seems to have a firm grasp on everything that will take place over the next 48 to 72 hours. Lydia, with Jared's encouragement, agreed to give a statement about what she has witnessed the past three years.

This is not the phone call Dahlia expected this morning, but she's glad Hunter was honest with her. Carly was right. She needs to be with him during this. She's his support, his anchor, and she never should have let him make this trip alone.

Once she's in her car, Dahlia calls her mom to let her know what is going on.

"Hey, honey! How are you? How's Hunter?" Bonnie answers.

"Hey. I'm actually going to the airport to fly to Tennessee. He called, and he's having to file for emergency custody of Faith and—I should be there with him."

"Emergency custody? What happened?"

"Faith's mother showed up early this morning on drugs of some kind. He can't leave her there, not knowing what Melanie is capable of."

Bonnie sighs. "You two can't catch a break."

Dahlia chokes out a laugh.

"Honey, if you need me or your father, you call. I don't know what we can do, but we'll fly down there if you need us to."

"You've never been on a plane," Dahlia teases, but she appreciates her mother more than she will ever know.

"For you, I'd travel across the world. I'd do it for any of you."

"I love you," Dahlia tells her. "You really are the best."

"I love you too, sweetie. Be careful and let us know when you make it."

Dahlia hangs up and settles in for the hour-long drive to the airport. She debates calling Hunter, but he has enough on his plate right now.

She'll show up and be whatever kind of support he needs. All the while, she tries to be pleasant with Lydia. It's like as soon as she and Hunter make progress, another secret pops up.

Hunter said Lydia ensured Faith was never with Melanie when she was like this, but that doesn't make it okay. One, Lydia should have told him as soon as he called he had a kid, and two, she should've voiced her concerns about Melanie's habits.

Dahlia sighs and turns up the radio. There isn't any point in getting caught up in how any of this should have been handled. She just needs to get there as soon as possible and see her soldier.

# Chapter Forty-Five

HUNTER SITS ON THE floor with Faith, his prosthetic leg stretched out in front of him. His daughter keeps making him dishes of food from her kitchen and bringing over for him to eat and asking if it's good.

He pretends to eat every bite, and she giggles with delight before going to make more. Something so simple can bring so much happiness.

Jared sits on the couch while Lydia fixes dinner in the kitchen. Nobody has talked about Hunter's trip to the lawyer's office first thing this morning. The pain was clear on his mother's face, but ultimately, she knows her son is right and Faith comes first. Hunter checks his phone for the time. It's nearly seven and Melanie still hasn't come downstairs.

"How long does she usually stay asleep?" he asks, keeping his features excited for Faith's benefit.

"Most of the day," Jared admits. "Are you going to tell her?"

Hunter nods. "She deserves to know. She's Faith's mother and I'm not keeping secrets. When she gets clean, then we'll reevaluate. I'm not trying to keep Faith from her mother," he says softly. He doesn't need Faith repeating anything.

Jared rubs his hands on his pants and Zip jumps and faces the stairs.

Melanie trudges down the stairs, her makeup smudged around her eyes and hair matted in a bun on top of her head. Hunter stands, and Faith glances at her mom, then goes back to playing with her toys.

"Melanie," Hunter starts. She waves him off and shuts her bedroom door behind her.

Jared stands, "Hey bug, you want to go for a ride with Papa?" he asks Faith. Her eyes light up.

"Ice cream?" she asks and Jared nods.

"Let's get Mamaw and we'll go."

Hunter waits for the front door to close and then knocks on Melanie's door until it cracks open and her narrow slits for eyes find him.

"What?"

"We need to talk," he says.

"No. You talked last night. I'm going to sleep."

Hunter shoves her door open and closes it behind them. "You've been sleeping all day. How long have you been using?"

She snorts and sits down on her bed. "Like you care."

"I care about Faith. And—" He takes a steadying breath. "Until you go to rehab and get the help you need, you won't be alone with her."

"Who do you think you are?! She's my daughter! A judge will never sign off on this. You can't just keep me from her!" She shoves past Hunter and races through the house, her frantic screams reaching new heights with each passing second.

"Faith?! Where is she? What did you do?!" She whirls on Hunter and slaps him across the face.

Zip growls, but Hunter tells him to sit and he listens.

"You need help," he tells Melanie as gently as possible. "This isn't you. Just let us help get you into a place and get you better."

Melanie's face turns red, and she throws punch after punch at Hunter. He grabs her wrists and holds her against him.

"I hate you! You should have never come back here. Just leave! Nobody wants you!"

Hunter takes every verbal jab and doesn't retaliate. "Melanie, I'm trying to help you."

She spins out of his grip and rushes past him. "No! You're just trying to help yourself."

"Wait!" Hunter shouts as she storms out the door. He races after her, but he isn't fast enough. Her tires squeal out of the subdivision.

"Fuck!" he shouts, pulling out his phone to call his parents.

"Hunter?" Lydia answers and Faith giggles in the background.

"She left."

"What do you mean, left?"

"I mean, she just drove off and I don't have a way to go after her."

Lydia hesitates before saying, "You should call dispatch. She isn't safe to be out driving. Someone could get seriously hurt."

Hunter paces the driveway and whistles for Zip, who is still sitting where he was told. "Okay. I'll call Brody. He works for the police department now."

"Okay. Keep us posted. We'll take our time coming back home."

Hunter quickly pulls up the number for Brody. They played football together in high school. "Johnson," he answers.

"Brody, it's Hunter. Look, Melanie just left and she's not okay, man. I'm worried she or someone else is going to get hurt."

"What do you mean, not okay?" he asks.

"I found out she has been on drugs and filed for emergency custody this morning. She totally flipped and left. She shouldn't be driving, but I don't have a way to go looking for her."

"Describe her car to me and we'll put a notice out for it. Hunter, she'll face jail time if she gets arrested and tests positive for drugs."

Hunter stares out the last place he saw her tail lights. "I know."

"I'll be there in a minute to pick you up."

***

Dahlia sits in the back of the Uber, twirling her wedding ring and engagement ring around her finger. She already called her parents and by the driver's GPS, she is about fifteen minutes away from Hunter's parents' house. She's excited to see her soldier but nervous about what is waiting for her.

Perhaps surprising Hunter in this situation was a bad idea. What if she's entering a war zone, and she becomes collateral damage? Dahlia pulls her phone from her purse and pulls up his messages.

**Can you talk?**

She holds her phone as bubbles appear and disappear. Waiting, she chews on her cheek and checks the GPS again. She jumps as her driver lies on his horn and headlights shine directly at them. Dahlia doesn't have time to blink before metal crunches against metal. The seat belt digs into her collarbone and her head slams into the backseat window.

Car horns blare and a disinfectant smell mixed with charred rubber burns her nose. The world spins as she lifts her head and fumbles for her car door. It's locked and won't open. "Hey," she tries to say and coughs through the words. She can't see the driver around the triggered airbags, and she searches for her phone.

It lights up from the floorboard with Hunter's name across the screen, but she can't reach it with the tight seat belt. She pushes on the button, but it won't release.

She's stuck, pinned in place, and her heart races with each passing second.

"Somebody!" she screams.

Her shoulder aches from shoving against the car door and her fingertips feel bruised from trying to claw the seat belt free.

She can't get out. All her fears of dying, stuck and alone, are rushing to the surface. She tries to focus on something like Hunter has her do, but it's useless. The car horns are too loud and the belt is too tight across her body.

Forcing herself to get some kind of control, she clutches the woven belt and takes a deep, steadying breath. She's on her own and she has to get it together. Panicking won't get her out of the car. It won't save her. Her phone lights up with a missed call and her sobs quiet down enough so she can talk.

"Call 911," she orders her phone.

"Calling emergency services," it responds and rings.

"911, what's your emergency?"

"Hello! Yes, there was an accident. I can't get out and I can't see the driver. I'm in an Uber close to 2 Cedar Pine Lane. We need an ambulance."

The dispatcher types on her end. "What is your name, ma'am?"

"Dahlia Brooks—no Haynes. I just got married on Monday." Her body trembles and she taps her fingers one at a time to focus on the phone call and not her surroundings.

"Okay, I'm going to keep you on the phone until help gets there. Okay? Are you hurt at all?"

Dahlia runs through her list of injuries. Aside from the path of the seat belt and her neck being sore, she feels fine. "I'm shaking," she tells dispatch, her throat tightens and eyes burn.

"You're probably going into shock. I'm going to stay right here and talk to you. Why were you in Tennessee? Visiting family?"

"I was—surprising my husband," she stammers. "He came to visit his parents, and I flew down today."

"What's his name?"

"Hunter Haynes." Dahlia closes her eyes and focuses on her soldier's features.

The dispatch grows quiet and types some more. "Our units are almost there, Dahlia."

"I can hear the sirens," she says. They're faint in the distance and growing closer.

"That's good. Is the driver still unresponsive?"

"Yes."

Red and blue lights flash outside the car and Dahlia chokes out a sob of relief.

***

Hunter stares out the windshield, his hand braced on the dashboard as Brody turns on his lights and siren.

*Dahlia Haynes.*

That's the name that came across the radio scanner when Brody was getting details of the car crash.

It's a coincidence. It can't be his little flower. It can't.

"Go faster," he begs Brody, his body trembling with horrific images of what they will find. They aren't far from the scene. Dispatch said it was close to his parents' house. They had his parent's address—which means Dahlia is here.

But no. He can't believe that because if that's true, then she was just in a wreck and is hurt.

"Please, no. We just—this can't be fucking happening," Hunter screams and Brody gives him a sympathetic glance.

Red tail lights and headlights shine in the distance and Hunter's heart plummets.

"You need to stay in the car until we block off the scene."

Hunter recognizes the bumper of Melanie's car and everything Brody said goes out the window. Hunter rips open his door and his boots hit the pavement.

"Dahlia!" he shouts, but it's muffled by the car horns blaring.

"Sir, you can't be here—" an officer grabs at his arm, but Hunter shoves them off.

He rushes past Melanie's car and peers into the driver's side of the Uber. The driver is slumped over the steering wheel and unconscious. He spots wild familiar curls in the back seat and he opens his mouth, but no sound comes out.

It's her.

She's here, and she's stuck in his fucking car.

Dahlia slams her head back when the seat belt won't give. A figure walks around the outside of the car and she shouts, "I'm back here!"

Someone knocks on her window and she lets loose the sob she's been holding back at the sight of Hunter's wide eyes and pale skin.

He doesn't trust his eyes at first. It's Dahlia. His fucking wife. But how? Why?

She jerks on the handle, but it's no use. "It's stuck!"

"Hang on. We're going to get you out." Hunter straightens and shouts over the top of the car. Dahlia pulls on the seat belt, desperate to get free. He steps back and she places her hands on the window, hating that distance between them.

A man in a firefighter hat and jacket steps between them. "Cover your eyes and look that way!" he orders and points across the back seat. Dahlia nods and raises her arms and turns her head. Glass shatters from the front passenger door and the shouts grow louder. The lock disengages at her door and Hunter is there, ripping it open.

"Dahlia!" He cups her face and tears fill his eyes. "I'm so sorry, baby. You're okay...you're okay," he repeats, and Dahlia rests her head in her hands.

"Sir, we need you to move," a firefighter guides him back, and an officer takes Hunter to the side.

"Hunter," Brody says, forcing his attention away from Dahlia. "It's Melanie—she's—" Hunter jerks his attention to the other car in the collision and Zip presses against his leg.

"No," Hunter flinches and spots the white sheet covering a person on a stretcher. "No!" he says louder, his body trembling as his two worlds collide. Brody grabs his arm and holds him back as he wars with himself. He's the reason Melanie was driving in a blind rage. He's the reason Dahlia was in Tennessee.

They pull his little flower out of the backseat and place her on a stretcher, securing her neck and head in a brace. Hunter's hands shake as he rushes to her side while they wheel her to the ambulance.

"I'll be right behind you, Little Flower. I'm so, so sorry."

Dahlia gives him a soft smile and winces as the stretched bumps into the back of the ambulance. "It's not your fault. I'm fine, just bruised and sore. I'll be okay." She takes his hand and squeezes it.

*But it is my fault*, Hunter thinks.

He's forced to let go as she's loaded into the ambulance and the doors close.

Jogging toward Brody's car, he falters as he comes upon Melanie's mangled vehicle and busted windshield. Brody steps up beside him. "She wasn't wearing a seat belt. Went through the windshield. It was almost instant."

Hunter swallows the lump in his throat and runs a hand over his mouth. "I can't—I have to go. My wife—" he watches as the ambulance takes the turn toward the hospital and goes out of sight.

Brody clasps his shoulder. "Come on. I'm driving you."

Hunter nods and he and Zip get into the back of the police cruiser. Brody turns on his flashers and Hunter's legs shake as he tries to process everything that just happened.

"Hunter, your phone," Brody states, knocking on the divider glass. Hunter snaps out of his spiral to realize his phone is ringing.

Taking a deep breath, he prepares to answer and tell his parents that Faith's mother is never coming back.

# Chapter Forty-Six

HUNTER AND ZIP LIFT their heads every time someone walks past the waiting room at the hospital. Flashes of the wreck fight for Hunter's attention.

Dahlia being stuck in the back seat, her face streaked with tears and eyes wide as she fought with the door handle and seat belt. He couldn't get to her. He was useless and couldn't get her out. He knows she has a fear of being stuck and he couldn't do a damn thing to help her.

His leg shakes as he rubs his hands together.

His heart pounds in his chest and he knows he's teetering on the edge of a panic attack.

Long inhale, slow exhale.

Again.

Zip sits and places his chin on Hunter's knee, nuzzling his hands to draw his attention to something else.

Melanie's dead.

He grew up with her. She was his first girlfriend, the person who wrote to him the entire time he was in the army. He may not be in love with her, but the fact that she's just gone doesn't seem real.

None of this seems real. It's a fucking nightmare. He clings to the fact that Dahlia looked fine. She said she was fine before getting into the ambulance. That's the only thing holding him together right now.

Footsteps approach, and Hunter glances up at his father, rushing into the waiting room. He stops when he spots his son.

"Hunter," he says softly, not knowing what else to say.

Hunter presses the heels of his hands into his eyes and chokes out a dry sob. "Hey," he says around the lump in his throat. "Where's Faith?"

Jared sits beside him and places a hand on his curved back. "She's at home with Mom."

"Good. That's good. I don't really want her to see me like this." His eyes burn with tears and he leans back, staring at the light on the ceiling until he can't see anything but white.

"You can't blame yourself—"

Hunter laughs and pushes to his feet. "No—no, you're right. I just let her leave the house, knowing she wasn't sober, and she crashed into my wife. Melanie's dead, Dad. Dahlia is in the hospital and I'm the connecting thread. Melanie was on the road because of me. Dahlia was here *because of me*. This is all my fault."

"No," Jared says sternly. "Melanie made her choices. You were right to take a stand for your daughter. You didn't force her to take the keys and drive that car. You didn't force Dahlia to buy a plane ticket and come down here. Everyone makes their own choices. *None* of this is your fault, son. And I'm sure Dahlia would be pissed if she heard you talking like this."

Hunter rolls his lips between his teeth and puts his hands behind his head. "How do I tell my little girl that her mommy is never coming back?"

His voice cracks and he braces himself on his knees. Gritting his teeth, he tries to keep himself from falling apart.

Jared wraps his arms around his son and holds him as Hunter shakes. "This isn't how it was supposed to go. None of this was supposed to happen."

"I know. I'm so sorry, son."

Hunter pushes out of his dad's embrace and walks to the edge of the waiting room. "It's not fair. To Dahlia, to Melanie, to Faith. This is how Dahlia felt when I was in the hospital. We didn't tell you or mom, of course. I didn't want to worry you guys."

Jared bristles. "Your arm?"

Hunter nods. "Her uh—her ex ran me down on my motorcycle. Totaled it. We didn't know it was him until the night he attacked her—my first night back in Wyoming. When is it too much, Dad? Loving someone is supposed to be easy, but I feel like I'm a fucking punching bag. I'm just dragging Dahlia down into the hell I've been trying to escape all these years."

"Nobody said love is easy. But when you find your person, you'll go through hell for them."

Hunter scoffs. "Well, I'm there. I don't see how I could go any lower."

Jared shoves his hands in his pockets and stands on the opposite wall. "You could if you didn't have Dahlia. When you got hurt because of her ex, did you blame her? I mean, she was the reason it all happened, right? If there was no Dahlia, you wouldn't have met the ex. It only makes sense that she's to blame for your accident."

"Hell no, she isn't. She had nothing to do with Peter. He was a fucking maniac."

Jared gives his son a knowing look.

Hunter rolls his eyes. "It's not the same—"

"It absolutely is. I guarantee she came here after you called her to fill her in. She wanted to be with you—to support you and be with her husband. She loves you and you love her. That's the only thing you need to cling to right now. Not blame or guilt because that is a useless emotion that won't help you through this next transition."

Hunter exhales loudly and nods.

"Mr. Haynes?" The nurse asks as he steps around the corner. "Your wife is settled into her room if you want to follow me."

Hunter glances back at his dad and Jared nods. "I'm going to find us some coffee and I'll meet you there."

Hunter greets the smiling nurse and Zip walks at his side, his toenails tapping on the linoleum flooring.

Dahlia sits in her bed, flipping through the horrible television channels, anxiously waiting for Hunter to arrive. He was distraught when they drove her away and she wanted more than anything to reassure him she was okay, but she knows logically he needs to see it for himself.

When her door creaks open, she pushes up in the bed, wincing at the tenderness around her collarbone and ribs. The doctor told her if she hadn't been wearing her seat belt, it could've been worse.

Zip's white snout comes into the room first, and Dahlia smiles at the excited dog as he comes over to the side of her bed.

"Hey buddy," she coos. "I'm okay. Just a little sore." She rubs down his head and Hunter's boots step closer.

He looks ten years older, and Dahlia holds her hands out to him. "Hey, Soldier."

Dropping to his knees, Hunter presses his head against her stomach and wraps his arms around her back. "I'm so sorry."

She threads her fingers through his hair. Her chest tightens at the sight of her cowboy falling apart on her lap. "Hunter, I'm fine. You have nothing to be sorry about. It's not like you were driving."

He lifts his head and something in his blue gaze tells her there is more than what she knows.

"You didn't hit the car—did you? Are you okay?" She studies his features for any sign of injuries or bruising. Zip appears fine too.

"No. No, it wasn't me—it—" He takes her hands in his and brushes his thumbs along her soft skin. "It was Melanie and she—" his voice breaks and Dahlia places a hand over her chest.

"I overheard the staff saying the other driver didn't make it. It was Melanie?"

Hunter nods.

"Oh, Hunter...I'm so sorry. What—what happened? Where's Faith? Is she okay? Was she with her?"

"No. Faith was with my parents. I tried to talk to Melanie, tried to get her help, and she snapped. I didn't recognize her. Then she took off, and I wasn't fast enough to catch her. Brody called me and said dispatch was talking to my wife that had been in a car accident. It didn't make sense because you weren't in Tennessee, but then I found you in the backseat and I couldn't get to you—I couldn't get you out."

"I wanted to be here for you. I left this morning after your call. I didn't want to call and you tell me not to come."

Hunter kisses her hands and shakes his head. "I'd never tell you not to come to me, Little Flower. I want you—I need you. Always."

"Come here," she urges, pulling him up off his knees. She slides to the side of the bed and pats an empty space for him to join. Zip jumps up before Hunter has a chance to move and makes himself comfortable beside Dahlia.

"I'll take the chair," Hunter says, pointing to the other side of the bed.

Dahlia smiles and runs her hand down Zip's fur.

"Have you gotten the results of your scans yet?" Hunter asks.

"No, but the doctor seems pretty positive it was just bruising and that I'll be tender for a week or two. They can't find my phone. It's probably still in the back of the Uber car."

"I'm not worried about your phone, Dahlia."

"I feel fine, just tired." She yawns as if to prove her point.

Hunter's phone rings and he answers. "Yeah, we're in room 267."

"Who was that?" Dahlia asks when he hangs up.

"Dad's here. He was waiting with me and is bringing coffee. He was worried about you."

"I'm worried about *you*," she says, angling herself to face Hunter. "What can I do?"

He leans his elbows on her bed. "Being here. Loving me. Choosing me. That's all I need. I wouldn't complain if you got some rest, too."

Dahlia smiles and lays back on the bed, taking Hunter's hand. "I can do that. But first, I need to call my parents and convince them not to fly down here."

Hunter smiles and hands her his phone. "I don't envy you."

# Chapter Forty-Seven

A PARENT'S JOB IS to ensure their children can be independent and be prepared to live without them. Parents never plan to be the ones to live without their children.

Hunter holds his hand out for Dahlia as he steps out of his rental truck at the cemetery. His lips set into a tense line and he avoids eye contact as he and Dahlia walk toward his parents. Faith reaches for him immediately as he approaches and he gathers her in his arms. She didn't understand when Hunter sat her down to explain that her mommy wasn't coming home. It breaks his heart each time she asks where her mommy is and Hunter explains again that she isn't coming.

Faith smiles over at Dahlia and then buries her face in Hunter's chest.

Dahlia scans the crowd and spots a woman with similar features as Melanie. The woman's gaze narrows at Hunter and his parents, then back at the casket. Her hair is pulled back tight, and her expression reminds Dahlia of beady-eyed shrews. Melanie's brother that she remembers from the lake and an older man stands beside her.

"Is that—?" Dahlia asks quietly.

Hunter nods, not giving them even a small glance. He took it upon himself to call them with the news. Melanie's mother hung up without saying anything. She didn't ask about her granddaughter or even thank Hunter for calling.

Dahlia wraps an arm around Hunter as more people approach and the pastor speaks about a life lost too soon. Lydia wipes her eyes as the casket lowers and Hunter's haunted gaze stays locked on the ground.

No matter how many times Dahlia tells him it wasn't his fault, he still feels responsible. He was the last person to see Melanie alive, and they fought. Maybe if he tried a different approach or was smart enough to take the keys first before talking—

Dahlia runs a hand up and down his spine and he blinks.

"It's over," she whispers. Faith's head rests on his shoulder in a blissful sleep.

He dips his chin and steps back from the grave as they fill it in. Lydia chokes out a sob as Jared leads her away and Dahlia places a hand on her arm and offers a soft smile. Her eyes widen at Dahlia, and she places her hand atop of her daughter-in-law's.

"I'm very sorry," Dahlia says, and Lydia tilts her head to the side and nods with a trembling expression.

"Me too," she responds, and somehow Dahlia knows she's apologizing for every decision that led to this spot.

"You!" A venomous voice cuts through the moment, and Dahlia whirls to stand in front of Hunter and Faith.

"Not here. It's your daughter's funeral for Christ's sake," Lydia hisses at Melanie's mother.

"She's dead because of you and you bunch of rednecks! She graduated from college, had a great job, and after one night with you, it all went down the drain. You should've never come home from the war."

Lydia gasps, and Dahlia steps forward, forcing the woman back. "It's no one's fault, but if you want to place blame, try looking in a mirror. Where were you when your daughter needed you most? Perhaps if you didn't kick her out, she wouldn't have felt so alone and went down the dark path to begin with. But that reality hurts too much for you to grasp." She eyes the woman up and down. "Don't *ever* speak to my husband again."

"This isn't your place—"

Dahlia cuts her off. "My place is with my husband and his daughter—with this family. And I'll defend them during their grief because that's what you do for those you love. You don't abandon them because they're inconvenient."

"Carol," Melanie's father says, reaching for his wife's arm. Melanie's brother drops his gaze.

"No! They stole our little girl from us. They corrupted her and now she's gone. She's dead, Benjamin. My daughter, my life and the reason for breathing is dead and they're just going to stand here and act like they're the ones grieving."

"We're sorry for *your* loss," Dahlia seethes and ushers Hunter and his parents past.

Hunter won't let himself form the words he wants to spew at Melanie's parents. He won't stoop to their level, not here.

Not today.

He puts his sleeping daughter in the car seat with Lydia and Jared and straps her in. "Are you coming to the reception?" Lydia asks.

Hunter closes Faith's door and his body feels like it's been geared up for a fight since he woke up. He clutches Dahlia's hand and pulls her close.

The idea of more people, crowds, and stares makes his skin crawl, and he shifts on his feet.

"I can't. I'm sorry—I just—"

Jared places a hand on his shoulder. "It's okay, son. We understand."

Those two words are some he never thought he would hear from his parents.

*We understand.*

"Thanks, Dad."

He leads Dahlia to his truck and Zip jumps into the back seat. It isn't until all the chatter and noise dies from outside that Hunter shows how badly his hands shake and he struggles to breathe.

"Can I drive?" Dahlia asks, her voice a cheery disposition compared to what is going on around them.

Hunter rolls his eyes and glares at her. "I know what you're doing."

She places her hands in her lap and shrugs. "I'm not doing anything. I simply asked a question."

"I'm fine, Little Flower. Just—it's a lot and then Carol and her bitchiness. I so wanted to lay into her, but then I thought of Faith and how I don't want to be that man for her to look up to."

Dahlia sighs and stares out the windshield at the emptying cemetery. "They didn't even ask about her—or want to see her," she scoffs. "I can't wrap my head around that."

"You'll make yourself crazy trying." He snorts and starts the truck. "I know you didn't sign up for this—for Faith. If—"

"I'm going to stop you right there, Soldier. If you're about to give me an out or whatever, don't. I married you for highs and lows, and this is just another trial for us to face. Together. Okay? So that is what we'll do. You aren't getting rid of me and I'm kind of fond of you, so I'll keep you, too."

Hunter scoffs. "Kind of fond of me?"

"Yup."

He laughs, and it sounds foreign to his ears. Guilt hits him at the fact he's laughing at all under the circumstances.

"I have to talk to my parents still," he mumbles. "It's going to suck."

Dahlia threads her fingers with his.

"Together. I'm here for whatever you need."

Hunter takes in a deep breath and brings her hand to his lips. "Right now, I just need you and some place quiet."

He drives down the winding Tennessee roads, lost in the music and pressure of Dahlia's hand in his. When they reach the lake, Hunter doesn't get out of the truck. He stares at the placid water surrounded by turning leaves.

"You like it here, don't you? At this spot—I mean."

Hunter sighs and runs his finger along his lips. "I do have some good memories here." Her cheeks flush and he chuckles. "I've always come here when everything feels like too much. The day I joined the army, I drove here and sat for three hours before going home to tell my parents."

"I used to have a place like that. Back when my parents still owned the ranch. Now I guess it's the back room of my shop after everyone has gone home for today."

"Wyoming feels like that to me. I'm drowning here. I miss our home." He runs his fingers along the steering wheel and sits in the silence.

Dahlia leans across the center console and lays her head on his arm. She misses Wyoming too, her parents, friends, and business. What will their life look like when they go back?

She'll never be the same after Peter and he'll never be the same after Melanie. But they'll be together and they're strong enough to withstand the trials of time.

"You're really good with her, you know."

Hunter arches a brow in question.

"Faith. You make a great dad, Hunter."

He sighs. "She went from having no dad to both parents and now no mom. And she's only three. None of that is fair."

"You'll raise her to be strong and kind. To stand up for herself when needed and to concede when the time calls for it. You'll make sure she has every opportunity in life and will be there supporting her every step of the way."

"We'll be there," he corrects. "I'm bringing her to Wyoming. I'm not staying here. This isn't the life I want for her, haunted by memories and family who don't want her. I just have to find a way to tell my parents. Maybe we'll get her some chickens...and a horse."

Dahlia stiffens at the picture of her future. She doesn't know the first thing about being a mom. Loving Hunter and being with him is one thing—but filling the shoes of a parental figure? Is there a book she can read for that?

"We should probably head back." Hunter puts the truck in reverse and Dahlia settles back into her seat.

Her stomach twists with anxiety and terror. She had her life all planned out until Hunter arrived. So, she found a way to make it fit because she didn't see a future where he didn't exist.

Now her plans involve a smiling blonde haired, blue-eyed toddler and nothing makes sense. Who will take care of Faith while she's working? Who will take care of the chickens? She hates chickens! And Hunter didn't want to live in the main cabin because he wasn't comfortable? Is he suddenly over that feeling or will he bottle it up until he explodes?

"You're spiraling," Hunter states evenly, and Dahlia jumps.

"Just tired," she lies.

She needs her mom. She'll know what to do and hopefully say just the right thing for all of this to make sense.

# Chapter Forty-Eight

HUNTER SITS ACROSS FROM his parents in the living area. Jared rubs his hand along Lydia's thigh with sad eyes, but they're nothing compared to the tears welling in Lydia's.

"All the way to Wyoming?" she asks, her voice cracking on the words.

"It's where I live and Dahlia," Hunter responds. "You guys can come visit, of course. But it's what is best for everyone, including Faith. You are grandparents and you should get to act like it. This is a good thing."

"Where's mommy?" Faith asks, and Lydia excuses herself from the room.

"Hey, Pumpkin," Hunter says as he slides off the couch. "What do you think about going on a trip to see Daddy's house with Dahlia?"

"Will mommy be there?"

Hunter looks over his shoulder at Dahlia. "Uh, no. But Zip will be and Daddy is going too."

She thinks over it for a minute while pouring some imaginary tea into her cup. "I guess so."

Hunter smiles and Dahlia's palms sweat.

"I'm going to let mom know how I'm doing. She's probably worried sick." Hunter's brows furrow at the tone of her voice, but doesn't stop her as she leaves.

Dahlia sits on the guest bed upstairs with her phone up to her ear.

"Dahlia, honey. Are you okay? Any pain?"

She immediately relaxes at hearing her mom's voice. "I'm a little sore, but not bad. I actually have a question. How did you know how to be a mom? Like, how did you know what to do or what to say?"

Bonnie chuckles. "Well, honey, there isn't exactly a book to teach you those things. You just try your best each day and hope you don't screw up your kid. Why? What's going on? Are you—"

Her mom inhales deeply and Dahlia panics. "No! No, no, no. Not that!"

"Well, what do you expect me to think when you ask about being a mom?"

Dahlia sighs. "It's Hunter. Faith is coming to Wyoming with us, and I don't know what to even say to her. I don't know how to be a mom."

Bonnie laughs and Dahlia groans. "Mom! This isn't funny. I'm literally freaking out."

"Honey, you'll be fine. Kids love you. Your little cousins love you. But I am slightly concerned about your living situation."

Dahlia plops back on the bed. "Hunter says we're moving into the main cabin."

"Well, you'll need a toddler bed for her. Are ya'll driving or flying back? You'll need toys and foods she likes. How is she on clothes? Do you know what size? And shoes?"

Dahlia's head spins and she places a hand over her eyes. "You're not helping."

"Oh, hush it. You and Hunter have got this, Dahlia. That man loves you and you love him. Everything else will fall into place. Don't worry about the cabin. Carly and I will have that taken care of."

Dahlia pops up off the bed. "What does that mean? Mom?"

"Nothing for you to worry about, dear. Just let me know when you're planning the trip back. I love you, my sweet girl."

"I love you too."

Tossing her phone to the bed, she paces the floor. That call was supposed to calm her nerves, not give her a whole list of things to be worried about. Hunter pushes open the door and glances from the bed, then the other side of the room where Dahlia is standing.

"You bite your nails?" he asks.

She immediately drops her hand. That's a habit she broke years ago. "No."

He steps fully into the room and crosses his arms. "Looked like it to me."

"You're imagining things."

"Am I?" he asks and walks closer to her. "What's going on, Little Flower?"

She huffs. "I don't know how to be a mom. And when I called my mom for advice, she basically said neither does anyone else and I'll be fine. Which was the most unhelpful thing ever! And she gave me a long list of things we need for the house which we don't have and—"

Hunter grabs her shoulders and presses his lips to hers, cutting off her words. When he finally pulls back, he wears a crooked grin. "Have you been holding all of that in since the lake?"

"No," she grumbles.

"Dahlia, this doesn't work unless we communicate and talk. Don't you think I'm terrified? I've been a dad for what? Two, three months? I don't know what the hell I'm doing either."

Dahlia drops her forehead to his chest. "What if I screw her up or if she hates me?"

Hunter traces her spine with his fingers. "She'll hate us both when she's a teenager, if that makes you feel better."

Dahlia groans and tries to push Hunter back, but he takes her hands and pulls her back.

"Together, remember?"

"Together," she says, and he brushes his lips across hers.

"I can't wait to have you back home on the ranch."

She relents and wraps her arms around his neck. "Me either. But I have to warn you, Mom may have made some changes to your cabin by the time we get back."

***

HUNTER WRESTLING FAITH'S CAR seat into Dahlia's SUV nearly had her in tears. Watching the man do it without cursing around his daughter was the tipping point. Her stomach hurts from laughing so much and Hunter's features grow redder with the longer she laughs sitting in the passenger seat.

"Ha-ha, you've had your fun." He grimaces.

"I really haven't."

"You're a piece of magical unicorns!" Faith shouts from the backseat and Dahlia laughs so hard she can't breathe.

"Do I need to drive or do you think you can hold it together until we get there?" Hunter deadpans.

"Magical unicorns," Dahlia repeats, but it sounds more like wheezing air than actual words.

"It's better than what I wanted to say. Seriously, who designed those things? We are never taking it out—ever."

Faith giggles and kicks her feet.

"At least she's in a better mood than the plane ride," Hunter adds, twisting to look at his smiling daughter.

"Yeah." Through her rear-view mirror, Faith sticks her tongue out at Hunter. Zip lays across the back seat beside her like he is bothered in the slightest by the noise.

"Dahlia? Why are you going so slow?" Hunter asks, leaning across the console to view the speedometer.

"I'm not."

"You're doing like sixty-five...on the interstate."

She scoffs. "Well, I have a child on board. So, I'm being cautious."

Hunter takes her hand in his and intertwine his fingers. "You're going to be a great mom." He kisses her hand and leans back against his seat, anxious to get home.

"I have to pee!" Faith shouts, and Dahlia and Hunter groan.

"Between your speed and stops, we'll get home in nearly three hours," Hunter teases.

"Whatever," Dahlia grumbles.

***

FAITH IS FAST ASLEEP when they reach Haynes Ranch. It only took them two hours after Faith demanded food. Traveling with a toddler is totally different. You're at their beck and call.

The lights are on inside, and Dahlia's parents' car sits in the driveway. Bonnie rushes out to the porch before Dahlia is even out of the car.

"My baby girl!" she shouts and rushes up to Dahlia for a hug.

"Hey momma." She opens the back door for Zip to jump out and he takes off to the grass.

"Where is that little firecracker? I can't wait to meet her," Walt exclaims as he steps outside.

"She's asleep," Hunter responds as Walt follows him to the back seat.

"How are you?" Bonnie asks. "Let me see your bruises." Dahlia swats her hands away.

"It can wait until we get inside. We have to figure out where Faith is going to sleep."

Hunter unbuckles her and brings her around. Bonnie gasps at the sight of her blonde hair.

"She looks just like her daddy," she coos. "Come inside. Walt and I have a surprise for you."

Dahlia and Hunter follow Bonnie past the kitchen to what used to be the bridal room on the first floor. The walls are painted a soft pink and a princess toddler bed sits in the middle of the room. A new white chest of drawers is against the wall, and Dahlia pulls out the top drawer to find it already fully stocked.

"Mom," she whispers, running her hands along the sheer pink glitter curtains on the window that face the woods. "This is too much."

Bonnie smiles with her hands folded under her chin. "It wasn't just us, dear. With one call to Susan, the whole town was ready to chip in and get whatever you guys needed. The fridge is fully stocked with casserole meals and drinks and the cabinets have snacks for Faith and you guys as well. We wanted to make this as easy as possible for you guys."

Hunter looks around in disbelief and wonder then lays Faith in her brand-new bed.

He backs into the hallway slowly and pulls the door to a crack.

"I don't know what to say."

Walt places a hand on Hunter's shoulder. "You say thank you, son. But no thanks are needed because we're family and this is what we do."

"Thank you, sir." Hunter looks at Dahlia and reaches for her hand. "I never dreamed this is what I'd find when moving across the country, but I'm so glad I did."

"Well, we will leave you guys for the night, but be prepared because we'll be here first thing in the morning to meet that little angel in there," Walt says.

"He's just a little excited for another little girl to spoil," Bonnie says with a sparkle in her eyes.

"I don't think he's the only one," Dahlia remarks and pulls her mom and dad in for a hug.

"Thank you both. I don't tell you enough how lucky I am to have you as parents."

She lets go and Bonnie cups her cheek. "And we're beyond lucky to have you as our daughter. And now you," she looks at Hunter. "As our son."

Emotion pools in Hunter's eyes and she dips his chin and clears his throat. "Wow," he says with a chuckle. "You guys don't hold back, do you?"

"Welcome to the family, kid," Walt says with a wink.

Hunter and Dahlia wave at her parents as they back out of the driveway. Zip races inside and finds his spot next to the fireplace.

"I'll bring some wood inside for the fire, then I think we deserve a long, hot shower." He kisses Dahlia's temple, then disappears outside. She unloads their bags from the car just as Hunter comes back in through the back with an armload of wood.

"They even stocked the woodshed," he says in disbelief.

"Small town strong," Dahlia says with a sense of pride wafting through her. Family is more than just blood, and this town is her family.

# Chapter Forty-Nine

HUNTER'S KNEE BRUSHES AGAINST Dahlia's as their horses come to a stop.

"See, it's not that bad," Dahlia says. Her hands set loosely on the horn of the saddle where Hunter is gripping his for dear life.

"Yeah, totally," he squeaks.

"Loosen up, Soldier. You're going to scare the horse."

Hunter lets go and tries to let his muscles relax. "I'm going to scare the horse? You just had me run up a mountain."

Dahlia laughs. "It was a hill. Besides, if you're wanting to get Faith a horse this spring, you need to know how to ride."

"Why? It's Faith's horse. I didn't plan to be on it."

Dahlia turns in her saddle. "So, you were just going to let her ride by herself? No way. You are getting your own horse and you're riding with her."

"And what about you miss bossy pants?"

"This is my horse. I've had her since I was fifteen." Dahlia pats the black mare's neck. "And that," she points at the red gelding Hunter is riding. "Is yours."

Hunter's eyes widen and he looks down at the horse between his legs. "Mine?"

Dahlia nods. "Pa can't ride them all and well, Wren was Graves' and it's not fair to the horse to get left alone."

"What about Faith?"

"She can ride Jellybean." Dahlia runs her hand down her horse's neck. "And then when she's old enough and we know she's serious, we can get her, her very own horse."

Hunter sits back and smiles proudly. "And you were worried you didn't have what it takes for this parenting thing. I think you're doing a fantastic job."

Dahlia blushes, and she takes her horse's reins. "We should get back. Dad has probably let Faith in the cookie jar already."

"Little Flower," Hunter says, his voice deep and full of need. Dahlia turns to see him dismount from his horse and tie it to a nearby tree. "We're way out here. All alone, and I just watched your ass bounce in that saddle for most of it. Get off that horse and come here."

Dahlia's thighs squeeze, and she swings her leg around the back of the saddle. "Good fucking girl," Hunter muses and her center stirs with a burning desire.

When her lips part and eyes widen, he knows he has her. He closes the distance between them and takes the reins from her hands. Pinching her chin between his finger and thumb, he pushes his hat back and devours her mouth.

His tongue pushes past her lips and dances with hers. Their teeth clash as he thrusts his body against her.

He pulls back and Dahlia's lips are swollen and her skin hot.

Hunter grins salaciously and ties her horse near his. He takes his belt and slips it free in one quick motion. "You like being told what to do, don't you, Little Flower?"

Dahlia's gaze darts from his hungry blue eyes to his hands at the button of his jeans.

"I think you were holding back before when you rode my cock. How about we try again? Hmm?"

His chest brushes up against hers and his biceps flex and underneath his short sleeves. Threading his fingers in her hair, he angles her head back and forces eye contact.

"Do you want my cock?" he asks, and Dahlia's eyes pop. "Part those pretty little lips and say it, Little Flower."

"Yes."

Hunter releases his hold and steps back, pushing his pants down his legs. "Then get over here and take it," he demands, laying back on the grass and pulling his dick free from his boxers.

Dahlia giggles at the absurdity of fucking him out in the open. There's no hiding out here. They're free under the falling sun on her grandparents' ranch with cattle roaming the valley below.

She slowly unbuttons her jeans, staring down at her cowboy laying on his back, waiting for her to use him for everything she wants. As she pushes her jeans down and shoves off her boots, his eyes grow hungrier and Dahlia worries she might explode from the heat banked in them alone.

Hunter grips his cock and squeezes at the base. Precum beads at the tip and Dahlia gets on her knees beside him. She bends, licking across his cock, and he squeezes his hand tighter around himself.

Dahlia swings her leg around and hovers her center over his cock before slowly sliding down. He stretches her until she's fully seated and rocks her hips for friction on her aching clit.

Hunter's fingers dig into her hips as he stares up at her, taking control of her pleasure. Dahlia runs her fingers through her hair and down to palm her breasts.

"You feel so good," she mewls. Hunter bites his lip and thrust his hips up, causing her to place her hands on either side of his head.

Her hair falls forward and Hunter tucks it behind her ear before guiding her lips to his. "Fuck me, Little Flower," he grits out against her lips and slaps her ass.

Dahlia leans back and braces her hands on his chest as she slides his cock nearly all the way out before dropping down. Their bodies slap together as she does it again and again.

Her orgasm coils inside her until she aches for a release.

"Take it," Hunter demands, as if he knows what she needs.

Leaning back, Dahlia dips her finger between her thighs until she finds her clit and she presses down on it, moving her finger back and forth.

She moans around the pleasure coursing through her body until her breath hitches and she cries out Hunter's name. Her pussy clenches around his cock and he grabs Dahlia's hips, thrusting himself deeper, and taking her for his own.

She braces herself on his knees with her hands behind her back and her sensitive clit zaps pleasure through her with each slap of Hunter's pelvis.

He jerks underneath her and fills her pussy with his hot cum. Sweat glistening off them both and Dahlia's hair sticking to her skin.

"I'm so glad you're my husband," Dahlia sighs as she leans down and kisses his lips. "Because when we get home, we're doing that again."

Hunter smirks and raises his hands above his head. "I love you, Little Flower."

"And I love you, Soldier."

***

"Hey Graves," Dahlia says to her brother's voicemail. "So much has happened since I last called you. I got married," she says with tears in her eyes and a lump in her throat. "To Hunter Haynes. Yeah, finally," she scoffs. "Peter, my ex that you never liked, remember? Well, he got arrested for basically trying to kill Hunter and kidnapping me—it's a funny story, only not really, if I ever get to tell you."

Giggles catches Dahlia's attention toward the barn and she steps around the porch of their cabin to spot Hunter spinning Faith around in the air.

"Oh, and I'm a mom now. I didn't have her, but she's amazing and I think you'd love her company. She's sassy and will put you in your place if you're out of line. She has Hunter and I wrapped around her finger. I guess I should rewind to tell you that Hunter had a child he didn't know about and then her mom…well she died, um, after hitting me in—not me exactly—I was in an Uber and she crashed into; it doesn't matter."

She drops her chin and picks at the wood on the porch railing. "I wish you were here to meet her and see Hunter. He's doing really, really great. I know you'll come home one day and when you do, I'm going to kick your ass for leaving us. At least you know you have that to look forward to."

Fresh buds cover the trees with the signs of spring, and a caravan of cars roll up the driveway. Faith squeals at the sight of Walt and abandons her game with her daddy. Hunter's parents get out of their parked car and wave with smiling faces.

"Wait until the cars stop!" Hunter shouts, chasing after her.

"It's Faith's birthday, that's her name," Dahlia says. "She's five already. Dad is her hero and Tripp is the fun uncle, just like I expected. He is teaching her pranks and I have to be careful of rubber snakes in the laundry. Sterling said he'll be close in the next month or so and that he plans to stop by. He's been around a couple of times, but I'll believe it when I see it. All we're missing is you. I love you, Graves. Until I see you."

She hangs up the phone as Hunter climbs the steps. "And I'm chopped liver."

He wraps his arms around Dahlia and pulls her back into his chest. "You're still my fillet mignon," she teases, and he barks out a laugh.

"Wow, that was—"

"Impressive?" She spins in his arms and tilts her head back.

"Sure, Little Flower. Impressive," he chuckles, kissing her forehead.

"Daddy! Mommy!" Dahlia's heart stills at the small word coming from Faith. It isn't the first time she's called her that, but it's still new and foreign. "Aunt Carly brought cupcakes from the good place!"

Faith runs across the porch, her tiny footfalls somehow resembling an elephant tromping along.

"She did?" Dahlia asks, crouching and bopping Faith on the nose. "Let's go steal one before Daddy notices."

Faith looks at Hunter with big eyes. "Stay here. Don't move. Okay? You can't come inside yet."

"Why not?" Hunter acts, pretending to be offended.

"Because it's girls only right now." She places her hands on her hips and Dahlia rolls her lips between her teeth to keep from laughing. "Okay?"

Hunter lifts his hands. "Okay, Pumpkin. But I'm counting to ten."

Faith grabs Dahlia's hand and pulls her along. "Run Mommy! Hurry!"

Hunter's eyes open at the sight of Faith's curls bouncing as she runs across the porch with Dahlia in tow behind her. Right before they disappear around the corner, Dahlia's mischievous smile flicks back to her soldier. They've been through so much together, but it's moments like this that she knows without a doubt it was all worth it.

# About the author

Lacy Chantell resides in Kentucky and owns a small business. She is a mom of two toddlers and lives on the family farm with her husband. She loves to read all genres, ride her horses, hiking, pretty much anything outdoors. Inspiration hits her everywhere she goes for new book ideas and she is excited to keep telling stories for others to enjoy. Romance and Fantasy are her favorite genres to write, and she loves to put her characters through hell for them to get their happy ending in the end.

Follow her on her social media accounts or join her newsletter to keep up with releases and her future works.

# Also by

**Lacy Chantell – Cowboy Romance**

**Curston Ranch Series**
Wild Heart–Book One
Tattered Heartstrings–Book Two
Wildflowers and Wild Horses–Book Three
**Langley Ranch Series**
The Reason Why - Book One
**Dreaming of Dahlias** – Cowboy Romance Standalone

**Lacie Chanel – Dark and Taboo Romance**

**Seeing Double** – Why Choose Romance
**The Games We Play** – Stalker Dark Romance
**Intracoastal Waters** - Dark Billionaire Romance